IN THE DARK

THE GRADIENT DUET

BRITT BEE

IN THE DARK
Copyright © 2024 by Britt Bee

All rights reserved. No part of this book may be used or reproduced in any manner whatsoever without written permission except in the case of brief quotations embodied in critical articles or reviews. This book is a work of fiction. Names, characters, businesses, organizations, places, events, and incidents are either the product of the author's imagination or used fictitiously. Any resemblance to actual persons, living or dead, events, or locales is entirely coincidental.

Contact Information: brittbeebooks@gmail.com

Cover Design by: Disturbed Valkyrie Designs
Editor: Ashlyn Harmon
Interior Formatting by: Disturbed Valkyrie Designs

Paperback ISBN: 979-8-9911090-0-0
eBook ISBN: 979-8-9911090-1-7
First Edition: July 2024
10 9 8 7 6 5 4 3 2 1

For Jordi and Eilis,
Without either of you, this simply would not exist.

Playlist

The Wolf in Your Darkest Room (Matthew Mayfield)
Right Here (Chase Atlantic)
Crown (WE ARE FURY)
Romance (Varials)
over her (One Hope)
O.K.? (Picturesque)
Gasoline (Version Eight)
Monster (PVRIS)
Where Did U Come From? (Jennings Couch)
Imagination (Tilian, Tim Henson)
Are You Tired? (Scene Queen)
Middle of the Night (Loveless)
Tangerine (Glass Animals)
Heat Waves (Living in Fiction)
She Thinks of Me (Landon Tewers)
Therefore I Am (Rain Paris)
Crazy in Love (Eden Project)
Dancing with the Devil (Alter.)
Where Are You? (Elvis Drew, Avivian)

Complete playlist can be found on Spotify:
In the Dark playlist

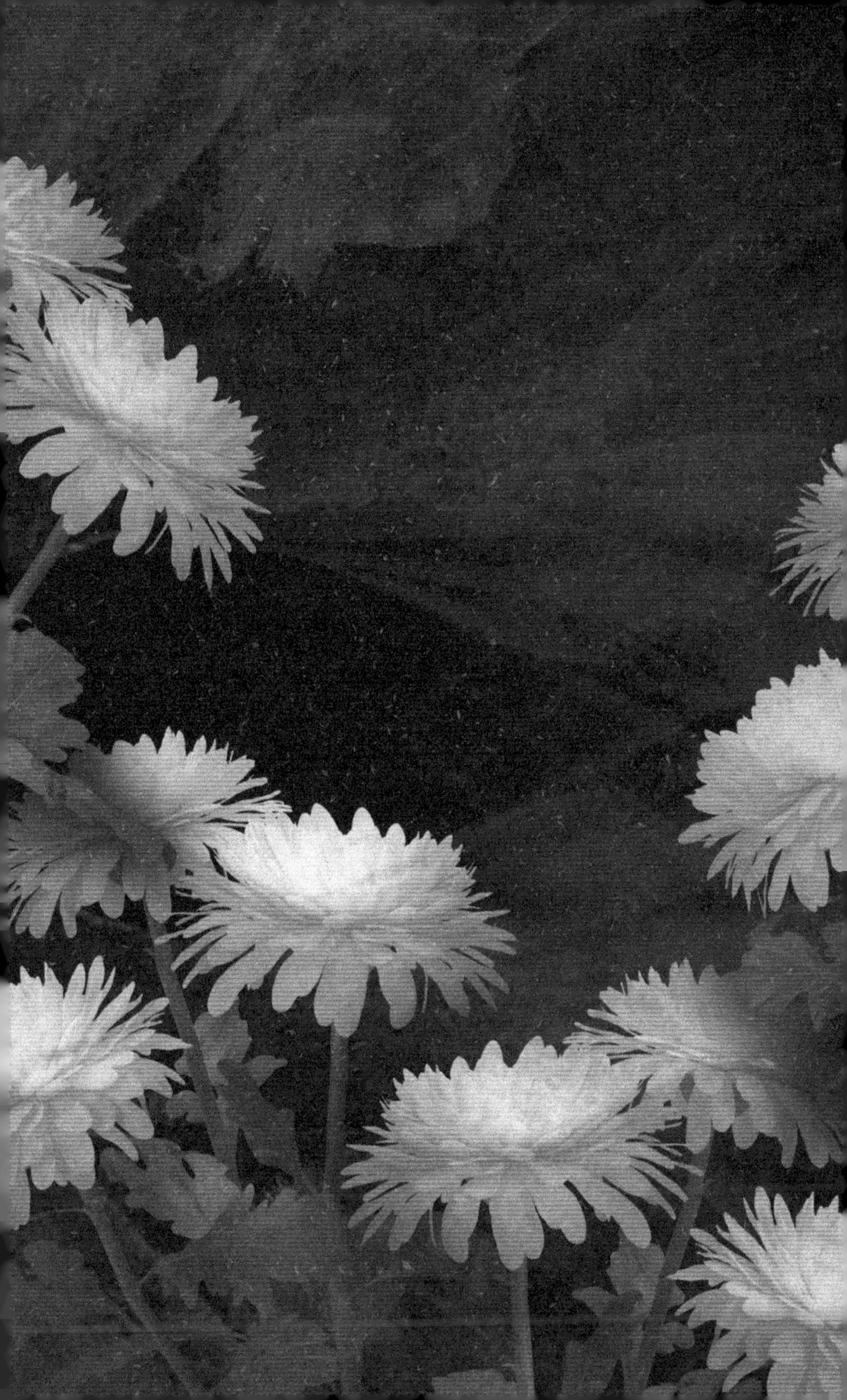

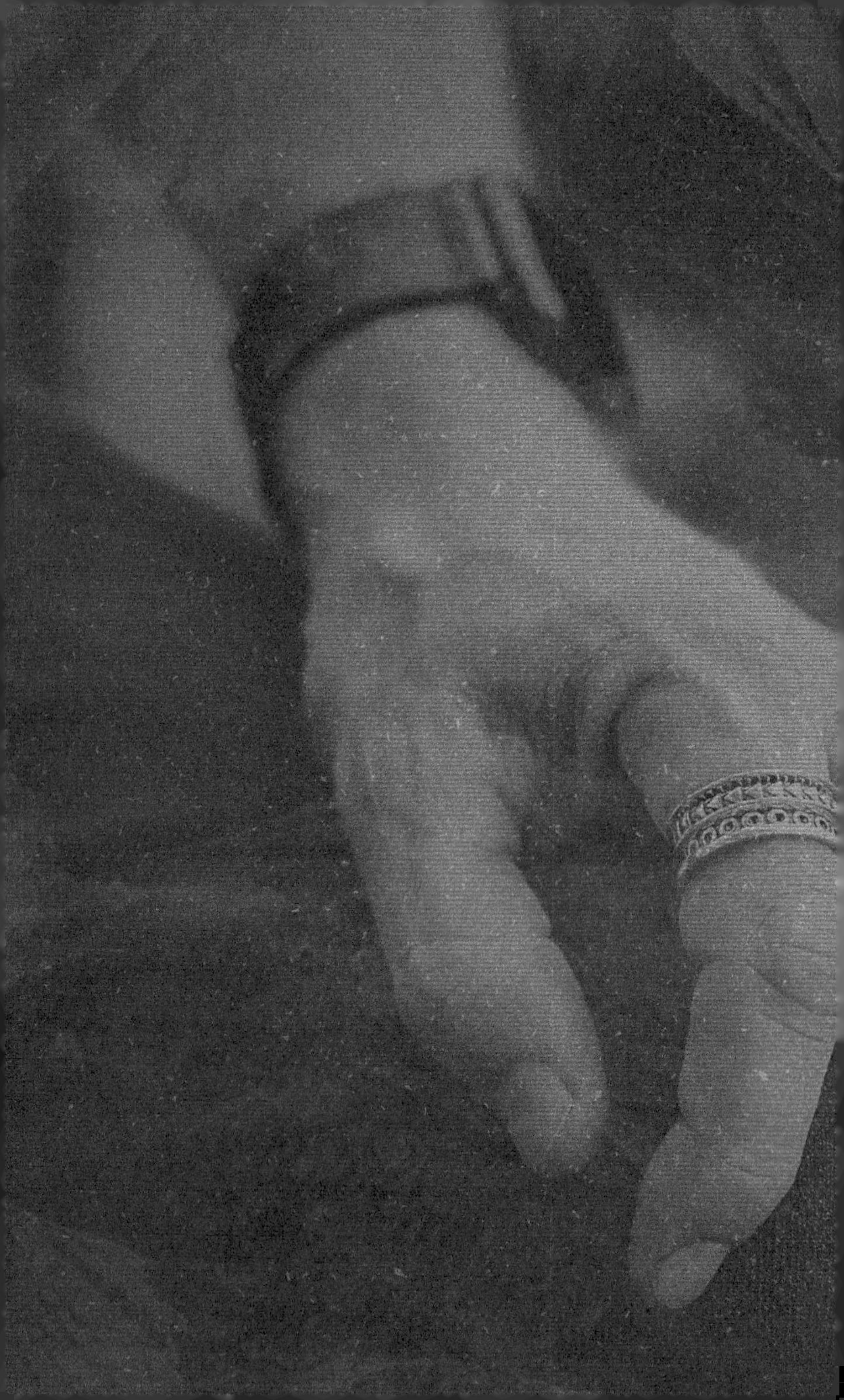

Content Warning

Please note that this book has darker themes, content, and situations that may be uncomfortable for some readers. Your mental health matters.

Stalking
On-page murder
Graphic torture
Spousal abuse mentioned, but not depicted
Explicit sexual interactions (on-page)
Kidnapping of FMC
Drugging of FMC
Aggressive bar patrons (groping)
Physical altercations
Forced captivity
Potential claustrophobia-inducing environments
Death of loved one(s)
Gunshot wounds, unprovoked violence
Enucleation

If you have any questions and/or concerns, please feel free to email brittbeebooks@gmail.com

If you are related to me (talking to you, Mom), do NOT proceed.

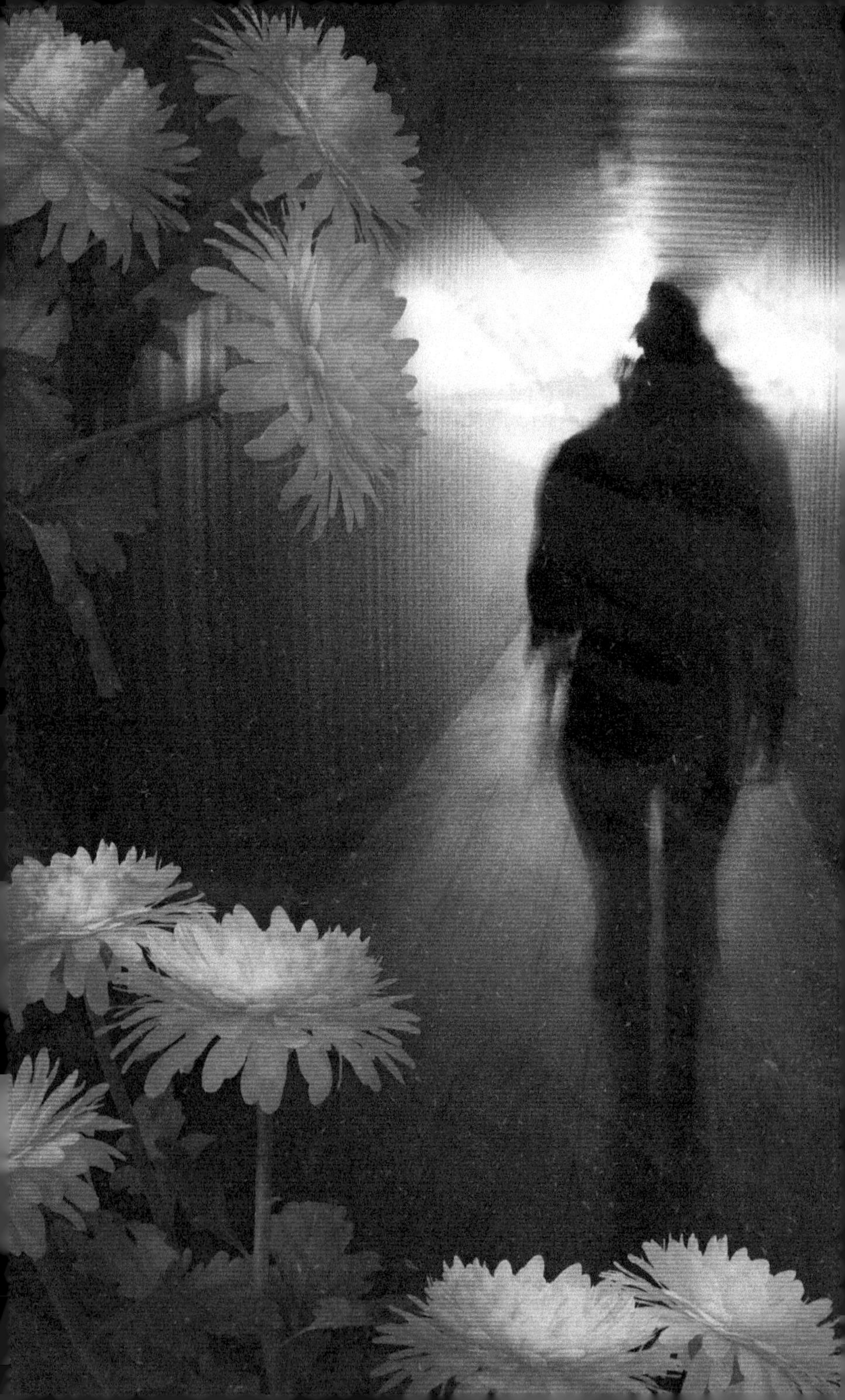

BEFORE

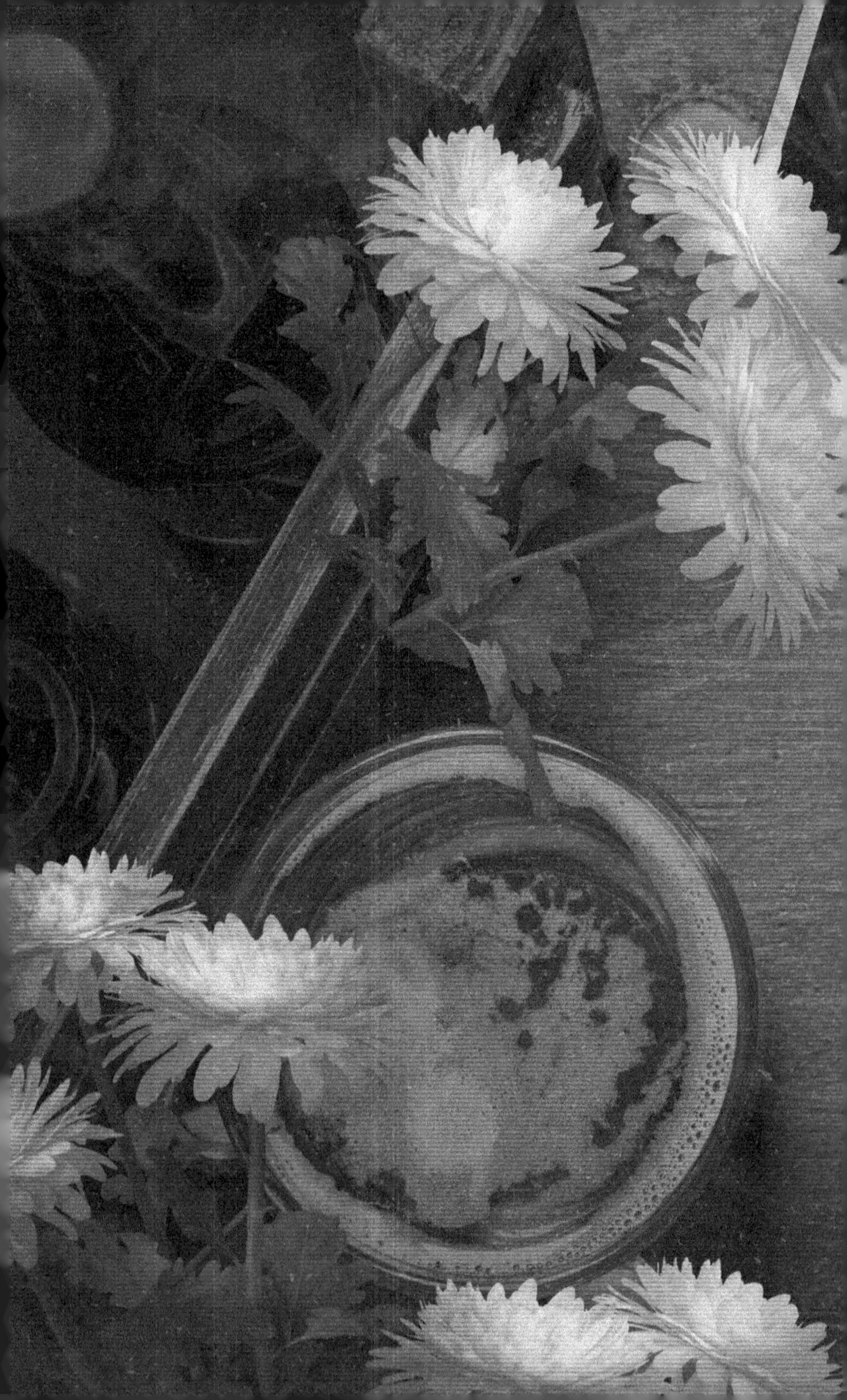

One
August 2018

DOMINIC

I push my button-up shirt into my slacks, tucking it in roughly. I instinctually straighten my black tie. I adjust my cufflinks that glimmer in the bathroom's harsh light. Taking one last glance at myself, I slide my blonde hair behind my ears. I can't have a single strand out of place tonight. This is a make-or-break type of meeting. A once-in-a-lifetime opportunity.

The meeting has been set for over a month. Our empires have been gnashing at one another for years. It is time to either combine forces or shoot the other. Tonight will decide it all.

Growing up with my father was difficult. There's no doubt about that. My mother, though? She brought life and love. She brought everything with her. Most nights as a child were spent with her, laid up in my racecar bed with her reading a superhero story. She would do different voices for the cast of characters, making me belly laugh so often my stomach would ache.

One day she was there, the next— gone. A stray bullet, I was told years later. My father never spoke of her after her death. He barely went to her funeral, stopping by to see her closed casket. His phone rang and off he went.

My hand was clasped in my nanny's. She was an older woman with graying hair at the time. Zoey was her name. She cared for me when my mother was around, but her time with me tripled once she died. She stepped up. She was the one who helped to shape me as I grew.

But my father had his talons digging deep in my back from the day I was sired. He dug until his claws pierced the skin on my back, drawing blood. I allowed it.

I didn't have a choice in the matter. My mother couldn't stop it. I couldn't as a child, either.

By the time I was a teenager, I didn't care anymore. I would do his bidding, do the dirty work, and keep my mouth shut.

"You about ready?" My good friend, Milo, who is also my second-in-command, walks into my bedroom. We're dressed identically, black everything. His cropped hair is gelled into place.

I come back to reality, leaving my mother in my thoughts, where she belongs.

I give Milo a quick nod.

"Then we better head out. Don't want to be late." Quick and to the point, that's Milo. We've been friends for over a decade, met back in middle school, and have been buds ever since.

The drive to the warehouse is silent and efficient. Milo powers down our headlights as we pull into the empty lot. I adjust my necktie once more before pushing open the door and climbing out. Milo meets me on the other side of the vehicle, shoving his hands in his pockets. We're both carrying weapons, tucked slyly into our waistbands. I don't want to engage in violence, but if there's no other option? Then it's a free for all.

We share a glance while walking into the decrepit building. The entry is guarded on the inside by two men who take one look at us and point toward the middle of the warehouse.

Once in the large open space, we stop walking and wait.

He will come to us.

I survey our surroundings, noting eight men. There are an additional two at the door. They are spread out around the perimeter of the space. They are nearly invisible with their black shirts, pants, shoes, and facial coverings. They hold military-grade weaponry against their chests, ready to fire at any given second.

If I were a different man, I might be nervous.

Keeping a grin from my face, I take to biting the inside of my cheeks. Enough to hurt, but not enough to bleed. No one likes the taste of blood, not even me. Not in public anyway.

Milo stands silently, patiently. After what seems like ages, but is more like ten minutes, we both hear a door open and close loudly. He must want us to know when he enters the space, hence no WD-40 for one specific door. Smart. I make a mental note.

He walks out. We look like a trio of friends all dressed the same, but we are far from that. I didn't come to this meeting expecting friendship. I expect a truce. Maybe a partnership.

"It's nice to see you showed." He looks at his silver watch. "On time as well." His face twists with a saccharine smile, one that doesn't quite meet his eyes. "Shall we get on with this, then?"

"Yes, let's, please." Polite to the teeth is what I'm determined to be. Straightening my jacket once more, I follow him to a secluded room off the side of the warehouse space. Milo is close on my heels, his own head turning and surveying. He waits and continues watching for any trouble.

He leads us into a bright room. A wooden table sits in the middle with exactly three chairs; we all take one.

"I have to admit, Dominic, I was surprised you asked for this."

I look The Sandman in the eyes. "It was, no, *is*, time for a change, Sandman. You know that better than anyone."

The Sandman nods once, twice. He raps his fingertips on the wooden surface, pausing before responding. "I hate to admit it, but you aren't wrong there. Things have been far too tense for far too long, unfortunately."

"Indeed, which is why I propose-,"

"I read your proposal, Dominic. While it's...heartwarming at best, it's a pipe dream. We won't be achieving those specific goals. Not here, not today, not between us." His words make my blood leaden. I want to sink into the chair, melt to the floor, but I hold my composure.

My hands turn to fists on the table. "What don't you agree with? Be straight with me here. We're businessmen, aren't we?" I keep my voice level, doing my best to maintain my hardened exterior.

Our empires used to be united, up until our fathers destroyed it. Hell, we grew up together. We fought together, trained together, got punished together, and fucked women together. But then our fathers had to go fuck it all up, and we were ripped from one another's lives. Nothing has been the same.

But now our fathers are dead. While we didn't plan it together, our thoughts cosmically aligned. We each carried out our parts perfectly. I'm impressed with our actions, kind of wish we planned it as such instead of being so distant.

The Sandman glares at me, his jaw set in stone. "We can't agree on the terms you provided because it doesn't make sense, Dominic. You want to merge our empires into one. But who would be in charge? I know I'm not going to step down, and I know you're not willing to either. Neither of us is married. We have no heirs. So how do you suggest we navigate these terms?"

He makes valid points. I desperately want to gnaw on my bottom lip, but I manage not to. "I won't deny it. I won't step down. I know you sure as shit won't either," I pause, swallowing, "and I would never ask you to. I think we could run the empire together. We could merge our businesses, our people. We could take special interests in certain things. You enjoy nightclubs. You run the nightclubs. I enjoy bars. I run the bars. We coordinate and we plan and, ugh," I let out a frustrated groan. "We work together for fuck's sake. That's all we need to do."

He taps a finger on the table. "And for our heirs?"

"We marry. We have at least one child. I don't give a shit about it being a son. Hell, our daughters would probably run this shit better than we could ever dream," I chuckle.

The Sandman joins me for once. "You're not wrong there. How long before we fully merge?"

I have thought about it. "Five years. Five years to fully merge and hopefully find ourselves women who actually want to be our brides."

"I agree. We don't want to be like our fathers. We won't force women to marry us. We need to start a new precedent. Find love, for real. Get married, for love. Have children with whomever we desire."

"Honestly it sounds like a decent plan." I murmur more to myself than to him. He gave me whiplash in this meeting. First outright refusing then coming to an amicable agreement. What are we? Adults?

The Sandman stands, smoothing his jacket. He reaches a hand out to me. "Five years until we're fully merged. Five years to find wives, to begin our lives."

I follow, grabbing his hand and giving it a firm shake. "It's a deal."

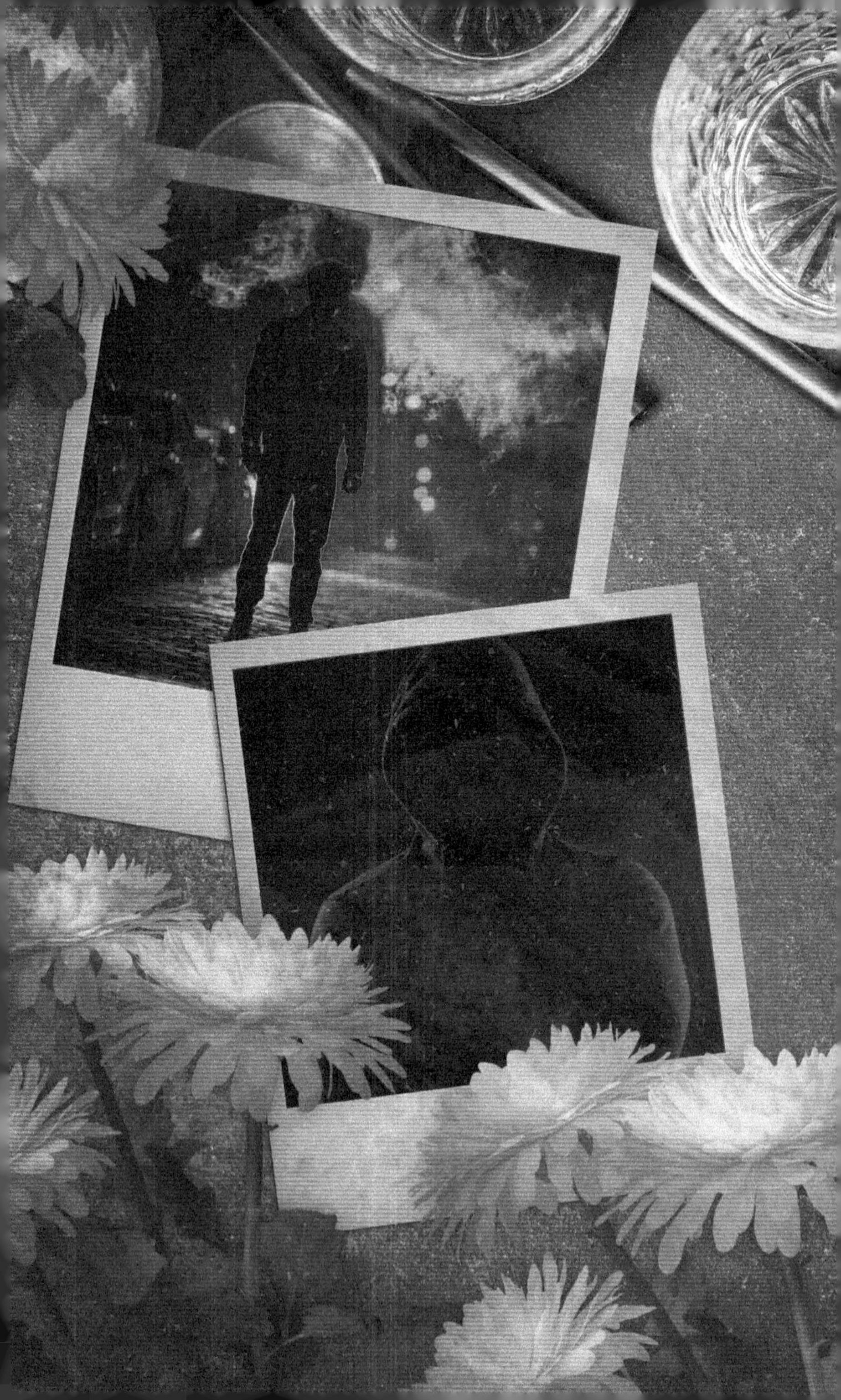

Two
October 2018

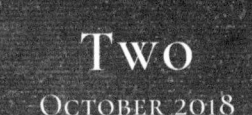

DOMINIC

I twist my cufflinks as I sit in the car. My suit is pressed, and my hair is gelled with my curls falling down the nape of my neck. Milo is driving us to the new bar I bought. This will be my first visit since signing the paperwork yesterday. It should be closed and quiet, letting us conduct our business without distractions.

"Did you gather all the necessary supplies for today's activities?"

"Everything is packed in the back and ready for installation, boss." Milo is fluent in technology and surveillance, so I don't need to hire anyone for this job. Makes the security for it less complex. All my businesses operate with full camera coverage. I keep tabs on all my employees. It comes in handy when customers inevitably go haywire. It is a bar after all; there will be punches thrown and more than one chair slinging over shoulders and smashing into the floor.

Luckily, the bar, coined Point B, is only a short drive from my penthouse downtown. The quick trip will prove beneficial when I need to storm the place to set things straight.

"We're here, boss," Milo calls from the driver's seat.

He's already shut the car off, exited the vehicle, and is rounding the front of it by the time I open my door. We both take a glance at the bar. The windows in the front need to be cleaned immediately. Handprints cover the mottled glass. I cough and motion to the front door.

The bar itself is old wood, something dark, but has so many rings from the overflowing alcohol that defining the type of specific wood is difficult. My gaze roams. The leather booths and barstools are cracked five ways to Sunday. They must be replaced immediately. I begin doing mental math to keep track of how much money I will be spending in the very near future.

I drag three fingers across the bar top, feeling the caked-on alcohol, bitters, and simple syrups that have coated the wood. Did no one know how to properly clean? I would be firing people tonight when they arrived for their shifts.

My original plan was to come in and get the new security equipment installed, but seeing the state of the place? I can't do that.

First things first. Clean.

I'm telling Milo the amended plan for the day when I hear sloshing water. A young woman who can't be more than twenty or twenty-one, with curves for days and midnight hair rounds the corner from the small washroom.

She carries a dull red bucket. It is nearly overflowing with soapy water. She comes to a screeching halt when her eyes meet my own. The water splashes over the sides of the bucket and coats her shoes. "Who are you? Why are you here?" She squeaks, not pausing to allow an answer to slip through.

My eyes harden. "Who the fuck are you, and why are you here at this hour? The bar is closed." My voice rings throughout the empty space, hitting her like a physical blow.

It makes my stomach clench with some type of emotion that I am unfamiliar with. Her eyes crinkle like she might cry, and I immediately want to take back my brash tone. Who is she? Why is she here? I need to know everything about her.

Her lips don't quiver and her eyes crinkle further, not in an emotional outburst, but rather annoyance. "I work here, obviously." Her voice is cold.

"Why don't you try again?" I cross my arms against my chest. Milo stands silently off the side of me, watching the interaction with hawk-like eyes.

The woman sighs, "I know it's closed. That's why I'm here!" She slams the bucket of water on the bar top, slopping it everywhere. She braces against the bar top. "I work tonight, and I worked last night. However, I wasn't the closer, but I fucking knew they wouldn't do their shit right, so I decided to come in a bit early today to fix all their fuck ups so I can grab a nap before my shift starts."

I digest her rushed words. "Who are you?"

She stares at me, her eyes never wavering. She can hold her own. "Katherine."

"Hmm, nice to meet you then, Katherine." I don't recognize her from the five minute debrief the previous owner gave me before I strung him from my warehouse's rafters. Her name on my tongue is sweeter than I expected. Will she taste similarly sweet? I stare at her for a few more moments before a slight blush raises to her cheeks and she grabs the bucket unceremoniously.

"I'm going to finish cleaning up the bar. It's disgusting." She scoffs.

I wring my hands together. "That's fine. We're here to get the new security cameras installed." I don't know why I think I owe her an explanation. This is my bar after all, not hers.

Katherine pops in an earbud, sliding a tendril of fallen night hair behind the ear. Her fingers are slim, and her nails are painted black. Several rings adorn her fingers, some with glittering gemstones and others just bands of silver and black. Her ears are similarly decorated with silver hoops and chains and gemstone studs.

She is ethereal, stunning. Plucked straight from my wildest dreams and manifested before me.

She might not realize it yet, hell, I barely recognize it myself, but I am going to be her everything.

KATHERINE

The two men stay in the bar like the taller one told me. He mentioned he was the owner, but I was unaware we were under new ownership. Go figure. I'm not too surprised given the reputation the bar has anyway. People come and go here, especially workers. I'm the only barkeep who has been here longer than a year. I'm freshly twenty-two and started working here as soon as I was legally able.

The men keep to themselves, going from one corner to the next. They bring in several large suitcases filled to the brim with cameras and devices to plant all around the facility. It makes me feel a little safer honestly. There have been many bar fights I had to endure.

As I scrub the bar top, I keep one eye on the pair of them. The blonde one, the taller of the two, exudes confidence. It pours out of him and lingers in the open space. His suit fits well. It must be tailored, which means he makes bank. His hair is perfect, falling to the back of his neck. It must normally be blonde, but the gel in place makes it a shade or two darker than normal.

His statuesque face pulls me in. A sharp jaw and cheekbones with a beautifully crafted nose. It is as if the Gods specifically made him to be devastating to all the women in the world.

I force my eyes away from him, focusing instead on the wooden bar top that will never be fully clean. I made no progress on the damned thing, though this is the third scrub I'm giving it. I sigh and scour like mad.

After cleaning for several hours, I'm finally caught up with everything the closer had mysteriously forgotten. I take a ten-minute break, smoking a few cigarettes out the back door of the kitchen. When I make my way back inside, the two men are still here.

They're installing so many cameras. I find myself a little surprised. How many can they possibly need? While the camera presence makes me feel safer, they also make me a little uneasy. It isn't like they're hanging up cams in the bathrooms or anything, but there are cameras in the main room, the back inventory space, the small kitchen, and behind the bar. No corner left unguarded, no blind spots.

My apartment is only a brisk walk away. That gives me plenty of time to curl up on my threadbare couch and drift off to bliss and get two hours of sleep before the night rocks on.

I dump the red bucket of chilled soapy water down the sink in the washroom. It runs a gross, gritty gray. Rinsing the bucket out, I leave it upside down in the sink to drain. I pull my small shoulder bag from the only hook on the wall and begin walking towards the front of the bar.

A deep voice stops me in my tracks. "Where are you going, Katherine?"

Facing the tall man. "My shift doesn't start for a few hours, so I'm gonna head home and grab a quick nap." I jerk my thumb behind my back, pointing in the vague direction of my apartment.

His eyebrows draw downwards, squinting at me. "You go through the alley to get home?" His voice is incredulous.

"I mean yeah, it's a short cut."

The blonde god doesn't say anything. He gives a singular nod, before pivoting and gliding back to his cohort. I guess that's that. I shrug and head out, ready for a fucking nap.

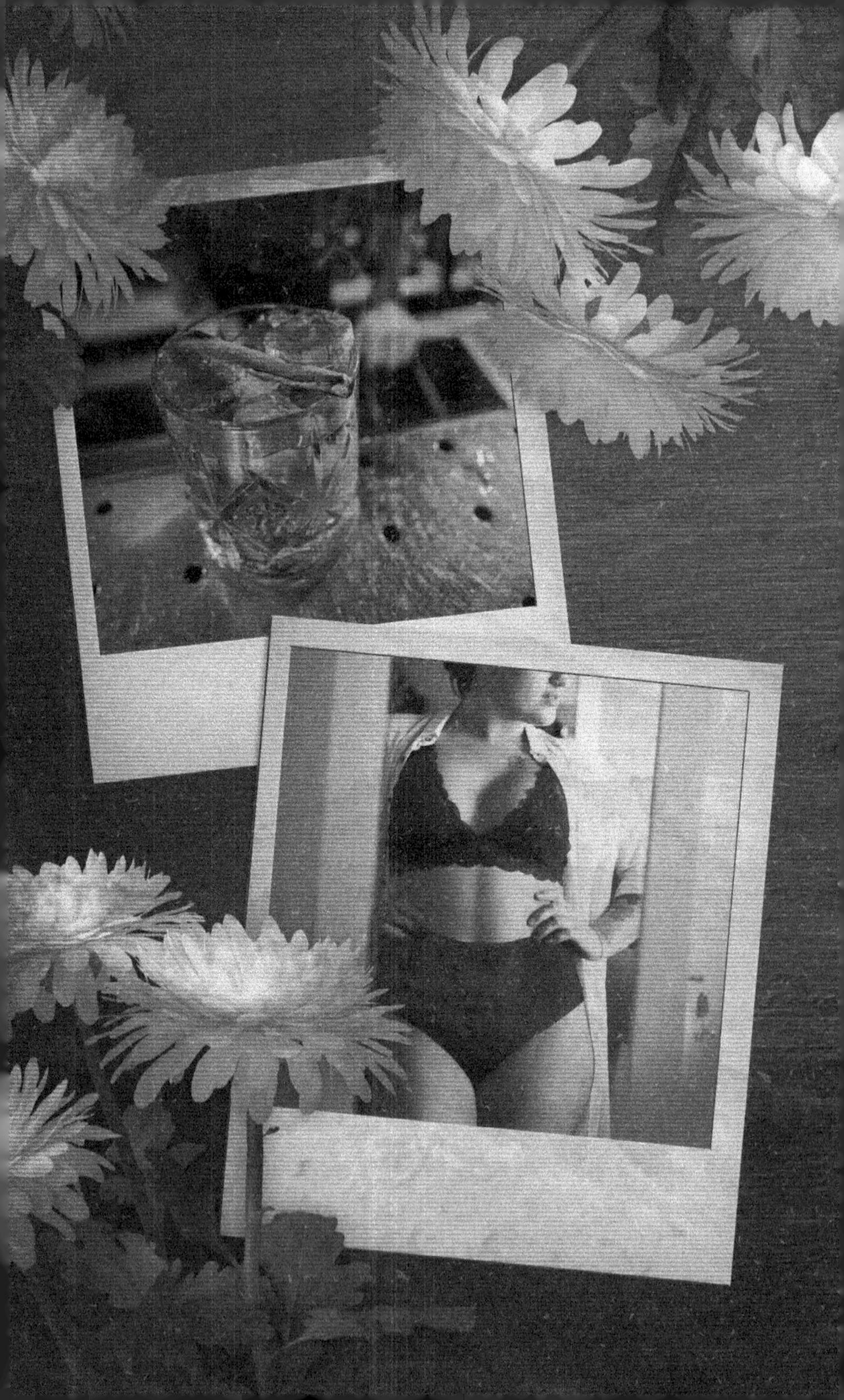

Three
November 2018

KATHERINE

Working at Point B isn't my favorite thing in the world. However, it does manage to keep me sane, allow me to hang with my bestie often, and pay my copious bills at the end of each month. I go above and beyond, and the manager knows. It's how I managed to find myself with a new title in less than a year.

I'm not only a bar keeper anymore. I'm the bar lead. Fuck yeah, I deserve that shit.

I study the lounge as I wipe down the bar top, the patrons drink their fill and slam their glasses down. I'll have to make a walk-through here soon and quickly wipe away as much disgust as I can. I roll my eyes, it's always the same shit.

My bestie, Marisol, trots up to the bar. Her untamed mane of red hair swings around her shoulders. Her curls are somewhat docile today. They are wild, each with a mind of its own. She could never contain them. She clutches her serving tray against her chest as she walks, then sets it on the bar as she leans against it.

"Hey, bitch, what are you doing later?"

I scoff. "Working. What are you doing?"

Marisol pops her elbows onto the bar, arching her back a smidge. The regulars cast gazes her way. She plays into it, giving her ass a subtle shake. She catches my stare. "What? I get better tips if I flaunt a little, ya know?"

I don't give a shit what Marisol does. The regulars are usually men who are old enough to be our fathers and for the most part they're harmless. They admire a little sashay occasionally and tip often. Hell, several give me tips when my shirt is a vee neck. I'll take what I can get.

"Hey, I know. We gotta do what we can to make money, honey." I mimic a Boston accent, really selling it.

She laughs, her arm brushing mine. "You're too good at that, Kirbs. It's almost as if you grew up there or some shit."

"Nope," I said, popping the *p*. "Grew up here, or well, this general area." I give a sweeping motion over the bar, signifying the whole town. I've bounced around all throughout my childhood, going from one foster family to another.

"Well anyway," Marisol pulls a tube of lip gloss from somewhere (no, seriously, where did she get that?) and applies a thick coat to her plump lips, "I was thinking we could go to this new club next month on its opening night. It's small and in a shitty part of town so I doubt there will be a huge line or anything." She smacks her lips together, smoothing out the gloss.

I start to shake my head, but she quickly cuts me off. "No! You can't possibly say no! It'll be fun. Please!" She gives me the ultimate weapon, her doe eyes.

I level a gaze at her. "You know I hate it when you pull out those fucking doe eyes, don't you?"

Marisol answers with a giggle.

The night wears on from there. Customer after customer bombards the bar and keeps me so busy I barely have time to wipe the counter down. There's at least an inch of nasty shit on every surface by the end of the night.

I finish mixing a few more cocktails, turning back to the bar to hand them over to the guests. A middle-aged man leans against the bar and gives me a blatant once over while leaning on his hand.

I plaster a fake-as-shit smile on my face. "What can I get for ya?" I pick up a glass and begin running a clean rag over it, collecting the water droplets left over from its wash.

His voice is thick. It's like molasses, and it instantly makes my skin itchy. "Get me a classic draft." Straight to the point. I can appreciate that at least.

"Comin' right up." I turn, grabbing a tall glass, and pull the lever for the draft. I watch the amber liquid churn into the pint, nearly no foam in sight. Damn I'm good.

I gingerly place the glass on the counter. The man glances at it, then taps the counter with two fingers. "This isn't going to do, sweetheart."

Clasping my hands in front of me, I lean in to hear what he has to say. "What seems to be the issue?"

"There's too much fucking foam in this shit. Do you not know how to do shit right?" He plows into me verbally. There isn't more than a centimeter of foam in the glass.

"I can get you another one if you want." I'm not going to bow down to the damned guy, but I can be a little polite, if not to get him off my back and away from my bar.

"I don't want another fucking glass of this shit!" He stands abruptly and reaches for me, his cold hand clamping tightly around my upper arm. He yanks me toward him.

My stomach crashes into the bar top, nearly knocking the wind out of me. "Get your fucking hand off me!"

The guy clamps harder on my skin, and I know it will bruise.

No way out of this one. Luckily, a mass of bright hair is coming toward me. Thank God for Marisol.

"Hey, Dickhead!" She yells, causing the guy to turn his head slightly towards her.

Marisol, as a drink runner, carries a circular tray around with her in the bar. She flips it around her hands. It arcs through the air, landing a solid *smack* against the guy's cheek.

The man stumbles backward. I yank my arm free and leap onto the top of the bar. I inwardly cringe as my boots stick to the disgusting surface. I point toward the door and level a hard gaze at the man. "Get the fuck out of this bar, jack ass! Go!"

The man blinks a few times.

"GET OUT!"

He high tails it the fuck out of here.

DOMINIC

The chair in my office does little to comfort me. I usually find it beyond comfortable, but in this instance? Hell no. I'd originally come into my office to check on the cameras at Point B; it was supposed to be a quick five- to ten-minute perusal of the different feeds then I would go downstairs and meet with Milo for drinks in my kitchen.

It's what we've been doing for months anyway. We are both bachelors, me by choice since I've been waiting for Katherine and Milo, well, by choice as well. We don't talk about his lack of female friends.

A slight knock disrupts my concentration on the bar's cameras. I take a few moments to glance around my office, not noticing anything out of place. The window is closed, nothing to be seen from the other side. I double-check my personal cameras throughout my house. Chalking it up to house-settling noises, I reopen the tab.

I log onto the server only to find a sleaze ball at the bar. The first few minutes of live footage goes alright, nothing too out of the ordinary. Katherine is slinging drinks as if she is made for it, mixing cocktails, and pulling drafts. It's a good thing the manager promoted her; we can't afford to lose her.

I watch with burning eyes as the man wraps a taloned hand

around her upper arm. Even through the somewhat grainy footage I could tell it was a punishing grip. I watch as she tries to pry away from him, but to no avail. As I am about to reach for my cell phone to call someone, her petite, red-headed friend rushes over. She yells at the creep, offering Katherine a reprieve long enough for her to rip out of his grip.

I sit at my desk, chin cradled in my hands, raptly paying attention to the screen as I watch Katherine hoist herself up on the bar top, her jeans molding to her perfect curves and ass. Her black, vee neck shirt is oversized, but shows off a tasteful amount of cleavage.

She stomps her tiny foot in her big ass black lace-up platforms and yells at this guy, threatening him. Tells him to basically get the fuck out and don't come back.

And I'll be damned, he leaves.

I quickly pull a screenshot of his face to send off to Milo. We will be hunting that sorry son of a bitch down one way or another. He didn't pay for his multiple drinks, and he touched her. Gripped her hard enough and now she's rubbing her upper arm in slow circles. It will undoubtedly leave a bruise.

I need to punch something, and Milo isn't an option. I push back from my desk, slamming the chair against it. Striding out of my office, I call out to Milo, "Get the car ready, man. We've got some hunting to do!"

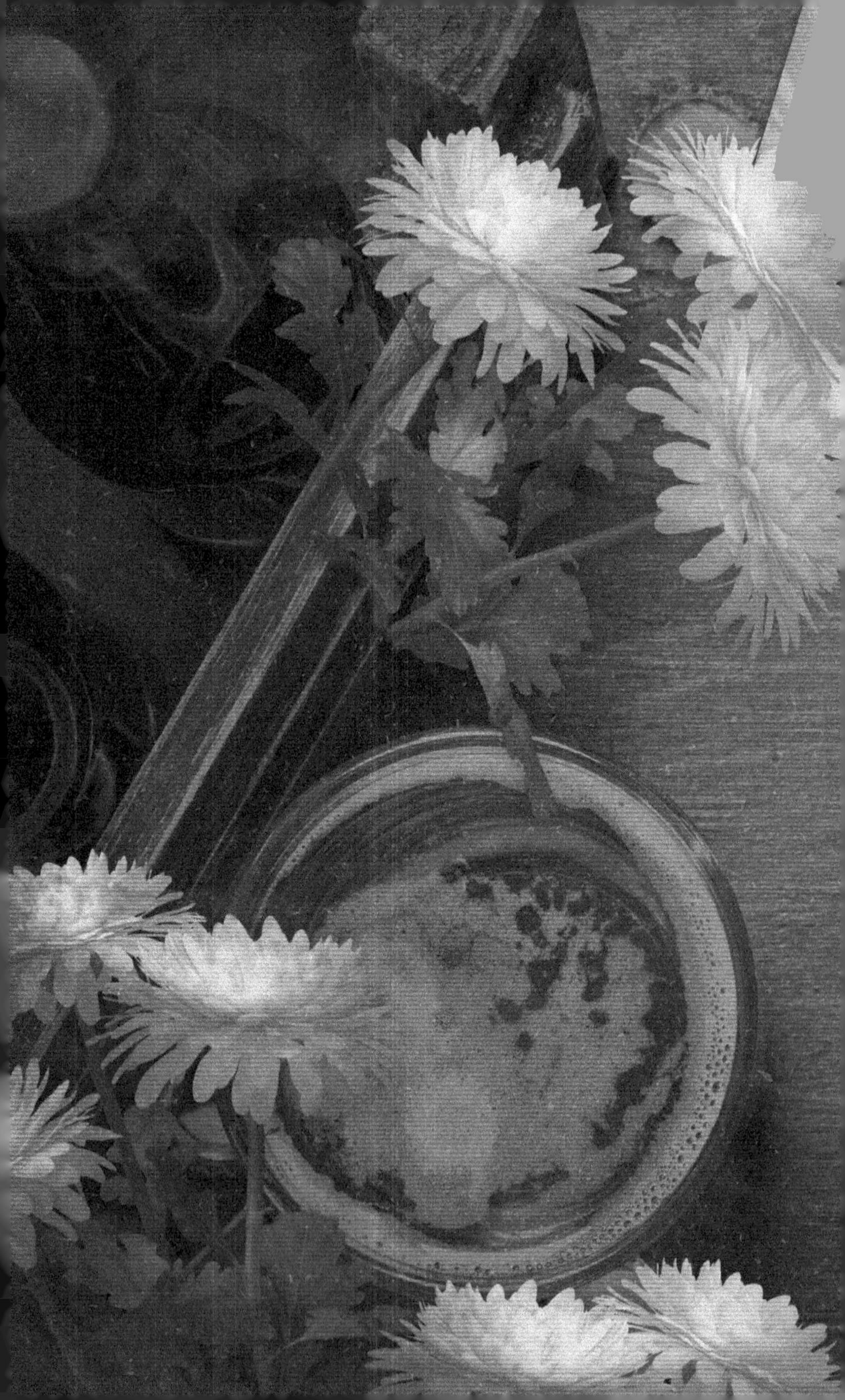

Four
March 2019

DOMINIC

The Sandman is getting on my last fucking nerve.

"We still have over four years to iron out all the finer details."

Even frustrated, the Sandman sports a level voice. I'm slightly impressed but will never admit it.

"We barely have over four years left, Dominic, before we both need to be married. We aren't even dating people! How are we supposed to find trustworthy wives who won't narc on us in four years? That's basically impossible from where I'm sitting."

I sigh, growing more exacerbated by the minute. "Listen, go out and find a random fucking woman and get her to sign an NDA. Who gives a shit man?"

"I fucking do!" He yells through the phone. "I give a shit because this will be my *wife*, you bastard. You should give a shit too, considering these women will eventually birth our heirs."

I chuckle, not ready to lavish him with all the nitty-gritty details. I let him in on the secret. "I've already found my future wife."

"What the fuck do you mean 'you've already found her'?"

"I mean exactly what I said. I'm going to marry her within the next few years. Although, the sooner the better since summer is right around the corner, and we would want to get married in the late fall, close to winter. Not too warm, but not too cold either."

"Jesus. Fuck. I get your point, jackass. You don't need to rub it the fuck in." His voice trails off.

It feels good to rub it in a little bit. Fuck, who am I kidding? I love it. He can get fucked for all I care. I tell him as much and hang up on the poor bastard. He'll find someone eventually. Will it be within the five-year deadline? Maybe, maybe not. Will they be up to his standards? Most definitely not.

That's something I can figure out when we cross that bridge. But for now? I'm going to relish his misery.

As soon as I hang up, my phone rings again. Milo's name flashes across the screen. "What's up?"

"We found him."

"On my way."

We've been hunting for a specific man for over a month now. He isn't a criminal, per say, but he's a complete piece of shit who is barely the equivalent of scum. I learned about him several weeks ago while watching the security cam feeds from Point B. They aren't so much for the bar anymore, but specifically for Katherine. I can check in with her daily, even when she isn't working since she spends so much free time at the bar outside of operating hours.

One night a few weeks ago, she was in the back room with her friend, the redhead. I wasn't overly concerned at first because they looked like they always do. But then Katherine's face crumpled ever so slightly. Her face reddened, tears leaking from her face.

It caused a whole slew of operations to occur. I scoured the bar's cameras, finding nothing. Then I located her apartment and found its shitty cameras. I saw the man force a boot in her door. It made my blood boil then and it continues to do so.

Now I make sure to always watch her at the bar when she's on shift, especially when she's closing.

It almost feels as if I'm talking to her directly. My favorite thing is when she faces the cameras head-on, like she knows I'm watching. I'm the boogeyman waiting in her closet.

THE WAREHOUSE IS COLD AND DARK WHEN I ARRIVE. Milo is already in the bowels of the building with the piece of shit he managed to pick up. My blood is hot and ready to punish the man who dared to hurt my Katherine.

It isn't acceptable.

I stroll into the warehouse. I take several flights of stairs and pass around multiple bends before stopping in front of a metal door. A thick bolt rests on the outside, but it's open now.

The short-dicked man is under six feet. He is slumped over to the best of his capabilities. His wrists are chained to the beam in the ceiling. His toes are about two feet off the ground causing all the muscles and tendons in his arms to take the brunt of the weight. Beautiful tension boils in his veins.

Milo stands off in the corner, behind the man. I give him a quick nod, and he lowers the beam the man is attached to. When his feet barely brush the ground, the sound he creates makes me think he's about to cum in his pants. I stifle a laugh as I approach his scrawny demeanor.

"Do you know why you're here?" His face is mottled with freckles, his nose harboring a deep scar across its bridge. One too many fights it seems. "Answer me."

His teeth chatter. I sigh. I whip my arm out, delivering a deep punch to his kidney. He crunches inward and wheezes. "I'll ask you one more fucking time."

"No! I don't!"

We're finally getting somewhere. "Are you positive you don't know why someone would want to end your fucking pathetic life?"

The man was barely holding it together before. Now tears leak from his eyes, drowning his face in salty wetness. I flick a finger out to his cheek. He startles. I chortle again as I sweep up a single tear droplet, the liquid thin and oddly relaxing as I rub it between two fingers.

His eyes flick upward, catching mine as an idea spreads. I give Milo another nod and he strides out of the room. The door, still cracked. He can handle a lot, but sometimes things become too much for him, and I respect that he knows his limits.

My victim stares me down. Does he think Milo leaving is a victory for him? He's sorely mistaken.

I wipe the other side of his face, collecting his tears like possessions. "Does the name Katherine Rigby ring a bell to you?" I ask casually though my heart demands for me to kill this fucker now.

The man shakes his head slowly, proving he's the idiot I think he is. I *tsk* at him. "What a shame, she's a beautiful woman."

Not that he will ever see her again.

As I toy with the droplets of liquid between my fingers, I lay them back on his face, right under his cheekbone. His skin is warm. His blood must be hotter. I swallow thickly at the thought.

I dance my fingertips up his cheekbone. I trace where the crow's feet begin marking their territory on his pock-marked skin. My pointer finger grazes his eyelid, prying open the tender skin. I sink my finger into the underbelly of his eyeball.

His screams vibrate my skull. Tears leak out of both eyes.

In two tugs his eye is loosened and pouring from his eye socket. The small ocular nerve barely holds its weight as it slops against his still moistened cheek.

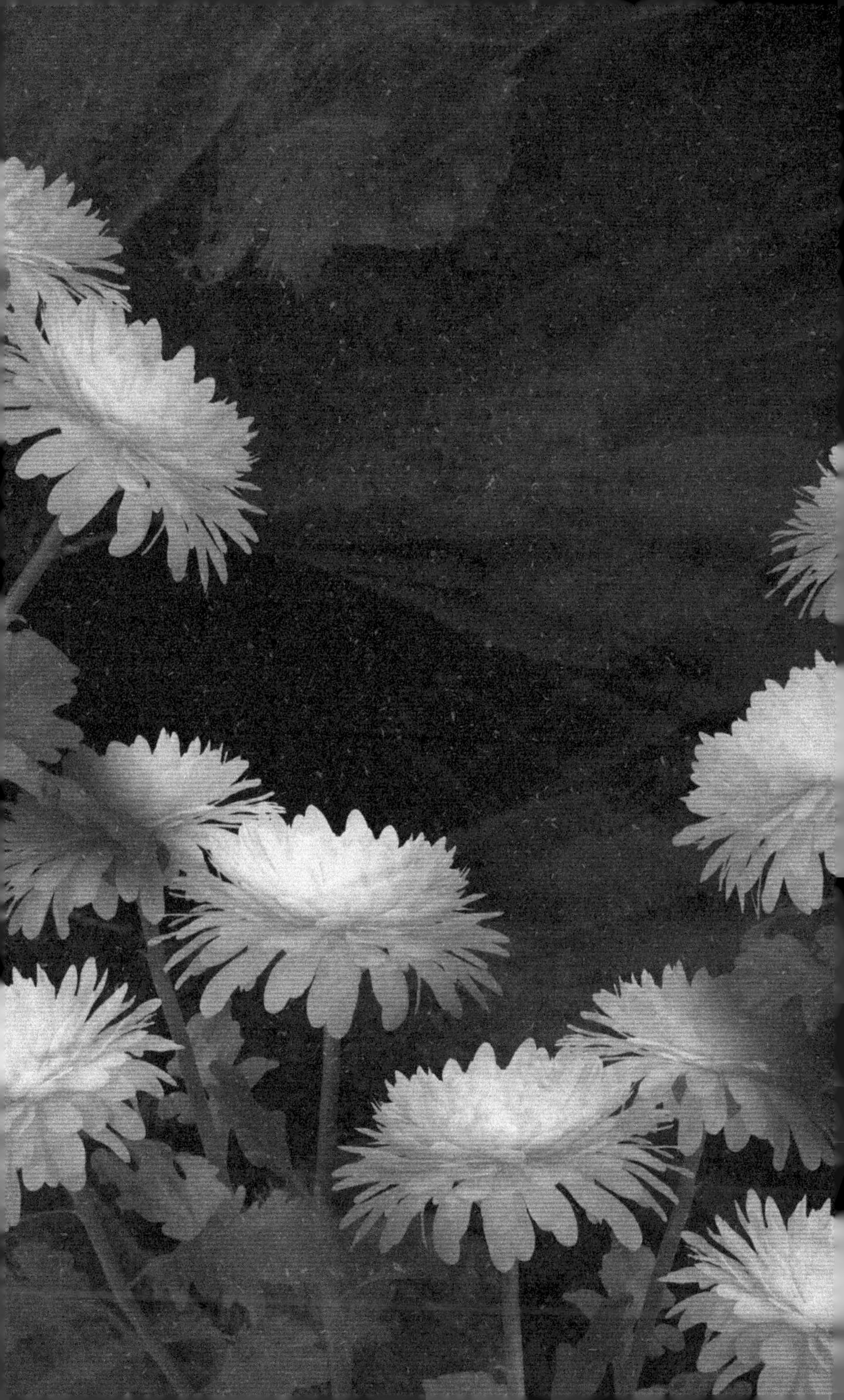

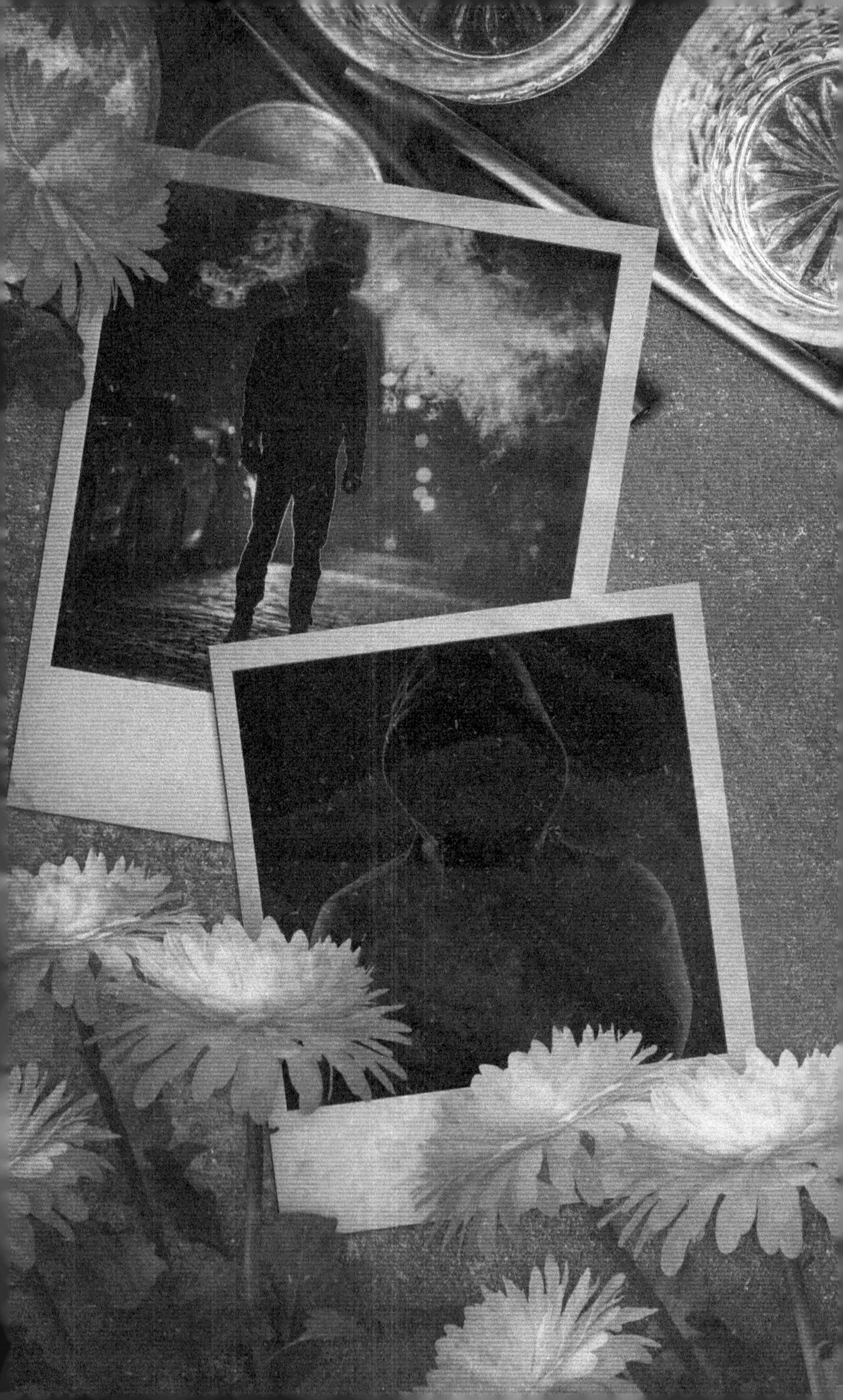

Five
June 2019

KATHERINE

The bar is monotonous on a good day and annoyingly shitty on an average day.

Today is an average day.

I've been here since two in the afternoon, and it's only approaching nine PM. Each hour creeps by slower and slower, like molasses pouring into mildly warm oatmeal. I'm making my rounds wiping off all the tabletops and booths. I glance at the large television hanging on the far wall every few minutes. The screen casts blue hues throughout the lounge area.

Marisol is around here somewhere, but I haven't seen her in a hot minute. She's probably around back, macking on her latest man. Someone I don't know or have seen before. She's being secretive about it, honestly. I try not to think of it too much.

I steal another glance at the droning television and recognize the face staring back at me. It's a man who had taken me out on a super shitty date several months back. I stare at the screen, unblinking, not hearing Marisol enter the lounge area. When she taps me on the shoulder, I nearly jump ten feet in the air. My hand flies to my chest as I try to slow my rapid breathing. "God damn it, Marisol! You scared the shit out of me!"

"I wasn't trying to scare you, bitch!" She leans closer. "What's got you so amped up? You're not normally this jumpy."

I glance back at the screen. I take note of the near-pristine skin looking back at me. The bright red banner dragging along the bottom of the screen tells the viewers he's missing.

"Hey, didn't you go out with someone with that name a while back?"

I nod, swallowing my words. We had a boring dinner. He walked me to my apartment like a gentleman, but when I turned to enter my door, he shoved his foot between the door and the frame. His front had pressed against my back. His breath reeked of the garlic and onion he had at dinner. I could feel it permeating my skin. I shudder at the memory. "Yeah, it was actually that guy I went on a date with."

Marisol's wide eyes look between me and the screen. "Oh my god. Are you sure?"

I swallow, not really knowing what to think. He was a scumbag, but that doesn't mean I *wanted* him to die. I glance at the screen one last time. Something uneasy settles in my gut.

TIME CONTINUES MOVING SLOWLY THE REST OF THE shift. We're ready to close around midnight. It's early in terms of closing since no one came into the bar for over an hour. No point in staying open for no customers. I rotate my shoulders as I count the money drawer, waiting for Marisol to bring me her roll of cash to add in.

She prances right up to the counter, her wild hair fluffing

around her. Speaking of the devil. "Hey, are you doing anything next month?"

I steal a glance at the redhead. "I work and I sleep, I don't really do anything else unless it's with you."

Marisol shrugs, unbothered by my attitude. "Well, there's another new club opening in the town over. We should totally go."

I try not to mimic vomiting. "Ugh, why would we do that?"

Her mouth props open. "Because opening night is themed, and you know I'm a sucker for a themed night." She juts her lower lip out by a mile.

I plant the money from the drawer into a small zipper bag for the boss to pick up in the morning. "What's the theme?" I ask, my voice lacking any emotion. I'm ready to go home, take the quickest shower of my life, and flop into bed completely naked.

"It's a masquerade, costume themed. Please, can we go?"

Fuck, I'm getting suckered into this, aren't I? I can't ever say no to Marisol, not when her lip reaches clear to California. I find myself nodding. "Sure, let's go. It sounds fun."

Marisol jumps up and down, clapping her hands and whooping loudly. Thankfully the bar is closed, and no patrons are inside, or I would be slightly embarrassed by her outburst, but that's Marisol, the life of the party.

DOMINIC

I'm getting increasingly irritated by the numerous phone meetings the Sandman requires. Is he opening another nightclub? Definitely. Is it the first? Or the second? Or the fifth? No, it isn't. So, why is he constantly calling me and bugging the fuck out of me about it?

I scratch my beard. I briefly think of shaving it but decide not to. I like the scruff and it gives me something to do with my hands when I am on the phone with the Sandman, which to seems to be all the fucking time at this point.

I'm currently listening to him drone on and, fucking, on about the new club he is opening in the town next to ours, Clivesdale. He isn't necessarily asking my permission for anything, just giving me the rundown of all the essential information. It's part of our merger deal, I suppose. It makes sense he's telling me all this shit, but that doesn't mean I have to enjoy all the yapping. I cup my cheek as I listen.

"We should do a themed event for opening night. What do you think?"

"It sounds like a solid plan. What theme do you have in mind?"

The Sandman is quiet for a few moments. For a second, I think he hangs up and I am eternally thankful before he speaks again. "Let's do a masked event. Like a modern-day masquerade where you have to cover your eyes and shit. That could be fun. Classy and sexy all at the same time."

I'm impressed, I admit. "Sounds like a good idea. We could definitely sell enough tickets to be at capacity. Do you need any assistance with prep or are you good?" I offer support not out of the good of my own heart, but because it makes me look amenable to the Sandman.

He chuckles. "Nah, Dominic, I'm good, but thanks for pretending to give a shit." And he hangs up on me.

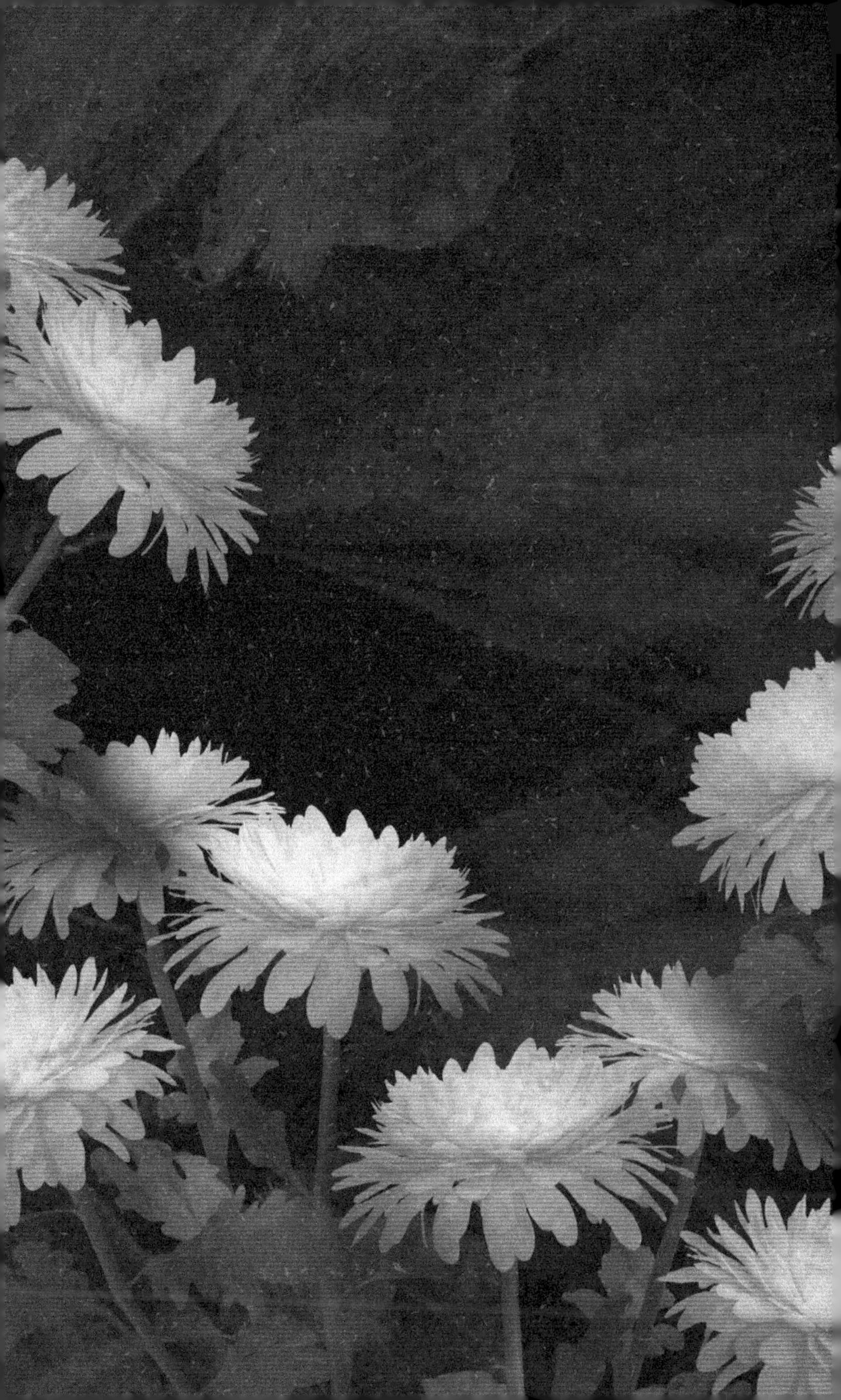

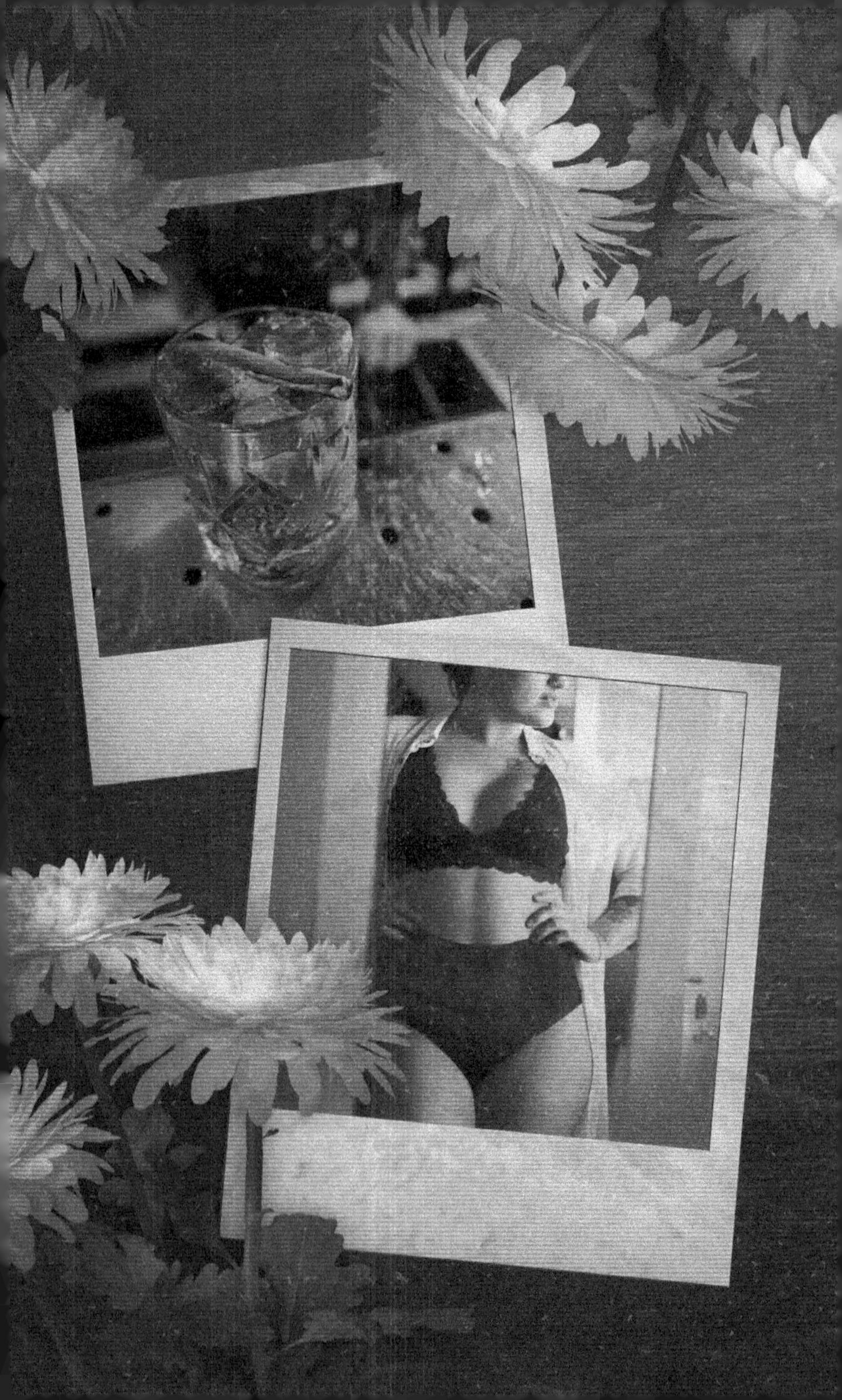

Six
July 2019

THE SANDMAN

This has been in the works for several months, and I'll be damned if it all goes to shit on the opening night. I pull my cuff links into place and stare into the mirror. Straightening my tie, I take a deep breath and allow myself a moment of clarity.

Everything was ordered, the staff is trained and ready to go, the bar is fully stocked, and the DJ is already onsite setting up. It will be perfectly fine. Who gives a shit if my blood pressure's a little high at the thought of something going askew?

The club is about two hours from my house and by the look of my watch, I need to get going now or I run the risk of being late to my own opening. I rush out of the house, slicking my hair as I stumble down the stairs and into my garage.

The club is empty when I arrive – thank fucking god. The inside is sleek and modern, the outside resembling an old Victorian. Duality. Change. I love the striking difference between the shell and the core.

Slipping inside, I make my way to my office, where my costume, if you can call it that, resides. I'm fully embracing my name, Sandman. My suit is a desert beige. My mask, an elaborate piece of cloth, lace, and weeping jewels rests well against my hot skin. It covers my eyes, a good portion of my forehead, my nose, and ends above my lips. No one will recognize me. Hell, I barely recognize myself. I secure the ties behind my head and adjust the mask to sit comfortably.

I face the corner mirror, noting the small diamonds littered across my nose and cheeks like adorned freckles. They resemble glittering sand. I commissioned a small business I found online to create the mask. The woman's craftsmanship was stunning and didn't even cost a hundo. I tipped her graciously.

I spend the final moments before the opening running around the club ensuring everything is where it needs to be. Staff is on point tonight. I haven't seen Dominic, but he didn't say he was coming, so I push that thought away.

Tonight is about the club.

It's approaching midnight and the club is bustling with noise and bodies in every corner. Couples are... coupling – groping and shoving their tongues down one another's throats. I slick my hair behind my ear and double check my mask's ties to ensure they're still tight.

So far, so good.

I plan to have the club open until dawn. After a long night of dancing and tongue fighting, the guests can crawl into the rising sun and pass out on their couches or beds. I wish I could have a semblance of something similar, but it isn't in the cards for me.

Instead, I'll stay here until at least ten in the morning, counting bills and cleaning the bar tops and booths, and helping the staff where I can. Most of them take off as soon as we close since they will have been here for over twelve hours at that point. We're closed tomorrow anyway, so I'm not too worried about the cleanup and logistics of getting that figured out.

I'm making a ninth round around the club, scoping out any problematic patrons lurking. Thankfully, I haven't seen any aggressive people tonight, which is rare at a nightclub unfortunately. There is always someone who tries taking things too far or slipping something in someone's drink. Hence why I hired so many security guards and bouncers. I don't want anyone to be harmed in my club.

I'm leaning against the back far wall when two women catch my eye. There's a short girl, rail thin and with a halo of red hair floating around her head. Her dress and mask are matching reds, as well as her stilettos and handbag. Most women, from what I've noticed, don't mix reds when they have fiery hair, but this woman is going all out. I'm impressed by her confidence.

But she isn't who my attention focuses on. Her friend, I assume, is a curvy woman a few inches taller than her. Her dark hair is wavy and hits her dress straps. Her dress is somehow modest, hitting her mid-thigh. It's a fabric made of the deepest green. It's smooth with a light layer of tulle on the lower half, giving it motion as she moves across the floor with her friend. She wears small heels and carries no bag. Her mask is also dark green. It melts down her face with large droplets covering her cheeks and caressing her throat.

It has to be a custom mask; I've never seen one like it. The green of it sparkles against the roving lights in the club, throwing off small splotches of color in any direction she turns.

When she fully faces me, my breath escapes. My mouth dries. I lock eyes with her, her mask failing to cover the sudden blush creeping up her neck. She licks her lips and offers a small uptick in the corner of her mouth.

She's only a dozen or less feet away. I could go up to her right now and ask for her name. Find out who she is and learn everything about her. But with the mask comes anonymity.

She wants to be unknown for the night and I present the same. There will be no names exchanged, no pertinent information. No matter how much it hurts to think of her not gasping my name.

KATHERINE

"Just go up to him already," Marisol scolds me for the fifth time in the last two minutes. Ever since I made direct eye contact with the hottest man I have ever seen; Marisol has relentlessly pestered me to introduce myself.

I hate myself for considering it. I don't know him. I'll probably never see him again.

But maybe that's why I should go up to him? He doesn't know I live in a super shitty apartment, work at a dead-end bar, and can barely afford the cheapest drink in this place tonight. He doesn't know my history or my lack thereof with the opposite sex.

"Fine. Fuck it." I throw a glance at Marisol who has the largest grin known to man spackled on her face. Fucking bitch, dragging me here and then encouraging me to talk to someone? Why were we friends again?

Swallowing down my nerves, I approach the stranger. He's better looking up close. He's at least a foot taller than me. His dark hair is cropped close to his head. His mask matches his suit, reminding me of sandy beaches. His gaze doesn't leave mine, never straying to my exposed chest or body. I hate to say it – but it makes me like him a bit more.

The expectations are on the fucking ground apparently.

"Hi," I manage to squeak out. Blood rushes to my cheeks, forever grateful for the homemade mask I had spent hours on the day before. It covers most of my face, hiding the blush and embarrassment.

"Hello." His voice is low and beautiful. "Are you enjoying the club?" His hands are holding a single wine glass, full of a deep ebony liquid. It must be some type of sweet wine.

"It seems like a great club."

He smiles. His white teeth gleam under the low lights. "I'm glad you're enjoying it. That's the whole point, isn't it?"

"What, to enjoy it? I mean, it is a club," I laugh then want to pinch myself.

The man chuckles back at me. I instinctively know he isn't laughing at me, but rather in solidarity. "The whole purpose of a night club is to enjoy oneself. It's all about the fun. Throw in the masquerade aspect of it and it's a hell of a party." He smooths his tie down his torso and my eyes fixate on how the shirt under his suit jacket stretches across his chest.

"Yeah, you're right, I suppose."

The man rakes his hand through his hair, ruffling it a bit from its position. "Would you like to dance?" His voice is lower, like he's suddenly shy.

"Sure."

He holds out his hand. He's wearing an array of golden rings that match beautifully with the colors of his suit and mask. I place my palm in his, letting his long fingers grip around mine as he leads me to the center of the floor.

The music has been loud since we stepped through the door. But out in the center of the dance floor? It is pulsing-- a drum beat like the heart of an animal. Bodies, in varying stages of dress, are everywhere. I let the man lead the way, his elbows and shoulders making plenty of room for the two of us to fit in wherever we choose.

He comes to a halt, spinning to face me. His smile lights up his face, his eyes twinkling in the low light. I do not need to see all his face to know how beautiful he is. His olive skin contrasts against the beige suit.

My mouth waters. How long has it been since I've kissed a

man? I'm really *considering it*. The man's full lips are screaming at me, begging to lavish them with attention.

Thankfully, the man interrupts my wayward thoughts by wrapping his strong arms around my waist. He pulls me closer until our chests are only a breadth apart. I want to close the small gap between us, but I don't want to seem desperate. Keep it together, I tell myself.

"Oh, fuck it," he says, reading my mind as he tugs me effortlessly closer.

My breasts mash against his sternum. My breath leaves my mouth as I peer up at him under my lashes, coated in several layers of waterproof mascara Marisol lent me. She spent ten minutes combing through my lashes with a spoolie, curling them, and applying the mascara in thick coats. Thank God for that woman. I will never curse her name again.

"You were too far away for my liking, *Ranuncolo*." He smiles at me.

What does it mean? I don't particularly care because coming from his mouth? Leaving his tongue? The name calls me like a lover lost at sea.

I wrap my arms around his neck, playing with the collar of his jacket and shirt. My thumbs dip into the neck of his button-up. His skin is hot against mine. It sends a burning sensation through my fingertips, up my arms, and into my chest. I'm afraid my heart will stop. I suck in a breath and look directly into his amber eyes.

"I felt it too."

How did he know what I would say?

His eyes are wide, almost moist with affection. The electric shock of emotion still harboring in my chest tells me to move closer if possible.

"Kiss me?"

"You don't need to ask me, *Ranuncolo*," he whispers before his head tilts down and his lips fall onto my own.

They are as plush as I imagined. Soft and smooth.

I let my lips mold to his as his tongue caresses the outer edges of my mouth. He licks at the seam, asking-- no, begging for entry. I take a quick breath, and he slips his tongue into my mouth.

I moan as his tongue sweeps from side to side, the two dancing a long-forgotten dance. He is all consuming. He pulls away a fraction, his breath hot.

He kisses the corners of my mouth, lavishing me with open-mouthed kisses. He trails my jaw and neck, brushing the edges of my mask. His arms hold me upright as my back bows to the pressure, like he wants to be one identity, one soul.

"You're so fucking beautiful." His eyes meet mine, his lips wet with the evidence of our dalliance.

His eyes devour me. I find myself near speechless. "T-thank you."

"Come home with me?" he asks in a rushed voice.

"Come home with you?" Surely my ears just stopped functioning correctly. Right?

He takes a small step backward, giving our bodies a tiny space to breathe. "Actually, fuck!" He runs one hand through his hair again, the other arm staying wrapped around me possessively. "I live over two hours away. That wouldn't work."

I shake my head, agreeing silently. That's a little too far for my comfort zone. "I didn't come here alone anyway. I came with my friend, and I can't just leave her. We don't live around here." I whisper-shout.

His face lights up. "I have a private office here. Upstairs."

"What? Why do you have an office here?"

His face shutters for a moment. "I invest in clubs."

I nod in shock. "Okay?"

"Okay to coming to my office or okay I invest in clubs?" He asks me, his lips barely quirking.

I shrug. "Both?"

Officially not giving a single fuck. He wants to go to his office for quick fuck? I can get behind that. I'm a single lady who has needs after all. He's a grown ass man who invests in clubs? He makes more money in a day than I do in a month no doubt. But what about that spark earlier? Is there something more here? Is it worth diving into?

"Okay, follow me, *Ranuncolo*." He grabs my hand and begins leading me away from the crowd.

I catch Marisol's eyes. She didn't stray far from us, always making sure that I'm safe. God, I love her. I give her a quick thumbs up and point to the unnamed man and back to myself. She gets the drift, and I continue following the Greek god of a man to his private office.

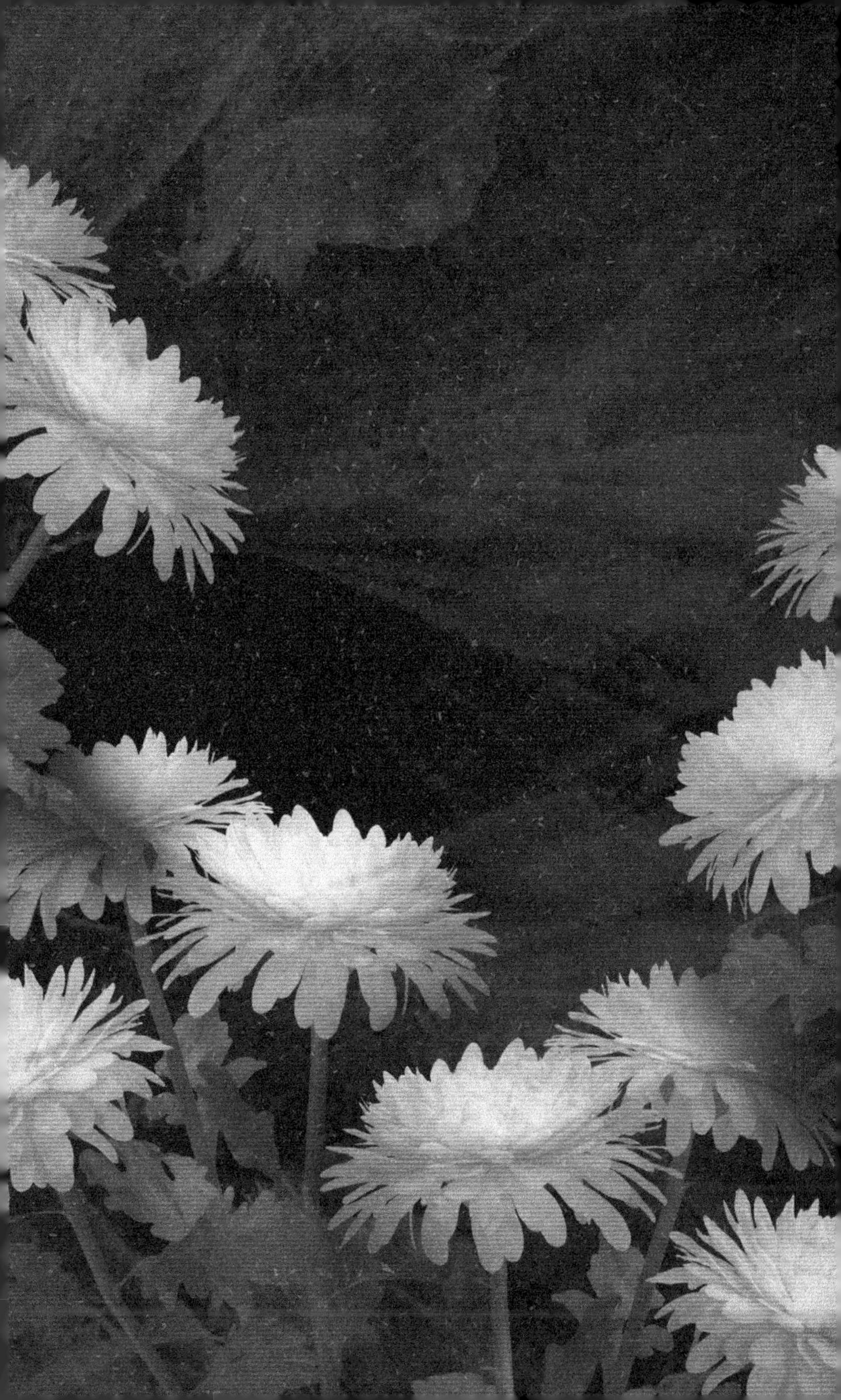

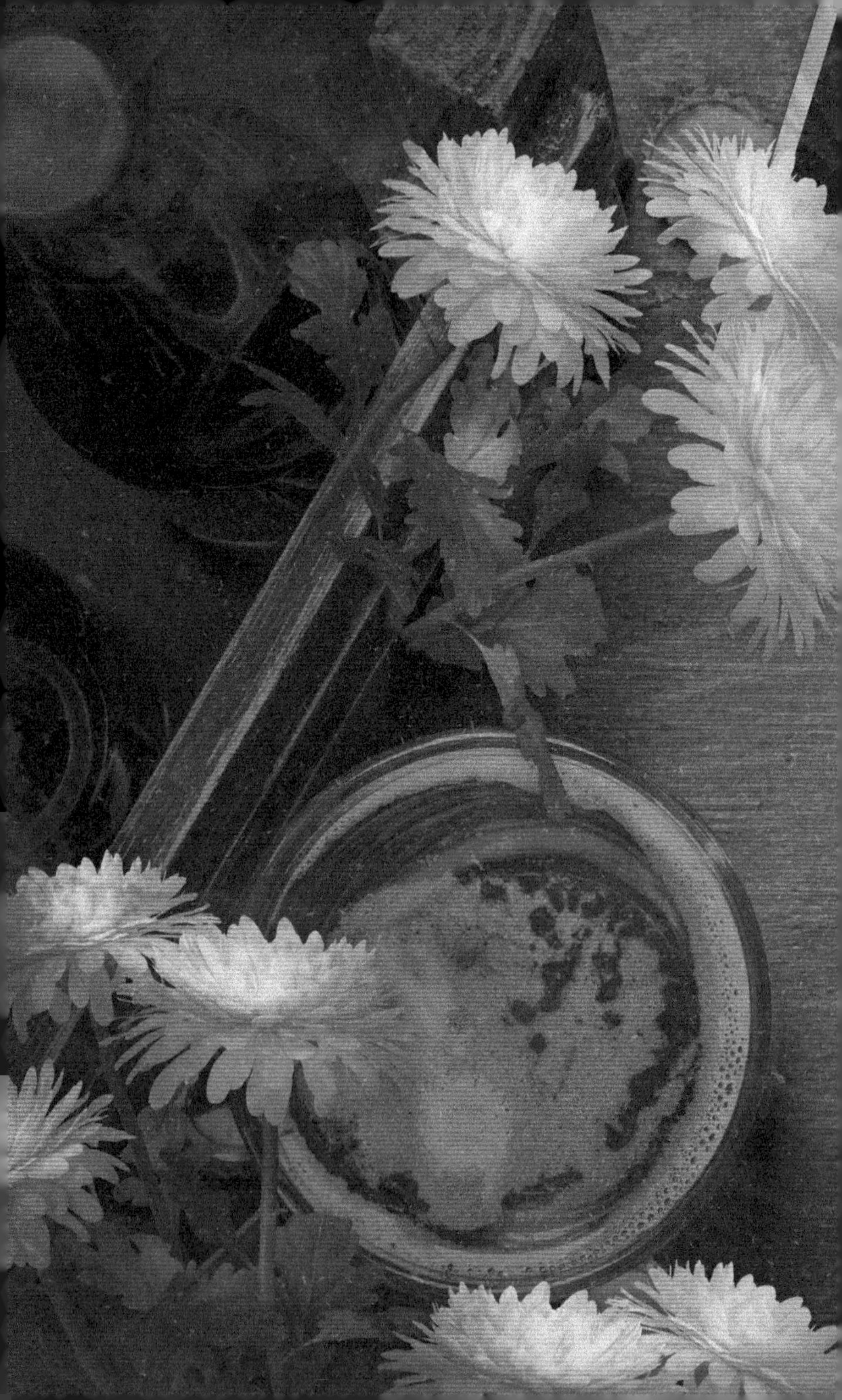

Seven
July 2019

THE SANDMAN

My mind races as I climb the stairs with the beautiful woman, her hand in mine. I take a risk and glance back toward her. Her face is angled down, watching her feet. Her hand clutches mine tightly, as if she's using me to steady herself. I lick my lips at the thought of her name, her career, her native city. I stop myself and focus on the anonymity.

We broach the top of the stairs, and my office door looms ahead. I face the beautiful goddess before me. I have to look down, my height hindering me from looking directly into her eyes. I've never wished to be shorter before, but damn am I now.

I close the small gap between us. I wrap my arms around her waist and secure her body to mine. I dip my head low, capturing her lips on a sigh. She tastes sweet like nectar. Amaretto and grenadine. I long to drown in it.

As her lips part for me, I wrap my arm under her ass. I lift her, and she wraps her legs around me. Our torsos crush together. We're two flames becoming one. Her skirt rides up her thick thighs. I caress the smooth skin. Skitters of electricity dance up my arms.

I pause my languid kisses as my forehead falls to hers. I look into her eyes. They are beautiful swirls of gray, like a storm approaching the horizon. A storm you must watch from your window even though it may be an F5 tornado coming to wrench your life apart. Her eyes hold the histories of a thousand suns and revolutions. I am lost.

I push her against the wall, separating her legs open for my hips to sink into.

"Is this for real?" His voice is low like she doesn't want me to hear.

I raise my hand to tuck a wayward strand of hair behind her ear. Her mask is dark in the dim light, but the intricacies astound me. The melting effect drags down her cheeks, highlighting her lips. They're wet and her mouth is slightly ajar. "It's real," I tell her, almost not believing it.

I kiss her once more, a little harsher and briefer before pulling us away from the wall and making it down the hallway to my office door. I grip the door handle and push our way in. My office is still sparse. I have no trouble carrying her to my large desk.

I plop her ass on the top. She looks up. Though her mask conceals much of her expression, I can make out the intense blush polishing her cheeks, neck, and bust. I wonder if I can make her blush brighter.

I want to savor this – enjoy her skin against mine. Enjoy how her eyes look as she peers up at me through those thick lashes. I take a small step back, propping my chin on my hand. I study her, memorizing everything. She's the most beautiful woman I'll ever have the pleasure of viewing.

If God himself created her, then she is filled with all the most delectable sins, overflowing from the bucket of life. She has lust sewn into her body. Envy coats her hands, turning her fingertips green from the jealousy of the other women who've crossed her path.

This woman, the goddess who I shall worship for the rest of my days, must bathe in pools of divinity, her skin glowing, like a siren calling out to captains, leading them to their watery deaths.

I would walk straight off a ship into the coldest waters to be surrounded by her song.

Her fingers gently tap the top of my desk. She leans back, pushing her shoulders and chest toward me. It draws me in, much like that captain. I close the gap between us. A full sea of stormy waters can no longer separate us.

I cup her knees, my thumbs running small circles over her skin. She trembles into my grasps. Windows line the wall behind her. The city illuminates my office in a sheen of colors. Pinks and blues coat the walls. Her dark emerald gown shimmers like liquid gems. I slide my hands up her thighs, leaning in close.

She licks her lips once more. The flame ignites my chest. I surge forward and catch her lips. I lick the seam and guide my tongue into her awaiting mouth.

Her dress bunches around her waist. My fingers find the waistband of her underwear. I pull back enough to ask, "Are you sure?" I gaze into her storm-ridden eyes as she surely shakes her head. "Words, please."

She gives me a light giggle, bringing her hand to her mouth. "Yes, please, sir."

I roll my neck, the small nickname making my pants stretch across my cock. "Since you asked so nicely, *Ranuncolo*." I grin.

I grip her underwear, maintaining direct eye contact with the vixen as I slowly pull them down. She shifts onto her hands and lifts her bountiful ass. I slip the thin fabric over the globes and down her thighs. I take a step back as I continue pulling the fabric down her legs and over her feet, her heels still in place.

I bring her underwear to my nose and inhale deeply. Her scent is sweet and earthy.

She gasps. "What are you doing?"

My gaze darkens as I look at her. "Saving these for later." I scrunch the fabric into my pocket. I want to remember every single detail. Her chest moves with deep breaths. "Open your legs and keep them apart." The goddess complies, widening her legs instantly. I can nearly see her center, but not quite. "Pull your dress up a little further." She does as I ask. "Good girl, *Ranuncolo*." I smile, and the grin I get in return sets my skin aflame once more. My dick, swollen and needy, is painful against the zipper in my pants. I long to give it a squeeze but keep my hands in my pockets as I watch my girl.

My girl? I'll dissect that later.

With her legs apart and her dress pulled up, I have a perfect, full-fledged view of her glistening pussy. It's covered in a layer of dark curls. My mouth waters, and I swallow deeply.

"Do you like what you see?" Her voice doesn't waver. She's still quiet, nervousness bleeding through her tone.

I don't take my eyes off the sight in front of me. I take one hand from my pocket and firmly grip my cock through my pants, giving it the squeeze I desperately needed earlier. It does nothing to sate me now.

"Take your hand and pull your lips apart," I command.

"W-what?"

I will ease her fear. "Pull your lips apart, let me see more of you, *Ranuncolo*."

She nods and takes one hand from the desk, briefly bringing it to her collarbone. She drags her fingers down her chest, over her breasts and down to where her navel would be. Her fingers walk over the bundled dress at her hips until they graze the apex of her legs.

I watch, raptly and fully, as her middle finger swipes between her folds. Her pointer finger and ring finger take each side and slowly pull apart her lips, showing her inner heat to me. Her middle finger is making languid circles around her clit. I glance at her face. Her eyes peer at me while her teeth dig into her bottom lip. With one more sultry glance from underneath her eyelashes, her mouth opens.

"Are you just going to stand there and stare?" Cheeky, brazen. My heart pounds. I squeeze my dick harder, almost wincing at the pain from being so swollen.

I step into the woman, her knees bracketing my hips. I pull her wider. My hips thrust on their own accord even though my dick is still behind my slacks. I groan at the heat that radiates from her core.

I pull her hand from her cunt, wrapping my fingers between hers in a harsh handhold. They are moist, the juices from her cunt visible in the multi-colored light from the city. I brush my nose against hers. "You're delectable, aren't you, *Ranuncolo*?"

Her free hand is at my waist. She pops the button and drags my zipper down in one movement. Before I can wrap my head around it, her hand is gripping my shaft, squeezing, and pulling it out from my boxers. I glance down at our meshed hips. My dick pulses at her proximity. I thrust involuntarily again, almost embarrassed, but she only squeezes me harder, pulling her hand down and around the head.

A drop of precum oozes from my head as her thumb swipes over it. Looking into my eyes, she brings her thumb to her lips. She paints it across her lips like it's the most expensive lipstick.

Her tongue darts out. "Delicious," she moans.

My cock is fully erect, reaching for her. I rally my thoughts. "Are you on birth control? I have a condom somewhere..." I begin looking around, then remember there's one in my desk, courtesy of Dominic. He gave it as an office gift.

She swallows. "I'm on birth control—have an IUD."

I barely stifle a groan, thankful she is safe. I tell her I'm clean and she says the same. "Ready then, *Ranuncolo*?" Her eyes are wide, pupils fully blown. I wish I could see her face. "Masks?"

"Leave them on." She's saccharine sweet, but there are hints of sassiness coming through that make me want to sink my teeth into her.

I take a breath, readying myself both physically and mentally.

Her heels dig into my waist nearing the top of my ass as she tries to pull me closer to her, to her core. She's weeping for me as I am for her. Two halves of one whole.

I surge forward, slamming into her rather harshly. Her ass moves backward on the desk as I plunge into her. I withdraw almost fully before diving back in. After several pumps of my hips, I wrap my arms around her torso, pulling her impossibly closer to my chest. Her breasts smash against my pecs, flattening and nearly spilling out of her top. "You're so goddamned hot, *Ranuncolo*," I moan into her ear.

I drag my tongue from the bottom of her ear before placing a sloppy kiss on her temple. I move one hand from her and drop it to where we connect. My cock slides in and out of her wet heat. I twist my wrist and find her clit, adding pressure to it and swirling in slow circles before adding pressure again. I repeat the pattern, listening to her gasps and moans as a guide to her pleasure.

Her hands are roaming my back, her sharp little talons scratching my shoulder blades before coasting down and back up my back. When did I take my shirt and jacket off? My mind is muddled, completely consumed by the woman in front of me, wrapped around me in more ways than one.

Her body shivers once more. I give her another open-mouthed kiss on her jawline, dragging my tongue along the bone and following the drips of her mask before kissing the corner of her mouth. "You're taking my cock so well, *Ranuncolo*," I breathe, "What else can you do?"

She moans, her eyes clamped shut as I pound into her harder. I pull out, completely, keeping her close. "Turn around."

She whimpers but does as I say. I give her space to hop down from the desk. Her dress is mussed and her hair more askew than it was earlier in the evening. Sweat glistens on her shoulders and collarbone. Slivers of her face and neck are red from the mask rubbing against her cheeks and throat.

My cock is at attention, still crying to be back inside of its new favorite place. I go to her, putting my hands on her hips and turning her so she's facing away from me. I meld my front to her back, using the pressure to slightly bend her over my desk. I find her ear once more. "Are you ready?"

She bites her lip hungrily. "Yes, please."

I push her back down with one hand. I clutch her wrists, bringing them behind her. My pupils dilate at her flattened breasts bulging against the desk. Her back bows as I tug her closer. "You're doing so well, *Ranuncolo*."

She shimmies her shoulders until she's laying comfortably. I shift both of her wrists to one hand and brace the other on her hip as I align my cock with her entrance. I slide home in one quick stroke.

We moan together. I drop her hands and she pulls them in front of her head, clasping the edge of my desk. The desk rocks with each pound.

I'm relentless as I meet her ass with my hips. Pistoning in and out of her is an out of body experience. If she's the goddess, then I'm the sole worshiper.

I push my arm underneath her, finding her heat from the front. I toy with her clit for a few moments, hoping to get my timing perfect. I want us to cum together. I'm nearly there but refuse to go over the top without her. I pinch her clit, softly at first, then a bit harder as the base of my spine tightens.

I bend over her back, keeping my ministrations with her clit constant and hard as I slide in and out of her pussy. "Come with me, *Ranuncolo*. Come on my cock and drench me."

She cries out her release. I pump into her, my cum coating her walls. I slump against her back. Her dress is scratchy against my bare torso. I press my cheek against her skin. I close my eyes and regulate my breathing. I keep my arms on either side of her, making sure to keep my weight off her.

What the fuck just happened? My ears are ringing. Sweat coats every inch of my skin and somehow my dick is still half hard even though it just ran a fucking marathon.

I peel off her and help her to stand. She tries to tuck her hands under her arms like she's hiding from me, but I won't accept that. Not after what we just did. "Don't hide from me, *Ranuncolo*." She gives me a small grin and nods. I help her adjust her dress, pulling it over her thighs to hide the mess. "Don't wash off until tomorrow morning when you shower."

"Excuse me?"

I smooth her dark hair behind each ear. I kiss her crown. "You heard me. Keep my cum between your legs until you shower in the morning. I want you to feel what we did, even while you sleep."

Was I being irrational? Perhaps. Did I give a shit? Not particularly.

I adjust her mask and tighten the knot holding it in place.

She wraps her arms around my neck and returns the favor. We take a few breaths, and I can't look away. She's gorgeous, a goddess. I'm convinced I've somehow died, and this is the afterlife.

She bends, picking up my shirt and jacket from the ground.

"I don't remember taking those off," I whisper.

"Me either, but you must have at some point," she laughs. This feels so natural. I don't want it to end.

I slip my shirt on, buttoning it up quickly, not wanting to look away from her. She holds out my jacket and I slip that on as well. She adjusts my lapels as if it's the most natural thing in the world for us to be doing. She glances up, her expression tight for the first time.

"What is it?" I ask. "Are you alright?" I frantically skim my hands down her arms, afraid I hurt her somehow. Was I too rough? Too greedy? Did she not cum hard enough?

"I like you. This was...an interesting evening to say the least."

I rake my hand through my hair. "It was the best sex of my life, honestly." I don't mean to say it out loud, but, well, my brain is quickly becoming useless.

The corner of her lips draw upward, her eyes crinkling at the edge. A genuine smile. "I enjoyed it as well."

Oh, thank fucking god. "So, what's wrong then?"

"This is all it can be."

"All what can be?" I'm confused. I know my face shows it.

She leans back onto my desk, crossing her arms. Her eyes are downcast, her jaw jutting out.

"This is all we can be. I don't know you and you don't know me."

"Well, we can fix-," I start. I go to untie the knot supporting my mask on, but her hands grab mine quickly.

"No, you don't understand."

"Then tell me, please, I'm losing it here." I try to play it off, but I can feel my heart breaking, the subtle echoes in the cavern of my chest quaking, changing the very DNA and blood that inhabits it.

"We can't see each other again. We don't know each other." She lets go of my hands and steps away from the desk, going toward the door.

I move to follow her, but she halts me. Her face is no longer red, but her eyes are misty.

"Please, stop. Don't follow me. Don't look for me." She wipes a finger under her mask, collecting tears. "This was just a fun night, a one-night stand and that's all it can be. I have things going on and you obviously have things happening in your life as well. This was fun and now it's over."

She pivots and walks out the door. It clicks shut.

I shove my hands in my pockets, finding her underwear. The only keepsake I'll have for the night I fell in love with a goddess and was left all in one breath. While I keep her underwear, she keeps my cum between her thighs and that will have to be enough to satiate me.

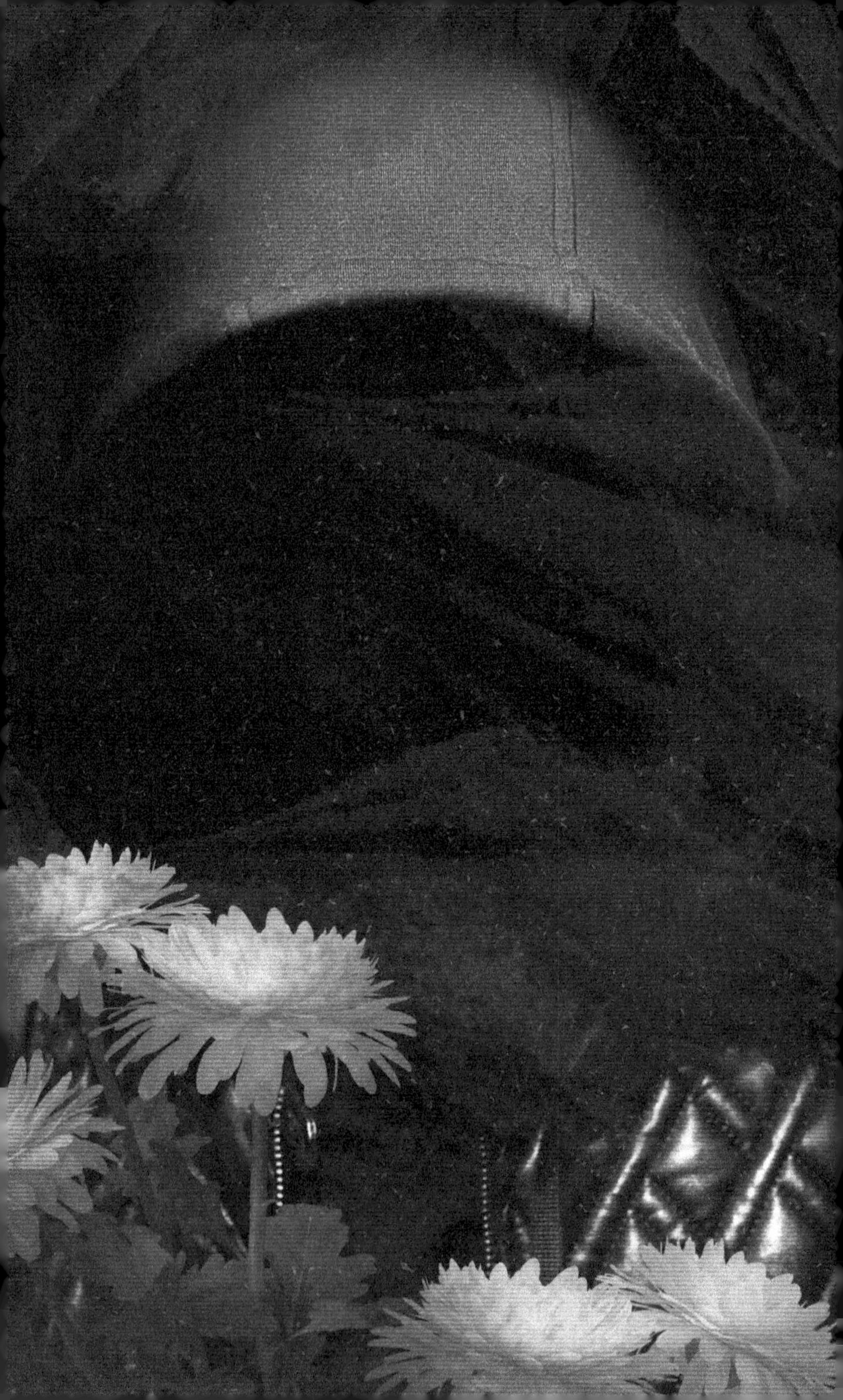

AFTER

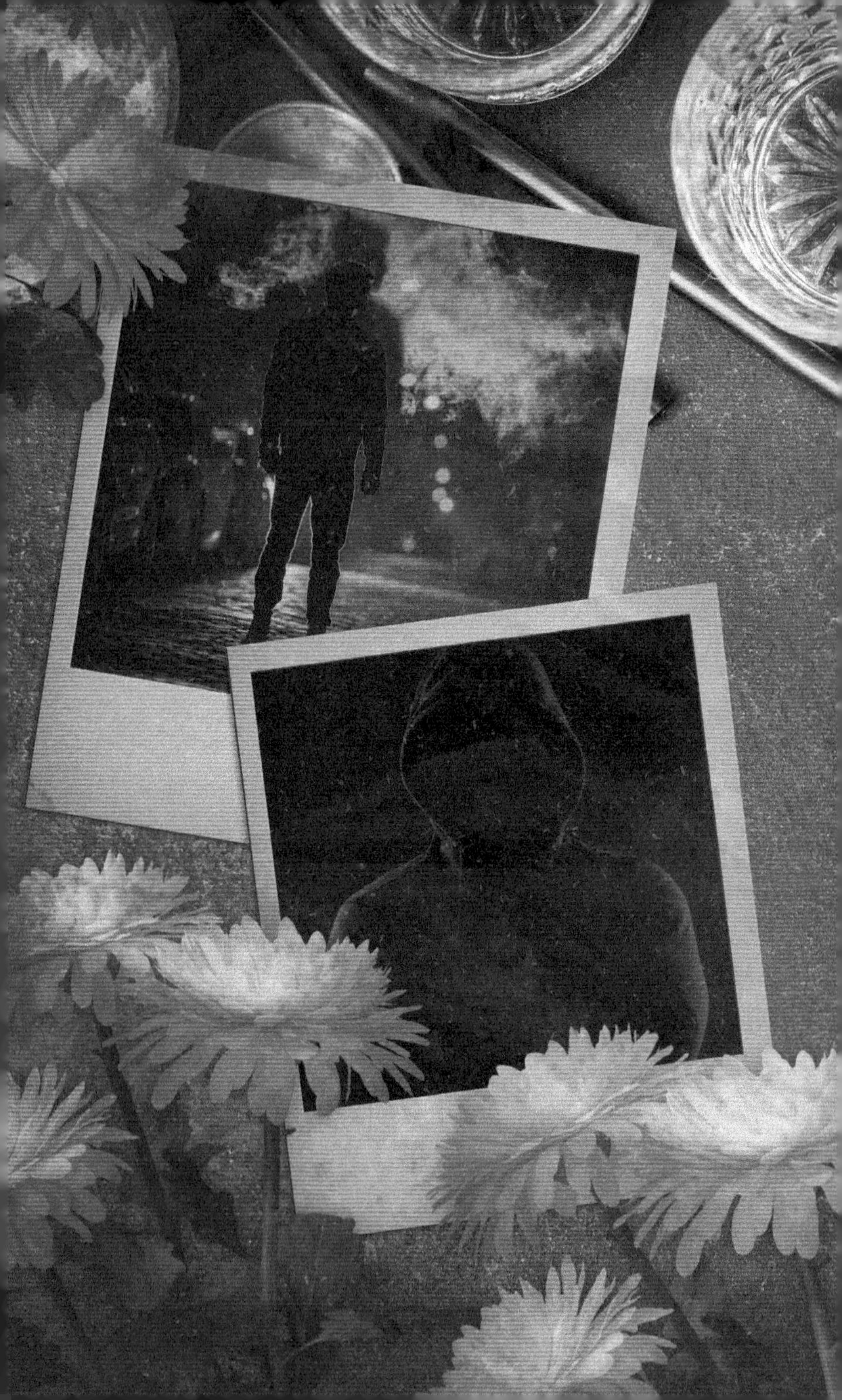

Eight
Five Years Later

DOMINIC

The alley is damp and smells like a basement that's been sealed for years. It might be an alley, but it offers the best vantage point to watch her.

Katherine Rigby is leaning against the bar top at Point B. The same as she's done for over ten days in a row. Will the routine continue tomorrow? What about the next day? My bet's on yes—yes it will since consistency seems to be her middle name. (It's actually Ruth).

Her hair is shorter than I'm used to, hitting just at her collarbones. It has a slight wave to it like she let it air dry. Like an endless void, I could lose myself in its darkness.

God, I want to.

I want to wrench her head back, feeling those short strands slip through my fingers as I pound into her from behind. Fuck, what a sight that would be.

But Katherine Rigby hasn't given me the time of day. She didn't steal any glances while Milo and I installed cameras. She didn't longingly gaze at me as I did her. She stayed behind the bar, cleaning.

Currently I'm seated with said best friend, Milo, talking over the specifics of an upcoming job. We speak of the target and what we will need to do to prepare.

Katherine's at the bar now, slinging drinks with some douchebag of a coworker whose name prickles my skin like thorns.

Joseph.

He doesn't deserve a last name. He's nearing thirty; his parents are both dead. He showed up about three years ago to Point B, looking for a job. I hired him then because he seemed nice enough, but not too nice, if you know what I mean. That kindness I showed him then is biting me in the ass now.

My mind slinks languidly back to the present. I shift in my seat and wonder why Joseph is in the bar tonight. He isn't on the schedule, and no one called in. He's just…working for no reason.

Except there is a reason and her name is Katherine.

My Katherine.

I digress, slipping my gaze back to Milo. His face tightens in annoyance. "Sorry, man," I say, trying to stifle a glance at the bar again, but ultimately failing, "you know how I can't help myself when it comes to her."

Milo nods, his voice barely audible in the loud bar, "It's alright, boss. I know how you get around her."

Thank God he's mildly understanding. He never complains, though my frequent loss of focus clearly agitates him.

Stealing a glance at the bar, I notice the douchebag coworker crowding around Katherine. He's all hands and shoulder bumps. I can't get the feeling of boiling rage filtered from my blood. I want to slam his head against the bar as his hand brushes her elbow, slightly turning her toward him.

I push up from my seat, shoving the unnailed table towards Milo.

"Dude, what the fuck are you doing?" he grunts.

"I have to talk to her."

Milo's eyebrows nearly touch his hairline. "Nic, come on. You're still after this one?"

I turn my body to him, leveling an icy glare. "That douchebag is touching her, grabbing her, feeling her up." I keep my voice even, but the rage wants to be let out. I need to do something.

Milo scoffs. "Man, he's just helping her do her job. You know, like coworkers do?" He's taking all of this in stride, mocking me. "Just sit down man, give yourself ten minutes to chill the fuck out and then go up to the bar," his hand drifts toward it, "and order a drink. Maybe flirt a bit." Now he gestures to me, still standing, my shoulders heaving with each breath I take. "But for now, you need to sit down and chill the fuck out, so you don't freak her out. *Sit*."

And, so, like a bitch, I sit down and begin planning my future, more so than I already had. It's an obsessed, ludicrous plan that will probably bite me in the ass. Or maybe she would.

KATHERINE

The first of the month always brings me a new level of anxiety – if that's even possible. But at this point in my life, I don't really give a shit. The anxiety of paying the bills and keeping myself alive are so intertwined with my being that I just continue existing, knowing I'll figure it out as I typically do. Why stress more when you stress the maximum amount?

It makes sense to me.

Walking to the bar, I keep my headphones in and my eyes on the sidewalk. The walk is short and there's not much to see other than the cracked sidewalk and weeds that refuse to die. There's usually dog shit around one set of apartments. I do my best to avoid the dehydrated stray turds.

As I walk, I fish my cigarettes from my bag. They're at the bottom, so the package is slightly concave. They'll still light and smoke the same, so I pop one between my lips. A quick flick of my lucky lighter and the cherry blossoms red, the smoke flowing across my tongue and down my throat. I inhale deeply and exhale gently. The cloud plumes wiggle away into the air.

I don't need to see everyone around me. I need to get from Point A (my shitty apartment) to Point B. Point B has become my home over the last few years. I basically live and breathe that bar, sometimes against my better judgment.

I have the closing shift tonight, as per usual. It's a Tuesday so the bar shouldn't be too busy as the regulars filter in and out after work before going home to their own shitty lives. That's the way of life around this part of town. Nothing you can do about it, not really.

My cigarette burns up and I pinch the end, extinguishing the tiny flame before stuffing it into the side pocket of my bag. I'm not adding fodder for the little birds to choke on around here. I ensure the butt won't fall out of the hole-riddled pocket.

I hurriedly light another cigarette, sucking the tobacco down in deep breaths. Once I start my shift, I won't have time for another until at least midday.

Five minutes later and the cigarette is ash on the sidewalk and another butt is added to my bag's side pocket.

I shrug my bag back onto my shoulder, pushing the unlocked door open.

Marisol must already be here. Either her or Joseph. Or both.

Joseph is a fellow bartender. We don't need two people working behind it tonight so maybe it's just Marisol. Glancing around the dimly lit bar, I see her satchel lying on top of one of the high-top tables, a little round thing that could maybe hold a few beers, but nothing more.

"Marisol?" I call just as she walks around the corner from the back, her red-tipped nails swiping at her equally red lips.

"Hey girl!" She runs faster than I believe possible in her four-inch stilettos. She throws her tanned arms around my neck, crushing my head to her chest. "I'm so glad you're working tonight! I was worried I'd be alone with the pricks." She rolls her eyes dramatically. She sniffs my hair as she pulls away from me. Her eyes narrow. "Did you just smoke a cigarette?"

I gently shove her off. "Put your hound nose away, Officer. And, for the record, those pricks pay your bills and mine."

"You need to quit that shit before it kills you," she admonishes. "And, yeah, for sure, but they're still grabby, pencil-dicked pricks."

I laugh with Marisol, tossing my bag down onto the bar and letting it slide down to the end by the register. "No Joseph tonight?"

Marisol rifles through her satchel, pulling out a small cosmetic mirror and applying a new slick layer of lip gloss to her plump lips. "Last I heard, which was last night, he wasn't going to be here tonight, but who knows with him?"

I *tsk*. Joseph is a good guy, don't get me wrong, but he's flakey at best and irresponsible at worst.

THE TUESDAY SHIFT IS GOING HOW I EXPECTED IT TO – slow. I drum my fingers against the bar, peering out at the handful of patrons that litter the booths. Marisol lingers a few feet from me, scrolling through her phone with puckered lips.

"What's got you making that face?"

She closes out her screen and glares, but I know she isn't angry with me. "I've been talking to this guy on Brimble."

"What the fuck is Brimble?"

"You know, that new dating app for hot singles. Duh."

"Oh right, of course," I chuckle. "My bad, please continue." I flourish my hand.

"Well, anyway, we've been messaging for a few days now and he was supposed to stop by the bar tonight, but the idiot has to cancel. Says he had a work thing come up." Now it's her turn to scoff, "A work thing? I mean, come on!" If Marisol was a cartoon character, smoke would be pouring from her ears.

Before I can ask about her mystery guy, a glass pounds on a booth across the bar. That's how the pencil dicks alert us their cups are too low and that we should bust ass to refill them.

Spinning around to the wall covered in bottles of liquor, I pull what the patron had previously and make the drink. Within a few moments I'm sliding the large glass to Marisol, letting her take the drink to the man.

The man is a regular. If I recall him, then Marisol definitely does. She knows almost all the regulars and their orders. Her memory is unmatched when it comes to people.

The regular must be in his fifties. His hair is thin and graying around the temples. His face isn't horrible to look at, but you can tell he spends every night at this bar. Marisol places the cup in front of him as he grabs her waist to pull her to his side.

On reflex, Marisol's hands fly to the guy's shoulders, keeping him at a distance. Since I saw her nearly knock that guy out a few years ago with nothing but her serving tray and gusto, I know she can handle herself.

That doesn't mean she has to do it alone, however.

The guy puffs out his lower lip. "Oh, come on, darlin', bring it in," he slurs. "Let me get a good look at ya." His eyes leave her face and travel from her bralette to her booty shorts. She looks hot, I'll be the first to say, but that doesn't give this prick a right to straight up ogle her.

Before I can think better of it, I hop over the bar, my ass sliding through the condensation left by countless drinks.

Great, I think, *I probably look like I pissed my pants.*

Oh well. My sneakered feet hit the bar floor and in no time I'm close enough to Marisol to smell her perfume. I place my hand over hers, still resting against the man's shoulder. "Hey girl, your boyfriend called behind the bar. He's looking for you."

It's always the story we use when some loser dude wants more than what we offer at Point B. We each have fabricated boyfriends, sometimes even husbands.

Marisol plays the part well, her eyes rounding. She pulls away from the man, cupping her mouth with her palms. "Tyler called? I've been waiting all day!" And with that, she tosses a casual glance at the man. "Sorry, hon, I gotta jet!" She all but sprints toward the bar, rounding the corner and heading straight to the office.

The man, who still hasn't touched his refill, glances at me. A sneer pulls his lips back and his eyes darken. "You think we don't know the score around here, girlie? Everyone knows that you two have boyfriends, but we ain't never seen one."

My heart stutters at his words.

The man guffaws, "You think just cause we're all drunk here most of the time that we're stupid fools?"

I don't know what to say to the man. He's exactly right. Marisol's fake man is Tyler and mine is Kane. We throw their names out left and right, never expecting any of the patrons to remember.

But this one does. Do others?

My heart pounds in my chest, keeping time with my racing thoughts.

He suddenly grabs my hips. "Just because you're behind that bar all the time doesn't mean shit to any of us, Kirbs."

Ah, shit. The bastard knows my name, or, well, at least my nickname.

Before I can think of a retort for the old creep, a finger taps on my shoulder. "Excuse me?" A masculine voice made of gritty sandpaper speaks.

The drunkard grabbing my hip squeezes harder, making me wince. Simultaneously, the body behind me steps forward. He faces the drunk, his back to me. My breath catches in my throat as I watch his back muscles flex through his shirt.

He is at least six feet tall. My head comes up to his chest –

maybe. I'm wearing thick sneakers, so even less than that barefoot. My words catch in my throat as this man with gorgeously blonde hair looks at me, his eyes smiling while his lips flatten. He looks vaguely familiar, but I can't quite place him.

"I've been waiting for you outside for nearly twenty minutes," he says.

"Oh, I, um." I want to bash my head against the table.

"I know it's slow here on Tuesdays, baby. That's why I'm usually alright with just waiting outside, but you didn't show. Are you okay?"

The longer I stare into this man's face, the more I recognize him. I rack my brain, going through face after face. It dawns on me then: this is Dominic.

He's the owner of this bar – my boss.

My face flushes red. He's here while I work. He hasn't come back into the bar during my shifts since he installed the cameras.

The delicious, yet slightly deranged, man pries (pries!) the old man's fingers from my hips and replaces them with his own. He shoves his thumb in my back pocket, pulling me to his side and kissing the top of my head.

The old man's jaw is slack as he stares at the two of us. "Well, I'll be damned," he mutters. "Maybe you have been telling the truth all this time, Kirbs." He looks away, utterly shell-shocked all the same.

"Come on, baby," Dominic says down to me.

I still can't find words as he wraps his arm around my shoulder and leads me to the alley. My heart is thrashing in its cage, but my feet carry through the lounge and into the dark street.

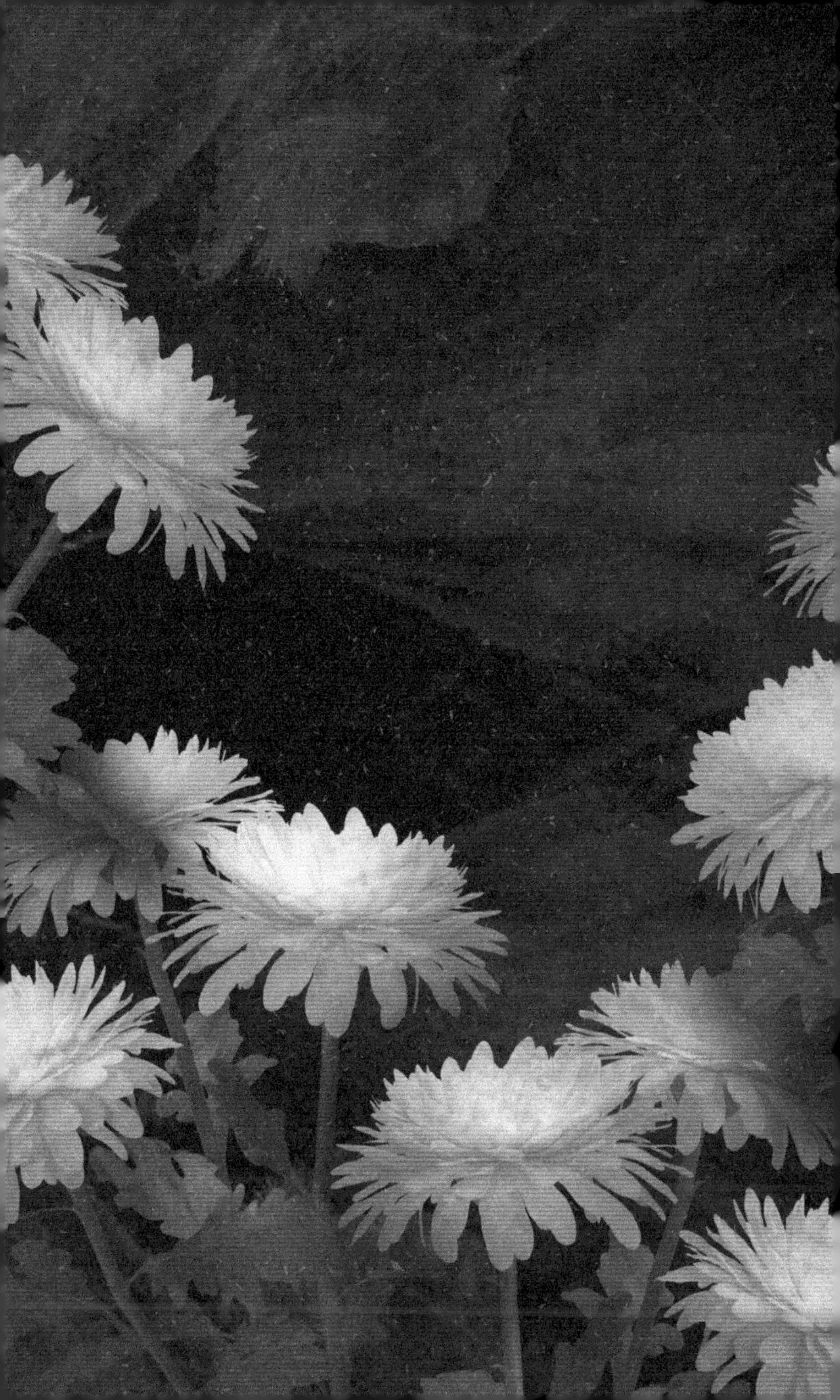

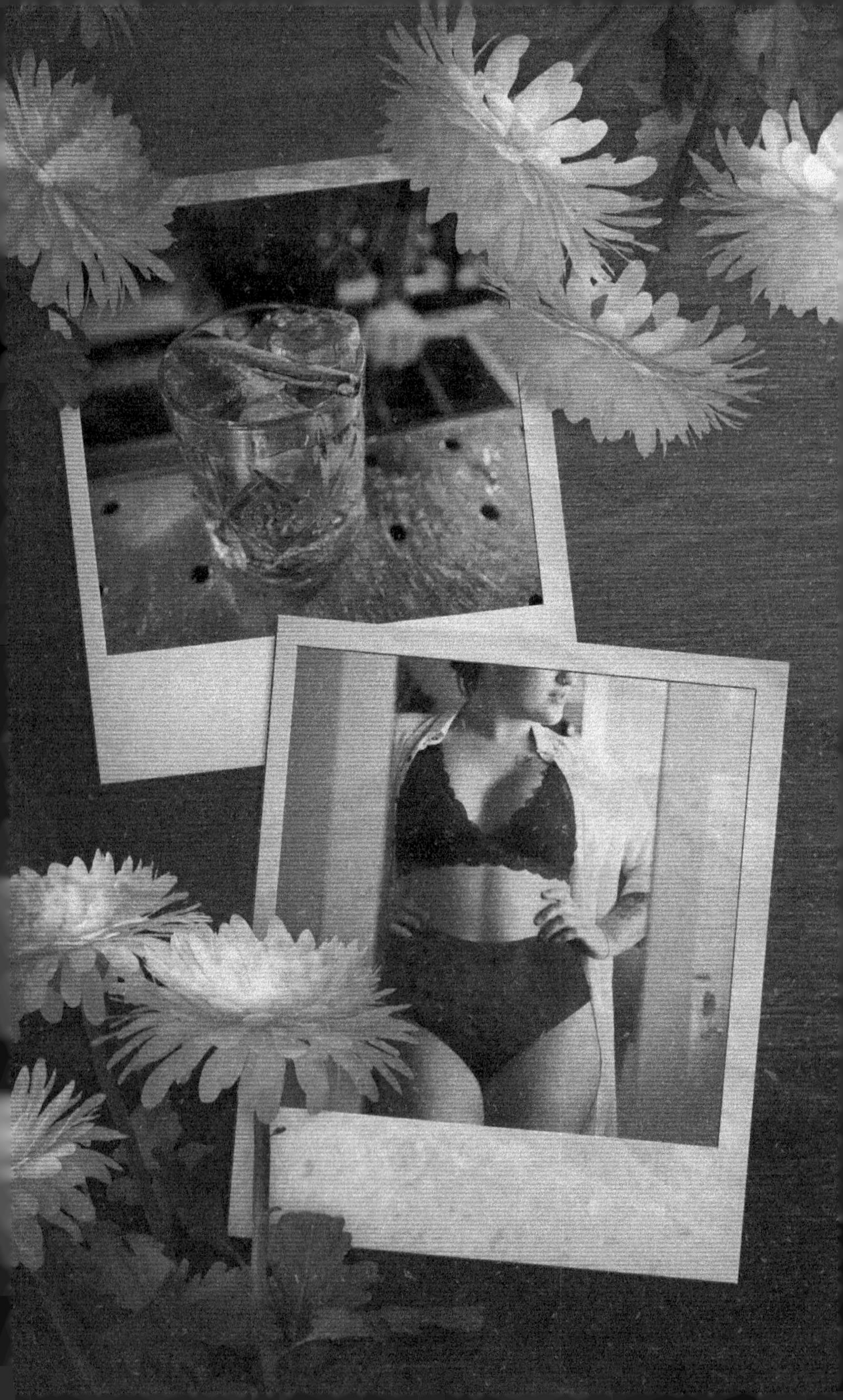

Nine

DOMINIC

I wasn't planning on approaching Katherine tonight. All these years watching through the bar's live feed (and recordings) have keyed me into her mannerisms and expressions, but they don't hold a flame to physically interacting with her.

I bite down on my tongue. I clench and unclench my hand, fighting a losing battle. While I don't want to lose the upper hand I have spent the last five years building, I can't help but to think maybe, perhaps, this is kismet and all will be right in the world. My world being Katherine, of course.

But here I am, leading her away from Point B and that old fucking loser. He thinks he can put hands on any of my employees? He'll get barred from the location for that, but threatening, no, *physically* touching Katherine?

He would pay with his life.

I've studied Katherine enough to know that she's going to yell at me. I continue to let my arm fall around her shoulders. Her skin is cool in the night air. I want to breathe in her scent and rub my nose into her neck. I shake my head, biting my tongue until copper floods my tastebuds.

I stifle those desires. I don't need her to pull out a hidden knife and gut me in the alley.

Katherine yanks away from my grasp the moment we're out of view. She rounds and stares me dead in the eyes. "What the fuck do you think you're doing?"

She is seething.

This is to be expected.

I drag my palm over my forehead, grappling for a clear way to handle the situation. I don't want her to know that I've been watching her. All hopes and dreams of claiming her will be out the proverbial window.

I sigh, deciding to go with chivalry. "I saw that old fuck bothering you, *harassing* you. And I didn't want him to."

Cool, calm, and collected. I am so relaxed – I could work at a day spa.

"Well, I had it handled," Katherine steams.

She's offended that I'd stand up for her? I suppose that tracks. "I watched you handle it, and he wouldn't stop, so I figured seeing someone who was larger than him would assist you."

Katherine's shoulders bunch to her ears, the tips of them turning crimson against the night sky. If I could paint her in this moment, in her vulnerability, I would do it repeatedly. She doesn't speak.

I spread my arms wide, conveying that I'm not a threat. "It looked like he was going to cop a feel and you seemed uncomfortable. I couldn't let that continue."

"Oh, so you're a knight in shining armor, are you?" She quips, her fire rekindling.

Does she not remember that we met all those years ago? Did she forget that I am technically her boss, the owner of the bar? Am I that forgettable? In the same moments I was falling in love with her, was she just having another day?

I raise my eyebrows. "If that's what you want me to be."

Katherine scoffs, "If that's what I want you to be." She plants her hands on her hips, taking a fighting stance across from me. She clenches her teeth. "I don't need you to be anything other than my fucking boss."

She does remember me. Thank fuck. "Well," I shove my hands into my pockets, "in that case I was acting in the capacity of your boss. No employee of mine will ever be treated like that."

Her shoulders fall to their normal stature. A two-part painting series then. I stretch my hand out to her. "Dominic," I remind her. I don't want to embarrass her.

"I remember who you are for fuck's sake." Katherine grasps my hand in a shitty attempt at a handshake. "But if you even think about having me call you Dom, I swear-,"

"People usually call me Nic," I quirk, doing my best to hide my growing beguilement. She's a spitfire.

Katherine's face eases a fraction. "Well, Nic. We need to get a few things clear here, do you understand?" She plants her hands on her hips, brows drawing together.

I swallow. "Okay, shoot." I school my features, lowering my smirk and widening my eyes a bit.

"First," she counts one finger in the air, "I don't want or need you to save me or do anything for me, actually."

I nod when she pauses, eager to hear her out. I want to please her, consume her, however she lets me.

"And secondly, now that you've shown your face around that regular, he isn't going to let me live it down. He's just going to dig in harder since he's going to see you as competition now."

Well, shit, I hadn't thought of that. But he's just some old man who probably has to pop a Viagra just to get it up and ready, so can he really be that big of a deal? I'll come back to that later.

Katherine's gaze lifts to Point B behind me. Her expression suddenly slackens, the corner of her lip shooting up. I quickly spin to investigate what's inducing this reaction.

Of course, it's that fucking bar hand who had been touching and talking to her all the damn time.

Joseph.

I didn't see him in the bar tonight, though, so why the fuck is he showing up now?

"Joseph! What are you doing here?" Katherine seems as flustered as I am.

Storing that information for later.

Joseph casually approaches me. He stops at my shoulder, and I instinctually step to the side.

"I figured I'd come hang out at the bar and see how your shift was going." He pauses. "I didn't think we were due for one-on-ones with the boss tonight."

Cheeky bastard.

Katherine giggles, but it sounds strange. I've heard her giggles with her redheaded friend. This isn't a genuine one. "Oh, you know me, Jo, just being friendly." Katherine glances around the alley, unease coating her skin.

Joseph nods in my direction. "Well, Kirby, there's still a few hours till close. Wanna grab me a Bud Light then I can walk you home after your shift?" He side-eyes me. "Nice to see you, bossman. Hope your night is going well."

He's definitely being a kiss ass. He doesn't give a fuck about how my night is going. He inches closer to Katherine. Does he think I'm a danger to her? Does he not remember how he gulped in his interview when I threatened to castrate him if he fucked up too much?

Also, did he just call her Kirby? Like the pink puffball action cartoon thing? What the fuck?

Katherine, I mean Kirby (nope, not calling her that ever again), clasps her hands together, wringing her fingers. "Yeah, Jo, I'll be right there. Just take whatever seat you want. I'll grab you that beer here in a few." She throws a quick, but hardened, glance toward him.

Joseph pivots on his heel and stalks back to the entrance of Point B. Once the doorbell chimes, Katherine turns. "Why do you have that look on your face?"

I scoff. "I don't know what you're talking about."

She raises her brows. "Sure, you don't, big guy." She walks past me and claps me on the fucking shoulder like I am her long-lost best friend. I watch her walk across the dimly lit street and re-enter Point B.

I'd be lying if I said I don't watch her ass sway as she walks. I imagine slapping it like she did my shoulder.

She is *pissed*. She doesn't need (or want) saving. Then she said the old fuck will be expecting me to hang around. Does she expect me to hang around? Was that a come on from her? No, I shake my head, she needs my protection now. It's clear as day. The patron will know my face as her boyfriend and now I'll have to be in the bar regularly on her shifts. It wouldn't be a hardship for me.

I plop my shoulder back against the concrete alley. I resume watching the bar – watching her. She might not want or need me, but I'll be her knight in obsidian amor regardless.

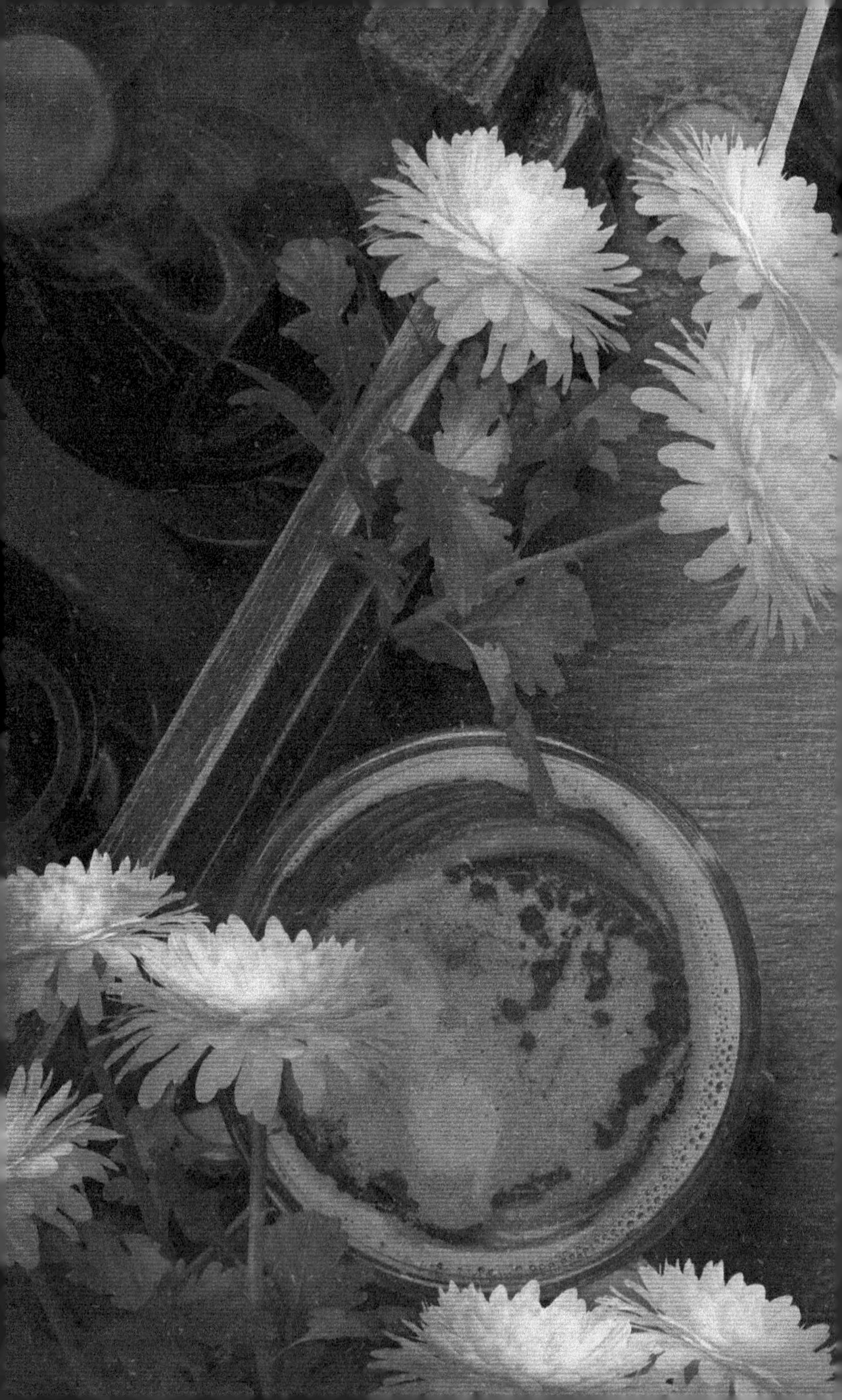

Ten

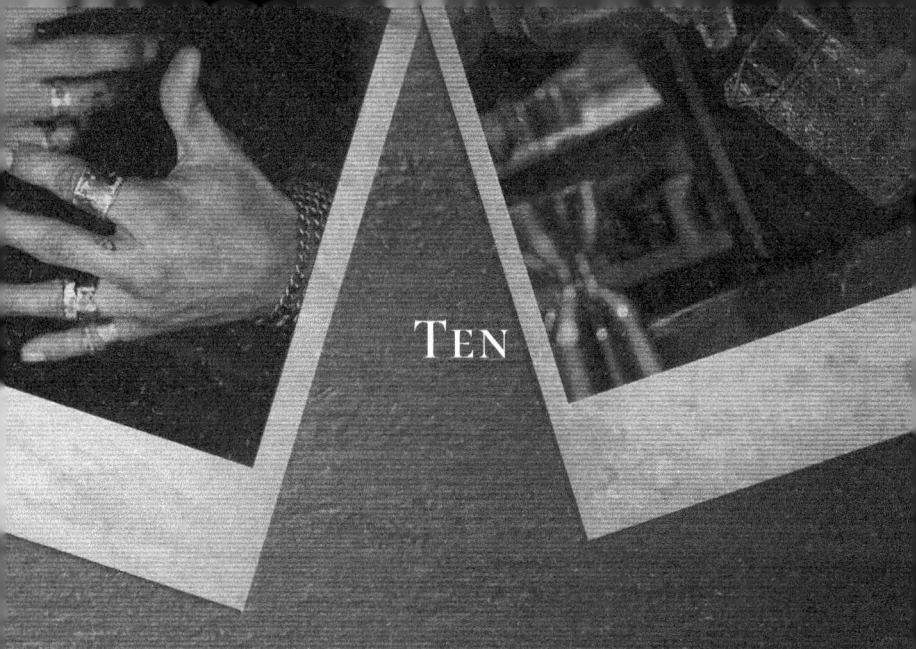

KATHERINE

My mind is swirling with a thousand conflicting thoughts.

Why would Point B's owner come to my aid? I tap my finger on the side of my face. He must want something.

I chew on my lower lip as I follow Joseph back. I want to glance over my shoulder to see if Dominic is still there in that dank ass alleyway, watching me.

I don't want him watching me.

Do I? Maybe I do?

Fuck.

My eyes flit to Joseph's back as I cross the threshold into the bar. He's decently tall, taller than me at least. His shoulders are wide, but he doesn't get my nether bits raging. He's been flirting with me endlessly for the past few years since I started working at the bar. He's always nice about it, but I can tell he wants anything I can give him.

It makes me feel grimy as he holds the bar top up for me to slide through. "Thanks," I reply monotonously.

He stares, his eyebrows scrunching. "Why were you talking to the bossman outside?"

I sigh, "Fuck if I know, Jo." I grab a rag and begin wiping down the alcohol that splashed on the bar, hoping Joseph will get the hint to leave me alone.

"He was looking at you like he owned you or some shit."

I huff, facing him. "He barely knows me, Jo. He couldn't possibly look at me like that."

Joseph laughs, full-bellied and loud. The sound ricochets throughout the bar causing several of the regs to give us stares like we're disturbing their family holiday dinner rather than their fifth rounds of stale beer. Joseph shoots a look back before returning his gaze to me. "Trust me when I tell you, Kirbs, that man was looking at you like he found you, paid for you, and kept you in his basement for years before letting you see the light of day."

One day bleeds into three, then into five, and I still haven't seen Dominic again.

It's a standard shitty day, not that any of the other days were great. It would be nice if something happened to perk me up or give me something else to think about rather than spending all hours of the night and daydreaming about that man's fucking delectable face.

I feel like I'm going insane. Or have ingested an aphrodisiac. I keep finding myself thinking of him, the way his chiseled jaw sloped down to meet his neck that was ablaze with dark swirls and roses. I still feel his arm draped over my shoulder. The heavy, sturdy weight of it lingering on my scorching skin.

My eyes pinch shut as I lie across my bed. I imagine his arm grazing my stomach as he leads his hand to my pants. I imagine, dream, *wish*.

His hand teases at the brim of my pants. He looks up, his eyes piercing and heated.

One finger slips under my waistband, ruffling the soft curls. I bite my lip and concentrate. One finger becomes two. His deep voice floods my ears, "Aren't you a good girl for me? Going to let me slip another here?"

I moan. The blood rushes to my bottom lip clamped between my teeth.

Imaginary Dominic gently prods. He locates my clit in record time, according to my track record. He swirls once, then twice. On the third round he presses down and starts the pattern again.

Instantly, liquid coats my thighs.

Dominic ushers me higher. I nearly plead for more pressure and friction. My hand tracks the movements I wish the *real* him would make.

I keep my thumb pressed to my clit as I add a third finger to my channel. They're instantly coated with wetness. I whimper. "Dominic," before I can stop myself. I keep the punishing pace.

"Come for me, baby," he whispers as he presses my clit harder, nearly pinching it between his fingers.

I can't hold it anymore.

My climax reaches its high and pushes through me without a second thought. I finally let my lip go and cringe at the blossoming bruise.

God damn.

I steady my breath before my hands slip from my panties. I sit up, finally greeting the day like I should have before I imagined my boss touching me. Shaking my head, I make my way to the bathroom to shower and get ready for yet another shift at Point B.

As I walk down the sidewalk to work, my phone rings. The only person who ever calls me is Marisol. I glance at the screen and pause.

It's an unknown number.

A scam caller? Really?

I slide the bar to answer the mysterious call. "I don't have time for the fucking IRS," I nearly shout down the line.

A deep, dark chuckle mists my ears. "This isn't a scam call, Katherine."

Him.

It's Dominic.

"How the hell did you get my number?" I stop on the sidewalk outside of the bar, craning my neck to look down the alleyway.

"You seem to keep forgetting that I own the bar you work at. I have the records." A brief pause. "I looked up your file."

No one is in the alley. "You're abusing your power! But why am I not fucking surprised? Is this about work? What do you need?"

"This isn't about work, Katherine."

"Then why the fuck are you calling me? You aren't my keeper and we're not fucking friends." My heart thumps heavily in my chest.

"I may not be your *keeper*, Katherine. But I do want to be friends." Dominic's voice is honey, thick with an undertone that reminds me of an angry hive of bees.

"You called for a reason. What is it?"

"I haven't noticed that old fucker hanging around the bar this week."

"How in the *hell* do you know that?"

I am seething. Was he watching me? Is he truly not down the alley? Instead of craning my neck again, I start for the alley, quickly glancing both ways before jogging across the street.

"I'm not in the alley, Katherine."

How does his voice caress my name so sweetly while also creeping me the fuck out?

"Are you watching me right now?" I want to facepalm myself for losing my momentum in the conversation.

"Look behind you, Katherine, above the door," he instructs.

I spin and glare at the door. There's a camera stationed above it, pointing at the street. Where I am. He's watching me now.

Dominic cackles, albeit softly this time. "You're free tomorrow."

"Are you asking?"

"No," he states plainly.

"Well, you're not fucking telling me."

"Also no, I just know you're not doing anything tomorrow. It's your day off work and you don't do much besides work. You don't have family around, so you're not visiting *them*. You don't volunteer or have another job." He sounds like he's reading the resume of my life.

"How do you know all that?" I scan the street, waiting to catch him leaning against a building with a ski mask covering his face like the villain in a bad story. I briefly think about my, uh, interlude from this morning and shame blossoms in my belly.

How can I think of him in that way when he's so fucking blood-curdling?

"Are you stalking me or something?" I'm only slightly afraid to learn the answer.

"No, of course not Katherine. I don't *stalk*. I'm just getting to know you." He's so confident in his answer that I nearly believe him. Nearly.

"Maybe you should crack open a dictionary or something, Dominic, because it sounds an awful lot like you're stalking me." Droplets of sweat form along the back of my neck and in between my shoulder blades. I've been standing outside the bar for what feels like ages. I need to go and clock in before I'm late. "I'm going to be late for work."

"No, you're not. You still have two minutes." Of course, he casually knows that. I'm not surprised.

"And yet again, I ask: what do you want?"

"I don't *want* anything, sweet Katherine," he pauses. "I *wish* you would come to dinner with me tomorrow evening."

Wish? What the hell?

I'm suddenly drowning in thoughts of being kidnapped and murdered, but others stray to my body plastered to his.

I spin and grab the door handle to Point B, clicking off his call without giving him an answer.

Work sucks ass.

My head is pounding, and I can't stop thinking about the phone call with Dominic.

He wants to go out to dinner tomorrow.

But why?

I don't really care why, honestly. Curiosity is killing this cat. I want to go out and see him. See if his fingers can work as magically as I imagined them.

"You closing up?" Marisol interrupts my daydreaming rather abruptly.

The bar is empty. I stack glasses, preparing to take them to the kitchen. I lean toward her. "Yeah, sure thing. Just about done."

After a few moments Marisol skips up to the bar. "You're off tomorrow, right?"

"Sure am. Only day this week."

"Hmm." She twists her mouth to the side.

I grab the bait. "What's up?"

Marisol bounces up and down, her hands slapping on the bar top before she comes to rest. "Let's go do something! We hardly ever go out unless it's to come here and work."

I plop the mountainous stack of glassware on the bar. I eye Marisol's curly red hair and her matching stilettos. "We went to that night club awhile back, remember? We DIY-d our own masks and shit?"

"Kirby, that was like," she puts her finger on her chin in contemplation, "five years ago maybe?" She wiggles her eyebrows. "And you got completely dicked."

I grab a rag, snapping it toward her arms. "Shut the fuck up!"

She raises her hands in mock surrender. "Hey now, you were the one who told me that, and I quote, 'His dick was the biggest dick I've seen, Marisol. It stung and I'll dream about it for the rest of my life'."

I belly laugh.

She's exaggerating. Kind of. Maybe. "His dick was huge, and it was the hottest sex of my life." I count the register quickly. "I'll never forget that night."

Marisol's eyes lower. "You could have told him who you were, though, you know?"

I'm not going over this again. I won't think of Rhett now. I *can't*. Marisol knows a bit about Rhett, but not all the sordid details. I'm instantly transported back to the last time I saw him.

The sun slowly sank into the horizon, dipping lower with each breath we took. It cast an orange glow around the street, the taller buildings silhouetted against the sky. The air was crisp, but enjoyable with the sweater I had thrown on. My foster family gave me their eldest daughter's hand-me-downs and, for once, I was grateful. I gripped it tighter as a gust of wind blew through my hair.

"You're off in your own land again, Kath."

I smiled, a shyness washing over me as his words coated my skin. "I'm admiring the sunlight, appreciating the wind." My eyes floated to him, looking up until I met his. They were a wonderous shade of green, bright and warm. His hand caught mine and we continued down the block. "What do you think of the sunset?"

He wrapped his arm around my shoulders, pulling me tightly against him. He dipped his head against my crown. "I think the sunset is beckoning us to walk into it, to feel its warmth. I think the sun is going home after being high in the sky all day." We paused on the sidewalk, his hand cupping my cheek. "I think the sunset's brilliance highlights how dark your hair is." He ran his fingers through my long mane, his fingertips pulling on the ends with a gentle tug. "It's as dark as the closet we were in that one time."

A giggle fell from my lips. "Of course, you'd remember that closet!" I playfully shoved his shoulder. Strong arms twined around my torso, bringing me impossibly closer. I folded my arms around him and lay my hands across the base of his spine.

"Now, how could I possibly forget our very first kiss?" He pecked my nose quickly then returned to smack his lips against mine.

I rolled my eyes. We unwrapped our bodies, and our hands found their places together.

"It's almost time for me to head back to the foster fam." I shrugged as his arms tightened.

"And I have to get back to the dorm to get some homework completed." He pouted.

"My eighteenth is close. Then we can finally have those sleepovers we've been dreaming about," I teased.

Rhett smiled. "At least we had those two years living there together before they separated us."

I barked a harsh laugh. "Well, the foster mom did see us kissing in the laundry room, Rhett." I sighed. "It created a huge shit storm."

Rhett pecked my forehead. "That foster mom was fucked up. She viewed us as true siblings, like what the fuck?"

I shake my head, stuck between wanting to forget the whole ordeal and laughing my ass off at the ridiculousness of it.

My foster family now wasn't too bad, and Rhett turned eighteen a few weeks after the incident anyway. He packed up, moved out, and graduated within a few weeks.

I peeked up at him as we walked. His hair was longer than he normally wore it, but the stark white streak in the front section was prevalent as ever. When I first asked him about his hair, he told me it was a birthmark, just in his hair. I didn't believe him at first, but when it never changed or moved, I started to. I wanted to run my fingertips across his scalp, pulling him closer to me until we were one.

"How many classes do you have tomorrow?"

"Only a few. I'll be done by four, I think." Rhett tugged me closer to one side of the pavement so a mother and stroller could pass.

"That's great. Do you want to do homework together at that one café in the middle?"

Rhett halted on the sidewalk. "I believe I can accommodate you, my sweet lady." He grinned. He pulled our clasped hands in the air and spun me.

Tires grinding on the road pulled my attention from Rhett.

A small car peeled down the road, tires almost hitting the curb. Rhett jerked my arm hard. He forced me behind him. I peeked around his arm.

The car barreled toward us.

A man, probably in his late twenties or early thirties, hung halfway out of the back window. His elbow leaned on the car door, supporting a long-barreled rifle.

My eyes widened.

Rhett backed up a step, slightly turning his jaw. "Do not say a word, Kath. I mean it."

The man leaned further out his window. "Boy, you've really fucked up this time, you know?" His voice didn't match his body. It was higher pitched than expected and didn't match his burly exterior.

When neither of us responded, the man continued. "You should have known better than to fuck with the Sandman!"

Rhett turned, his face full of determination. I went to grab his arms, but he shoved me down.

A spattering of pops erupted.

Rhett pulsed once.

Twice.

Three times.

He staggered as the tires grinded the pavement. The car peeled away, leaving the smell of burnt rubber heavy in the air.

Rhett collapsed as I reached for him.

Marisol's hand touches my arm, snapping me to the present. Her eyes are wide and her mouth parts, but I quickly come up with an excuse for leaving the masked man.

"He was an investor, Marisol. An investor!"

Marisol gives me a once over until she's satisfied with what she sees. "Okay, and?"

I slam the register drawer closed. My head pounds.

"I'm *this*!" I motion to the bar, to myself. "Our worlds are wildly different." I take a deep breath, briefly closing my eyes. "Just drop it, please? I don't want to talk about him anymore. He's probably off to Wall Street or something by now."

The memories of my mystery man's glittering mask and Rhett's tear-soaked face clash. I swallow deeply, blinking until I only see the mystery man's large hands cupping my hips.

I throw the remaining rags from the night into a dirty laundry basket under the counter and turn back to Marisol. "Anyway, what were you thinking about doing?"

Her face pinches, but she quickly schools it. "Well, there's a new night club a few blocks from my place. Why don't you come over, say about eight, and get ready with me and then we can head out to the club and dance our asses off."

Her large eyes expand, begging. I immediately think of my earlier phone call with Dominic. At least if I go out to the nightclub with Marisol, I have an excuse why I can't meet him. I won't call him and tell him I was busy. I'll just ignore him.

He will never compare to the man of my memories anyway.

"That sounds like a great idea."

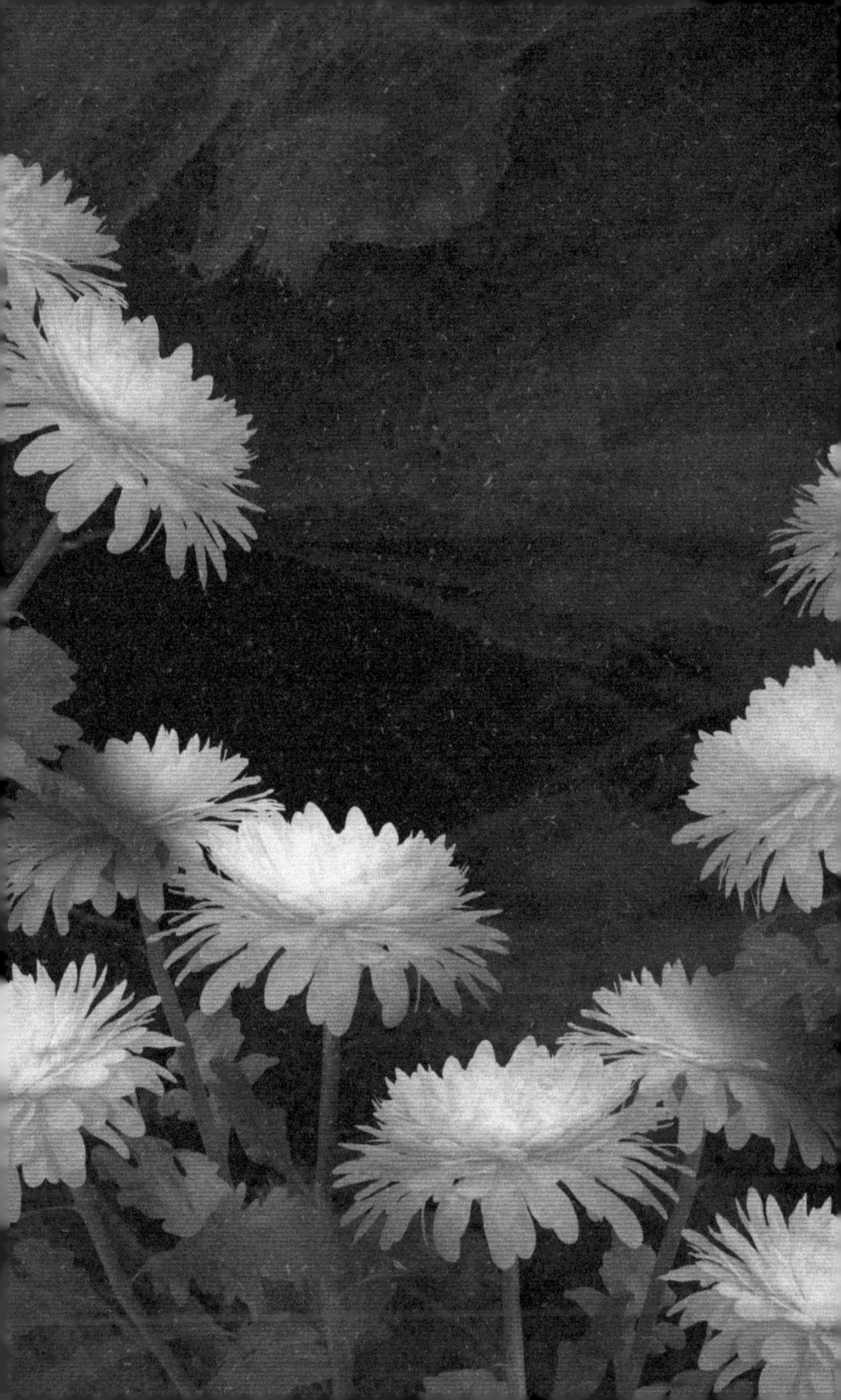

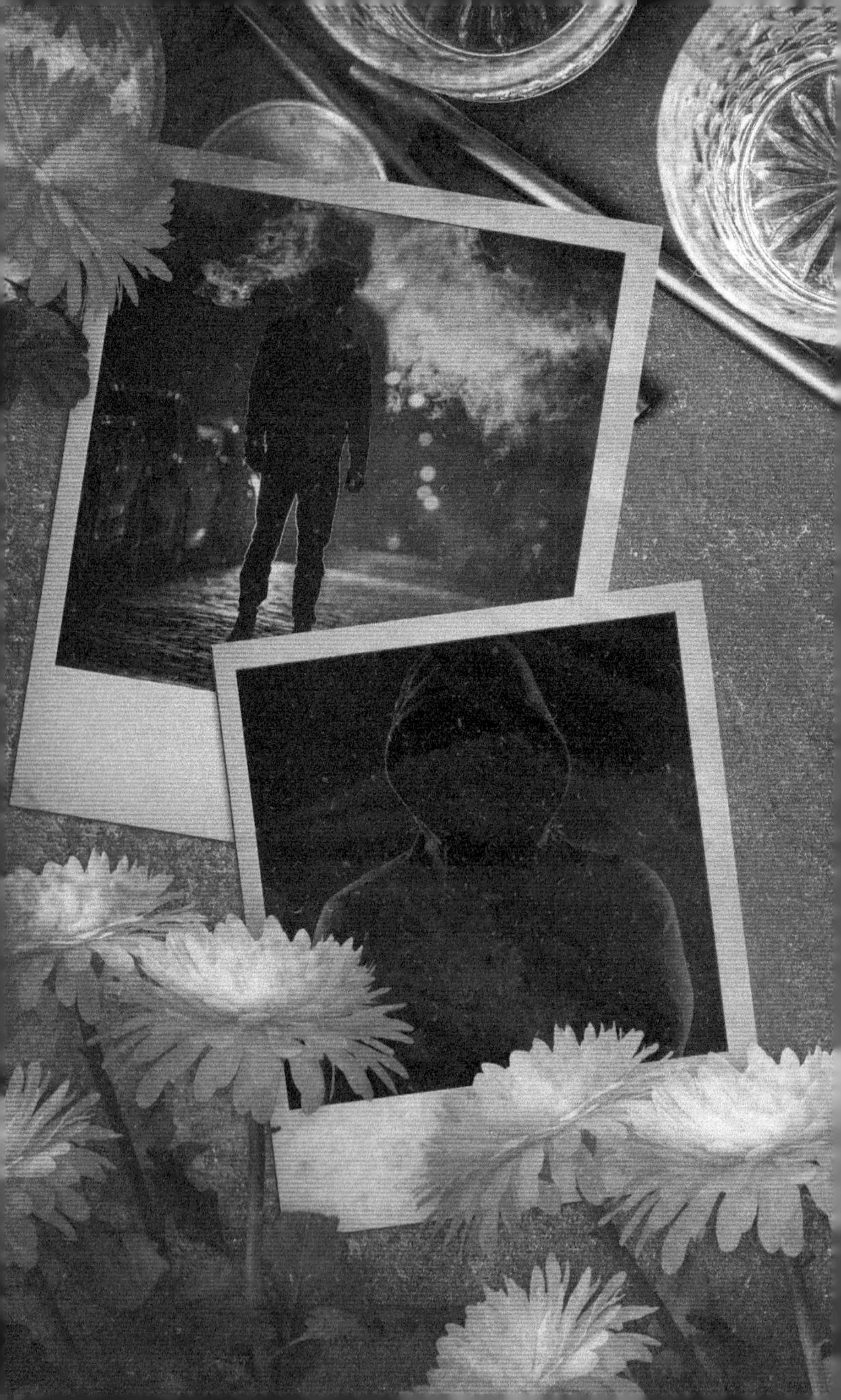

Eleven

KATHERINE

Sleeping in a was a great decision. I was out for eight hours, but it felt like days. Who knew that could generate a good mood?

My clothes and makeup are packed in a small backpack, ready to head to Marisol's, when my phone buzzes in my palm. I've recognized Dominic's number twice now, flashing across the screen. I watch until the call switches to voicemail.

He doesn't leave any messages.

Marisol's place is a short bus ride away, and by the time I arrive, I'm beginning to feel excited about our rare night out. I knock on her door and the redhead opens it immediately, throwing her arms around my torso and pulling me inside.

I laugh. "I'm here, I'm here!"

Marisol releases me, taking a step back. She levels a harsh glare. "It's about fucking time! We only have an hour until the doors open!"

"Well," I hug my backpack to my chest, "I brought all my stuff to get ready so why don't you let me?"

She huffs. I imagine smoke billowing from her ears as if she were a cartoon character. She ushers me down the hall and into her extra bedroom (it's actually her closet). It's fitted with a tall mirror behind a ramshackle desk with makeup products strew across the top.

"Just dump your stuff out and get to work! I still need to get dressed." She looks at me, head to toe, "And so do you!" And with that, she turns her back on me, and faces her clothing wall. Marisol puts her finger to her chin, rifling through the hangers.

Not wanting to incite her wrath further, I let my backpack go and sit at the little desk. Moving her products to one side, I begin unpacking my own. Within ten minutes, my makeup is complete. Nothing too crazy – just a little winged liner and blush so I don't look completely dead on the outside.

"Hey Marisol, do you have any of that lipstick you wore a few weeks back? That burnt, burgundy shad that I complimented you on?" It will accentuate my cupid bow perfectly.

Marisol pops a gum bubble against her lips as she spins toward me. Her hands clap in front of her chest. "Do I ever! I know, for a fact I'll add, that it would look amazing on you." Marisol becomes a flurry of motion. "Let me find it real quick."

Real quick turns into ten minutes.

Marisol rummages through her desk drawers, until finally grasping the tube. She pops it up like bread in a toaster. "Found it!"

I lean toward my friend, pouting my lips like she'd shown me numerous times. She opens the tube and scrunches her eyebrows, nibbling her lip. She concentrates on coloring between the contours of my lips. She swipes once, twice, three times before signaling me to smack my lips together.

"Ah! It looks perfect. Your whole face looks hot as shit!" Marisol swipes the lacquered wand over her lips, greedily applying several thick layers. "Are you ready to go?"

"I just need to slip into my dress, then I will be." I pull out a dark green, decently short, dress. It's fitted, but not overly. It hugs my figure but helps compact the fluffy stomach I've packed on throughout the years.

The neckline plummets, appearing like two strips of fabric are conjoined at the base of my breasts. It makes them look good. Without too much thought, I strip out of my jeans and tee and pull the dress on, maneuvering my breasts to fit and sit how I want them to. After a moment of finagling, they sit pretty, and I am finally ready. I slip on low-heeled, open-toed shoes.

"You look drop-dead hot. I wonder if you'll see anyone that strikes your fancy tonight. Maybe you could take a ride and release some of that...stress."

She knows it's been a while – four years since I've slept with anyone. I momentarily drift back to the masked man of my dreams. I shake my head, and Rhett flashes through. I put him away in the box I store him in. Marisol doesn't need to bring it up though, not when I feel pretty good.

"I'm not taking anyone home tonight, Marisol." I wrap my arm around her shoulders and we head from her closet/dressing room to her entryway. "It is a true girls' night, and we will go out together and crash at one of our houses. No boys allowed." I feel stupid saying it, but I'm a bit nervous as it is, and I don't need to worry about taking home some random man to fuck.

THE NIGHTCLUB IS A BRISK WALK FROM MARISOL'S house. It's swanky, in my unprofessional opinion. The outside is sleek gray metal with no adorning windows in sight. There's a large double door at the front, solid metal to match the outside. On either side is a stereotypical bouncer swathed in black. SECURITY is written across their chests. They're also wearing cargo pants (do they carry tasers?) and combat boots in case, I don't know, they need to kick down a door or kick a handsy dude's ass. A hat with the night club's logo on the front sits on their heads. At first glance, the place feels opulent. Desire leaks from every surface I can see.

Marisol lets out a small squeal, the sound ricocheting off my ears and pounding into my skull like a hammer. She shimmies down the sidewalk and into the relatively short line. I guess we're early.

"Aren't you stoked, Kirbs?" Her smile stretches wide across her face, her joy palpable.

"I am. I can't believe I haven't heard of this before." The line is slowly moving.

"I haven't heard of it either until recently. I guess some guy bought the location and overhauled it." Her eyes are trained on the bouncer closest to us. Her elbow digs into my side swiftly, catching my attention. "Look, Kirby. Do you think he could do you well?"

I want to groan out loud. "Marisol, for the last time, I am not here to meet any guys. Let's dance and drink and have fun, okay?" I am not above begging my best friend.

Marisol pouts, her bottom lip jutting out. She is the fucking queen of pouting.

After a few minutes in line, we make it to the bouncers, who are bigger up close. Don't get me wrong, they're both good looking, but I don't feel anything other than that surface level attraction.

My mind drifts to the man who *did* cause something inside to stir.

Dominic – my fucking boss.

He wanted to go to dinner tonight, but I blew him off. He called but left no messages. He wasn't serious. If he were, he would have at least left a message or sent a text. I shake my head to toss the thoughts away, stomping over them with my low heels.

Why can't I get these men out of my head?

After flashing our IDs to the bouncers, we're allowed into the dimly lit club with no worries. It's popping off. The music vibrates my chest. The bass thrums through my feet and into my legs. I'm already shining with sweat, and we haven't made it to the bar yet.

Marisol's red-painted nails clutch my hand, dragging me behind her like a rag doll. "Come on! We need to grab some shots!"

I brought a clutch with me to hold any necessities. It suddenly vibrates against my leg. It's probably Joseph wondering if we will stop by Point B tonight. No dice there, buddy.

Pulling my phone out while trying to keep up with Marisol is harder than I imagine, but I manage. The text is from an unknown, yet known, number.

Dominic.

> **UNKNOWN**
> Where are you?

How am I supposed to respond? And why is he asking? I'm clearly not going to dinner with him. Why text me now? I continue to ignore him.

The bar area is packed, but Marisol, being as tiny as she is, squeezes through the throng of people, leaving me to my own devices about twelve feet behind her. My phone vibrates again.

> **UNKNOWN**
> Katherine, where the hell are you? You aren't at home and you're not at the bar.

What the fuck?

Of course he knows where I'm not. I'm fed up, ready to toss my phone into the garbage, but the urge to strike is too strong. I type a hasty response.

> **ME**
> It doesn't matter where I am. Forget about the dinner, I'm not interested. Better yet, forget about me you egotistical, stalker douchebag.

I hit send before I can re-read and overthink.

Within seconds, my phone buzzes. I sigh down at the screen for a moment before hitting the power button and watching the screen go dark. Before I tuck my phone away, Marisol sways back over, shots in hand. "Here you go, bitch! Drink up!"

We dance.

We dance hard.

Marisol grinds up against me as I shake my ass. We each have a red solo cup in hand. We gulp down mouthfuls in between songs. We've been alternating between water and drinks for several hours now. Hopefully I won't wake up with a hangover.

As the song fades and a new one starts bursting through speakers, Marisol and I lock arms and drink with the other. Her face is red and splotchy, and I'm sure I'm not fairing much better. Tiny drops of sweat cling to my nape and my thighs stick together.

"You wanna sit down at a booth for a sec? I think I might die out here," Marisol groans.

We locate a lone booth to the far-right side of the crowded club. Plopping down on the cool leather seats is heaven against my flushed legs. I move each thigh up and down to prevent them suctioning to the seat.

Marisol plops down across from me. She cradles her chin in her hands as her elbows dig into the rustic wooden table. She flicks her wide-ass eyes to me. "Aren't you loving this place?"

I chuckle and down a swig of good ole H2O. "Yeah, this place is actually pretty fun." I shrug. "The music has been great, too."

"Hasn't it though? Do you want to continue dancing, or would you like to sit here for a bit? Honestly, I'd be cool with chilling. I feel like I'm about to have a heat stroke!" She fans herself, pressing her solo cup, dripping with condensation, onto her forehead. "Ah, now *that* feels nice."

I click my phone back to life. After rebooting, I notice several missed calls from...him. I'm not surprised. He's *too* pushy. The longer I stare at my now-lit screen, the more I wonder, no, question, myself

Do I want to go to dinner with him?

Surely not, or I would have answered one of his calls or his message in a better way. I made plans with Marisol, plans I have no intention of changing, especially for Dominic. But he asked me to dinner before Marisol invited me to the night club that looks like a can of tuna on the outside. My mind races. Dominic confuses me, and he, quite frankly, scares me too. But there is...something? Something about him that makes me gravitate toward him, something dark and shiny as if I was raven seeking trinkets.

Maybe it's the thrill of it. I haven't felt a tingle since that night several years ago. I try not to think of it. I don't want to relive the endless nights of confusion, anger, and regret.

Why did I leave the way I did? The night plagues me, but it's been worse these past weeks. Those first few months, he was all I could think of – dream of. Rhett's memory grew fainter with time, and now? They mystery man encroaches on my mind once again. He reminds me of Rhett. Knuckles rapt on our table.

I'm ripped out of my thoughts. I glance up, and *wow*.

The man, no, the *God* before us is immaculate at worst and perfection at best. His hair is dark and cropped above his ears, leaving tendrils to torment his temples. His eyes are molten honey.

And he's staring.

At. Me.

Completely oblivious to anything he might've already stated, I choke out, "Um, hey?"

I want to slap myself against the head. What the hell?

The new addition to our table titters as he spreads his fist on the surface. He splays his fingers across the wood, melding into it. Rings adorn three of the five digits. "I was wondering if I could buy you a drink?"

Me?

I glance at Marisol, sporting the widest, cheesiest fucking grin I've ever seen. "Yes, you!" she harshly whispers.

Did I say that out loud?

I face the tanned-like-a-God man, his eyes never wavering from mine. Instead of fumbling my words again, I settle for a nod.

He offers me his silver-adorned fingers. I gingerly lower my palm to his. The man helps me to my feet, my thighs (thankfully) not pulling on the leather cushion. Thank God for small miracles.

He leads me to the bar, and I glance over my shoulder. Marisol still wears that big smile. She gives me a thumbs up with both hands. I simultaneously want to hug her tightly and throw a shoe at her.

It's late into the night now. Many patrons have returned home, leaving behind empty tables and drained glasses. My escort leans against the bar, offering me the barstool. I greedily accept and peer up at him.

Before I know it, he's passing me a cocktail. I raise the small glass in question.

"That would be an amaretto sour for you and one for me." He lifts his glass and clinks it against mine.

I stare over the rim. Who is this man? Why are there suddenly two new men in my life? What is happening?

"Whoareyou?" The question erupts from my lips in a jumbled mess. My cheeks grow aflame.

The corner of his lips twitch upwards. "Sorry, I've been so rude. My name is Alecsander." He takes a quick swallow of his sour. I watch as his throat moves. My eyes dip to his shoulders and back to his lips.

"I walked in here a few minutes ago, and I was immediately entranced by you. I had to talk to you."

I stretch out my hand with a shy smile. I am a little drunk, admittedly. "Well, Alecsander, my name's Katherine, but people call me Kirby. It's nice to meet you." His rough hand meets mine and suddenly they're locked together. It's a different feeling than when he guided me to the bar. Shockwaves pulse from my fingertips to my forearm. His shake is gentle, but firm.

"It's nice to meet you, Kirby." Another long swallow.

My blush deepens, spreading down my neck and to my collarbone. Something about Alecsander feels...I can't quite put my finger on it.

It isn't new to me, but it's definitely different than my feelings for Dominic. I want to cringe. Why should I feel bad? I don't, surely. I told him off in that text. There is a hotter, taller, and *nicer* man sitting in front of me, and buying me sweet drinks.

I need to take a chance, have fun, stop thinking about the stalker I possess. I steal a glance at Marisol, and she offers the wriggling eyebrows. I give her a slight no, looking back at Alecsander. His face is so relaxed and carefree.

"Hey, Alecsander."

"You can call me Alec, if you want." His eyes latch onto my own, drawing me in, and devouring me in one look.

"I need to tell my friend I'm heading out."

"Oh." His grin slips. "You're leaving?"

I squeeze his shoulder, leaning my upper body over his lap. I press my chest into his arm and whisper, "We're leaving."

I don't stop to think it through. I'm so sick of battling my mind, wondering about that man from years ago and now Dominic? No. I need to take control of my own fucking life. I know I told Marisol this would be a girls' night, but she'll understand.

"That we are," he responds before quickly turning his head toward me, his nose brushing mine, sending more shocks through my skin. His eyes are heated. His brows sinch low. "I'll wait here for you."

I simply nod before dragging my nose against his, pushing away from him, and heading in Marisol's direction.

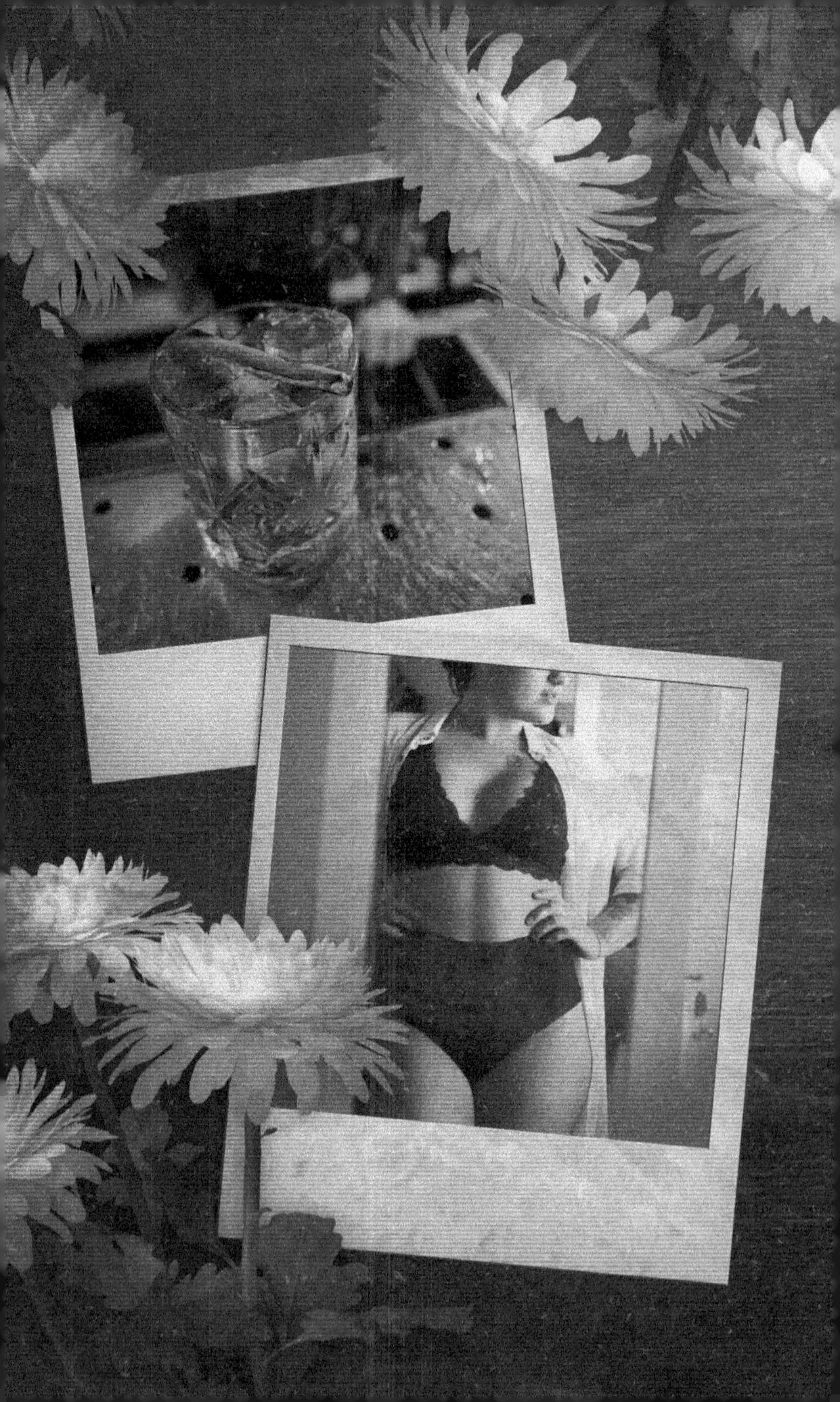

Twelve

DOMINIC

I'm pacing around my living room. Moonlight pours through the tall windows, spilling across the hardwood floor. I catch a glimpse of my reflection in the glass. My hair is mussed and sticking up at odd angles.

Handprints dot the glass. The maid must have missed them. I shake my head. There are other things to focus on now, damn it!

I run my hands through to the ends of my hair again, again, again.

Where is she? My Katherine Rigby.

She isn't at her shitty apartment. I've walked there and back. I strayed to Point B, wondering if she picked up a shift, but a quick trip inside the establishment proved my suspicion to be aimless.

She's ignored my calls all fucking day. Ignoring them, not answering, or responding. I called so frequently that I figured she would at least send a message telling me to get fucked, but not even that.

I'm finally at my breaking point when I text her demanding to know where she is. Her response: calling me an egotistical douchebag! Though holding a semblance of truth, it doesn't quell the aching. I need to know where she is, what she is doing.

Why is she ignoring me?

Why can't she meet for dinner so we can get to know one another? Or at least so she can get to know me better. Her actions astound me.

However.

I know she's interested in me to some degree. I saw how her eyes licked up my body, saw her pupils dilate.

I know she felt *something*, at least found me worthy of lust. But I want – no – need more.

She *must* want me as I want her—animalistic and complete.

I rub my palms down my face. I walk to the kitchen and pound one fist against the granite counter. Pain explodes through my knuckles and into my hand.

Fuck!

I need Katherine out of my head.

Though it's utter agony, I must. I'll go out and grab a shot of whiskey...ore ten.

Yeah, that's it.

I can't convince Katherine to go to a single fucking dinner with me?

Fuck it...I'll get drunk. That's my new plan.

I take a brisk shower, only fucking my hand twice, and pull on my best clothes. The charcoal buttons on the black shirt match the slacks. I want to be dark tonight. I need to feel something else than this fucking pain.

My chest hurts.

My head hurts.

Hell, my fucking hand hurts from busting it on the countertop.

Within twenty minutes I'm in my underground garage, loading into my car. Once I drop into the seat, I pull my phone from my pocket. Seeing no texts from Katherine, I pull up an associate's number and send him a quick message:

> **ME**
> Hey, Sandman, are you in town tonight?

Two minutes pass before he responds:

> **SANDMAN**
> Hell yeah man, I'm down at the new nightclub. There's some hot ass here tonight.

Ugh, I don't want to think about "hot ass". I want to drown my sorrows in the bottle of top shelf liquor they keep for me, and me alone, hidden underneath the bar.

Maybe I'll mention Katherine to Sandman.

He is a flirt—he'll know how to win her over.

THE NEW NIGHTCLUB IS A SIGHT, BUT PERSONALLY, I think it resembles a box. Maybe a prison cell? Hell, it's all metal so in the summer it must be hot as shit inside.

The line isn't as long as I expected, so I gain entry in no time. Perks of being friends with the Sandman, who happens to own this joint. May as well use connections when you have them, I suppose.

It's hot and heavy in the club. Women and men are grinding on one another in every corner and nook and cranny. The women are scantily clad, but none of them catch my attention. None of them are *her*.

I push my way through the crowd to get to the bar. The Sandman will be there. He likes to scope out the place as if he's a common patron. He always says it's a good business practice to immerse yourself in the atmosphere, to get a feel for the vibes or whatever the fuck. Good for him, I guess.

There are several lines in front of the three bartenders. I wonder if Katherine has thought of applying here. The Sandman pays more than her current gig, but I don't want her working for him. He'll take one look, chew her up, then spit her out on the sidewalk. Nightclub shifts are significantly worse than bar shifts. It's common knowledge around here.

Katherine is too sweet, too sassy for someone like him and a place like this.

I keep my eyes peeled for the Sandman. He's around here somewhere. I nudge my way through the multiple lines. A head of glossy black hair catches my attention.

She is facing the opposite direction, so I can't see her face. But I know who it is.

Katherine.

She is clad in a short dress that accentuates her thighs and legs. Her hair is satin on her neck. She's in a conversation with someone, holding their hand like they're about to leave.

What the fuck?

Her companion leans closer to her, practically yelling in the loud environment, "One sec, let me say goodbye to a mate of mine." Then he leans down and gives her a peck on the cheek. I see a flush rise to the surface of her skin.

As I stand no more than two feet from the pair, the Sandman beams. "Hey, man, glad you could make it out tonight. I actually can't stay much longer." His eyes drift to Katherine.

My Katherine.

She finally turns towards me, and the light in her eyes dim, widening. "Dominic?"

The Sandman gives her an odd look. "How do you know Nic?"

"Dominic?" Her voice is low, questioning.

The Sandman gives her an odd look. "How do you know Dom?"

Katherine looks between us. She's at a loss for words, but I'll be damned if I am. My blood is hot, my skin flushed. I attempt to keep my voice at an acceptable decibel. "The better question is, Alecsander, how the fuck do you know Katherine?"

"We met tonight." Alecsander shoves one hand in his pocket and drapes the other across Katherine's shoulders. He circles gentle fingers over her bare skin.

Katherine steps aside, and his arm falls back to his side. Her eyes shine like she's holding back some emotion.

She blows me off and now she is here? With him of all fucking people? She couldn't have known the connection between Alecsander and me. I turn my body, only speaking to her. "I see I found you, Katherine."

"Um, well," she starts, her voice teetering off.

I snigger, surprised and a little anguished at the outcome of tonight. "Were you going to go home with him, Katherine?" I need to know. Is she going to get under him and let him take off her clothes? Is she going to kiss him and let him kiss her back? My heart aches, my fingers itch for blood. "Answer me."

Katherine's voice is low, embarrassment coating her skin like a shroud. "I was planning on it, yes."

I can't blame her for this. I scan the club and find her red-headed friend in a booth not too far away. They must have come together. So, this isn't exactly a date.

"Hm, I see." Looking at Alecsander, I keep my voice cool and monotonous. "Was this the hot piece of ass you were telling me about?" I don't need to look at Katherine to see the words slice through her like a knife. Her face falls, her eyes closing once, twice. She shakes her head slightly.

"I think I'm going to go back to my friend." She turns her now tear-streaked face to Alecsander. "It was nice meeting you Alec, but

I need to go." She pivots and is across the bar before either of us can stop her.

I slowly count to fifteen in my head to cool off. I don't need to cause a scene in Alecsander's bar. But, fuck, do I want to. What the fuck is going on? I am no less confused than when I left my house, yet here I stand, wondering what was going through Katherine's mind.

Sure, I know where she lives and works. I know who she is friends with and all about her history that I could find, but do I *truly* know her? Definitely not. Which is the whole fucking reason that I wanted to have dinner with her. I know she doesn't go out often, so a logical conclusion would be that her friend, Marisol, brought her here tonight. I imagine she had to beg her. Katherine, being a good friend and person, and hell, maybe wanting an excuse to not see me, obliged.

No, I won't, *can't,* fault Katherine for this. This is between me and the Sandman. We might be friends, but in our business world, we couldn't be further apart. Some would dare say we are rivals. I turn back to him, shoving my hands in my pockets. "Let's take a walk, Alecsander. I think it's best we discuss what the fuck was happening here tonight."

He smirks.

I want to throttle him.

"Kirby didn't mention you, Dominic. Surely that's a sign." He lets out a loose laugh, mocking me. And he calls her Kirby. *I fucking hate that nickname for her.*

Fuck protocol and logistics and our businesses and causing a scene.

I rear back one arm and punch the fucker square in the jaw. Something snaps. Is it my knuckle or his jaw? I don't give a fuck. As his ass hits the nightclub's floor, I walk out, leaving the tin can club behind me. I go the fuck home to put a bag of peas on my hand.

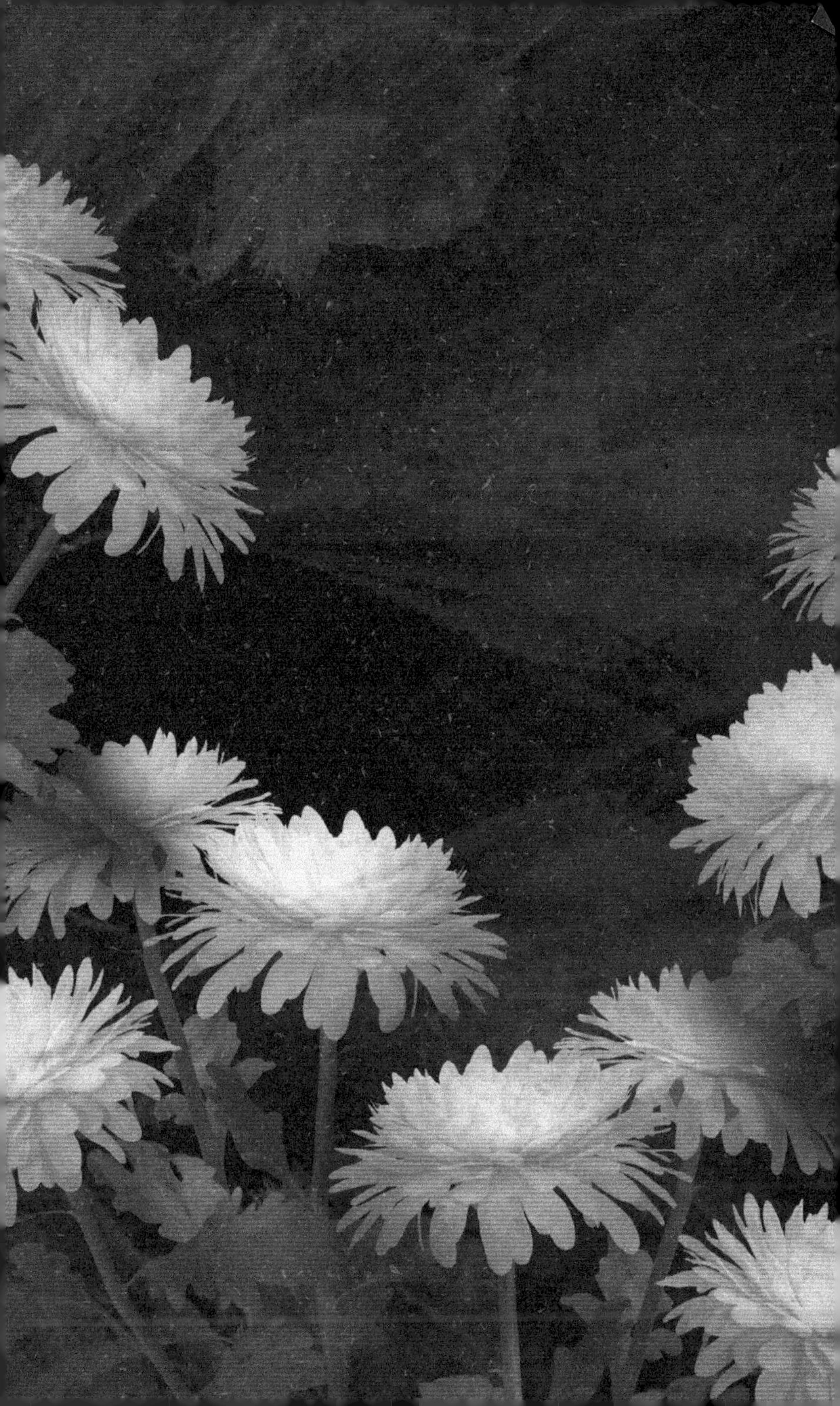

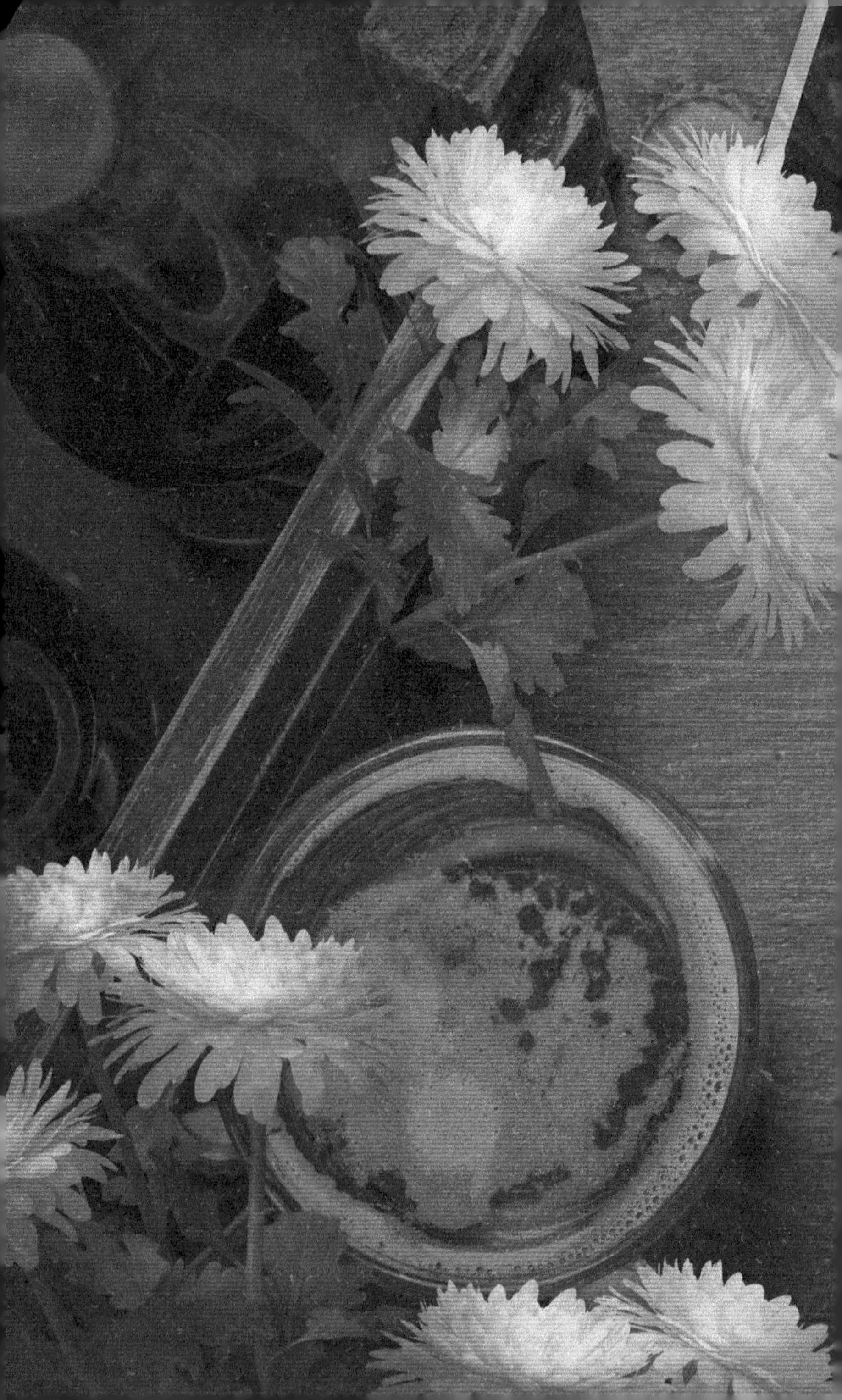

Thirteen

DOMINIC

I make my way down the street, letting my feet take me back to the alley. I need to at least see Katherine, even if she wants nothing to do with me. Even if she hates me now.

God, please don't let that be the case. Surely, we can get past last night. It's quarter past ten now. I timed my arrival to the alley perfectly.

I stand in the shadows of the early morning sun. The shade conceals my profile as Katherine walks up to the bar's doors and unlocks them. She stubs out a cigarette on the ledge of the window and shoves the butt into her pocket.

She's smoked for as long as I've known her. It's a filthy habit. From what I can ascertain, she doesn't chain smoke and usually only lights one, maybe two in succession.

She's a workaholic. I want her home, pursuing her passions, doing something she actually likes rather than only trying to meet rent.

If I hadn't seen her at the club last night, I would've never guessed she was out partying and drinking. She is put together this morning with tight jeans molding to her round ass. Her short hair is pulled in a half-up, half-down bun, highlighting her face. I'm too far to see the freckles on her cheeks, but I can imagine them. One look at her face and I had it memorized. The splattering sunspots caress her nose and hug her under eyes. I'd love nothing more than to count them individually while running my finger from her temple to her jaw. What I wouldn't do...

The sudden urge to be closer to her overwhelms me. I find myself in front of Point B's door before I can think it through. I shake my head and open the door against my better judgement. It is nearly nonexistent when it comes to Katherine.

The bell above the door chimes. I scan the empty room, the stools sitting atop the bar top. The lights flip on slowly. I stay put, not wanting to alarm Katherine or, God forbid, scare her.

She rounds the corner, and her eyes catch mine instantly. She nearly trips over her feet. "What are you doing here?" Her voice is solid, but it holds an edge, reminding me of our interaction in the alley. She is pissed.

I clasp my hands at my torso, trying my best to show her that I'm not here to threaten her. "I came to apologize."

Katherine crosses her arms, pushing her tits towards the vee in her shirt. "Oh, did you come to apologize for stalking me last night." Her eyes harden. "Or did you come to apologize for ruining my date?"

"Your date?" I chuckle, "Is that right?" I want to hear all about this. Then I will find the Sandman and punch *him* in the dick this time.

Katherine huffs, "We were about to leave before you showed up out of fucking nowhere."

"Do you know who you were talking to last night, sweet Katherine?"

"Yes, his name was Alecsander. He did introduce himself to me, you know."

"Yes, but do you know who *Alecsander* is?" She obviously

doesn't. They were flirting and talking about going home together. And now she's mad? My emotions flip through stages of anger, jealousy, and sorrow. I've upset her.

Katherine throws her hands in the air. "I knew enough, okay? What the fuck do you want, Dominic?"

The perfect question indeed. I stalk toward her, my steps steady and purposeful. The less intimidating I am, the better. I need her to want me.

I stop a foot away from her. My nose welcomes her floral body wash. I can't pinpoint the exact scent. I need to stock it in the bathroom at home. "Oh, sweet Katherine." I stretch my arm towards her. Will she flinch? Will she retreat? She does neither. It's both surprising and not.

My fingers find her chin and direct her face to mine. I gaze into her eyes, large and questioning. Is she questioning me or herself? Probably a little bit of both. "Katherine, you know what I want."

Her breaths come harder, her chest flushing. "I do?"

I grin. "Yes, sweet Katherine, all I want is *you*."

I yank her towards me, and our chests collide. I claim her in a crushing kiss. She is mine and, most importantly, I am hers.

My tongue caresses her lips, seeking entry. When she grants it, a moan rumbles in my throat. I wrap my hand around the side of her neck. I squeeze gently until her moan meets mine.

I pull back. She stares at me, wide-eyed. I flick my gaze to her lips. Her tongue darts out to lick her bottom lip, and I can't control myself any longer. I sink into her and walk her back until her ass hits the bar.

Her lips are plump and delicious. I could feast on them for days. But that's not all I desire.

Our tongues duel for dominance. I push her further. Her back arches against the bar top as I grip her hip harder. I leave her lips and slather her neck with open-mouthed kisses. When I'm eye level with her chest, I look up. She is panting, her eyes dilated. "Tell me you want this, sweet Katherine."

I hold her gaze, searching. What is she thinking? "Tell me, Katherine. Tell me what you want, and I'll give it to you."

KATHERINE

Dominic's chin is in between my breasts. He looks so soft and sweet that I want nothing more than to grasp his face and pull it to my own. I know he asked me a question, but I can't find the answer. Words have left the building, the building being my brain.

I didn't wake up this morning expecting to see Dominic, but I should have. Especially after last night. Even though I was pissed beyond belief, I couldn't stop myself from finger fucking myself to the thought of him...and Alec. They are so different, but there's something about each of them. Something about the two of them together.

Alec seemed so soft and delicate and, well, sweet last night. The total opposite of Dominic, the stalker, the man who knows my moves before I do. That's what I thought before I had Dominic practically on his knees before me, pleading with me, telling me he'll do whatever I want.

There's something endearing about him and his cold, hard exterior.

My hands move to his face. I capture his lips with glutinous need. I take the lead this time, separating his lips and diving in. His tongue clashes with mine. We knock teeth as we ravish one another's mouths. I push him back until we crash into a booth. I shove him down in the leather seat, straddling him before I can think it through.

He grips my arms, halting my descent.

I rear back in rejection.

What am I thinking?

Dominic catches my face in his palm. "No, Katherine, sweet Katherine. Don't look away. Look at me."

I keep my eyes downcast, focusing instead on his plain black shirt.

The pressure increases. "Katherine. Look at me." His voice is firmer, but I don't look. "Now," he commands, and my eyes instantly lift at their own accord.

"Good girl." My belly stirs. "You like being a good girl, Katherine?"

A blush creeps to my cheeks and spreads down my chest. I start to pull away, but he holds me still. "Sweet Katherine. You have nothing, you hear me? *Nothing* to be embarrassed about."

I shake my head numbly.

His eyes melt into mine. "Words, Katherine. I need words."

"Yes, I hear you," I mumble.

Dominic sits up with me still on his lap. His hands wrap around my waist, pulling my chest to his. Dominic is crafted of more sides than I was aware of. He can be sweet and charming, but he can also be a dark storm cloud, rolling in to rain on one's day. I need to woman-up and figure this shit out. "What are we doing, Dominic?"

"I'm not quite sure, sweet Katherine," he sighs. "What do you want us to do?"

My fingers twitch, suddenly nervous. What is it about Dominic that sets me aflame? What is it that burns my skin and tightens my stomach with butterflies? I shouldn't have these feelings for him. He stalks me at Point B from the alley. He knows my phone number. He learned intimate details about my personal life that I sure as shit didn't offer, but he somehow discovered them anyway. At the same time, his insatiable need has infected me.

This tryst doesn't have to mean anything.

We can appease our desires and part ways. He will probably continue stalking me, though, but am I truly bothered? Dare I say it makes me feel safer knowing there is a man like Dominic Alcutti protecting me?

Fuck, I need to talk to Marisol about this shit. Better yet, I should find a therapist whose specialty is in wack-a-doodle women who fancy their fucking stalkers.

I look back to Dominic. His brows clench together, awaiting my answer. I let out a breath. "I want you to fuck me, Dominic." Somehow my voice doesn't waver. A slight blush inches up my face. I shove it down.

Dominic's eyes harden. "Oh you do, sweet Katherine?" He leans forward, and his lips brush the shell of my ear. His hands roam over my back and dip into my waistband. He cups my ass, grinding against my pelvis. The hard outline of his erection pulses through his jeans.

I moan and Dominic responds in seconds. He guides me to a booth, hungry. My legs brush leather and a quick gasp pushes through my lips as I fall onto my back. He leans over me, inching his jeans-clad dick closer. My breath shudders and he chuckles darkly. "Oh, Katherine, we aren't doing that quite yet."

I open my eyes and stare at him. *What the fuck?*

Before I can protest, Dominic leans down and licks a stripe between my breasts. "I can't have our first time being in a dirty bar, baby. But I can help you out a bit before your shift starts." *God, yes.*

"Nothing holy about this, sweet Katherine."

I guess I said that out loud. Jesus.

Dominic snakes a hand from my ribcage to the seam of my pants. He finds my clit through the material. The friction is beautiful, but not enough. I'm panting, near desperation. "More, Dominic. Please."

"Begging looks good on you, Katherine, but there's no need. I'll give you what you crave, baby."

Dominic lavishes my neck and jaw with small kisses. His fingers work my jeans loose. He slips his hand under my panties and caresses my swollen bud. I arch my neck, inviting his mouth to the smooth skin. I bit his lip as he descends on me.

His deft fingers work tirelessly. As he groans into my mouth, my fantasy floods back. I close my eyes, chasing my orgasm.

Dominic snickers breathlessly, "Sweet Katherine, the things you do to me." He sinks two fingers between my folds and curls them inside me. My legs tremble. "Breathe, my Katherine, give it to me."

My climax barrels through me. I squeeze my legs tighter, feeling the release through my entire body. Dominic doesn't release me until I deflate against the bench. He slowly withdraws, zipping my pants back over my belly.

I'm still shaking when he wraps an arm around me and guides me upright. He adjusts my V-neck tee to cover my breasts. I meet his eyes. They shine with a newness that I can't place.

He takes my hand and holds it to his lips like it's something precious. "Thank you, Katherine."

I scrunch my nose, why is he thanking me? I should be the one thanking and praising him for a job well done. I thought my fantasy was hot, but it was nothing compared to his actual hands and mouth. I must stay silent too long because Dominic starts speaking again.

"Don't worry, Katherine. I understand. We don't need to talk about this right now, but you best believe we will be discussing things later. Once your shift is over and you're free?"

I find myself nodding, giving him a wide-eyed look. He stands gracefully. I see the tent in his pants, his need palpable. He isn't asking me to take care of it, like so many men would do. He offers his hand. "Let's get you back to work. Can't have someone walking in with you over here looking confused." The slight curve of his lips makes me think of a cat, a predator with a playful side.

"Yeah, I should probably get everything set up for the night." I take Dominic's hand and let him lead me to the bar. He grips it tightly. A feeling of dread washes over me. I wonder what I've gotten myself into and who I've found myself under. Dominic leans down and gives me a chaste peck on the cheek, but I remain silent.

"Have a good shift, sweet Katherine." He pivots, and leaves me staring after him, wondering if I've just made a massive mistake.

DOMINIC

I don't look back when I exit Point B. The memory of her soft skin causes me physical pain.

The air outside is wet like a rainstorm approaches. I should have grabbed a better suited jacket for the day. I'm will regret it later when my clothes are soaked. I shake my head, focusing instead on turning the corner. I would have crossed the street in front of Point B, choosing to take the famous alley, but this time I didn't have the urge to linger.

Maybe, being around Katherine helps me feel at ease. Do I need to watch her constantly if I'm seeing her consistently? My mind wanders. I begin to imagine scenarios of something bad happening to her while I'm distracted. I decide, then and there, that I will continue watching her through the cameras, regardless of if I'm seeing her in person now.

I round the corner, and a thick-as-fuck arm clotheslines me. My body careens to the pavement, and I gnash my teeth as pain shoots down my recruit,

I angle myself, taking stock of the fucker who thinks they can assault *me*. My eyes widen in recognition. I cough before finding my voice. "What the fuck was that for?" I stare at Alec's bodyguard. He's a burly fucker, but I can't place his name. I slowly rise to my feet, palms flashing. "Look, whatever the Sandman wants, just send him to my apartment, yeah?" The brute cracks his knuckles in a display of aggression.

"He's ordered your presence. You can either come willing or I force you." I square my shoulders. Alec has never sent his goons after me before. He usually only calls until I answer since he refuses to leave me voicemails.

"You've got about two seconds to decide."

"Fuck! Fine, I'll come with you."

As soon as the words leave my mouth, the man grabs my upper arm hard. He towers over me and must outweigh me by fifty pounds. There's no way I have the advantage to send him to the ground.

The bodyguard hauls me fifteen feet to a dark SUV. He unceremoniously throws me in the back where I'm met with two other beefy goons. They grab at my clothes, tossing me inside. "Watch what the fuck you're doing, damn!"

They ignore me.

I slouch in the backseat, surrounded. The driver quickly puts the van into gear and peels out. All I can do is shake my head as he meets my gaze in the rearview mirror.

"Do you know why the Sandman is wantin' you?" The goon on my left asks.

"Fuck if I know, man." I sift through memories, trying to piece together why Alec would act like this toward me, his partner.

"Word on the street is you laid him out flat the other night." The man on my right quips.

Fuck.

"By the look on your ugly mug, that rings a few bells," he laughs. He wipes his face with his hand, his smile fading like a mask. "Yeah, the Sandman told us to make sure you got what's comin'."

"What the hell—,"

His fist coils back. He punches me in my nose, a sickening crunch ricocheting through the cab. My hands fly up. I cup my bleeding nose as the other guy lays a few quick jabs to my ribs.

Within seconds, their fists are flying rapidly. I don't have time to fight them in such close quarters.

A blow to the temple, and my teeth rattle.

A punch to the chest, right below the neck, has me gasping for air.

Another blow to the other temple.

The last thing I see is a fist barreling toward my eyes.

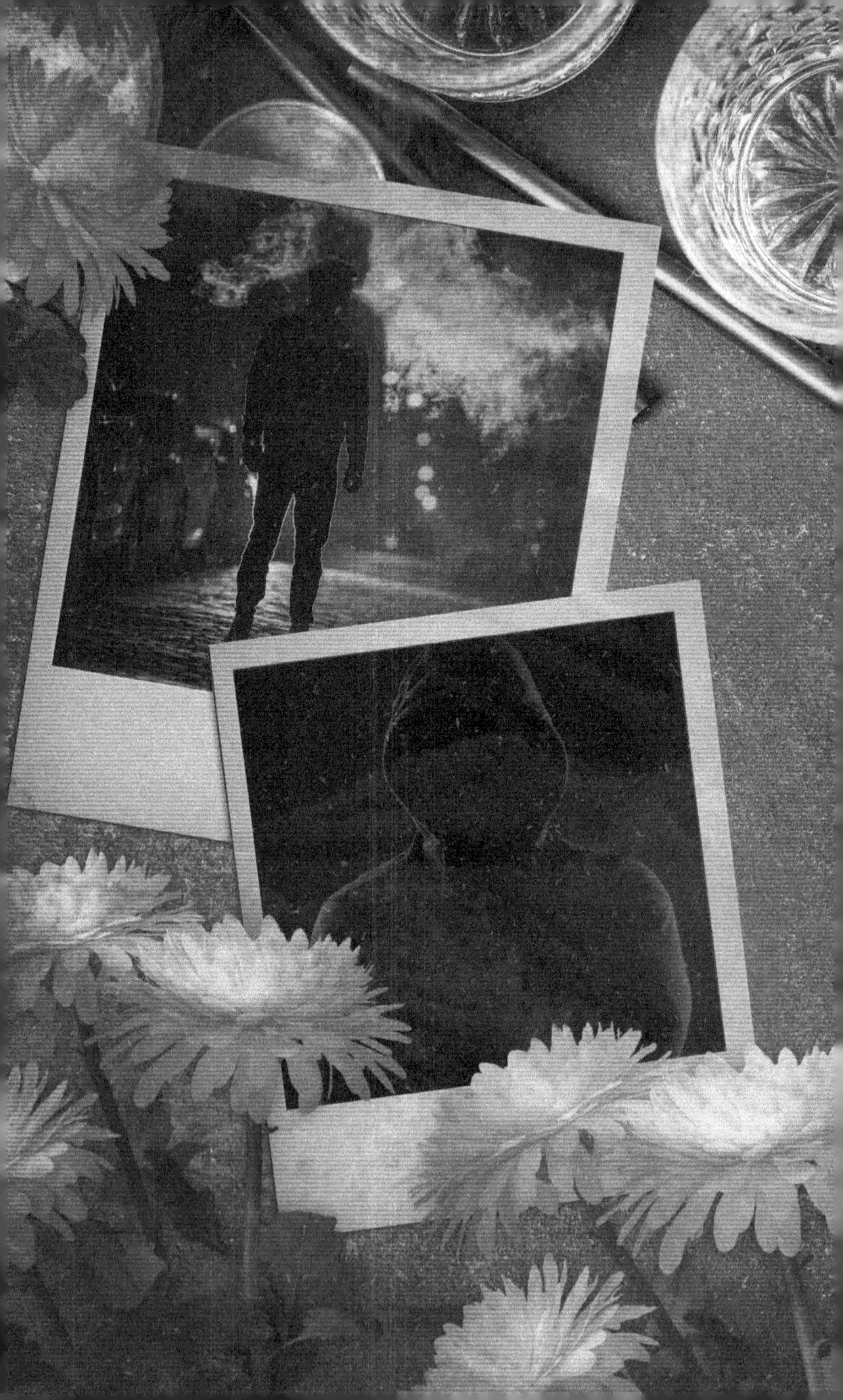

Fourteen

KATHERINE

The next few days follow a similar pattern: wake up, go to work, work til I nearly drop, and go home. Then I rub one or two out, pass out in bliss, have dreams involving tattooed hands, wake up, rinse and repeat.

Dominic hasn't contacted me. I should be glad he's done with his stalking, but my brain won't shut the hell up. I remember how he nestled his chin between my breasts. The vision haunts me throughout the day. I wonder what he's doing and where he is.

Can he see me? Does he know what I'm doing?

Then there's Alecsander. He was such a smooth talker, but Dominic made it seem like I was just a piece of ass to him. I roll my eyes at the hypocrisy.

He touched me. He kissed me. And then he had the audacity to ghost me?

Something is wrong with both of them. Something is wrong with *me* because I'm still, somehow, into both.

It's baffling to me how quickly Dominic can change his game. One second, he's stalking and the next? Well, I haven't heard from him in two days. Am I the one who's obsessed now? The thought only pisses me off further.

I plan to spend my day off wrapped in a robe, sitting on my couch, and watching trash television. Maybe a movie, who knows? I have a quart of ice cream that is calling my name, and I plan to eat the whole damned thing.

Hours later, I finished my quart of ice cream and binged a whole season of some cooking show that's barely entertaining. I need to do chores around the house but can't be bothered. As I stand in my tiny shower stall, I run my fingertips over my scalp, emulsifying the shampoo into sudsy goodness. I keep thinking back to the night at the club.

How Alecsander looked at me.

His eyes were molten while speaking. I thought he was interested in me, but Dominic showed and basically called me nothing more than a hook-up. And, honestly, I know he was right.

I practically offered Alecsander a quick fuck. I didn't care because I'd accepted what it was. I wanted to stop thinking about Dominic, but he literally showed and ruined it. It was different when it was voiced out loud. It felt like a cruel dagger stabbing through my heart.

Realistically, I know the Alec ordeal wasn't anything more than what I intended it to be. Sleep together, and The End. Why did it bother me so much when Dominic pointed it out? Is it because I thought Alec looked at me as more than a single fuck or that his molten eyes seared me from the inside out? Something was happening between us, and I was willing to go to great lengths to experience it.

I quickly rinse the shampoo out of my hair before moving

onto conditioner and body wash. Before I know it, I am scrubbed and ready to get out of the steamy bathroom. I wrap my bathrobe around my slightly wet skin and slink into my tiny living room.

Now there really is nothing to do.

I contemplate going to the corner store to grab another quart of ice cream when my phone starts ringing. I pluck it from between the couch cushions and glare at the unknown number. It isn't Dominic though, which only irritates me more.

If it isn't his crazy ass, then who can it be?

I say, "fuck it" and answer it anyway.

"Katherine, we met the other night at the bar. This is Alecsander."

ALECSANDER

I walk around my basement. The concrete is freshly washed, and the drains are clean. It isn't the basement at my house, but one of the many warehouses I own. This one, however, happens to be the closest and most efficient for the latest job I acquired.

This section of the basement is a blank seven-by-seven room with no windows or anything denoting it as special or customized. The floors are partially sloped toward the drain that lives in the center of the floor. Several hoses are attached to the wall, hooked up to various cleaning agents.

A single metal chair sits behind the drain, facing the entrance. Can't be wood in case someone tips it over and breaks it into a million pieces. Legs can become weapons or, et cetera.

Dominic Alcutti's head lolls forward in the chair. His reddened blonde hair clings to his forehead, and his arms are cuffed behind his back.

My loafers hit the concrete floor, clacking through the thin layer of water and blood swirling down the drain. I'll wash my shoes later, but that's the least of my concerns. Right now, I can only afford to think about Dominic and what his role is in everything. He will give me answers one way or another.

"Time to wake up, Dominic." My voice is hard and calculating. He won't respect me if it isn't. His legs are spread with his ankles cuffed to the chair legs. He won't brute his way out of this. My hand flexes across my jaw, soothing the ache creeping in, thanks to the punch he landed two days later.

Dominic groans as he lifts his head. His stare is cold, as to be expected. "What the fuck, Alecsander? Why the hell am I here?"

I step closer, bending my knees until I am eye-level. "You know what the fuck you did, asshole." I bare my teeth. He doesn't buckle. He isn't like everyone else I deal with. We aged and trained together. We understand, most of the time, one another on a deep, almost cellular, level.

Dominic does his best to square his shoulders. "What the fuck, Alec?" He spits onto the concrete, adding more blood to the drain.

I crack my knuckles and steeple my fingers. I lean towards his face. "You tell me, *partner,*" I pause, pulling back slightly. "It's been five years asshole! We're merged on all things legitimate. Nightclubs, bars, hotels. You fucking name it and our names are on it somewhere. So, tell me why, *why in the fuck*, neither of us have filled the rest of our deal?" I laugh bitterly. "Oh wait, I was working on part when you happened to saunter into *my* club and lay me on my ass, acting like you knew the woman I was with!" My vocal cords grind in agony. I never yell, not when it comes to business. It is more intimidating to be lethally calm, but Dominic? Fuck, he brings out the worst in me.

My thoughts bleed back to Katherine, the dark-haired goddess who walked through my club like she fucking owned it. I noticed her short, haunting hair when I entered. I had my suspicions about her identity. I haven't forgotten that night years ago. When I walked up to her booth, she sat with her redheaded friend, and her eyes locked on mine. I was sure she would remember me or ask how I found her.

Except, I didn't *find* her. I stumbled upon the goddess from my past, the woman who left my office and never returned. The woman who I could never quite track down. I sweep my hand down my face, cooling my features. Looking back at Dominic, he's ramrod straight. His face is drawn, his eyebrows scrunching together in mock confusion.

"You called her, and I repeat, a 'piece of ass' in your text message jackass." He draws in a deep breath, schooling his features. "You called my sweet Katherine a 'piece of ass'! You fucking asshole!"

My eyes widen. He *does* know Katherine.

I assumed wrong.

I thought he was fucking with me, seeing I was with a woman for the first time in what felt like ages and one as gorgeous as sin itself. I assumed he was there to bruise my ego, knock me down a peg, and somehow infiltrate my plans to find a woman and marry her.

It is so much worse, though.

I go back to Dominic, lowering my face to his. "How the fuck do you know Kirby? And don't fucking lie to me, man." I pace in front of him. "Yeah, I met her at the fucking nightclub. She was with a little redhead. And I saw her and, *shit*," I laugh, deciding not to tell him the identity of the woman I fell in love with several years ago. "She pulled me in like a god damned siren, Dom. I don't know if it was her green eyes or her curves that flowed like a river, but fuck!" I pull my hair up and away from my scalp.

"Katherine isn't *yours*, Alecsander. I've known Katherine for years. She works at *my fucking bar*, prick."

Years?

She works at *his* bar. "Which bar?"

Dominic sighs, "Point B."

The worst there is.

Point B has been on the back burner. We focus on the larger bars, the ones that are downtown and hopping with people every night of the week. Our callous, low-level attention to Point B put Kirby on the back burner. It kept me from finding her. "How long has she worked there?"

"About four years."

What?

I pace my way to the wall, slamming my hands against the cool concrete. "FUCK!"

"Untie me and we can figure this shit out like partners."

Dominic has a point.

But does he?

He doesn't know half of it. Sure, he knows I fell in love with a woman in a single night years ago. I haven't divulged much more information. I never mentioned her looks or how she glittered in her gown and mask. I never mentioned her dark, void-filled hair.

I shuffle to his chair and make quick work of releasing him. As soon as the ties are undone, he slumps forward. Dominic sucks in breaths through an open mouth. He grunts a few times while doing his best to stand tall. Dominic glares while still hunched.

"Did you really have to have your fucking goons beat the shit out of me?"

I catalog his body for the first time. His lip is cut. Bruising mars his cheekbones, giving way to two black eyes and a newly crooked nose. I shrug.

"Sorry about that man, but, I mean, you did sock me pretty hard at the club." I turn and walk to the door. I let the Kirby issue take the back burner, at least on the outside.

"One fucking punch to the jaw doesn't equate to two fucking days of being beat and waterboarded you fucking jackass." His voice is harsh.

I know he'll get over it. We have work to do, after all.

"And anyway, how'd you know where I'd be the other day? Your guys jumped me like a block from Point B."

This is news to me.

I was under the impression my lackeys found him walking out of his house, which is a short walk to Point B. The distinction makes my skin crawl. "Why the hell were you at Point B, Dominic?"

A sheepish grin splits his face. A droplet of blood pours from his reopened lip. "Had to stop and see Katherine. Make sure we were straight after the move you fucking pulled the night prior."

"What's going on between you two? She didn't seem too thrilled to see you the other night."

Dominic releases a slight laugh, "She's mine. Has been and will be. Don't fucking touch her, talk to her. Fuck, don't *look* at her." His gaze is aflame, burning with something underneath.

I make a horrifying realization in that moment. He's dead fucking serious.

As much as I respect Dominic as a business partner, I want to throttle him for his thoughts on Katherine. His claim on her? It won't stand. I can't let it. I found her in that old club, we made love, and I fell instantly for the woman in a beautiful mask. I won't let Dominic steal her from me, not when I finally found her.

"Sure thing, man, no problem."

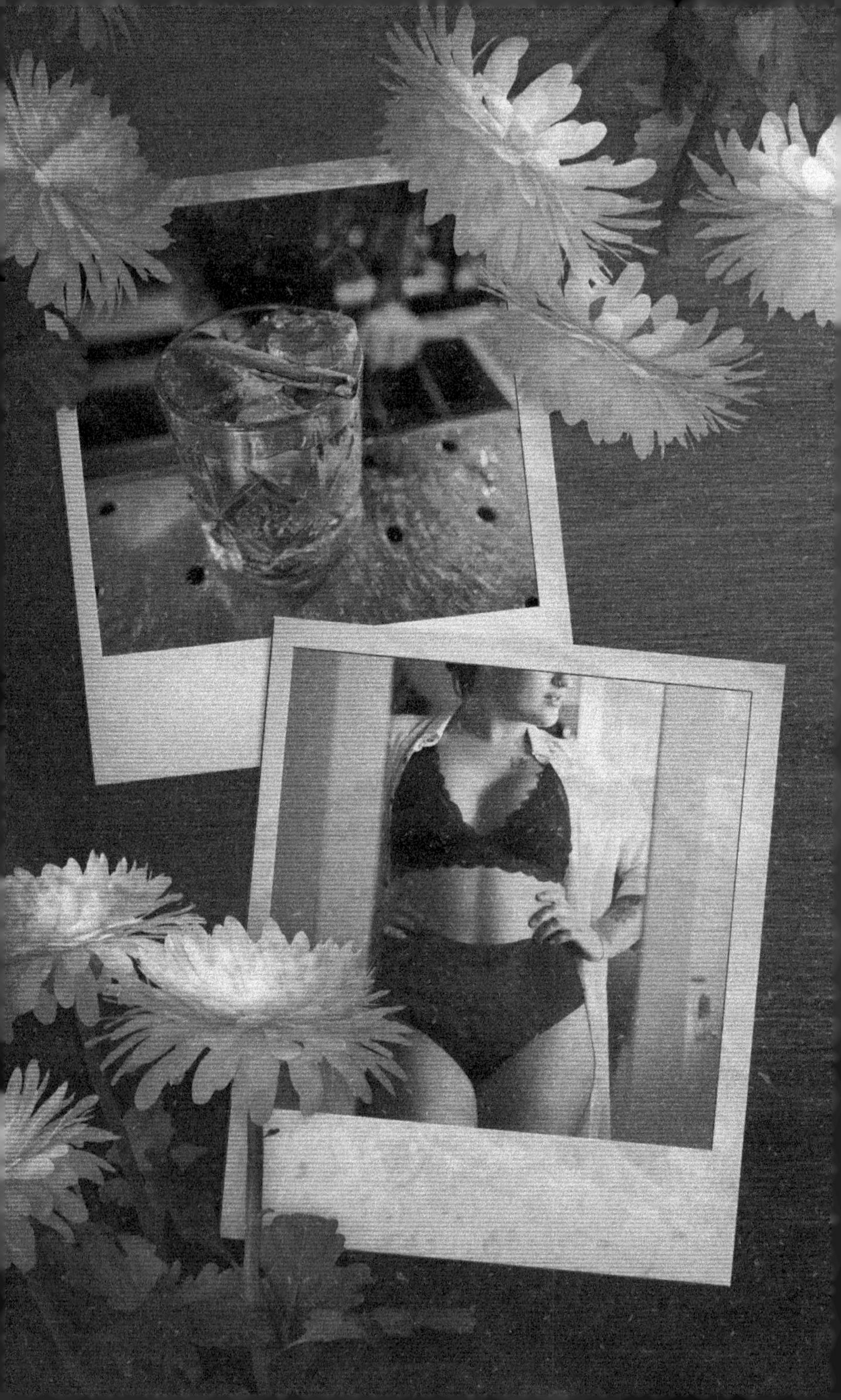

Fifteen

DOMINIC

I'm not going to lie – I haul ass getting out of Alecsander's dank fucking warehouse. The bastard. I'm fuming, trying to keep my face blank as I hurry along the pavement. I'm anxious to get back to my place. As I left Point B and Kirby the other day, I rounded the corner and was clotheslined by some big ass dude. I was so giddy with satisfaction that I made some level of progress with Kirby, therefore I didn't have my wits about me.

Now, two whole fucking days later, I'm sore as shit and fucking tired. I was tied to that chair from the moment I was hauled into that warehouse. My ankles and wrists were bound and anytime I thought about ways to get out of dodge, the beefy dude punched me or threw ice water over my head. What made it better was the sweaty rag that he pulled over my face beforehand. I felt like I was going to drown. Fuck, I believed it a few times.

Shit.

Alecsander's goal wasn't to murder me. He wanted revenge for getting his ass handed to him. He thought he had some claim over Katherine. Well, the fucker was wrong. On all counts.

Katherine is *mine*. He isn't about to steal her away if I have anything to do with it.

I walk for over an hour before hailing a cab. The driver, a mousy man, gives me a shocked look as I climb into his backseat. I'm filthy and there's a splattering of blood on my shirt. My face is black and blue. I give him a cold stare, signaling for him to shut the fuck up and drive. After giving him my address, I lean my head back against the headrest, finally drawing in a deep breath.

My mind wanders. Where is Katherine now? What is she doing? Is she safe? This is the longest amount of time I have spent without seeing her or looking at her through the bar's cameras in years. She caught my sight four fateful years ago and I'll be damned if she wasn't going to be in my sight for a few days now.

My apartment is on the top floor of a tall building. I bought the penthouse about seven or so years ago. It keeps me close to the city and downtown but also offers me a place of solitude. It's a place where I can *be* without having to be the Dominic that everyone knows, the Dominic that runs businesses and fights and makes people bleed.

The elevator ride to the penthouse goes by at a snail's pace. My heart thunders in my chest. At what, I can't decipher. I'm anxious to be back in my zone.

I'm not new to beatings and methods of torture. Most of my childhood and teenage years were spent fighting against my father. He wanted to beat me into compliance. As a kid, I was bull-headed and strong willed. He would tell me one thing and then I would do the exact opposite to spite him. Look at me now and look where he is and try telling me that I didn't make the right decisions.

The apartment is dark as I open my door. The lights flicker above me as I wade through the entryway, living room, and kitchen. The lights fade from one room to the next. A small package catches my eye. It's sitting on the kitchen island. It's perfectly wrapped. I paw at it, ripping it open to find a scrawled note from none other than Alecsander. In the box is a new phone. I chuff, it's the least he can do considering his fucking goonies smashed mine to bits prior to tying me to the god-forsaken chair.

The phone is set up and my contacts are synced, as are my messages. Feeling a little off about the whole situation, I quickly hoof it across the penthouse to my office. I plug the phone into my computer. My keyboard is misaligned. I shrug it off, making note to remind my cleaning lady to not come into my office, even if it's to dust.

I run a few diagnostic tests and exhale when I discover nothing suspicious about the new phone. I half expected Alecsander to plant a recording device or have installed a cryptic app to clone the phone. Thank fuck he's still semi-trustworthy.

Unplugging the phone, I come to a horrific realization. I never called Katherine.

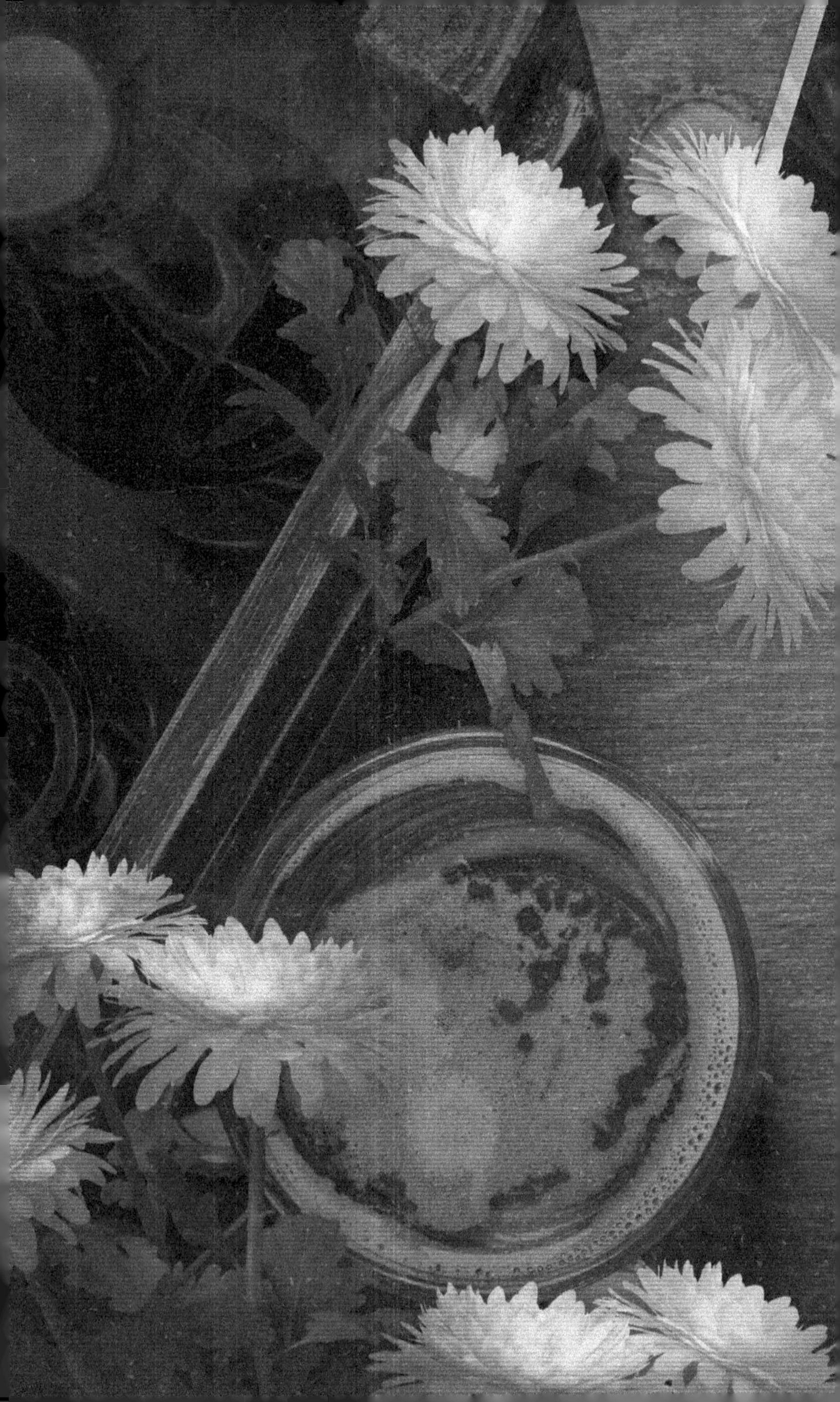

Sixteen

KATHERINE

How did Alecsander get my number?

If he's anything like Dominic, he would pay someone to get it for him. Even as I hold the phone up to my ear, vaguely listening to him, my mind won't stop wandering.

"What do you want, Alecsander?" I do my best to sound mildly threatening.

A soft chuckle meets my ear. "I would like to ask you one question, Kirby."

I find myself nodding, though he can't see me. Plucking my nails, I respond with a subtle, "Okay." I'm still lying on the couch with my robe stretched out around me.

Alecsander clears his throat before answering. "Would you like to go on a date with me, Kirby?" His voice is polite and albeit a little stiff.

I'm caught off guard. I was hoping for Dominic to call me (was I really?), but instead here's Alecsander. He's calling and *asking* if I would like to go on a date. What are the chances?

I sit up straight. I clear my throat. "Well, um, I'm pretty busy, Alecsander." I bite my lip, anticipating what he'll say next.

"That's alright, love. I'm available whenever you are free. If it needs to be a quick breakfast date before your commitments, then that's perfectly fine with me."

"Oh, well, that's really sweet of you, Alecsander-,"

"Call me Alec. Alecsander makes me sound too professional." A light laugh trickles down the phone line. A subtle *zap* moves across my scalp.

"Okay, Alec, like I was saying— I'm fairly busy with work and everything. I don't have a day off for at least two more weeks." Am I kind of bullshitting him? Definitely. While he was sweet at the nightclub, the whole interaction between him and Dominic threw me for a loop. It makes me question my original assessment of Alecsander. Is he a good guy? Or is he a player trying to get in my pants? I can't tell, but this whole conversation is beginning to change my mind. Even if it's just a fraction.

"That's okay, Kirby. Work is work and we all must do it, don't we? Are you working today? Tonight?" Alec seems, dare I say, excited?

"I'm off today, yeah, but I'm doing things around my apartment. Cleaning. Tidying up." Now I'm rambling. I need to get the hell off this phone call.

"Let me ask you this, Kirby."

"Okay?"

"Say yes to one date, hell, even one conversation in person. Chalk it up to coffee or pancakes at the diner. Go out with me, one time? After that you can wipe your hands clean of me and shove me in the river. I just want an hour."

"You're awfully confident. A little cocky, are you?" I tease him, but he seems so genuine that my chest hurts.

"Confident? Maybe. Cocky? You can find out if you're willing." There it is. The slight manwhore-ism. But hell, the way he says it, casual and a little flirty makes me wet.

"One hour? One date?" I ask him, wanting to be sure.

"Yes, wherever you'd like. You choose."

Such a gentleman.

"How about Point B? I have to go there later anyway to pick up the cash for the day."

Alec doesn't say anything for a moment. "That's perfect, Kirby. Six o'clock?"

"Sure, that's fine." What time is it now?

"Perfection, I'll see you there." The line goes dead. He hung up! And I agreed to meet him at Point B? What the fuck was I thinking?

I glance at my phone screen.

It's already after five! *Fuck!*

Point B is mildly busy. There aren't lines wrapping around the side of the building or anything akin to that, but it's busy enough to warrant my coworkers not noticing me when I walk in. I try to flag them down like a diseased banshee. However, after several failed attempts, I relent. I make my way to the bar.

"Marisol!" I call my friend, but her head is turning and assessing her tablet of drinks. Arranging them into perfect rows, she struts in her death-trap heels across the lounge and hovers by the pool tables. She's waiting for a handsy man to demand a drink. Her ass shakes of its own volition as she walks. Several heads turn and follow her.

I powerwalk to a booth against the far wall of the bar. I changed and threw on light makeup before I left my apartment, and then immediately came over here. It isn't six yet and I'm already beginning to sweat. My baggy jeans want to stick to my legs. Why is it so fucking hot in this damned bar? I need a fan for fuck's sake. I dig through my purse, looking for a piece of cardstock or a thick pamphlet to use as a makeshift fan, anything to bring a slight breeze to my scorching skin. Not finding any paper products, I pull out my whole ass wallet. I quickly bring it back and forth to displace the air in front of my face. Just a little breeze to cool my skin.

I try to cool myself down. I'm beginning to panic. Between the "date" and everything else going on, I'm frazzled. I try to focus on the *now*, but my mind keeps pinging back to Dominic. Why hasn't he called me? That isn't exactly his MO. He *is* stalking me for fuck's sake. He finally gets a little taste of me and now, what? He's over it, over me? I don't buy it and that's not because I'm self-assured or whatever the hell. It doesn't add up. I shake my head, dislodging the thoughts. I try to focus once more.

I must not have been focusing as much as I was hoping for because next thing I know, a velvet voice is greeting my ears. My eyes pull from the table to the sculpted face hovering a few feet from me.

Alecsander.

My mouth is suddenly filled with cotton. I lick my lips. "I'm sorry, what did you say?"

Alec laughs, his cheeks crinkling and the crow's feet by his eyes scrunching. "I was asking how you're doing."

My cheeks burn from embarrassment. "I'm alright, thanks."

Alec braces one elbow on the table as he gracefully folds into the small booth. When fully seated, his knees brush my own. Even sitting down, he's towering over me. How fucking tall is this man?

"Have you already ordered something, Kirby, or do you want me to grab you something from the bar?" His voice is screaming 'casual', but his eyes are fucking me. They're dark, smoldering. They're how you imagine bedroom eyes looking, but we're in public.

"I haven't ordered anything. The place isn't usually this busy on a night like tonight. You know, a weekday," I joke.

Alec knocks once, twice on the table as he stands. He unfolds his tall self casually. "I'll grab us drinks and be right back." Before he's more than a foot away, he glances back over his shoulder. His eyes are hooded. "Don't go anywhere, Kirbs."

With a demand like that, how can I?

I stay planted in my booth, ass to leather, for the next ten minutes. I watch as Alec walks up to the bar, to Joseph no less, and orders effortlessly. He doesn't pay attention to the countless eyes that follow him or the woman who materializes out of thin fucking air next to him, rubbing her chest on his arm. He gives her a quick glance, his eyes beaming down in a quick delivery of rejection. His expression is cold, glaring daggers at the poor woman. She backs off and he retrieves our drinks. He makes his way back over to our booth where my elbows are propped up on the table cradling my chin. If I was swinging my feet, I would look like a swoon-stricken girl. This isn't a fairy tale, I remind myself.

"What did you get for me?"

Alecsander smirks as he sets the glasses on the table. "A little amaretto sour for you and a whisky sour for myself." Alec twirls the mixer straw around the outer edge of his glass using the pad of his pointer finger. His silver rings gleam in the dimly lit bar, throwing shadows in every corner.

"You remembered what I ordered at the nightclub?" I ask before I can stop myself. I hurriedly take a sip of my drink. The icy sweetness of it clashes with the residual toothpaste from my hasty getting ready.

"Of course I did, Kirbs. Have a little faith!" Alec is gingerly sipping his sour. His eyes crinkle with each swallow. It's endearing. I want to kick myself in the ass, what the fuck am I thinking? What am I doing here? With him? Making bad fucking decisions, apparently.

Alec's hand meets mine, encasing my fingers as he rubs gentle circles over the back of my hand. "Where'd you go, Kirbs? Is this too much?" His voice lowers, caressing me like a warm hug on a rainy day.

I blink, centering myself. I start to pull my hand from his, but he only squeezes my fingers harder before letting go.

"No, no, I'm fine. I'm sorry, I got carried away. I've been pretty busy lately, dealing with a lot of things." I ramble.

"I see, I get that, I do. But we're both here, at this bar, drinking some drinks and, well, hopefully, enjoying one another's company. Try to relax, breathe. You're off." If anyone else said that to me, I would be instantly pissed, but something in Alec's voice is soothing. It's like balm to my burned soul. I inhale deeply and let it out. I relish the fact that I'm not working tonight at least.

"You're right. Okay. Deep breath, two, three. Gotcha. Okay, I'm good." I open my eyes to see Alec smiling. His finger still toys with the thin straw of his drink. It's like a waterfall is spewing from my mouth, and I can't stop it.

"You're good."

"So, anyway," I redirect, tired of the subject being myself. "How are you doing?" Casual. Yep, that's me.

"I'm alright, nothing to write home about." Alec takes another sip. "How long have you worked here?"

"How do you know I work here?"

Alec has the decency to look slightly ashamed. His face reddens. "Dominic told me."

"Ah, I see. Did Dominic tell you anything else?" I fire back.

Alec straightens in his seat. "Not really, no. Do you know him well?"

I laugh. "Know him well? I barely know him at all!"

Alec steeples his fingers. His eyes never leave mine. "That's interesting because Dominic is under a different impression."

There's something about his tone that's beginning to piss me off. He sounds accusatory.

I lay my hands on the table, leveling his gaze with one of my own. "Say whatever the fuck you want to say, Alecsander. Stop playing weird fucking mind games." Take that, douche canoe.

Alec's eyes widen. "Dominic told me that you were together. As in, *together*, dating, something like that. I must admit I was a little perturbed considering you talked to me at the nightclub and went out with me tonight."

"Oh, so you baited me tonight? Wanted to see if I would be the type of person who would cheat on my significant other?"

"So, you guys are dating then?"

I throw my hands up. "No! We're not together! I barely know him, but he knows a lot more about me than I do him. Stop jumping to fucking conclusions you have no right to jump to!"

Alec sets his glass down, taking in my frantic state. "Kirbs, I didn't know that. Dominic told me you guys were together. I was confused and assumed things. Incorrectly, apparently." He takes a breath, "I apologize."

I search his face, trying to figure out if he's lying, scheming, or part of Dominic's plans. I'm still on the fence about Dominic anyway. I'm warming up to him, enough to let him in my pants. Then he drops off the face of the planet for two whole freaking days. The man doesn't make sense. Ugh.

I shake my head again, dislodging that thought once more. Alec peers at me like I'm a rabid animal about to bite his leg clean off. His full attention is on me, and it makes my skin crawl. I want to move around and get the feeling away from me.

I sit on my palms, forcing them into compliance. "Thanks for apologizing, I guess. But it doesn't really change anything," I bite out. I want to verbally lash him for all the hoops he's jumping through in his conclusions.

Alec reaches a hand toward me, palm up. He offers his hand like it's a beacon in the night. I slowly unpeel my hand from the back of my thigh and leather seat and place it gently in his upturned one. He gives my fingers another subtle squeeze, reassuring me that he is here. Comforting.

"I'm sorry for making assumptions, Katherine." He gives me a small grin. "I'll do my best not to do so in the future."

I start to remove my hand, but he holds it firmly. "There doesn't need to be a future here, Alecsander." I want to stare into his eyes and say it, but I can only gaze at his nose.

Alec scoffs. "You think you're going to run me off that quickly?"

"Run you off?"

"You think I'm going to run for the hills because we had a disagreement, which, to be fair, was my fault. I apologized and I'm attempting to move on," he rambles.

Fuck, I'm nervous. But why?

"Alecsander-,"

"Alec, please."

I roll my eyes at the man sitting across from me. Somehow, he's so polite and sweet while also being somewhat of that douche canoe from earlier. My skin crawls, or is it electrifying? I can't tell the difference. I don't trust myself completely thanks to Dominic and his whiplash.

"Okay, Alec," I drag out his name like a petulant child. "Alec, just because I agreed to come to the bar with you for one hour doesn't mean jack shit, honestly. I don't owe you shit." I steal a glance at my phone, sitting on the booth by my leg. We've been here for over half an hour at this point. I did my dues; I can leave and not feel shitty about it.

"Kirby, come on. Talk to me here," he starts.

I rip my hand from Alec's, standing up from the booth in one solid movement. "Alecsander, I said this doesn't matter. I don't need more fucking drama in my

life, okay? I have enough shit to worry about without adding you into the mix."

Alec stands from his side of the booth, approaching me like a cat would a mouse. He stops a breath away from my chest. I crane my neck to look at his face, his sun-kissed skin gleaming in the dim lighting of the bar. He smells expensive, like cologne I don't have the nose to identify. "Kirby, you're not giving me a chance to explain."

"Exactly, I don't get why you keep stating the obvious here, Alecsander." I cross my arms over my chest, my elbows brushing against his upper abdomen.

As I stare into Alec's eyes, my skin tightens. I become aware of exactly how close we are. How we're nearly chest to chest in a semi-crowded bar. "Alec-," I begin.

Alec grabs my upper arms and pulls me in closer to him. I uncross my arms and drape them by my sides, letting him pull me in closer until our chests are crushed together. He wraps his arms around my torso, effectively giving me a soul-crushing hug.

I feel a kiss to the top of my head as Alec's lips descend to the shell of my ear, "Kirbs, go on a date with me. Please? Say no and I'll walk away right now. I swear. You won't see me again."

My cheek rests against his chest, and I hear his heart pumping wildly. I nod as his teeth scrape the shell of the ear he was whispering into.

"Okay."

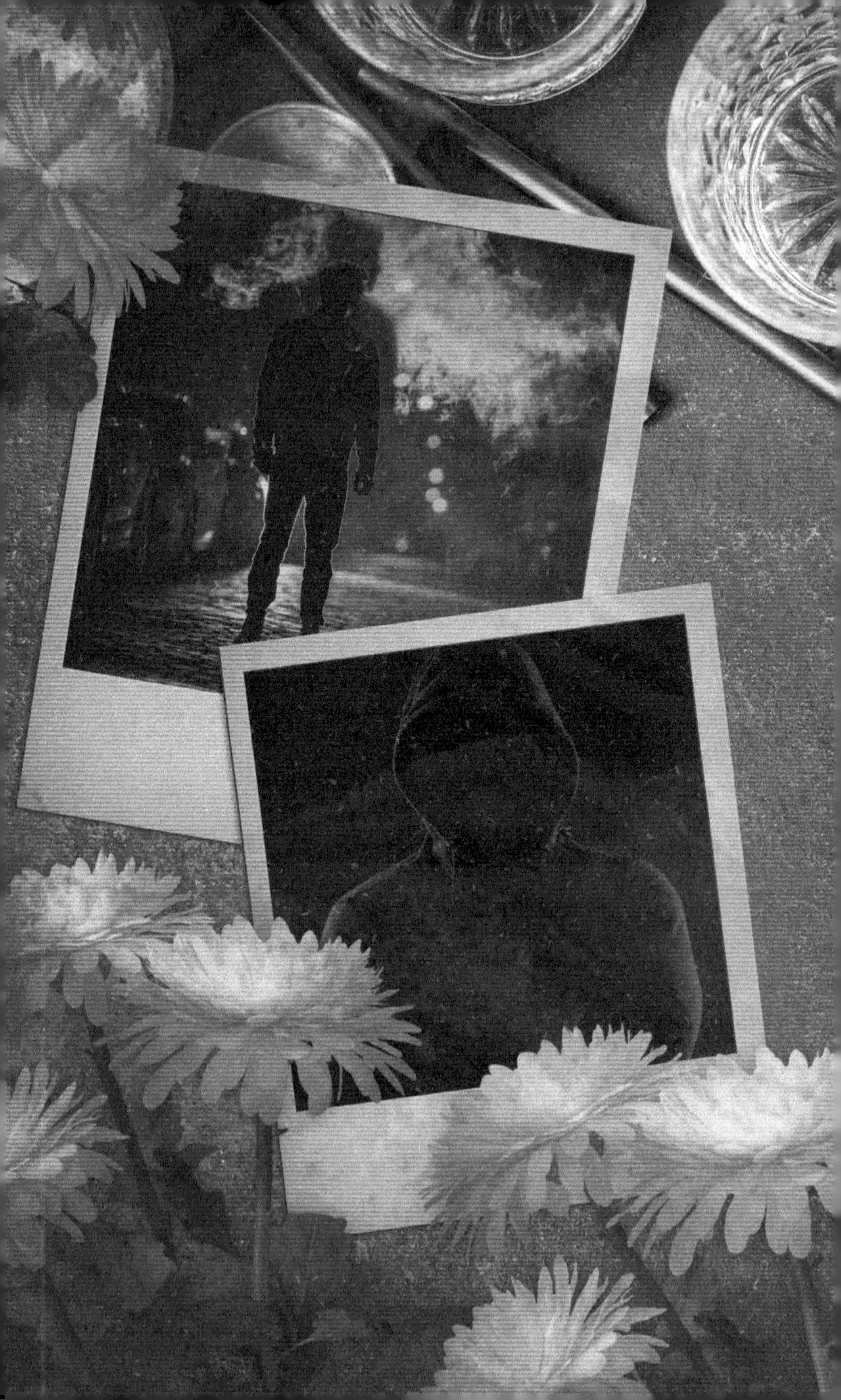

Seventeen

ALECSANDER

Everything is going according to plan.

I must admit, however, that it was supremely difficult leaving Kirby last night after she finally agreed to go out on a date. As I kissed the crown of her head, a deep pang shuddered in my chest, making me want to fold in on myself. I held fast and gave her a quick peck on the cheek before we parted and went our separate ways for the night.

I sit in my office, in my house, on the outskirts of town. I stay as far away as I can manage when I don't have meetings to attend or skulls to bust. Dominic typically rules the inner city anyway, something our merger brought together. It makes my job easier, for sure, but it also gives him quite a lot of territory and power.

I knead my forehead with the tips of my fingers, doing my best to erase the skepticism and paranoia that usually clouds my thoughts when they involve Dominic Alcutti. We are no longer enemies. We aren't necessarily back to being best buds like when we were younger, but we have made tremendous efforts and progress in the past five years.

But this whole situation with Kirby? I don't know how to navigate it.

Dominic is all I have these days. He's a friend when I need one and an ear when I can convince myself to trust him. I know he keeps a guy around. Milo, I think. But I don't have a Milo. It's just me. In this house. Alone. My thoughts constantly drift to the woman I met nearly five years ago, the woman who turned out to be Kirby.

It's enough to drive anyone to madness. I can feel myself petering on that edge between madness and sanity. Standing up, I dust my legs off. They have a complete layer of white fur on them from where my large, Maine Coon cat, Birdy, has been sitting the past several hours.

Speak of the devil, Birdy trots around the corner leading into my office. She pauses, her big blue eyes gazing at me. I often think if she had eyebrows, she would be scowling. She blinks, meows, then turns and leaves the office. Typical Birdy.

I shake my head and go to the kitchen. It's state-of-the-art with a large island and a deep sink. It doesn't excite me. I don't cook very often. Usually, the chef does it since it's what I pay her for and I'm pretty lazy when I'm home.

But I need to brush up on my pasta recipe if I have plans to invite Kirby over for dinner. Glancing at the stove, I notice evening is quickly approaching. If I want to invite her to dinner tonight, then I need to call her soon so she can get here. I pluck my phone and dial her number without thinking.

She answers on the second ring. "Hello?"

"Kirby, dear, how's your day going?" I cringe at how awkwardly forced I sound.

"Um, it's okay so far. How are you doing, Alec?" Her voice is a melody that I long to hear.

"I'm suffering here, Kirby."

"What? What's wrong?"

I chuckle lightly. "I'm lonely and could use a dinner date if you're available tonight?"

"Tonight? Like when tonight?"

"A few hours maybe? I could send a car to you if you'd like."

Silence for a few beats. "Um, could you actually pick me up, Alec? I don't know if I feel comfortable with a stranger picking me up." Her voice is small, like she's nervous about asking for the bare minimum. Surely this is something I can blame Dominic for. What an ass. Hell, even if he had nothing to do with it, I'm blaming him.

"Of course, Kirby. I can leave here soon, maybe in an hour. It will be an hour drive, so, I'll be at your place in two hours? Does that sound fitting?"

"Yeah, that should work."

"That's perfect. I'll see you then."

"Alec?"

"Yes, Kirby?" I smile.

"You don't have my address."

Such simple matters and simple, easy answers. "Don't worry Kirbs, I know where you live."

She exults and hangs up the phone. No argument from her as I expected. Maybe this is going in my favor after all.

I'M DOUBLE-PARKED ON THE STREET IN FRONT OF HER apartment. Looking up into the sky, her apartment climbs toward the clouds. It's in a crowded section of town, a section with higher rates of crime. Which means it's cheap and that's what I assume Kirby needs.

I can't believe she works at Dominic's bar, Point B. And has been for years. I've never seen her when I go in, but admittedly, I don't go very often. I will be rectifying that soon that's for damn sure.

I send her a quick text telling her I'm here and waiting in the car. It takes several minutes, but eventually she bursts through the front door of the complex in a flurry of motion. She has a beanie on her head and is clamping it on with a free hand while her other hand clutches a tote bag of some sort to her chest. Her jacket is open, not buttoned as it should be, and flowing in the wind around her torso. Half of her dark shirt is tucked into her jeans, but the other half isn't. Is that a fashion thing? Or did she forget to tuck in the other half? Her head jerks back and forth along the street, searching for me. I give the horn a quick tap to catch her attention.

It does and she's not happy about it. Her face scrunches in such a manner that, frankly, kind of terrifies me as she storms up to my car. Clutching her bag still, she rips open the car door, casually throwing the tote bag into the back seat as she all but falls into the low-seated car. Not missing a beat, she pulls off her beanie, releasing her dark hair in waves to her shoulders and throws it in the back seat as well.

I clear my throat.

Her head whips in my direction, her eyebrows drawn low. "What?" Her face is slightly flushed. Her breathing is labored.

Did she go down all the flights of stairs? She pulls her seat belt free and clips it into place.

"Well?"

"Did you walk down all the flights of stairs?"

"What?"

"Did you walk down the stairs instead of taking the elevator?" Trying not to sound like a crazy motherfucker, I quickly add, "You sound out of breath is all."

Foot? Inserted into mouth.

Kirby sighs, not placating me with an answer. I take her silence as a reprieve from my own stupidity. Am I flustered? No, surely not. I'm never flustered. I'm around women all the damn time and the cat never catches my tongue, yet one measly car ride with Kirby and suddenly I'm questioning whether Birdy stole it or not.

We don't converse on the ride to the house. Kirby sits angled toward the window, looking out it with her head on her curled fist. I glance over every few moments, hoping to catch her looking at me. She never is. I eventually grow sick of the silence and turn the volume on the radio up enough to hear it rather than the sound of blood rushing to my head.

After what feels like hours, we pull into my long drive. "We're here," I tell her.

Coming out of her trance-like state, Kirby faces me. "This is where you live?" Her voice doesn't sound judgmental, but rather, interested.

I park the car and begin opening my car door. "Sure do. Want to see the inside?"

As I'm walking to her side of the car to open her door for her, Kirby leans over the middle console. She reaches in the back for her tossed beanie and tote bag. I lose all focus when her plump ass is staring me in the face with only a window between us. Her jeans aren't super form fitting, but they hug her waist and ass with such care that I can't look away. Not even if I want to. And fuck, I do *not* want to.

Once on stable ground, I look at Kirby. Her face is glued to the outside of the house, her eyebrows hitching a ride to her hairline. "Ready to go inside?"

She nods enthusiastically and wraps her arm around my arm. We climb the few stairs to the front door. Instead of rifling through my pockets for keys, I pull one hand from my pocket and hover it over a square next to the doorknob.

"Are you scanning your hand to get into your house?"

I throw a quick smirk in her direction, glad I can keep her on her toes. "Of course, Kirbs. Gotta have the latest tech."

Kirby gives me a noncommittal shrug as I push open the door and let her go around me. The entry is small. Her chest grazes mine as she inches her way around me. I feel her nipples through her shirt. I want to yank her inside and sink into her soft curves and luscious skin. I hold back. I give her a pained smile as I hold the door open and then quickly follow behind her.

Kirby walks through my house like she owns it. It looks damn good on her. Her head is on a swivel as she slowly walks through the entryway, living room, dining room, and eventually the kitchen. She doesn't utter a word and I don't offer any. She leads the way even though it's a slower route than I would have taken. I'm mesmerized by her, the enigma of Katherine Rigby. With her face turned upwards, staring at the chandelier in the kitchen, her nose is sloped elegantly. It leads to lips that are only just upturned at the corners.

She glances around the pristine kitchen, and she throws her tote bag unceremoniously onto the island. It lands with a thud. What the fuck does she have in there? Bricks? Books? Something to murder me with? Hands shoved in my pockets, I approach her cautiously. No need to scare the mouse.

"What's in your tote bag, Kirbs? It sounds like a weapon." I chuckle, trying to ease her into conversation.

She looks through her large gray eyes, no emotion shining through, just blatant disinterest. It contrasts so greatly with what I thought she was thinking that it takes my breath away. How can she go from staring at everything in my house with wonder to giving me such a dead look that I'm afraid she's nothing but a ghost in a matter of seconds? Kirby *is* duality, discourse.

I am forever baffled.

"Maybe it *is* a weapon," she utters.

I plant my hands on the island, facing her across the counter. "Show me, would you? I want to know what you'd hurt me with."

Maybe she doesn't need to be eased into anything. Maybe she harbors a kindred form of darkness.

She huffs but abides. Kirby grabs her tote bag and instead of rifling through it, she up-ends it. The contents spill onto the island. Little pieces of her life flutter before me. Scrap receipts are crumbled and beyond saving. A random pamphlet from something or another. Several pens and pencils and markers roll on the counter, all worn. A slab of sticky notes, crunched up like they have been at the bottom holding the weight of everything else in the bag. There are a few hair ties, some large and some tiny. A clip. A clothespin. A tube of lip gloss so old the label is illegible. But what really catches my eye, what must be the weight I heard, is the dull and rusty hammer that lay there.

My eyes widen. "A hammer, Kirby?"

She only nods, not giving me the satisfaction of seeing her eyes as she turns away.

"Why do you have a hammer in your tote bag, Kirbs?" I whisper. I don't want to startle her or embarrass her.

Kirby sighs, the sound coming from deep within her. She rubs her palm against her forehead, seemingly trying to straighten the lines that form there. "It's my just-in-case hammer."

"Just-in-case hammer?"

"Yeah, you know, the hammer I might need...just in case." She refuses to look at me.

"Just in case what, Katherine?"

Her face slowly brightens, turning a dark shade of pink. She's frustrated about how obtuse I'm being. Yes, I have a good idea what a "just-in-case hammer" is, but I want, no, need, to hear her say it. To confess it to me. To tell me *everything*.

"It's just in case you try anything. I was going to pull it out and beat you over the head with it." At the last phrase, she turns her doe eyes to me. They are aflame. She isn't fucking around. My chest tightens with an unknown emotion.

I bring my hand to my chest, appalled. "I wouldn't hurt you."

Katherine shrugs. She shoves everything back into her dingy tote bag. "Doesn't matter if I think you would or not, I wasn't going to come to your fucking house without something to protect myself with."

This woman keeps surprising me. "I want to make you a nice dinner and maybe start a fire in the fireplace afterwards to drink some wine."

Kirby picks up her tote and places it on the kitchen table several feet away. Turning back to me, with her arms crossed against her chest, she juts out her chin. "Well, then you'd better get started because I'm ravenous."

KATHERINE

Alecsander's house makes my mouth water with how extravagant it is. It isn't blatantly luxurious. His style is more on the minimalist side, with few pieces of décor hanging from the walls and lining the shelves and bookcases. It's casual luxury. I touch one wall, letting my fingertips glide across the dark gray paint as I eye the photos that are hanging.

They are black and white photographs. All of them are streets, roads, or trains. Older than modernity. No people are in the photographs. In each photo, there is a singular piece of color, something to grab your attention as you walk by, I'm sure. In the photo of the train, the only color is the illumination from the headlight on the locomotive. In the photograph of a town car from the fifties, the only burst of color comes from the equally old-fashioned stop sign. The rest of the wall's photographs are similarly done. One striking flash of color in the otherwise black and white world.

"Dinner's ready." Alec stands adjacent to my back. I turn, watching his amber eyes follow mine as I drink in his physique. How can he look so good standing in his own home? It must be some type of trick, some kind of pagan ritual that he completed years ago that bestowed such beauty upon him. It's sinful and delicious all at the same time.

I follow Alec into the formal dining room. The table is large enough for a dozen or so people, but Alec sat our places at the head of the table. I assume he will man the head and I'll sit to his side. However, he surprises me by pulling back the head chair and offering it to me. I smile dumbly as I plop into the velvet chair, embarrassment flooding my cheeks.

I gaze over the table. The layout is refreshing and alluring. Alec made a simple dinner of chicken parmesan, but it smells divine. "This looks tasty."

Alec gifts me with a small smile. The corners of his eyes crinkle. "It's simple enough, but I enjoy it all the same."

I nod while picking up my fork and twirling noodles around the tines. Upon the first bite I know it's good. But the second bite with a cut of chicken added to it? Perfection. I do my best to stifle my moans as I devour the noodles.

As we're both digging in, a loud *yowl* meets my ears. I twist in my chair, craning my neck to see what made the noise. I chew and swallow quickly. "Was that a cat? Do you have a cat?" The idea of a feline friend makes my heart ache.

Alec finishes his bite, looking at me like I'm the one to be devoured. He chuckles. "Yeah, that would be Birdy making her appearance." He juts his head in the direction of the kitchen.

I quickly turn, seeing a large, white fluff of fur speed walk around the corner and into the dining room. She walks figure eights through my legs and mews at me. I stare down my torso at her. Her white cloak is thick and poofy, making her appear larger than she probably is. "This is Birdy?"

Alec takes a swig of his wine. "Sure is. I've had her for years now. She might sound mean and judgmental, but, trust me, she's wonderful."

I lean an open hand toward the feline, keeping my voice low.

"Hey, Birdy. You're such a pretty girl," I coo. Birdy rewards me by slowly licking one of my fingers.

I giggle as she continues licking my hand. After a few moments, I peel my hand back to my chest. I give it a quick rub with a napkin and look up to meet Alecsander's eyes. He's already staring at me, his eyes twinkling.

"Birdy must like you," he smiles.

I shrug my shoulders. "She probably likes everyone."

Alecsander wags a finger at me. "No, no, no. Birdy is a great judge of character. She hates most people. Hell, you're probably the first new person she's seen in years."

Years? Has it been that long since he's brought anyone over?

Why does the thought excite me?

I give Alec a sheepish grin, petting Birdy one last time before she trots over to his legs and lays on the floor. She quickly falls asleep and we're back to eating dinner.

WE MAKE POLITE CONVERSATION. I LEARN THAT ALEC IS an only child, and his parents are dead. His father died in the last five years. His mother died when he was a teenager, but he doesn't disclose how, and I don't ask him.

"Tell me about you, Kirbs." His voice is smooth and rich.

I shrug non-committedly. "There's not much to tell. I grew up alone, my parents are either MIA or dead. I was in the system for a while. Aged out and now I'm here." Short and simple, but not very sweet.

You get what you see. Just me.

It's always been just me. That's what I'll continue telling myself. I don't-- I *can't* think about him. If I do, the nightmares will return, and I'll break. For good. There will be no return for me then. I shake my head, dislodging Rhett from my mind.

Alec stands from the table, collecting our empty dishes without hesitation. He marches them to the attached kitchen, making me spin around in my chair to follow him with my eyes. He pads across his house with ease and comfort, something I silently envy him for. His life seems so casual and carefree, existing in a way that I can only dream of. Comfort.

I stare after him. He puts the dishes into the sink and begins rinsing them off. I make my way over to him. I don't want to crowd him, but I stand a foot or so away, leaning my back against the countertop.

Alec looks at me while he continues rubbing a sponge over the plate, suds up to his wrists. "There's some more wine in the fridge if you'd like another glass," he offers.

We each had one glass of red wine with our chicken parmesan. It's a strange feeling having a man pour me a swirl of wine into a long-stemmed glass and setting it before me like I was royalty. I kind of liked it and wished he would pour me another one personally. The way his palm engulfed the whole bulb of the glass was mesmerizing.

I tap my fingers along the counter. "I think I'm okay wine-wise."

"What about everything else-wise?" Alec asks me, his smirk slowly creeping up his face.

I shrug once more. "I'm alright considering everything that's happened the past few weeks."

"Oh yeah? You're *fine* considering everything?" He raises his eyebrows.

I cross my arms on my chest. "Yeah, I mean, it's nothing I can't handle, you know?"

Alec flicks his wrists into the sink, allowing the water to sluice off his skin. He braces his forearms against the edge of the sink, peering through his thick, dark eyelashes. His eyes are a crime and I want to commit a felony.

"I actually don't know much, Kirby. Not really, anyway. Not where it matters." His voice fades.

"What do you want to know then, Alecsander?"

Please don't ask about my history. Don't ask anything, actually. Let's live in this bubble we've created where we're attracted to one another, and nothing stops us.

His eyes are wide and honest. It doesn't seem like he's hiding anything, at least, not at the current moment. That's more than I can say for other parties in my life. Hell, even Rhett managed to hide so much from me. I mentally huff and puff before continuing with the dangerous conversation I suddenly find myself in.

He speaks before I can build up the necessary courage. "Tell me anything, Katherine. Tell me your secrets, your desires. Your wants and your fears. Give it to me. Let me help you."

"What gives you the impression that I need or want your help?" I shoot back, but I lack mirth.

Alec chuffs like a damn cat. His eyes sparkle as he looks at me. "I think Dominic coming into my night club and laying me out flat on my ass gives me plenty of an impression about what you might be involved in."

The world pauses in an instant.

Alecsander mentioning Dominic.

Dominic bleeds into my life in every nook and cranny he can, even if he isn't around physically. How can one person be so involved yet so far away?

"How loud do I need to be for you to hear me when I say that Dominic isn't a fixture in my life?" My voice notches up an octave. I can feel the blood rush to my face.

Alecsander chortles. "Oh, Kirbs. You're a little delusional, I'll give you that, but are you really that deep in it?"

"What are you talking about?"

"I know Dominic went to Point B the other day and saw you."

He lifts his eyes to meet my own, our gazes clashing in a war that isn't soon to be won.

"Okay, what's your point? Point B is a bar after all, plenty of people come and go during my shifts there."

"Sure, they do. I've heard you come as you please too."

My arm shoots across the gap between us, hitting him square in the chest. A well-muscled chest, at that. I can't believe my ears. He's bringing *that* up right now? Better yet, how does he know about the encounter? My eyes widen, realization slamming into me. "You're like him, aren't you?" I stutter, "You, you know things I haven't told you. That's what he's like too." I turn and take a step backwards.

Alecsander isn't deterred. He follows me, inching closer with each tiny step forward he takes. "Kirby, I'm not stalking you."

"Yeah, well, says you. You who knows things!" I'm nearly incoherent, my heart pounding rapidly, my chest caving in. I'm on the edge of a panic attack. I need to get the fuck out of here. I get away from one stalker and somehow, I'm in the house of another. Who will believe this shit? Not me, yet here I am, living it.

Alec's eyes scrunch together, concern marring his features. "Katherine, are you alright? You're looking a little pale all of the sudden."

My heart continues galloping along my rib cage. I bring my hand to my chest, clutching the neckline of my sweater. With my heart racing and my head holding a dance marathon, I try to remain focused. I start a slow count in my head, trying to steady myself. I reach out with my free hand to feel for the counter, to offer myself some type of crutch to keep my body upright.

"Katherine, can you hear me?" Alec's voice is far off, seemingly in another room. I glance around, noticing him standing directly in front of me. His form is blurry, my vision turning black around the edges. Tunnel vision. I'm going to pass out if I don't calm down and settle myself.

Strong fingers grip my upper arms and the sensation borders

on pain. The quick sting of the fingers brings me a little closer to my senses. My vision brightens a smidge. I keep counting and breathing. I focus on what Alecsander is saying.

"Let's bring it down, Katherine. Easy." He puts slight pressure on my arms, pushing me down, down, until my ass hits the floor. I cross my legs haphazardly, not caring if a foot kicks him or bends in a weird way. Stability. That's what the floor offers.

As I settle on the cold, tiled floor, Alecsander's grip on my arms lessens. His hands move down to my elbows, skirting along my forearms until his hands are clasped over my own. He rubs his hands over mine, the friction warming my fingers. His breath is hot as he blows open-mouthed breaths on my palms, speeding the process.

"God damn, you're so fucking cold, Kirbs." His voice is lowered, like he isn't talking to me, but more so to himself.

My teeth chatter with anxiety. The pressure in my chest begins to lift. "T-thank you," I manage to breathe out.

Alec's hands hold mine steady as he looks up from his spot in front of me. He's kneeling on the tile, our knees practically touching. When his eyes meet mine, the atmosphere shifts. Taking a deep breath, I inhale his subtle cologne. The woodsy scent is grounding.

"You don't need to thank me, Kirbs. Trying to help you out."

I nod, not feeling quite up for conversation yet. My heart settles, and my fingers and hands regain warmth quickly with Alec's assistance. I chew on my lower lip, worrying it between my teeth until I taste the metallic zing of a droplet of blood. I flick my tongue out to catch the bead before it falls, but a calloused, ringed finger touches my face before I can.

I look up, homing in on Alec's beautiful face. His hair is wild, curling around the ends and sweeping around his ears. His eyebrows and eyes are no longer cinched in concern, but rather inviting as I drink him in. His finger brushes against my lip, swollen from the torture of my teeth. He catches the droplet of blood, barely there really, more like a smear. I watch, completely enraptured, as Alec brings his thumb to his own plush lips, gently pushing it into his mouth, sucking the tiny bead of blood off like it's honey.

My lips part and my breath quicken, but not in panic. My gaze never wavers from Alec's piercing eyes. His thumb lingers on his lip for a moment before breaching the gap between us once more and finding my jaw. His palm caresses my jaw as his fingers spread across my cheek and onto my neck. His metal rings are cold against my flaming skin, a welcome reprieve that I focus on.

"We should probably get you home, yeah?" he asks slowly. His words are wrapped in a barely veiled wisp of emotion, his throat clogged with something that I can't quite place but want to.

I find myself shaking my head. His eyebrows crawl up his forehead, "No?" He asks me for reassurance.

"No," I whisper.

Alec wastes no time. His lips descend on mine as if they're going through the nine circles of hell to get their home. They are hot, wet, and ravenous as they claim me. In one motion he licks the seam of my lips, causing me to part mine so he can sweep his tongue against mine and caress the inside of my mouth.

Something about the way his lips mold to mine lingers in my mind. His hands are back on my upper arms as I coil my body towards and around his, planting a leg on either side of his torso as we collapse together on the tiled floor. I moan into his mouth and our tongues dance together. Alecsander's hands roam up to my shoulders then back down to my hips, pulling me closer to him, closer to the hardy erection I can feel through his slacks.

"Alec," I moan, a question on the edge of my mind.

Alec backs away, taking a second to catch his breath as his cheeks flush crimson. "Yes?"

His fingers deftly trace circles directly under the hem of my sweater on my lower sides and back. His touch is electric, sending zaps throughout my body and straight to my core. I want to feel the heat of his erection seated deep within me, feeling myself clench around him as he makes me come. Thinking about it makes me wet with desire, solidifying the plans I didn't know I had.

"Alec, take me upstairs and fuck me," I groan. His hands grip me tighter, pulling me up with him as he stands. "Please," I beg him and, for once, I'm not feeling ashamed.

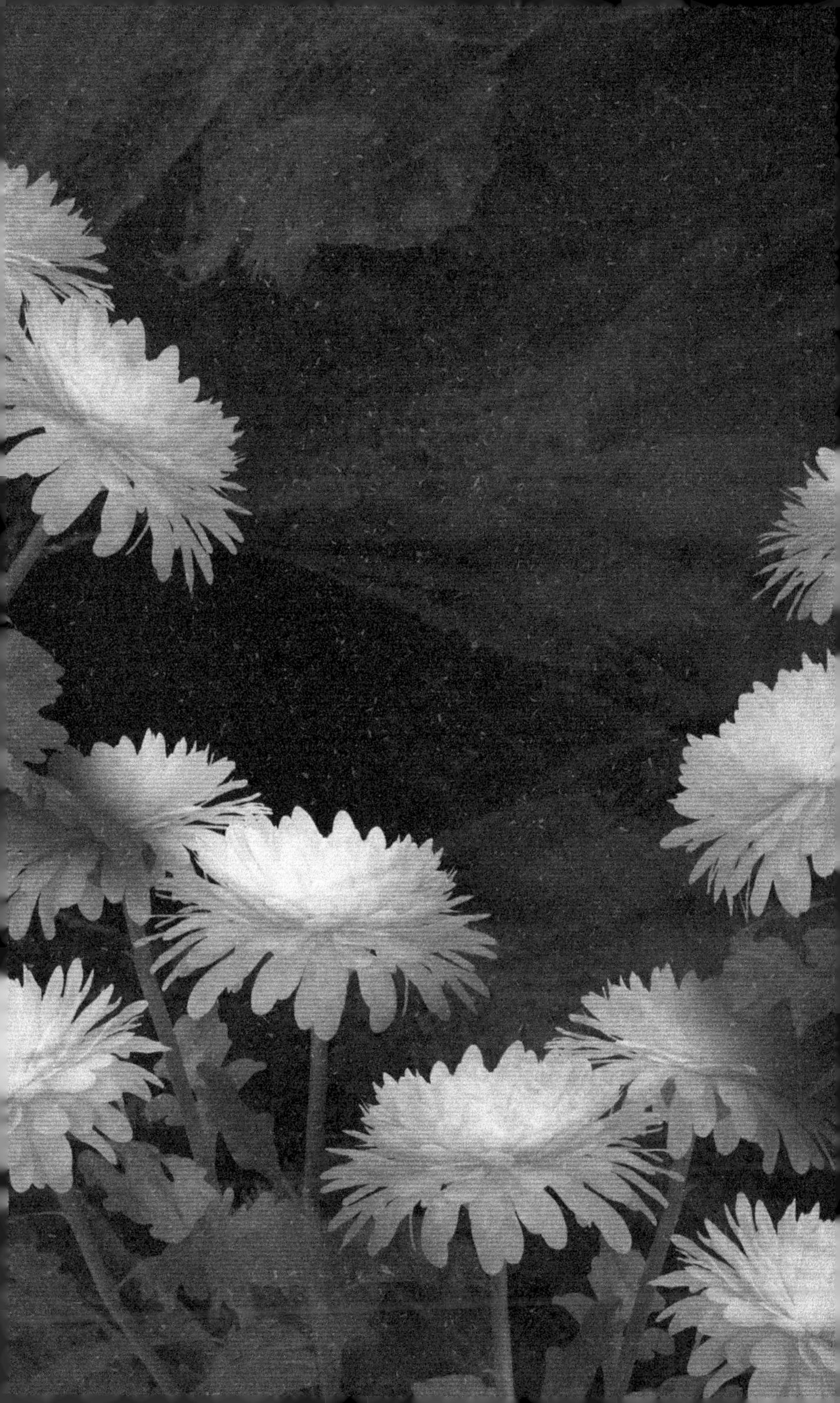

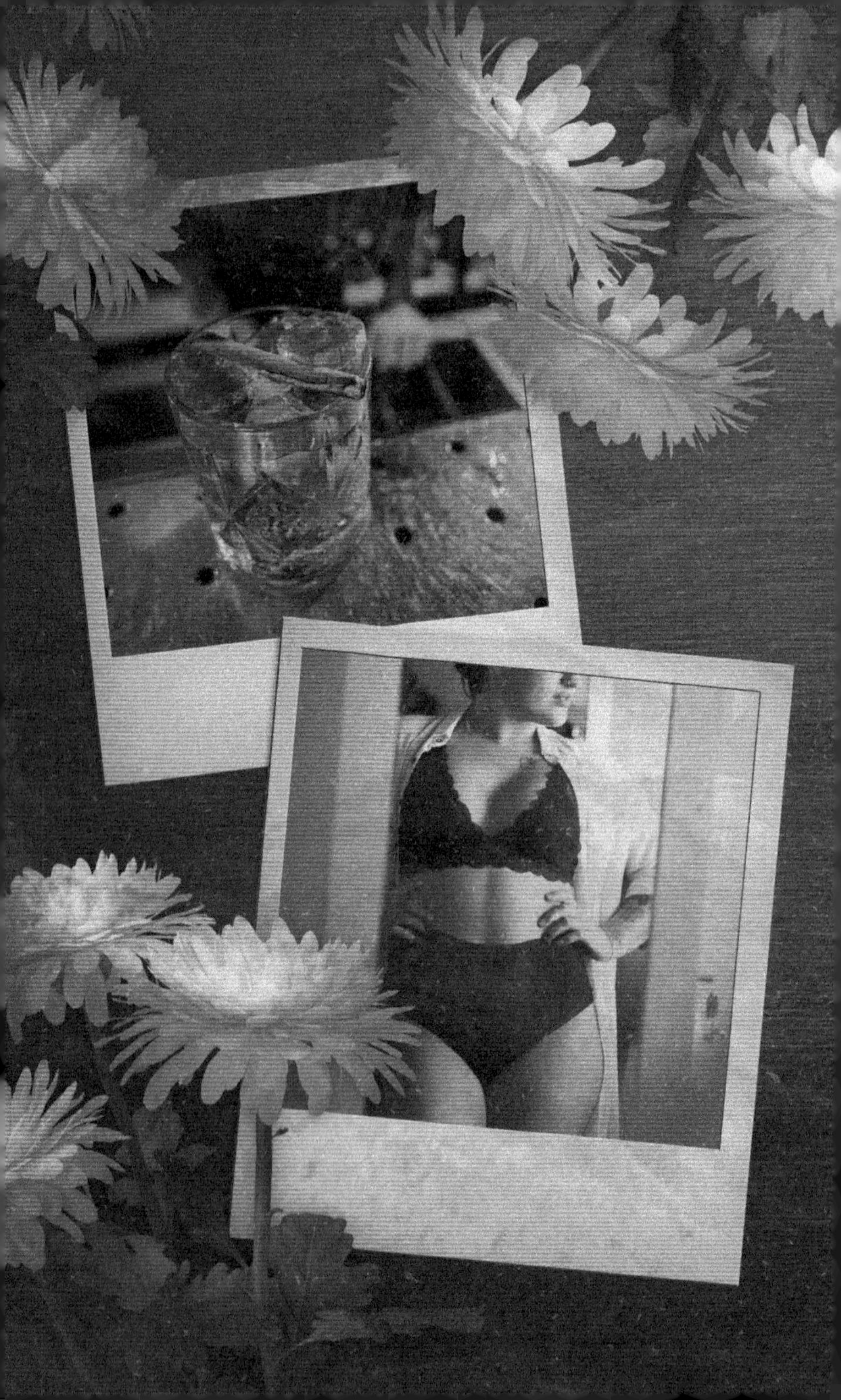

Eighteen

KATHERINE

Alec picks me up effortlessly. He cups my upper thighs, pulling me close. My legs wrap around his waist as he begins striding out of the kitchen. Our lips fuse. My heartbeat is rapid, but in a good way this time around. Our hearts sync as Alec walks into what I assume is his bedroom.

His bedroom is soothingly dark. When Alecsander leans forward and lets me sink into his plush bed, he continues further. He kneels on his bedroom floor between my spread knees. His pupils fully dilate and the desire coursing through his body mirrors my own. He braces his hands on each of my knees, giving them a subtle push wider. His eyes gleam with untamed lust. His tongue flicks along his bottom lip. "Are you sure?"

I nod, looking down my nose between my legs. What a beautiful sight it is. "Yes, please," I beg.

Alec flashes me a smirk as he places a hand on my shoulder. He pushes me down onto the bed with my legs hanging off the side. I'm positioned for perfect access. I feel, rather than see, his hands pull the button on my pants. He tugs down the zipper. In one movement, my pants, along with my panties, are around my knees. Alec's hands brush down my thighs, the warmth leaving gooseflesh in its wake.

Alec pulls my pants and underwear off my legs. He rocks backward on his heels, his fingers on his chin, staring. I stare back, but his attention isn't on my face. He's staring directly at my pussy. My entire body flushes. He scrubs his hands down his face, holding them on his jaw for a beat. "God, you're fucking beautiful Katherine."

Before I can offer my gratitude at the compliment, Alec dives in. His mouth latches onto the crease of my knee. His tongue meets my flesh, hot and wet as he begins leaving open-mouthed kisses up my thigh. Within moments, he's at the apex of my legs, his breath cascading over my center. I clench in need. "Alec-," I moan, but he stops me.

"One second, Katherine."

I watch, completely enraptured, as Alec pushes two fingers against my lips. "Open."

I allow him to place his fingers into my mouth.

"Close and suck."

I comply, closing my mouth and swirling my tongue around his two fingers. I release them with a pop.

"Very good," Alec mutters. "Stay still."

I throw my head back against the bed, preparing myself for *something*, but not knowing what.

Alec takes his sodden fingers and trickles them up my thigh. They make tiny circles as his mouth descends upon my center. His teeth nibble around the edges of my folds before he finds and latches onto my clit, sucking me thoroughly. He's a fucking vacuum. My back arches, the pleasure undeniable. I fist the sheets as his fingers prod my entrance.

Alec continues to lavish my clit with kisses and languid swipes of his tongue. His fingers press into me. They curl ever-so-slightly once they are seated within me. They hit the magic spot seamlessly as his tongue continues its torture.

The heat within builds. The mounting pressure concentrates at my center. I flutter around his fingers, causing him to moan around my clit. The vibrations of his moans feel incredible.

I'm *so* close.

Alec pulls away. I whimper at the loss.

He chuckles darkly. "You're not allowed to come yet, *Ranuncolo*. Not unless it's on my cock." He smiles wickedly, his voice deepening. His voice is so far away, yet so close.

I only nod, truly at a loss for words. Because what do you say to that? Fuck if I know. Alec withdraws his fingers from my core, the sudden movement shocking.

In a flurry of movement, Alecsander has his slacks and boxers pulled low, exposing his thick cock. It glistens at the head with precum. My mouth waters. Alec notices my line of sight as he grips his hardened length. He leans toward me. He pumps his shaft once, twice, three times.

"Are you ready, Katherine?" He leans forward, his lips dangerously close to my ear as his cock nudges my entrance. His skin is velvet, hot. "Don't you fucking think about coming until I give you the command." His eyes meet mine. "Do you understand?"

I thought being dominated would be a turn off, but it's promising to be a hell of a time. "Yes sir." I comply.

His eyes twinkle. He darts forward, sinking his full cock into my pussy in one swift movement. He's large, large enough to sting. My eyes widen as I feel him sink to the hilt.

He gives me a once-over. "Are you okay, Katherine?" His earlier demanding voice is gone, instead replaced by warmth and concern.

I nod quickly, meeting his gaze. "I'm okay. Please move." I beg him. This man has me begging more than I ever have in my whole life.

"Yes, ma'am. Remember what I told you." He withdraws fully, pausing for a moment before slamming back into me.

I gasp as Alec's hands wind behind my back, pulling me to his chest. I'm nearly sitting on top of him as he ruthlessly pounds into me. My threshold is rushing towards me, but I keep his demand in mind.

I don't know if I will make it.

"More," I plead.

Alec's lips are on my neck and jaw. They climb to my ear. He bites my earlobe, gripping the tiny stud earring I'm wearing in his teeth and giving it a slight tug. The pinch of pain is quick as he nips my lobe, pulling it and the earring into his mouth. He travels lower. He keeps the kisses and licks to my collarbone before dipping his hand into my shirt. He pulls my breast free from my bra and pops it out of my sweater. My sweater sticks to my back.

He turns his attention to my nipple. He pulls it into his mouth as he continues to slam into me. He plants his hips against my pelvis for a moment before unseating himself and slamming back into me. He does this over and over, all while focusing on my breast and nipple. When he pulls my nipple between his teeth, I clench around his dick aggressively.

"Not yet, Katherine," Alec groans into my chest.

"Alec, please," I beg breathlessly.

He drifts one of his hands from my back to my lower belly, caressing my skin and pinching it between his fingers. As he claims my nipple with his teeth and my pussy with his cock, he claims my clit with his deft fingertips, pushing and pulling it until liquid fire is burning me from his touch. I'm right on the edge as he simultaneously pinches my clit and whispers directly into chest, "Right now, Katherine. Give me your sweet come."

He pulls away from my breast and clit. His hands find my hips and pull me impossibly closer as he stalls his hips, locking them against my own. His cock pulses within me as I come harder than I have in a long time. His come mixes with my own, dripping down his shaft and onto my inner thighs. When I open my eyes, I immediately see his brimming with unnamed emotion. "Holy fuck," I breathe.

Alec nods, agreeing with me. "Holy fuck indeed."

ALECSANDER

Holy fucking shit.

My ears ring. My skin swelters. Sweat builds along my tailbone and collarbone. My hands hold fast to Kirby's hips, pinning her against me. Her full chest smashes against mine. Our breathing is hard, but in rhythm with one another. I kiss her on the forehead, holding my lips there for a moment.

After several minutes, we each pull away, albeit hesitantly. I drag my slowly deflating dick out of her wet heat, letting the excess cum dribble down her thighs. My eyes are fixated on her glistening skin. I watch the rivulets of pearly essence ooze out of her swollen lips. Without thinking, I quickly swipe two fingers along her inner thigh, wiping away the sticky substance and deftly shoving my fingers back into her tight channel. Kirby tenses then releases a breathy sigh, "Did you put your cum back inside me?"

I gulp, not sure what to say other than, "Sure did, *Ranuncolo*."

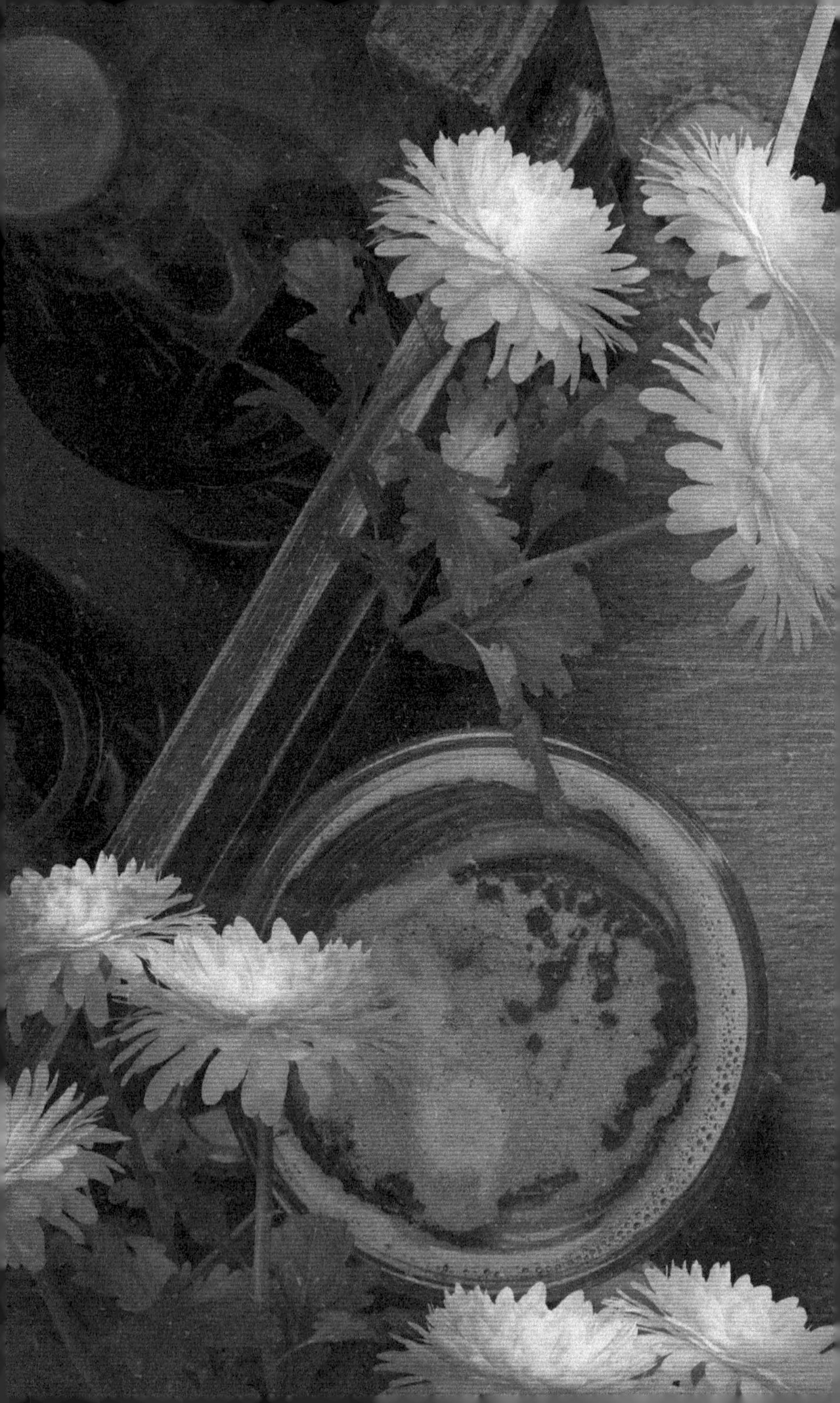

Nineteen

KATHERINE

A SINGULAR WORD BRINGS ME BACK TO LIFE AND THEN proceeds to stab me in the chest.

Ranuncolo.

I've heard it before.

Several times over the course of an hour or so.

One night.

Five years ago.

I heard that word and something was forever etched into my brain due to the gravity of the situation that occurred *that* night.

I push away from Alecsander. I study his sweaty appearance, his hair disheveled and his breathing labored. Does he remember? Does he call everyone that name? The more I gaze upon him, laying in his bed in all his naked glory, the more betrayal I feel settling behind my ribs, in a place where my heart should be.

I sit up, bringing my knees to my chest, trying to slyly cover myself. Alec is sprawled on his back with his arm draped over his eyes. A small smile dances across his lips. At my sudden departure, his arm moves and reveals his heavy eyes. "Where are you going?"

I want to climb back over his body, feel his still warm skin. But I hold back. I swing my legs over the edge of the bed, letting my feet hit the cold, tiled floor.

"I can turn on the heated floors for you if that'll be more comfortable, Katherine." Alec still lies on his back, but his gaze remains on me. His amber eyes follow my every move, like he wants to capture me and keep me here.

I shake my head, forcing a grin to my lips. "I'm fine. It's just a floor." My voice comes out a bit hollower than I intended. I hope he doesn't see through me even though I feel near translucent now.

I have replayed that night over and over in my head throughout the years. How his voice sounded. It's almost the same, but it is deeper now. I imagined the planes of his face but I never saw the full thing that night between the dimly lit room and the mask that covered the majority. How could I not instantly recognize the one man I had cried for years over? The man I was forced, albeit by my own doing, to leave behind as if it never mattered, as if that singular night didn't change my entire life?

Rhett would be disappointed in me right now and that's more hallowing than the feelings that break through the dams within my heart.

I sigh, standing up. I pad to the attached bathroom and glance over my shoulder at the man of my literal dreams. The man who either doesn't remember me or does and hasn't told me. I don't know which option is worse.

The bathroom is opulent but understated. The soaking tub is large and circular, taking up so much space when it has no right to. I peek in his cupboards, finding towels and linens for his bed. I scope out the largest shower I have ever seen and find nothing but his necessities and a few of the same products I use at home. I inspect the objects, but they are still sealed and brand new. Was he prepared for me to come over?

It's beginning to look that way.

I hear my heart crack.

I check his medicine cabinet as well. Nothing too shocking there. Aspirin. Tylenol. Toothbrush and paste. Deodorant. Nothing out of place and everything perfectly spaced. The opposite of my cabinet at home. When I exhaust all my nosey capabilities, I quickly do what I need to do and open the door to the bedroom.

Alecsander sits on the edge of the bed with his pants slung low on his hips, unbuttoned. "Find anything worth mentioning in there?" He smiles at me, but it doesn't reach his eyes.

My face reddens as I stand before him, completely naked. I want to cover myself but withhold the urge. I'll stand here confidently even if it fucking kills me. Let him look at my tits and still-wet thighs.

Let him look at me while he tries to explain himself.

I stare at him, not bothering to answer. I strut (including some ass wiggle) to the opposite side of the bed. I quickly gather my things and pull on clothes as I continue walking.

I walk out of Alecsander's bedroom and into the hall. He's behind me within seconds. "Where are you going, Katherine?"

I continue walking down the hall, hating that I have to recall how to get back to the kitchen.

"Katherine, what's the matter? Are you alright?"

If by alright you mean I have your cum between my legs still, then sure, I'm alright. But that's not what he's wondering. When I find the kitchen, I book it over to the bar where my tote bag resides.

"Katherine, are you-," he begins, but I cut him off.

I face him, my hand firmly clutching my just-in-case hammer against my chest. "I'm going to ask you this one time and one time only."

Alecsander gulps. "Ask away Katherine."

I stare, daring him to lie to me. I knock the hammer gently against his expensive ass counters. Not enough to crack them, but enough to make noise. "Did you know?"

"Know what?"

Is that sweat on his forehead? "Who I am? What we shared all those years ago?"

"Katherine, I can explain-," he starts.

"No." I slam the hammer against my hand, cushioning it. "Tell me the truth, Alecsander. Did you know who I was?"

Alecsander says nothing, but his face does enough talking. It's red, his eyes glazing with tears. I feel nothing. Or that's what I tell myself.

"I knew," he whispers.

That's all I need to hear. I step up to him, peering up with dead eyes.

He isn't expecting it.

I swing the hammer and crack him above the ear. His face registers a split moment of surprise before his eyes crinkle and fall shut. His body thuds to the floor in a messy heap of limbs.

I quickly throw the hammer back into my tote. I place the bag on my shoulder and go back to Alecsander's bedroom, nestling under the sheets. As I snuggle deeper into the expensive sheets, a fluff ball weighs down the bed. Birdy canters up the bed until she's lying next to me. She loafs up as I lean my head against the cold pillow. The tears begin to flow.

We will have to figure it out tomorrow.

DOMINIC

I've been holed up in my apartment for days.

It's only been mere moments since I witnessed the worst thing I've ever seen. My eyes need to be bleached. Either that or I'll scratch them out with my bare fucking hands.

It's worse than the sight of blood drenching my palms and stabbing my father in the chest. I shudder.

It's worse than when I blacked out while torturing someone in the basement of the warehouse for the syndicate.

That moment when I flipped the "on" switch on my computer and witnessed what happened in the confines of the Sandman's bedroom is seared into my brain.

Sure, one could argue that it's a massive invasion of privacy, but I'm not about to let the Sandman be on the up when it comes to our merger. I'm giving too much already, and I have to make sure he's keeping his end of the bargains.

I invited him to a dinner a few months back and while I was out wining and dining the motherfucker, Milo did the real work. There are cameras in nearly every room at Alecsander's house.

And they paid for themselves today.

I know our time is ending. The five-year mark for when we were supposed to find wives is quickly approaching.

I thought I had found mine.

I never expected to see him, *watch him*, fuck my girl on his bed.

I never expected her to be into it. She clawed his back and threw her head back in ecstasy as his flesh pounded into her, their combined cum leaking out of her.

The cameras I installed are of great quality. They're 4k and have sound. It's a personal porn video, but I watched it in real-time.

I don't think anything could have prepared me for what I saw, however.

I watch as Alec crumples to the tiled floor of his own kitchen. My lips turn up. She hit him. She, *my Katherine*, hit that fucker over the head.

I want to laugh at the absurdity of it all; I never thought she would do something like this. I can see her friend, Marisol, doing something of the sort, but Katherine? My sweet Katherine? Nah, I couldn't see it.

But now I can.

The thoughts won't leave my mind.

There are so many possibilities for us now that I know she has that inkling deep inside her. She isn't all light. She owns a shred of darkness that is beginning to bloom within her.

And I want to nurture it, encourage it.

I stalk Katherine back through the house. I figure she'll grab her shit and leave after clubbing Alecsander over the head. Instead, I find her making her way back through the way she came, ending up in his bedroom. I watch, my chin against my knuckles, as she climbs into his bed and pulls his duvet over herself. She tucks it under her chin. Katherine takes deep breaths, her body expanding then dipping with each one. Soon she is fast asleep, and I think I fall a little more in love with her.

ALECSANDER

Before I open my eyes, I know it's going to hurt. Actually opening my eyes, however, proves not only I was right but how I also underestimated how fucking bright my kitchen lights are.

I wince as I slowly bring my knees to my chest. I squint, trying to provide a bit of cover for my overstimulated retinas. Fuck my head hurts. What the hell happened?

I pull myself up by gripping the kitchen island. My thoughts shoot back to Kirby. She was here and we had spectacular sex, much like that first time all those years ago. Then, suddenly, she was up and gone and I followed her through my house to the kitchen. Where I am now.

But where is she? Is she still here?

I rub my scalp, trying to soothe away the tension that builds behind my skull.

As I pivot to walk to my bedroom, I realize that I'm still naked. Full on naked. I wince again and almost cover myself but then think, why does it matter? I'm most likely home alone anyway.

Did Katherine hit me with something?

I bring my hands up to my head, shuffling them softly through my hair. I grimace when I graze behind my ear. I pull my hand away and see a tinge of pink covering my fingertips. Am I still bleeding, or has it stopped? How long ago did I get hit? What did I get hit with?

Go fucking figure. I sidestep to my living room, grab a throw blanket, and wrap it around my waist as I creep through my home. I stop in my bedroom door frame, seeing a lump under my sheet with Birdy perched on top. Katherine is still here. She isn't hurt, from what little I can see, so I glance around the room. I take note of her tote bag thrown to the side of the bed nearest her, with a shiny metal object sticking half out of the bag.

Her just-in-case hammer.

It all rushes back to me. Katherine remembered me then she fucking clocked me upside the head.

A light bulb brightens my mind's eye. She knows that I knew who she was. She remembered that lucky night, and realized who I am after all. But she, somehow, knew that I already knew. And being distraught and most likely angry, she hit me.

I want to be pissed, want to scream, and lash out. I mean, she knocked me the fuck out! I scrunch my eyes, trying to locate the anger and burning hatred, but come up with nothing.

I don't hate her. I don't want to lash out at her for hurting me. If it were anyone else, they'd be strung up and bled dry.

Katherine isn't anyone else, though.

She is herself, just Katherine.

A woman I met fatefully nearly five years ago, who I made love with that first time and have dreamt of every night since.

I was baffled to see her in my nightclub. The dark-haired, jewel-eyed woman who stole my heart once again before Dominic showed up and punched me in the jaw.

I invited her here tonight for dinner and somehow, we both know how, ended up in bed with yet again. She is the one I am in love with, the one I want to marry and call mine for the rest of our time together.

Katherine is it for me. I knew it then before she waltzed out of my office without a word. I know it now, standing in my door frame to my bedroom. I clutch a throw blanket around my waist while my head kind of bleeds from a, I assume, small laceration where she pummeled me with a *fucking hammer.*

Katherine is Katherine to me, just Kirby. She is perfect however she is. And I'll be damned if I somehow fuck this up again.

I enter my bedroom, stopping at the end of the bed. I sit down, keeping the throw blanket in place and wait for Katherine to wake up.

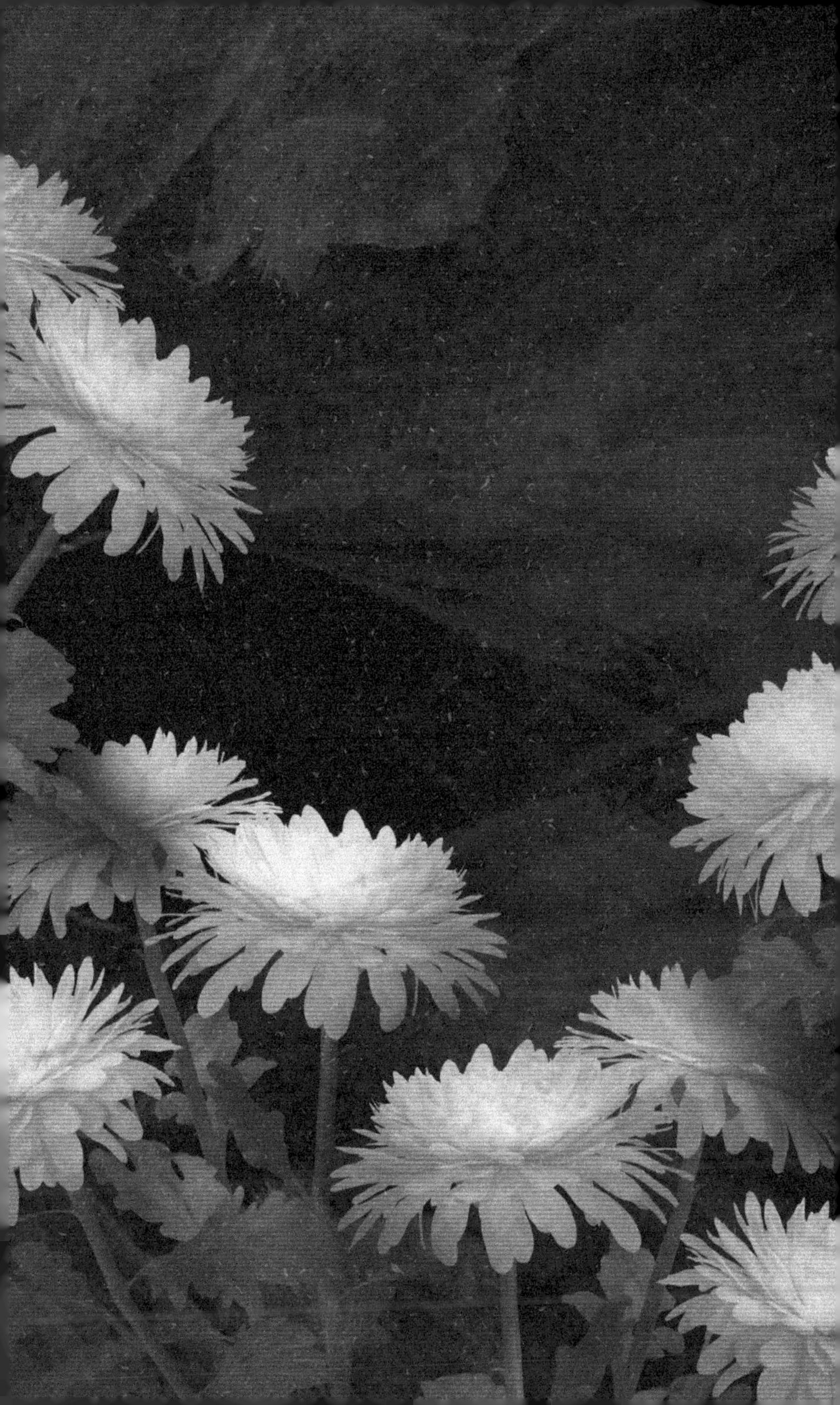

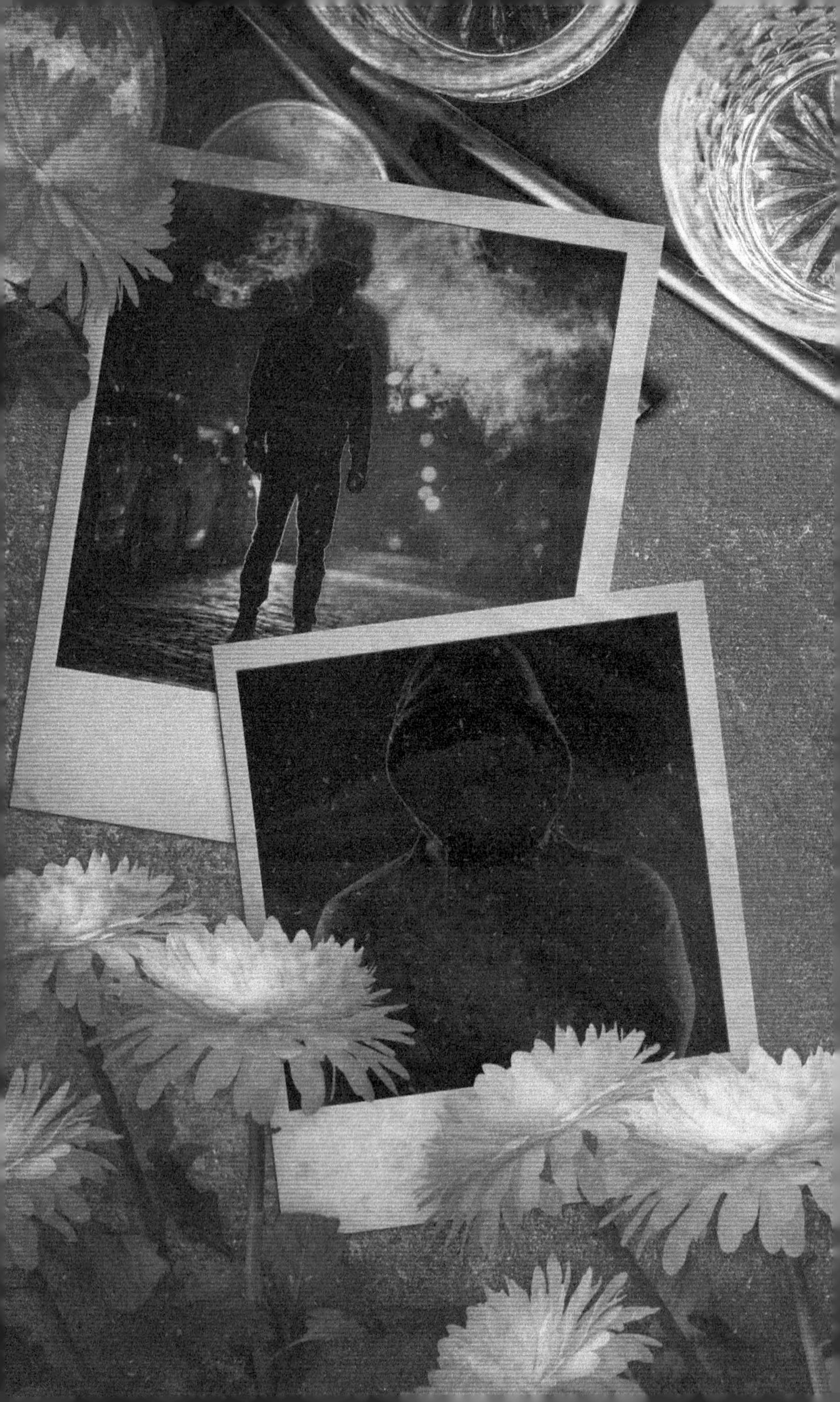

Twenty

KATHERINE

"Kath, are you coming or not?"

Rhett grabbed my hand, tugging me along behind him as we moved through the thin alleyway. "Where are you taking me, Rhett?"

He glanced back at me, his hair falling into his eyes. "We're going to our place."

"Our place?"

His smile was full wattage as we turned and approached a dilapidated, boarded up house. Rhett let go of my hand and walked a few paces in front of me. He threw his hands out wide. "This is ours, Kath!"

I raised a brow, "What do you mean exactly?" There's no way he could have bought this, not with his current position and not while I was still in school.

Rhett knocked my chin with his fingers, tilting it upward. "Don't fret, Kath. I've not done anything stupid...yet." He grinned and all my worries melted away.

"This is just a picture of what we will have one day. A house, for us. We'll do whatever we want with it." He painted a pretty picture of our future and I fell more in love with him.

We trudged up the bare steps, the old wood groaning beneath our combined weights. Rhett sped to the door that was missing hinges and knocked on it. "Welcome," he started.

Bang. Bang. Bang.

And Rhett fell.

I sit straight up in bed. Sweat thickens along the back of my neck. Rays of sunshine plunder through the tall windows and cast their gleams directly onto my face. I press the heels of my hands into my eye sockets, trying to rub away the dream.

It doesn't work.

I groan and stretch my arms out wide, going above my head then back down, arcing around my torso which allows a nice loud *pop* to sing through my spine. I yawn, still dead tired.

I twist at the waist, looking in the opposite direction while also stretching those muscles. Simultaneously, a tanned body flops down next to me, jolting me out of my weariness. My back goes ramrod straight.

"Good morning, Katherine." The silken voice muses.

I squint and tense. "Good morning?" I mumble.

His eyes are droopy with dark circles underneath. "How'd you sleep?"

"Um?" I croak out, embarrassment clawing up my neck as the man I knocked upside the head last night turns. He's lying on his side, staring me in the face.

His lips quirk, the deep smile line on his cheek making an appearance. How can he be smiling right now? Why isn't he throwing me out or murdering me in the basement?

Never in my life, maybe besides one or two times, have I been as upset and hurt as I was last night. I wasn't planning on *actually* using my just-in-case hammer when I brought it along with me. I only wanted the reassurance that it provided. But I used it.

I could have killed him.

Alecsander's large hand cups my knee, drawing his body closer to mine. I take stock of his body. His pants are still unbuttoned and slung low on his hips, his torso is gloriously bare, and his hair is tousled. A small smear of red marks his ear and jawbone

I gently cup his cheek with my hand, titling it to gain a better viewpoint. I suck in a quick breath. "I'm so *sorry*, Alecsander," I plead. My chest grows tighter as my throat constricts. What was I thinking last night?

Alecsander allows me to move his head back and forth, checking all over. I go to leave the bed, my plan to grab a warm cloth to rinse his blood away, but he cups my knee harder, keeping me in place.

A soft chuckle leaves his mouth, something I wasn't sure if I'd hear again. "Oh Katherine, don't think too much about it."

"Don't think too much about it? I knocked you out with a *hammer* last night. I could have killed you!" I screech.

"You really think a slight club upside the head is enough to take me down?"

My nerves fray. "You crumpled like a wet piece of paper, Alecsander! I knocked you clean out, left you half-naked on your own floor, and then slept in your bed!"

Alecsander sweeps upwards. Our knees touch as he places his hands on either side of my head, directing my face to his for a quick peck on my lips. I close my eyes, savoring how his lips mold to mine, and the distant saltiness that lingers on them.

He braces his forehead on mine, staring into my eyes. I blink, trying to ensure that he really is here, with me.

"Katherine, you reacted appropriately."

"W-what?"

Another quick kiss to my lips. "Katherine, I knew who you were when I saw you at the nightclub. I wasn't one hundred percent sure but before the end of that night, I was. I knew you were the woman I fell in love with five years ago. I knew it and I didn't tell you."

I suck in a breath.

Alecsander keeps going. "Katherine, I am terribly sorry for how I hurt you. I should have told you as soon as I knew."

I nod mutely, tears brimming my eyes. "I've been thinking of you every day since then, you know?"

Alecsander's lips lift, that beloved cheek line gracing me with its presence. "I've been thinking and dreaming of *you* since then, Katherine."

I pull back, trying to regain focus. My heart still burns with betrayal, but I swallow it down. "I need time, Alecsander." I risk a glance.

He casts his eyes down for the first time. He swallows. "I understand, Katherine."

He isn't going to argue with me? My chest hurts as a tiny fissure forms on my heart. This is what I want, right?

"I'm not going to lie and say it's okay with me, Kirbs. I want you." He throws his arms out wide. "I want you in my bed, in my home. I want you in my life every day. So, no, I won't lie and say I'm okay with this, but I also respect you and understand where you're coming from." He pauses, his eyes flicking to the crumpled sheets we sit on. "Take your time, but don't shut me out forever. I can't take it, Katherine." Alecsander's hands grasp mine, rubbing small circles on the back of each one. He's still wearing all his rings and my eyes lock on them.

After several breaths, I pull my hands from his slowly. His fingertips caress mine as I pull all the way back. "I can't promise you anything, Alecsander," I mutter, doing my best to stay upright. "I need time. Time to think and really digest everything." I'm losing my battle against my tear ducts. "I don't like the type of person I was last night when I hit you. I don't want to be that person." I *can't* be that person.

Alecsander nods, sucking his lip in contemplation. "You do whatever you feel you need to do, Kirbs. I get it."

I have a sinking suspicion that he doesn't fully understand, but I let it go.

I stand, finally sturdy enough to do so. I gather my belongings. I don't bother showering or brushing my teeth. I pick up my clothes and my tote. I pull the comforter back up onto the side of the bed where I slept.

As I'm tucking the hem under the pillow, Alecsander's hand appears on top of my own. "Katherine, you don't need to do that."

Throat tight once more, I simply nod and pivot, walking to his bedroom door. I spin once, to look back. I can feel the wetness of tears splashing against my cheekbones. He looks as broken as I feel standing here. His face is taut, his eyes dark and brooding. The blood smear is still apparent on his jaw and the side of his head. What I would give to wipe it away. I shake my bed, feeling like I'm reliving the night we spent together in his office all those years ago. I'm doing exactly what I did then.

"It's not the same this time around, Katherine."

How does he always know what I'm thinking?

I don't ask. I don't stay around to find out. I walk through his bedroom door and make my way through his house until I'm at the entrance. Taking a final glance over my shoulder, I don't see him. Sighing, I pull open the heavy door and step through the frame. I let the door click shut behind me and leave.

I pull up the drive share app on my phone and within five minutes I'm sitting in the back of a four-door regular car with a random woman. She tries talking to me, but I don't feel up for conversation. I lean my head back against the headrest and let my thoughts run wild.

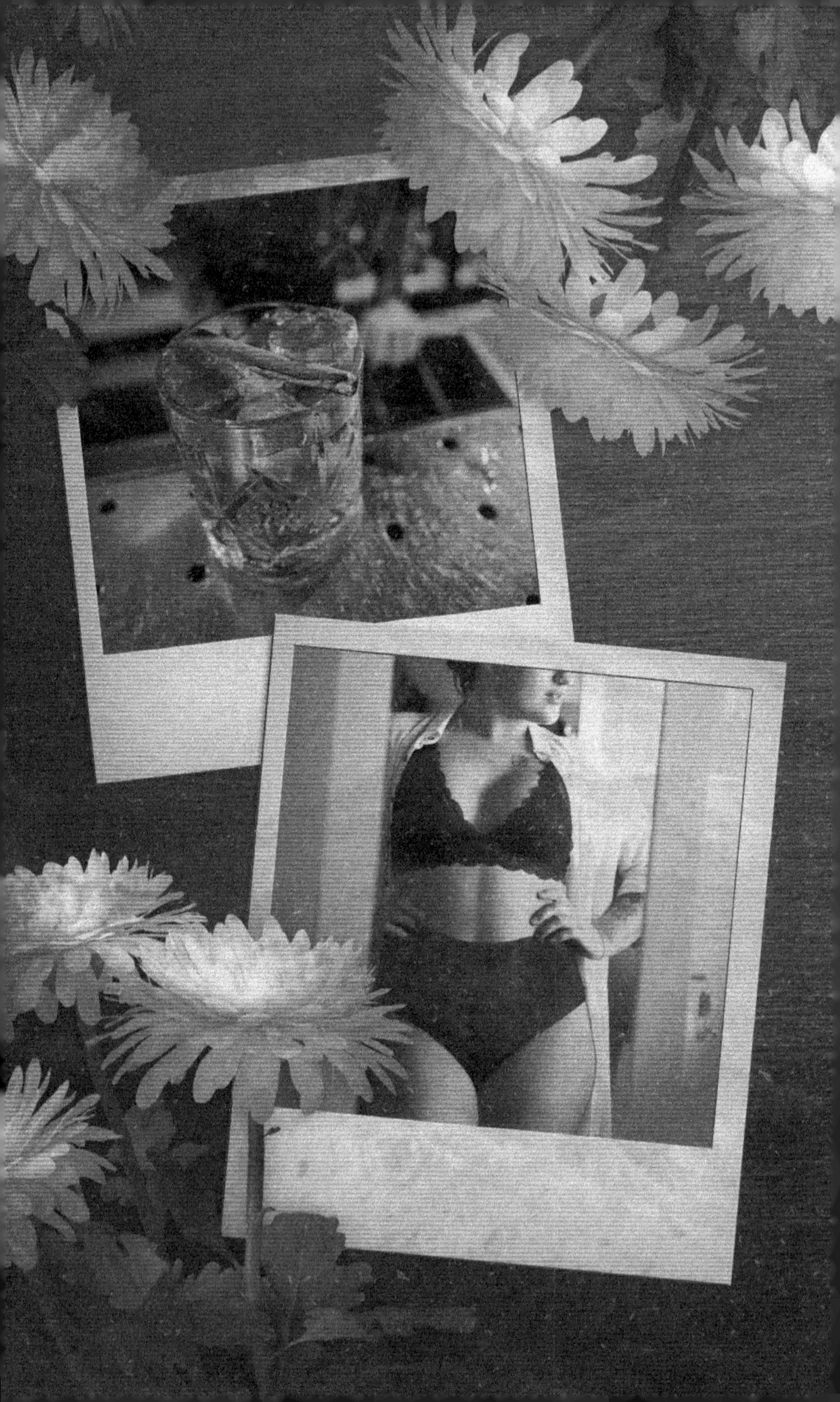

Twenty-One

KATHERINE

I don't know what I was expecting.

Honestly, I hadn't realized who Alecsander was until he whispered that fucking nickname into my ear mid-thrust. It took me a second to understand exactly what he was saying, but when I realized, it made me vibrate.

Then to learn that he *knew*? He fucking *knew*.

How could he know and then make the decision not to tell me?

I need to get out of there before I do something else that I might regret. I can't believe I hit him. I hit him with a hammer, and he was knocked out on his kitchen floor. I run my hand across my wet forehead. How much am I sweating? Jesus Christ, I'm beginning to lose it aren't I? I squeeze my eyes closed in aggravation.

The car stops. I stare up at my apartment complex. Who would have thought I would be relieved to see it in all its glory? Definitely not me, but, alas, here I am.

I scrub my face with my hands as I trudge up to my apartment.

Alecsander wasn't incorrect in his earlier assessment regarding the elevator and stairs situation in my building. I did have to huff it up and down multiple flights of stairs to get to and leave my apartment.

I quickly unlock my apartment and step inside. The temperature isn't warm, but at least the air conditioning hasn't made the apartment an icebox like it did last year. I flop directly onto my comforter, clothes and all. Sleep immediately overtakes me.

I CRACK OPEN MY EYES. DARKNESS SURROUNDS ME. I smack my lips together, my mouth drier than the desert. My small alarm clock shows me it's after midnight and my whole afternoon and evening were wasted.

I sit up, my head pounding behind my eyes with the fierceness of a timpani. I need a fucking pain killer.

Throwing myself out of bed, I rifle through the bathroom drawers trying to find a measly bottle of expired pain relief. I finally hit the jackpot and shovel three white pills down my throat, dry. I cap the bottle and toss it back in the opened drawer before toeing it shut and leaving the bathroom.

Ah, my living room.

My sofa looks plush as ever (hint, it's threadbare). I sit with my legs spread and propped up on my wooden coffee table. I'm still wearing my jacket, so I let it fall down my arms. I look around: my curtains are thumb-tacked to the frame of the windows. Their light fabric from the local thrift store means that light can still enter my space with the curtains fully shut. It has its perks (and its cons).

The wooden coffee table rests on top of another thrift store gem, a lovely deep red rug that somehow only put me out twenty bucks rather than the several hundred it's probably worth. The rest of the room is clad with tiny knick-knacks that I've collected over the years. Some of the small ornaments on the walls are from Marisol. Cheap frames line two of the walls, photos pinned in them. Marisol prints me handfuls of photos she's taken a few times a year. I would never spend the money on photos, but she does it for me. It's always my birthday gift. And I love it. I need to call the bitch and make plans soon. I miss her.

After scrutinizing my living room, I stand and sigh. What the fuck am I going to do now? My sleep schedule is completely fucked. I don't have to work until four in the afternoon and that's still hours away. I go back into my room and put away my jacket and unpack my tote bag.

DOMINIC

The air is crisp as I walk across town. I cancelled all my meetings for the next several days because, well, I have a fucking plan of course.

A plan that involves me and a beautiful lady who happens to be named Katherine.

She doesn't know we have these big, magnificent plans yet. But she will soon! I know where she lives and by God, I plan to see it today. Up close and personal with her. Alone. I adjust my crotch as I walk, keeping a low profile amongst the throng of people going about their daily activities.

I know Katherine is home. I'd given her nearly twelve hours which is more than I wanted. I convinced myself she needed some time to herself. I can be accommodating when necessary.

I will accommodate her for the rest of our lives if she'll let me.

I scrub my face with my cold fingers. The wind whips around my head and fluffs my hair. I forgot my beanie at home. It was sitting on my kitchen island. The weather is colder by the day and soon soft snow flurries will whistle down from the overbearing clouds and coat our streets with their muck.

It will only be pretty for a few hours before all the cars and foot traffic turn the pristine snow powder into harsh, grueling gray sludge that will stick to our boots regardless of how hard we'll knock them on the concrete stairs leading to our front doors. I shake my head, dislodging the thought of a fucking blizzard from my mind. I have plans and I need to begin. *Stay focused*, I remind myself.

Katherine's apartment complex is tall. It's brick and rises from the pavement as a massive fucking eyesore. Beggars can't be choosers and I know Katherine isn't exactly rolling in it.

An oversight I plan on correcting immediately. It's time for her employee evaluation at Point B and it's time for her to get a raise.

I bite my lip as the wind slaps against my coat. I stand in front of her building. Not because I need a pep talk or anything, but because I'm categorizing all the issues I see with the building.

The brick is haphazard in areas. The outdoor stairs have no railing, and the concrete is crumbling along the edges. Talk about a fucking safety hazard.

I pull out my phone, scrolling and clicking on different websites until I find the property. It's overpriced, but I find my realtor's number and call him anyway.

"Hey, this is Dominic Alcutti. I need you to look at a property for me."

"Yes, sir. I can do that for you. Do you have the address of the location?"

I check my watch quickly, noting the time. I rattle off the apartment's address and stare up at the building.

"Okay, Mr. Alcutti. I'll get things drafted and send you some documents to e-sign tomorrow morning. How does that sound?"

I nod my head even though he can't see me. The man's always been a dream worker. He's gotten me every property and location I've asked him to for far below the asking price.

It helps that I tip him generously and keep his family safe from the inner city's gangs.

"Sounds great, Rafeal. Keep up the good work and say hello to Brenna and the kids for me." My voice is thick with amusement, my business voice shining through.

Rafeal chuckles. "Sure thing, Mr. Alcutti. Have a good day."

I return the sentiment and hang up the phone. As I tuck it into my coat pocket, I climb the crumbling concrete stairs and enter the lobby of Katherine's building.

Luckily her apartment is old enough and cheap enough that it doesn't require tenants to ring up their visitors. On second thought, however, maybe it should? Her safety is the top priority here and I don't want anyone waltzing up to her apartment unannounced.

I keep the mental list of projects going in my head as I see the elevator fitted with bright yellow caution tape and a handwritten note stating it's out of order. Scoffing, I turn and locate the stairwell. Katherine lives up several floors and as I hike up the stairs, I'm glad I've kept myself in such great condition. I tuck my blonde hair behind my ears as I land on her floor. I push my way through the door that feeds into the general corridor.

Apartment 17 is my destination. I knock on the door several times. The doorbell hangs from a measly wire on the wall next to her door frame. It's probably older than I am.

"Who is it?" She calls through the thin wood. There's no peep hole in sight. That could be both beneficial and annoying.

I cough, clearing my throat, "It's me, sweet Katherine."

I hear a slight bang on the other side of the door before several deadbolts slide out of place. The door opens a bit. "What the fuck do you want?" Katherine is in the clothes she left Alecsander's place in, but she's added an old fluffy robe over the top.

"Katherine, Katherine. Why do you speak to me in such a way?" I smile.

She rolls her eyes.

When has a woman ever rolled their eyes at me?

I blink, awaiting her response.

The door opens a little further. Katherine's whole torso is visible now. She crosses her arms against her chest, pushing her tits up higher. The cleavage pokes through her robe's neckline. I swallow. *Fuck, she's beautiful.* She's a radiant sun against the midnight black of my heart.

"Maybe because you're an egotistical asshole who ate me out in my workplace, bad idea by the way, and then left and didn't bother calling me afterwards." Her face reddens. She's pissed.

"Katherine, I can-," I start, but she holds up a single palm, silently telling me to shut the fuck up, so like a pussy-whipped boy, I do.

She scrunches her nose. "How fucking dare you come here? To my home?" She looks around the hallway on either side of me. "How the hell did you know where I live anyway? My apartment number?"

"Your address is listed at Point B, in the records." Obviously.

She brings a hand to her forehead, swiping some lost pieces of black hair out of her face. "Oh, for fuck's sake." She takes a deep inhale and slowly loses it. "Tell me what you want so I can get back to doing what the fuck I was doing."

"I wanted to make sure you were okay."

"Why wouldn't I be?"

"You've had a rough few days, hell, so have I." I supply.

"How the hell would you know what the past few days have been like for me, Dominic?"

"Please call me-," I start, only to be interrupted again. That's twice now.

"Nic, I know. I don't give a shit what you want me to call you," she huffs.

I shove my hands in my pockets. My blood simmers as she casually tosses hurtful words at me. This isn't how I imagined our meeting going today. It's still salvageable. I try again.

"Katherine, please, hear me out."

She doesn't offer me a response. Katherine stands in her door frame with her arms still crossed against her ample chest.

I swallow, taking my time in picking my next words. "Katherine, I know the last time we saw one another, we were close and personal and, well, I was between your thighs." She scoffs, but I continue. "I was planning on calling you the next day once you had rested from your shift. I wanted to take you to a real dinner. However," I look at her, her face blank and unmoving at my words. But I'm determined.

"I was ambushed on the street on my walk from the bar. Some of the Sandman's guys found me and picked me up, took me back to one of their warehouses, and I spent the next few days being waterboarded and fucking beat to shit." I let the words rush out, not wanting to keep secrets from my sweet Katherine.

She visibly swallows, her eyes tracking my face and hands. Her eyes widen, then squint a fraction. She's tracking the cuts that mar my face, the swelling under my eyes and around my nose.

"Did you say the Sandman?" she asks quietly.

I stare at her blankly. How could she not know who the Sandman is? "Yes, he's one of the biggest, if not *the* biggest, crime lord in this part of the state," I tell her.

Her face pales, her red lips dulling. "*The* Sandman?"

I scratch my head. "Yeah, the Sandman—,"

"Why do you have business with him? What are you doing?" she asks quickly.

I tell her a white lie. "We run in the same circles once in a while." I see her face shudder, so I quickly add, "But not very often. It's occasional."

Katherine looks down at her shoes, her chin in her hand. "So, let me get this straight," she starts, pointing a hand toward me. "You run in the same circles as the Sandman?"

Is this not what I said? "Yes, Katherine, once in a while our business paths cross."

"You know he does awful things, right? Like he murders people, shoots them, and walks away like it's no big deal?"

I nod at her. "That's part of the whole 'crime lord' thing, Katherine."

She splays her arms wide. "Do you hear yourself right now, Dominic? The Sandman *murders* people. He, he has no hesitation. He'll do it because it's a Tuesday or something asinine like that. He has no mercy, *nothing*."

I swallow to keep my tone in check. Katherine is starting to piss me off. If she's this bothered by the Sandman's deeds, what will she think of me? Better yet, if this pisses her off so much, what will she think if she knows who the Sandman is? Her sweet Alecsander, turns out, isn't so sweet. I gnaw at the inside of my cheek. I'll keep that tidbit of information to myself, for now.

"Katherine, we don't do business together, per se. We more so have a similar clientele with my bars and his properties."

She takes a tentative step back, leaving a larger gap between us than I wish. "I don't want anything to do with the Sandman, Dominic. Not a damned thing." She chews on her bottom lip. "Promise me, Dominic. Swear to me, right now, that the Sandman isn't someone you're close to, someone you work with regularly. Promise me that you aren't like *him*." Her voice is dipped in venom.

I wonder what her aversion to the Sandman is about. Yeah, he's the main crime lord around here, but I do most of the dirty work. I've had more kills than him, though. I think I'm the only one who keeps track of that information. I make a mental note to dive deeper into her repulsion for the Sandman.

"Sweet Katherine," I say as I grip her shoulders. I'm doing my best to redirect her, so I pull her closer to me. "I wanted to see you after the other day. Fuck, I wanted to take you back to my house and never let you leave."

She offers a slight shake of her shoulders at my admission, as if

I'm joking. I'm not. I thought about doing that very thing, but of fucking course, Alecsander ruined my plans.

He won't ruin this one, however, because Katherine grips the doorknob on her side of the door, letting the door squeak open a little further. She tips her head to the side, her eyes never leaving mine. "I guess you can come in and make it up to me then, Nic."

I grin, my cheeks hurting with the pressure against my nose. "Yes, ma'am."

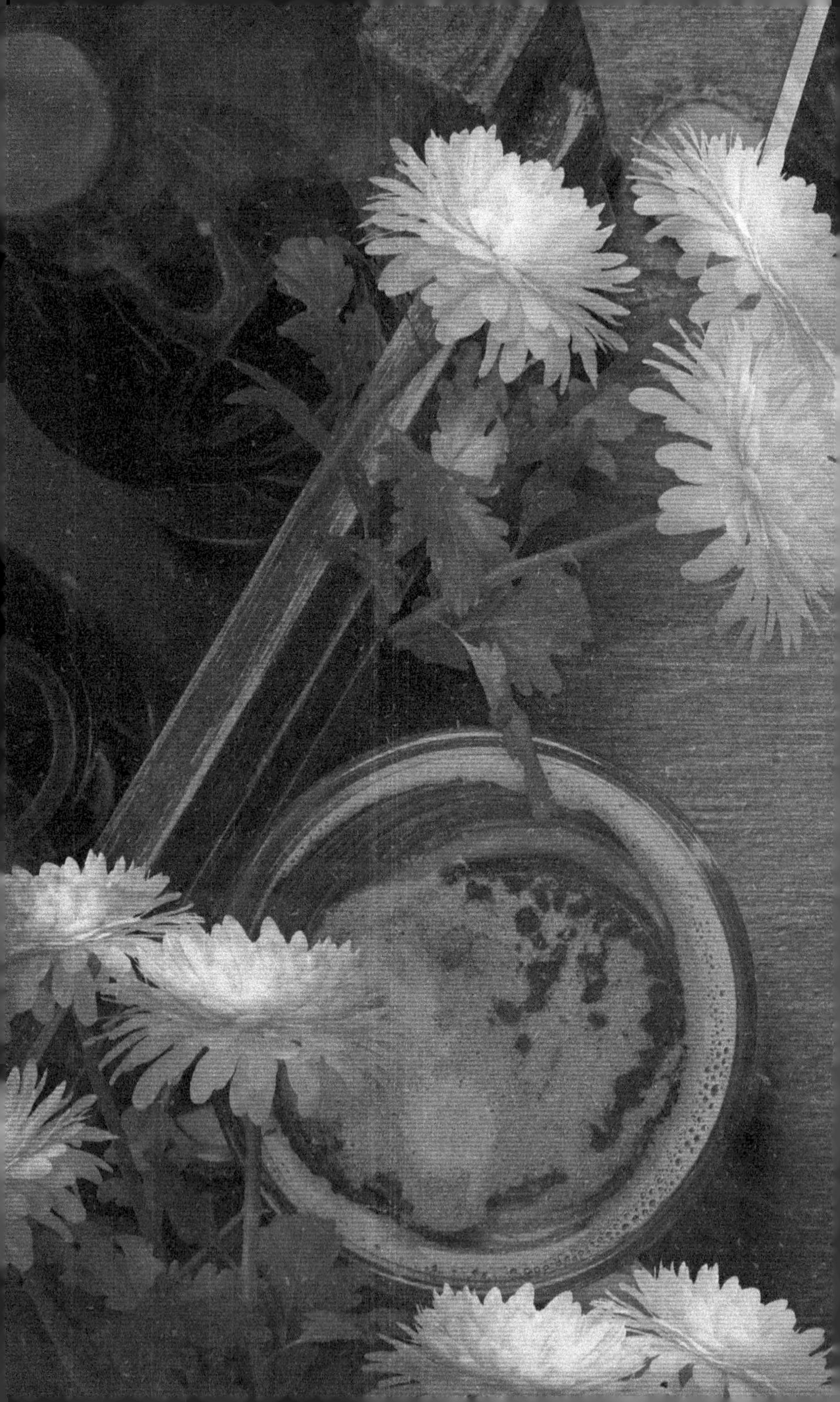

Twenty-Two

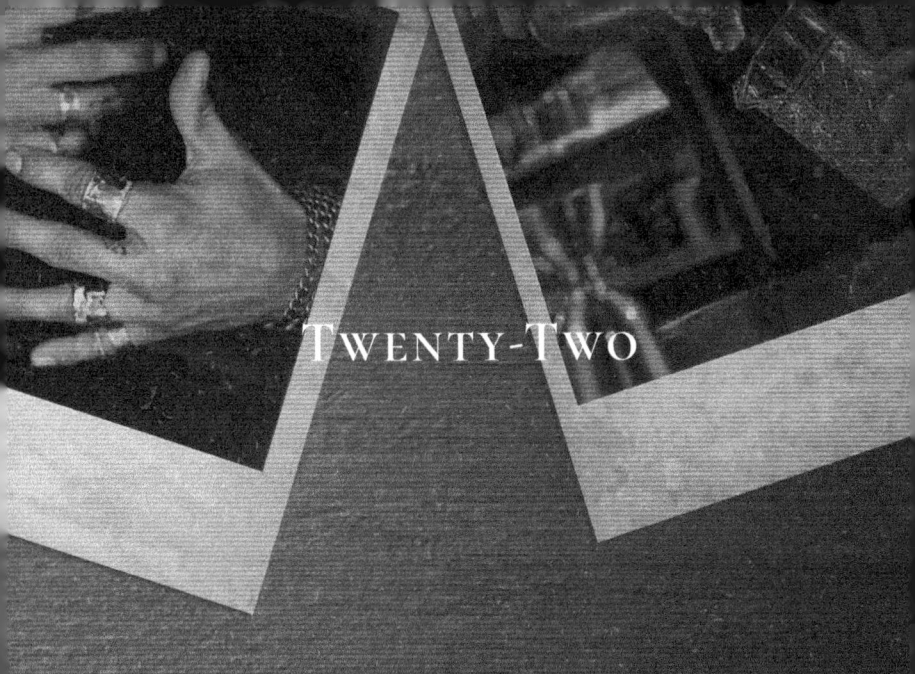

KATHERINE

Dominic crowds my small living room. He looks around the space. Why is he here? What does he want? The questions bounce around my brain as I bite my lip watching him.

"Kind of a small place, huh?" he asks, though it sounds more like a statement.

I cross my arms. Was he judging my apartment? Sure, it was shitty, but it isn't really his place to comment on it. I don't reward him with a response. Fucking dog.

Dominic ruffles his hair. "Fuck," he mutters under his breath. "I'm fucking this all up." His eyes meet mine and the clarity I see there is astounding. I almost want to drown in their crystal-clear blueness. *Get a grip, woman!*

"Get on with it, Dominic."

He rattles out a breath. "Katherine, I've been going about this," he motions to the both of us, "all fucking wrong. I've come on too strong then not strong enough. I saw you at Point B and you tasted *delicious*, but then I had circumstances that led me to not be able to call you or contact you for days." Dominic stares directly at me. "I wanted to call you, Katherine. I wanted to see you, hold you, take you out on an actual date. Fuck! I want to now!"

I swallow, gathering my wits as if they're a shield. His words are pretty, but his actions are screaming at me to pay attention. He is here now. It isn't like he completely ghosted me, is it? Not really. I shift my weight from one foot to the other, thinking about my response.

"Do you want to sit down?" Standing in the kitchen/entryway is beginning to feel crowded. Sitting down will help ease some of the stress I feel crawling up my throat.

Dominic only nods, bringing his arm out in a gesture that says, "I'll follow you anywhere" and, in that moment, I just might believe the bastard.

My living room only has the couch for seating, so I take a seat against one arm rest and motion for Dominic to take the other side. He plants his ass on my couch, and I take note of the fact that there's still a whole cushion between us. No contact whatsoever.

Dominic's side profile makes me want to do bad things. His elbows are on his knees with his chin resting on his clasped hands. His blonde hair falls around his ears in golden swoops as it brushes his shoulders. I want to run my hands and nails across his scalp.

I nearly choke on my spit when Dominic moves his face to stare at me directly. "Katherine," his voice is silk. "You're so goddamn beautiful it hurts."

I choke. "Stop trying to appease me, Dominic."

He scowls. "I'm not appeasing you, Katherine." He scoots a little closer to me, reaching an arm out so his palm can rest on my knee. My back is against the armrest with my legs bent underneath me. His palm is warm, and I feel it through the fabric of my pants.

My mouth is dry. My willpower slides out of my body. I'm warm and my clothes are causing my skin to itch. "Dominic, I-," I begin.

"Katherine," he interrupts me with his other palm caressing

my other knee. "Please give me another chance. I promise it will be worth it; *I* will be worth it," he amends.

I blink, not knowing what to say. Do I believe him and give my heart another shot or do I tell him to get out of my apartment. What about Alecsander?

Fuck, what about Alecsander?

I push against the armrest, hoping Dominic will move his hands. He doesn't. "Dominic, you need to know that I'm already, kind of, seeing someone." I think of how I left Alecsander in his apartment, but he didn't come after me. He didn't need to. We both know where we stand at this point.

Dominic's gaze loses warmth. "Are you referring to Alecsander, Katherine?" His eyes lock on mine.

"Yes, Alecsander and I, we both, well, we're figuring it out," I mumble.

"Hm, I see." Dominic sighs as he runs his palms up higher, stopping mid-thigh. Even though my legs are covered, my skin burns with his touch. "Well, if you're figuring things out with Alecsander, then you can figure things out with me, no?" His gaze is predatory. His lips quirk in a lopsided grin that doesn't quite meet his eyes.

I gulp, wishing for a tall glass of water or a shot or both.

"Katherine, if I must share you, then so be it. I want you."

DOMINIC

I will not be sharing her.

But she doesn't need to know that at this exact moment. I can see the war behind her eyes. Her mind screams at her to pick one, choose one. While I agree with her, I need her to think differently now. I need to believe that I don't mind her sharing her time with Alecsander.

While I don't necessarily find it horrible what she does with her time with Alecsander, I also don't need to keep replaying it in my head. Her, standing in his kitchen in all her naked glory, swinging that beautiful dinky hammer up and in an arc. I swallow, my throat thick with emotions and my pants tight with similar ones.

My hands are still positioned on Katherine's thighs. I yearn to hitch them higher, but we haven't quite made it there. I'll let her take the reins on this one. Her eyes are jeweled, staring at me with a new hint of life I haven't seen in a while. Her cheeks are properly flushed and her tongue darts out to wet her bottom lip.

"Katherine," I begin.

"Yes, Dominic?"

"Call me Nic." I tell her. Again. I blink and refocus. "Let me worship you, please." I look at her. Her large, doe-like eyes stare back at me. Her dark hair is down, flitting over her shoulders and curling around her exposed collarbone. The rivulets of night are begging to be wrapped around my hands.

Katherine's words evade her, so I prod once more. "I need verbal confirmation, Katherine. Please." I swallow thickly.

"Yes, worship me." Her eyes darken. "Worship me like it's the last time you'll ever see me." She grins like she's reveling in making me squirm in anticipation. Maybe she is.

"Katherine, don't say things you don't mean."

She wraps her tiny hands around my wrists, pulling my hands up her thighs to rest on her hips. The fabric of her thin shirt ruffles upward. My fingertips brush her supple skin. If I were a lesser man, I'd be moaning already.

"I might mean them, Dominic."

"Nic."

"Nuh-uh, *Dominic*." Her lips form the word as I watch. Her tongue peeks from behind her teeth, tempting me. "You get down and you fucking worship me like you should have last time." Her gaze is casual, but her eyes burn brightly. Her skin is warm beneath my fingers.

I stroke back and forth along her hips. I guide my hands to her back to find the hem of her shirt as she shimmies her robe off. Once she is free from her garments, I steady my hands on her waist once more. "Bedroom, Katherine," I demand. "Lead me there so I can christen it as my new house of worship."

Her cheeks glow as she stands and grips my hands. She slowly walks backward toward an archway. Her bed is on the other side, reminding me that her apartment is too fucking small for her. "Katherine," I groan. "We need to discuss this apartment."

"Shut the fuck up for once Dominic and take your clothes off."

I raise my brows but do as she commands. Katherine stands at the foot of her bed watching me. I pull my shirt up and over my body. I fling it to the ground.

She's in her underwear. She watches me as I flick open my belt, pulling it free from my belt loops and letting it fall to the ground. Next comes my shoes, which I toe off quickly and efficiently.

Or so I thought.

Katherine huffs like I've somehow offended her. She pops open the button on my jeans and runs her hands along my waist, under the band of my pants. Her hands are frigid, but soothing.

"Katherine," I groan as she pushes my jeans down. She lets me take the reins to step out of my pants and push them aside. I march her back to the foot of the bed until her calves hit. She flops on her back unceremoniously.

I stand above her with her legs on either side of mine. She's partially on the bed. Her hair fans out around her head like a crown.

"Take your bra off, Katherine."

Her hands trail from the sides of her body to her waist and up the valley between her lush breasts. She leans forward enough for her back to rise off the bed. Her hands fly behind her, flicking the clasps of the bra until it's undone and she's sliding the straps from her shoulders.

"Do you like what you see?" She dares to ask as she throws her bra off to the side of the bed. Her tits are beautiful. Her nipples harden as I continue to linger, my eyes eating her from the waist up.

"If you were to lead me to hell then I would make my residence there happily, Katherine." I vow to her. She could lead me nowhere I wouldn't desire her.

I prop a knee between her legs, taking my time in peeling her pants from her body. She squirms as I slide the fabric down past her knees, my fingertips brushing against her calves and ankles as I take one leg, then the other out. When she's finally pantless, I move back up her body. I tug at the waist of her underwear. They're standard black and hug her skin. Her thighs round out of the fabric.

"God damn, Katherine. You're divine."

"Prove it to me, Dominic," she demands.

"Yes, ma'am," I promise her. I lean down, taking my tongue to her stomach and licking upwards, gliding it between her breasts and planting an open-mouthed kiss on the hollow of her collarbone. She squirms and arches her back. She goes to move her hand to my head, but I grab her wrist and plant it on the bed. Looking into her dark eyes, I command, "Don't move this hand, Katherine. Do you understand?"

"Yes," she breathes heavily.

I pull her underwear down and off without much preamble. She wiggles her legs as I chuck them off, but before she can press her pretty thighs back together, I'm there.

I blow hot air on her pussy, watching her dark curls move with the breath. Her hand twitches.

"Don't fucking move, Katherine," I remind her. Her eyes are on me between her legs, and I hold her gaze as I part my lips and take a deep lick from her asshole to her clit. She shivers.

I lick each lip before suctioning my mouth over her clit. She tenses. I suck harder after a few seconds. I take turns between light pressure and heavier pressure for several moments before I bring my hand up. I tease her opening with two fingers, going around the edges. I split my fingers, opening her wider before pushing both in.

She moans.

My dick to hardens. I scissor my fingers, feeling her contract around them as she approaches her climax. I can't have that yet. I flick my tongue out to caress her clitoris, making X's and circles around the flesh before taking it between my teeth and giving it a gentle bite.

"Fuck!" Katherine bellows, her moan coating my skin in ecstasy.

I release her clit, pulling in a deep breath as I coach her, "That's right, sweet Katherine. Give it to me."

I reattach to her, continuing to massage her clit with my tongue as I spear a third finger into her. I rotate all my fingers and separate them before bringing them back together. I rub upwards, finding the section of her flesh that feels slightly different than the rest. I rub and circle it while sucking her clit further into my mouth.

My free hand presses her abdomen down as I work my fingers faster against her flesh. Within moments, she's gripping my head with her thighs. Her tits are high and a beautiful sight as I lavish her pussy with thorough licks and kisses "That's it, baby, come on my fingers. Soak me," I beg.

Katherine sinks back to the bed with a small huff. Her arm covers her eyes as her mouth opens. I finally remove my fingers from her vagina and lean over her. I grip her arm and push it back into the bed.

"I told you not to move this fucking arm, Katherine." Her eyes are wide, her skin slick with sweat. I trail a hand up her chest, holding one breast and massaging it roughly. "Do you know what happens when you don't listen, Katherine?" I inquire.

She shakes her head.

"*Tsk, tsk*, Katherine. Words please."

"N-no," she replies breathlessly.

I chuckle darkly at the woman laid out before me. Her body is sin incarnate, tempting me to the depths of hell. I run my hands up and down her torso and upper legs.

"Katherine." I pause my ministrations, causing her to glare at me. "When you don't listen to me, I must punish you. You understand?"

She starts to shake her head but stops herself. "Yes, tell me."

I knead her skin. "When you don't obey, Katherine, I am drawn to think you don't wish to be worshiped as is your divine right."

She scrunches her eyebrows.

"Ah-ah, Katherine. You need to believe me when I tell you that I'll worship you until I'm dust in the wind. I'd give you anything if you so much as I asked." I pause, "And since you haven't asked, I'll give you what I wish to. I'll give you orgasms and bliss and protection." I stare directly into her dark eyes. "I'll protect you, Katherine."

She mutely nods, her eyes glistening.

I don't waste time on proclamations. I grab my weeping cock and guide it towards the apex of her thighs. I find her opening with my head and work it inside an inch, then pull it back out before plunging the full length inside of her hot, wet heat.

"Nic!" She moans.

I push my hands onto her chest, massaging her tits. I roll her nipples between my fingers, giving them light pinches as she writhes beneath me.

I dive into her, pulling nearly all the way out and plunging back inside. Over and over, I rut into her. She devours me from the inside out. I grab her hips and keep her steady. Our first union is more than I could have wished for. My hair hits my face, sticking to my cheeks thanks to the sweat that coats my face and body.

"Katherine," I moan. "Katherine, sweet, divine." I continue lavishing her with names. She's beautiful in the throes of passion.

Her skin is slick, and her thighs are coated with my pre-cum and her own. The only sounds in the room are our breathing and the slapping of our skin together.

A beautiful symphony.

I move a hand to her clit, circling and tugging it. She thrashes her head back and forth, her hands gripping the bed sheet on either side of her body. My release builds at the base of my spine, but I refuse to reach it before she gives me another of her own.

I fuck into her harder, gripping her hip harshly with one hand while pinching her clit with the other. My hips stutter at the same moment her walls contract around my cock. She tightens, milking me for all I'm worth. I press into her once, twice, thrice more as my cum drenches her pussy.

"Alec," she moans low.

My breath shutters.

I catch myself on my hands as I lean over her. Our heads nearly touch in the low light of her bedroom. I'm still attached to her, right where I want to be. I quickly tuck and roll us to where we're both on our sides, still connected.

I give her a few moments to sink into my chest as I hold her tightly against me. A thousand thoughts race through my mind as I hear the whispers of what she moaned. She couldn't have meant it, right? The video I saw of them together last night was good and well, but would she call out his name while I was inside her?

I pepper soft kisses along her hairline and forehead anyway, whispering into the shell of her ear, "You did so beautifully." I worship her as she asked. My thoughts race and I'm stuck. My heart is splitting.

My plan of coming over and winning her over doesn't seem to be working. What more do I need to do? An original plan comes back to the forefront of my mind and suddenly my mind is made up. My thoughts are aligned, and I know what I must do. I know how to win her *and* keep her.

I hope it's enough.

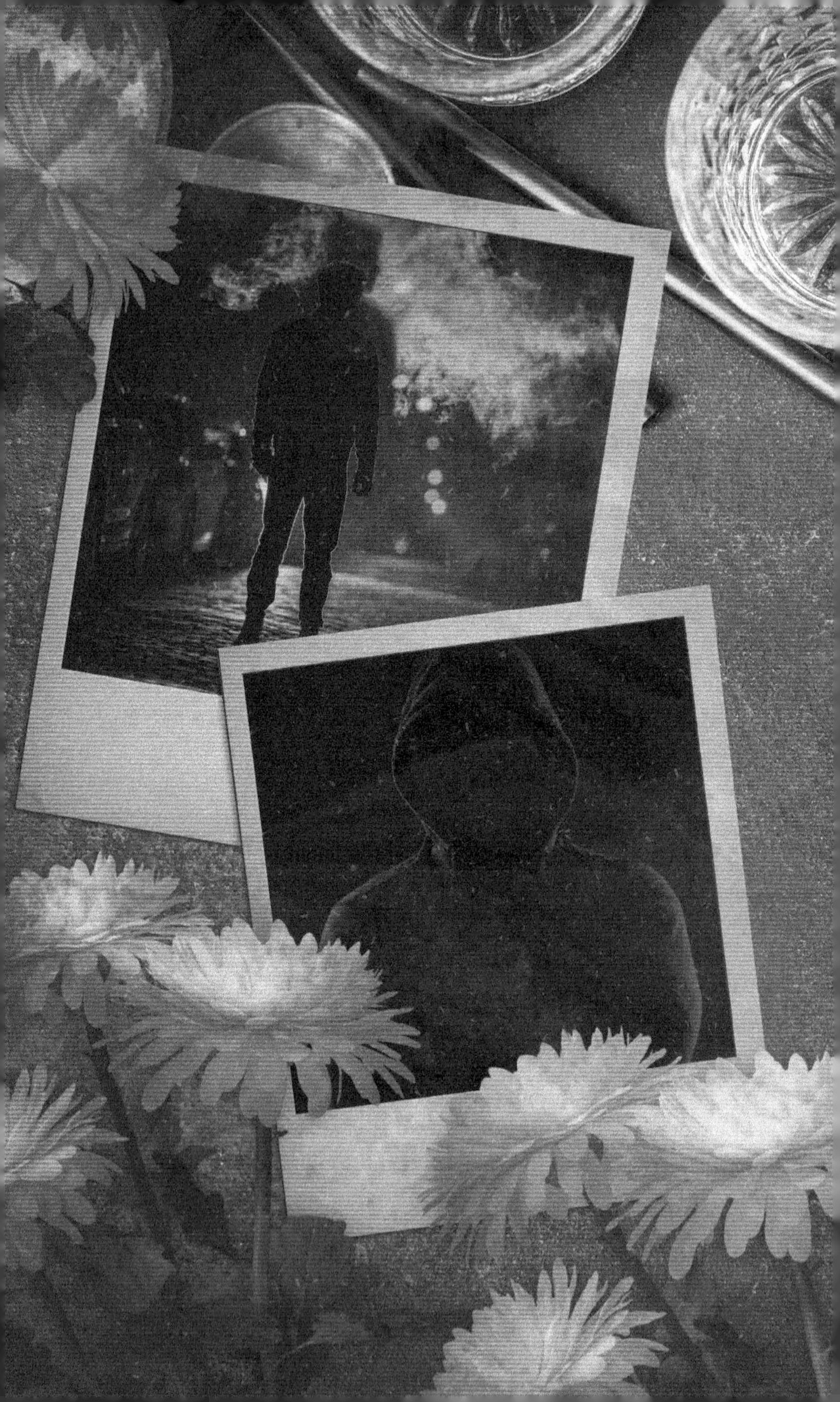

Twenty-Three

KATHERINE

I know I said it.

It wasn't a conscious action. Not truly.

But my subconscious? She's a gnarly bitch. I wasn't planning on letting Dominic into my apartment, wasn't planning on allowing him to seduce me and definitely was not planning on going through with it and letting him rail me to high heaven.

I'm on my side, still connected to Dominic at the waist while my head leans on his upper arm. He's breathing heavily and I know he heard whose name I moaned at the end. I'm debating on bringing it up or acting like it never happened.

Acting like it never happened seems to be the best choice, so I go with that. I gently remove myself from Dominic's dominant hold on my upper body and then slowly pull off his still half-hardened cock.

After several embarrassing sounds, I'm on the edge of the bed. I run my hands through my knotty hair, trying to tame it. I don't expect to feel his rough, calloused hands on my shoulders and back, but they're there, nonetheless. "Hmm?" I don't move to turn around and face him.

"Lay back down, Katherine. Rest." His hands gently pull on my shoulders until I'm lying next to him once again. Our shoulders brush. Dominic sighs, puts his hands on his stomach, and rolls to face me.

"I know you know that I heard what you said."

I swallow, my saliva suddenly thick. "Okay." I have no idea how to continue the conversation. All I want to do is run far, far away from the whole situation and not look back. My face burns.

Dominic sighs again. He scrubs his face with his hand, leveling his gaze once more on me. His eyes are dull. "Katherine, I want us to build this relationship on a foundation of honesty, on trust."

I bite my lip. Honestly? Is he serious? I roll my eyes, dumbfounded that that's where he wants this conversation to go. "Dominic," I sigh. "I don't know what you want from me, and, honestly, I'm not quite sure I give a shit." I want to pat myself on the back for standing my ground. It feels good. I know Alecsander would be proud of me. The thought makes my stomach ache.

I pull away from his body. I don't want to be around it. I don't want to be around *him*.

"Katherine, I don't understand-,"

I'm on the edge of the bed again, facing Dominic. I'm still naked, but I refuse to cover myself. "You don't need to understand, Dominic. That's the thing. *You* don't get to be the only deciding factor in this." I motion between our two bodies. "Whatever the fuck it is."

I stand and pad into my bathroom. I quickly pull on my threadbare robe and cinch it around my waist, covering my body while also keeping my chin to the ceiling. I won't be backing down. Not anymore. Not with fucking Dominic.

Dominic is still laying on his back on my bed. "Get the fuck off my bed." I keep my tone neutral. I don't want to seem too emotional. He seems like the type of guy who would find that a weakness of mine.

His eyes widen at my tone. "Katherine."

I hold up a hand. "Nope, I don't want to hear it. Get dressed. Get off my bed. Get out of my apartment." I stare him down like my life depends on it. "Now."

I pivot, leaving my bedroom and going to my living room. I don't need to watch him get dressed. His body may be hot and delicious and begging to be licked, but his attitude? It's trash.

When Dominic doesn't magically emerge from my bedroom, I stride back into the small room. He's, thankfully, pulling on his boots and zipping his pants. His shirt and other clothes are on, and his hair is loosely tied at the nape of his neck, showcasing the inky swirls that line his throat.

I fight the urge to tap my foot. Why is he taking so long? "Hurry up," I scold him.

Dominic doesn't glare or look in my general direction as he finishes tying his boots and exits my room. He's at my front door, about to pull on the handle, when I make it out to the living room. He tosses a glance over his shoulder, his face drawn, and his lips in a frown. "I'll see you when I see you, Kirby." Dominic pulls the door open and steps out into the dusty hallway, softly closing the door behind himself.

I don't respond to him. He won't be seeing me anytime soon. I need to find a new job. At a bar that isn't owned by him. I could ask Alecsander if he knows of anything that's outside Dominic's reach. He would know.

I go back to the bedroom and pull the sheets and pillows off my bed. Time to wash them and clean my apartment. I need to wash Dominic out of my life completely, starting here.

DOMINIC

I desperately want to look back at Katherine's apartment as I leave, but I don't. She laid it all out. I wasn't expecting her to be so forceful and confident in her words.

I must change strategies. Even out the playing field. I have to get back in the game since it seems I've been kicked out.

I'm sure Alecsander, *the bastard*, is to blame. What did I miss in the videos? There had to be something, a conversation or *something*, that explains all this. Katherine walked out of his apartment, and he didn't even go after her. It boggles my mind. Sure, I walked out of her apartment without looking back, but that was because she requested, no, *demanded* I do so.

She was brilliant in her execution, her commands. I wanted to stand in awe of her, but I had to leave. That's what she wanted, and I had to oblige.

I don't have to like it, though.

Once I'm back home in my apartment, I head straight to my office. Pulling up the cameras that hide in Alecsander's home is second nature at this point. I scan his rooms and hallways, nodding to myself when I find that he's working out in his home gym. Him being home means he's not out trying to be with Katherine.

I open a new server and connect my newest cameras. Katherine's bedroom comes up on the screen in 4K and is beautiful. While I was dressing myself, I spared a few moments to stick thumbtack-sized cameras in a corner of her room. Thankfully her apartment is super small, so the range I can see is vast. I can see the beginning of the living room and the door to the bathroom. It's more than enough to keep an eye on her.

For instance, at this moment, she's lying on her bed, staring up at the ceiling. She's gnawing at her lip like she's contemplating a multitude of tasks. If she is, then we're finally on the same page because this is only the first phase of my plan to win her over.

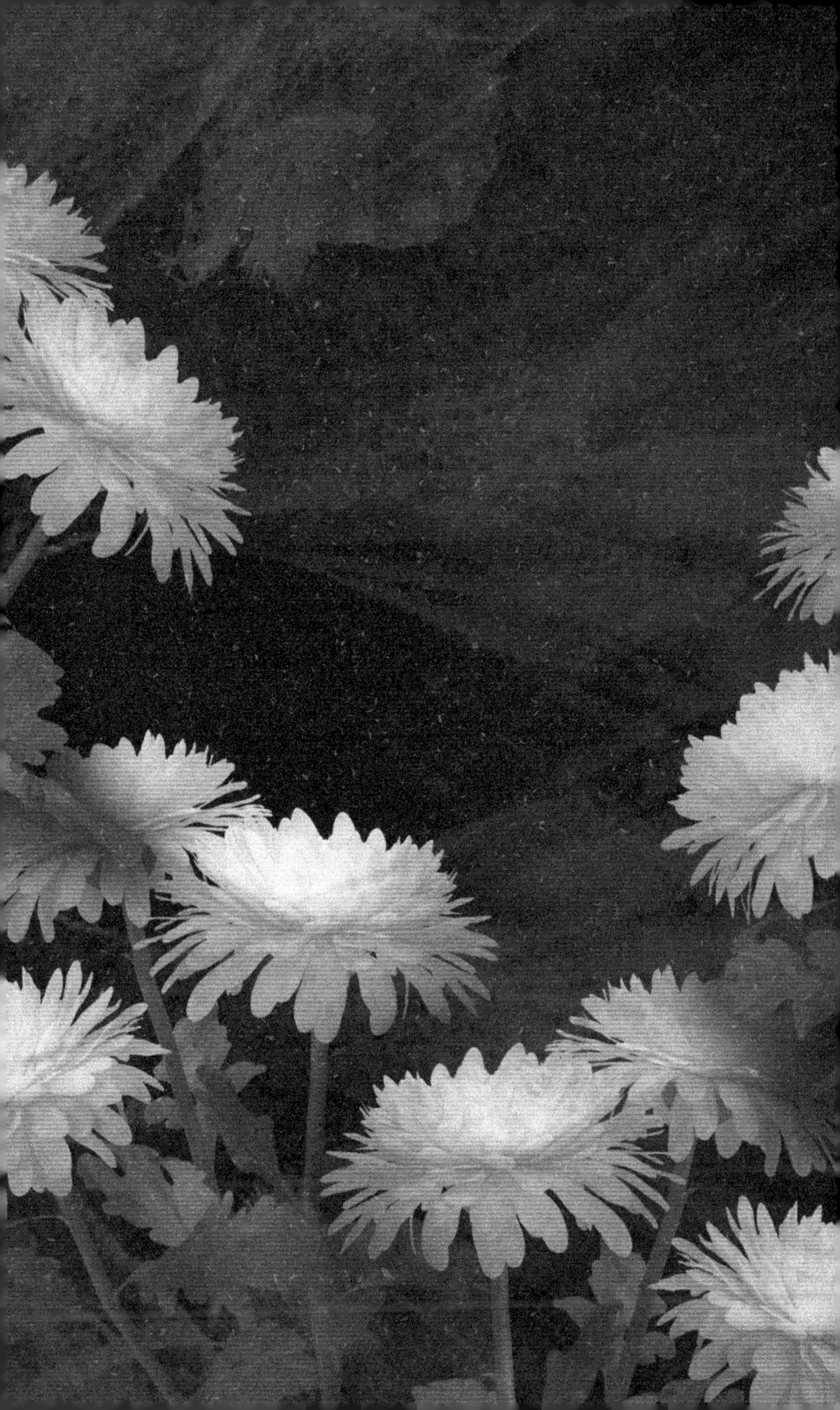

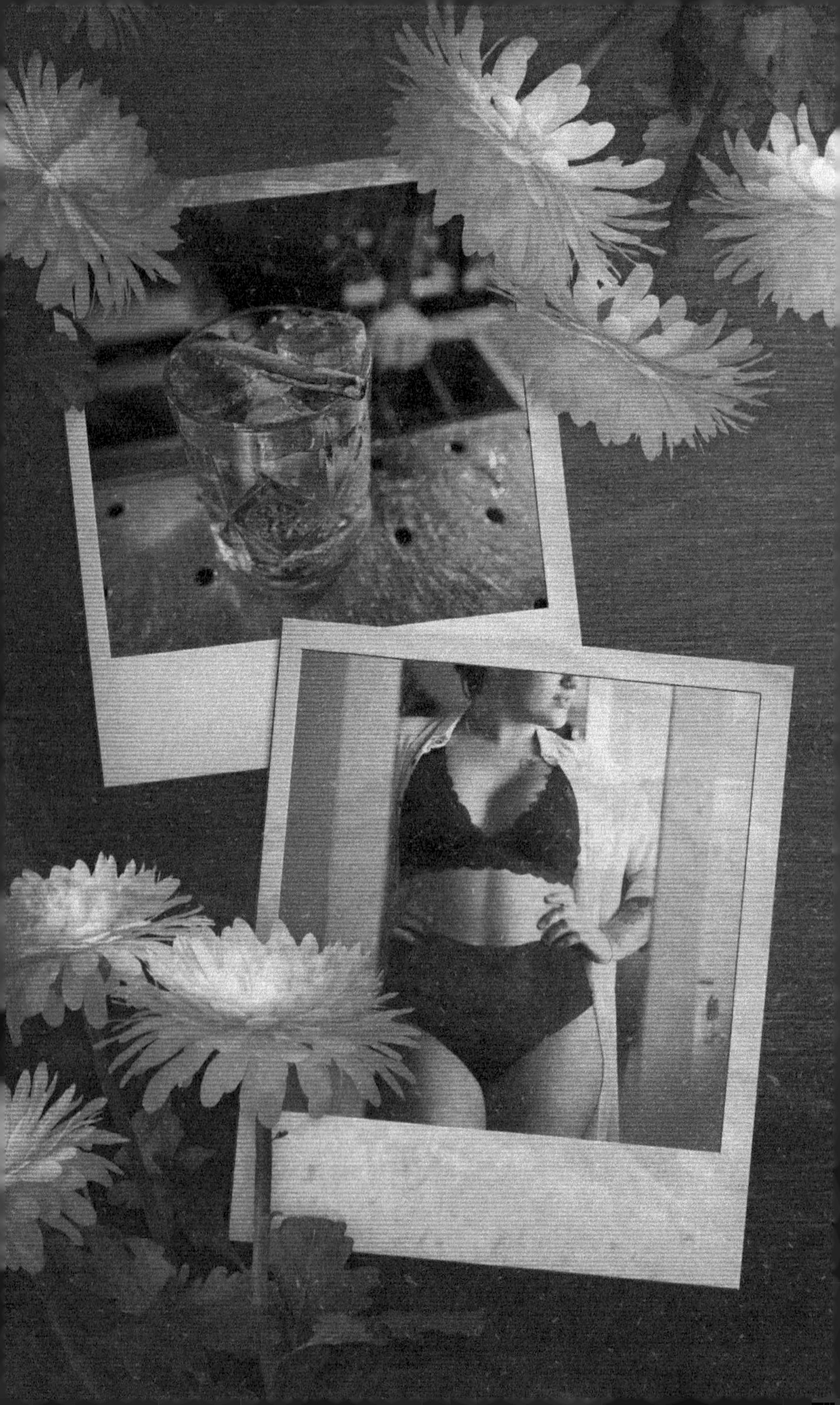

Twenty-Four

KATHERINE

The next several weeks simultaneously crawl and fly by.

I go to work.

I see Marisol.

I go home. Rinse and repeat.

Every day is essentially the same, as it was before Dominic and Alecsander bled into my life. My vibrator even broke the other day and that was the fucking cherry on top.

Fuck!

Today was just another day. I'm already dressed and ready for work. My shift starts in an hour, so I have enough time to leisurely stroll to Point B.

I grab my jacket and bag and slam my front door shut. Forcing the key in the knob, I twist and lock the door before turning on my heel and heading to the stairs. The apartment complex has been cleaned up a bit the past few weeks. The elevator was fixed a few weeks ago, but I need the cardio that the stairs provide so I continue taking those.

Even the walls in the corridors have been patched and painted fresh colors. The yellow, cigarette-stained walls no longer exist. Instead, cool blue walls catch my eye every time I walk by.

The air is crisp outside as I step onto the pavement. The stairs have a handrail now which helps my elderly neighbor extensively. She no longer needs a hand when she comes and goes. I've caught her smiling several times since the addition of the handrail and the corrected elevator.

I pop my earbuds in my ears and head off. I keep a brisk pace to make the walk count as a workout for the day. I almost laugh at myself, thinking I'll be consistent enough to work out when, in reality, I want to lay in bed all day and dream of Alecsander. His hands with his rings. His dark brown hair and how it falls into his eyebrows when he laughs. All the little things. I think back to the opening at his night club when I let him take me on his desk. Past me didn't even realize he was the owner of the fucking club. I laugh at myself. Past me was so naïve.

I don't bother avoiding the alley in front of Point B. There's no point. I figure if Dominic wants to watch me, he'll activate the cameras that are planted in every nook and cranny in Point B. Maybe I'll spend my break in a bathroom stall so I can be sure he isn't watching. I bite my nails, now down to the nubs on each finger. My anxiety has grown the past few weeks and the men that plague my life aren't even in it currently.

Walking into Point B, I strain to hear the music. The bar is bare bones. Marisol whips around the counter, coming straight for me. I cringe at her loud voice.

"I haven't seen you in a week! Where have you been?"

I stare, dumbfounded. "I've been here; what are you talking about?"

"Seeing you at work doesn't count as quality friend time," she complains. She crosses her arms over her chest.

I shrug my shoulders in her general direction as I go around her. I head for the back where I can store my shit.

"Don't you walk away from me, Kirbs." I hear her heels clacking on the floor as she stalks me to the back room. "Katherine Rigby."

Fuck. Throwing my bag in my locker quickly, I turn and face my friend's wrath. She never pulls out my full name unless it's either dire or out of anger. Seems like both this time around.

She waggles a finger at me like she's a mother lecturing her young child. "Now, you listen to me, *Katherine*." My name sounds like a curse when she says it like that, making me pay even more attention to her words. "We haven't hung out in forever!" She throws her arms wide. "We haven't done anything besides work, work, and work some fucking more!" Her face is red, a few shades lighter than her vibrant hair.

My shoulders sag as her words sink in. She only speaks the truth. I have canceled her plans the last few times she's tried making them. I haven't felt like going out to the bars or going, well, anywhere. "I'm sorry," I begin, but she cuts me off.

"Nope, nope. You aren't allowed to apologize. You're going to commit to going out tomorrow night or I swear to God, Katherine, I will find you and punch you in the tit." She stares holes into my head.

I nod to her request. Damn, Marisol can be downright terrifying when, and if, she wants to be.

That's enough to placate her at the moment. She rushes me then, wrapping me tightly in her pale arms. She crushes her head to my neck. "We're going to have so much fun. I have so much to tell you!" she mumbles into my throat.

I gently pat her on the back. It's the only type of hug I can afford with her arms trapping mine. I end up tapping her on the ass. And, thanks to the shit luck I've been having lately, that's the exact moment that Joseph walks into the back room.

His eyes are wide as he smirks. "And what do we have here, ladies?" He raises his brows at us suggestively. "Are you guys finally going to kiss? Let me tell you, I've been waiting ages to get tickets to *that* show." He chuckles and tosses his shit in his locker before spinning and leaving the room with a wink.

"What the fuck is up with him lately?" Marisol wonders, extracting herself from around me.

"I have no idea, honestly."

"Ugh, let's get through this shift and then we can go home and then it will be tomorrow, and we can hang out all day and maybe even end the day with watching a movie and eating ice cream in bed or something."

I nod, interested in the idea. "That sounds perfect. Come over whenever. You still have that key?"

"Bitch, you know I do." She smirks as she exits the room.

I sigh, the air leaving my body in one long huff. My shoulders sag, but I pick them up and try my best to put a smile on my face. I'm not feeling it. Only eight measly hours then I can leave and crawl back into my comfy bed.

That's my mantra for the next eight hours.

Closing the bar is easy enough, especially when both Marisol and Joseph are working alongside me. Point B never gets busy enough to warrant having three of us there, but we were having a decent enough time once Joseph stopped trying to tell jokes.

I swipe the towel over the bar for the hundredth time, feeling no resistance. The stickiness of the alcohol and beer that had been spilt all day is finally gone. My work is officially caught up and over.

Tossing the rag into the bin below the bar top, I wave to Marisol as she heads out the front door, her bag held up against her side. "See you tomorrow, right?" I confirm.

"Yes, ma'am," she sings to me. "I'll swing by that cafe down the street and pick us up some breakfast and I'll be over there after that, say, like ten or so."

"That sounds perfect to me. Get home safe!"

Marisol salutes me, her hair catching on one of her clunky, gumball machine rings. She yanks it free with a snit. "See you, Kirbs!" Then she's out the door and catching a cab to her place.

I sigh, letting the tension roll from my shoulders as I hunch my back then straighten. The muscles in my back are absolutely slaying me tonight. A hot shower is calling my name. I all but skip into the back room to grab my shit and yell a barely there goodbye to Joseph. He counts the drawer and does the final counts for the night. He waves, his eyes still on the money, saying goodbye without saying a word.

I take that as a win.

I clutch my jacket to my torso as I plunge out the door and into the abandoned street. It's gotten colder, the air nipping at my heels like a rabid dog. I make a split-second decision to take the alley home since it cuts a chunk of time from my walk. The sooner I get home, the better. The faster I get home, the quicker I can strip and hop into the shower, filling my bathroom with steam.

I smile to myself, finally feeling a bit better after weeks of stagnation. I'm coming out of the rut I've been in and it's...liberating. I breathe in the crisp, chilled air, filling my lungs to capacity before exhaling and doing it over and over. It's akin to a rebirth.

The alley has been cleaned recently as well. The large dumpster isn't overflowing, and the ground isn't littered with boxes and debris from deliveries. It almost smells...not bad? I hustle my way down the loosely lit alley, the few lights providing barely enough light to not trip.

Glass shattering against the concrete wall in front of me stops me in my tracks.

The alleyway is shaped like an L, taking a sharp turn to the right. The glass was thrown from further down the bend, where I can't see from my current vantage point. I bunch my shoulders to my ears, trying to figure out what the best course of action is.

Do I continue down the alley when someone, somewhere, threw a glass bottle at the wall for no discernable reason? Or do I turn around and make my walk even longer?

Definitely turning around. There's literally no question about it. I'm not going around that corner to find out who smashed that damned bottle.

I pick up my pace, quickly re-routing back to the point where I can take a left and be on the main street that runs between Point B and the entrance to the alley. As I round the corner, a hard arm catches my neck. My back bows and my knees are lost from underneath me. In one fell swoop, someone's thick arms are swinging under my kneecaps, into the ditch of my knees, as their other arm catches my back, along my shoulder blades. I go from standing, to nearly falling on my back, to being carried like a child in under five seconds.

My head spins. The grip on my arm tightens, and I look up at the person for the first time.

The male is wearing a black shirt and zipped jacket. The hood is drawn low on their face. I try to crane my neck to see their face but get nowhere as their arms wrap around me tighter. Their hold is punishing. Bruises will line by skin soon.

I try to swing my hands away from my sides and into the man. My arms refuse to budge. One is trapped against his hard stomach and my fluffy one, and the other arm is trapped against my hip by their hand. I wiggle and get nowhere.

"Stop moving." His voice is lethal and calm. Like he's done this a million times before. Has he?

Oh, God.

I kick my feet, barely brushing his hips. "Let me go!" I scream, finding my voice. "Let me fucking go, you damned creep!" I pull in breath after breath of air but find no relief.

"I told you to stop moving." His eyes are crystal clear and, somehow, familiar. He looks at me like he knows all my deepest secrets.

"Or what?" I don't know why I ask.

Probably because I'm stupid.

The man looks down, his face concealed by a black mask with holes cut for the eyes. It must be breathable. I feel a sharp sting against my arm and frantically look around.

The man's hand deftly traps a syringe between his fingers. He must have poked it through my jacket and into my skin. I felt the sting of the needle. It definitely hit me.

What the fuck was in it?

My breathing stutters. My heart pounds in my chest. It's doing its best to break free and escape.

My head lolls. I jerk it upright, trying to stare at the man. "D-did you drug me?" I ask, my voice still uneven. I can hear my own voice, but I sound submerged.

Is it raining?

I peer up at the sky, or I think I do? Which way is up? Down? I'm floating, floating...

A deep voice resonates through the fog, anchoring me back to the frightening reality. "Yes," he answers the question I nearly forgot I asked. "You're going home."

My eyes flutter shut, coating my consciousness in a black shroud of nothingness.

Twenty-Five

ALECSANDER

It's been weeks since I've heard from or seen Kirby.

Letting her walk out on me for the second time is no less rough than the first time. Five years ago, when I had her then lost her within the same breath, I searched for her. I spent countless hours and endless money trying to find her identity. I didn't have a name to work with. I didn't see her full face, so I couldn't even recognize her with complete assuredness. It ate me alive then, and it's going to eat me alive now if I don't do something about it.

I let her walk out of my home, and it was purposeful. I refuse to disrespect her boundaries, even if I want nothing more than to chase after her and slap a ring on her finger.

I didn't want to let her go, but I knew I had to.

Now I spend my days how I used to: working and thinking of her.

Except now I know more and have seen more of her. I miss her more vigorously than I did five years ago. I thought I had it bad then?

It is nothing compared to how I feel currently.

My body aches. My soul aches. My heart *aches*.

I clutch my chest throughout the day, wondering if this is going to send me to an early grave.

However, today is another typical workday where I go from club to club to ensure that everything is running smoothly.

As I walk into one club, *the club* to be specific, my mind is plagued with memories. Masks and lace, sequins, and shimmering stones. Dripping colors that poured down her throat and the way her skirt bunched around her thick waist. My sandy suit is stuck in the back of my closet. I usually donate expensive custom suits once I have worn them to their function, but I can't get rid of that one. It's too sentimental. The lapels are still slightly ruffled from where she grabbed them and held me to her body.

I savor the memory even as it rips through my mind and serrates my heart. The club is closed, set to open within the next several hours as the sun dips below the horizon.

The club has stayed the same for the past five years. It's one of the most profitable ones I own, raking in cash like it's no one's business. Dominic has been questioning me lately, wondering when I might snatch up another location. He's constantly asking when I might venture a little further south or north. Places that are hours away and wouldn't be as easily accessible as the locations I currently own.

He wants me out and I can't ascertain why.

Although I do have an inkling suspicion. A suspicion that has dark, wavy hair that kisses her shoulders.

Our five-year merger deadline is rapidly approaching. My head spins just thinking about the looming deadline. We have most things figured out and have been operating as one unit for a time. There are still bits and pieces of our work that haven't been merged, though.

And if I'm being frank, which I am for clarity, I'm a little worried about how the next few months are going to go. We've made strides: uniting our work forces into one, splitting them into departments and delegating certain tasks for certain groups. We've made a headquarters that we operate from together.

There's a fissure opening, its maw wide and waiting on either of us, or both of us, to slip and fall. I shake my head, going about my day. I check with my managers and employees that are onsite.

Everything is running well and effortlessly. It wasn't always like this, though. The first few years where I was in charge rather than my narcissistic father, employees quit left and right, valued ones who had been with our family for years, decades even.

They left because they knew the truth behind my father's demise. I haven't hidden that from any of my workers. I've been truthful and honest about how the trash needed to be taken out.

It was over quickly, and I was wiping the proverbial blood from my hands before his body ever hit the concrete.

I haven't lost any sleep over it, and I won't be starting now.

MY BED IS COLD AGAINST MY SKIN AS MY EYES FLITTER open. My phone chimes.

I groan, stretching my arm toward the device. I grab the phone and immediately pull it to my ear. My voice feels heavy in my throat as I answer. "Hello?"

"Alecsander?" A small voice greets my ears.

I blink rapidly, trying to place the voice, but come up with nothing. The clock on my nightstand reads close to midnight.

I sit up, my back pressing into my headboard. "This is Alecsander. Who is this?" I rub my forehead, trying to dislodge the sleepiness.

"You might not remember me," the voice continues in a

slightly higher pitch. "But I've seen you once, or well, I guess twice at this point," she rambles.

I sigh loudly into the receiver. "Tell me who you are."

"Yeah, yeah, my name is Marisol. I have red hair and I'm friends with Kirby. You know Kirby?" Her voice doesn't break as her words smash together into one long sentence.

I rifle through my brain, finding and locating Marisol. She was with Katherine when we first met, and she was with her the other time as well. Why is she calling me? Hell, how did she even get my number?

"Marisol, yeah? I remember you," I tell her. "What do you need?" I keep my voice calm since hers has taken all the stress from the room.

"I can't get a hold of Kirby," she groans. "We were supposed to hang out all day. We were going to have a girls' day, watching movies and eating ice cream but when I stopped by her house at like ten this morning, she didn't answer!" Her voice climbs an octave.

I'm out of bed, my feet hitting the tile floor with a small thud. I stumble into my closet and start pulling out clothes to change into. "Where are you now Marisol?"

"I'm outside Kirb's apartment, by the door. I thought maybe she was sick or something and was sleeping but she hasn't answered her phone or texts and she's still not answering her fucking door!"

"Okay, okay, take a breath with me, okay, Marisol?" I inhale and let the breath exit through my nostrils. I listen to Marisol mimic my actions. "Good, good job, Marisol. Listen, I'm getting dressed now and I'm going to meet you at Katherine's apartment, alright? It will take me a bit to get there, but I'll be there soon, okay?"

The phone shakes with her bracelet-clad wrist. "Okay, I-I'll wait here then. You're coming now?"

"Yes, I'm heading out to my garage and car now, Marisol. I'll be there soon, okay?" I unlock my car. "We can figure this out together when I get there, alright?"

More shaking of her head and bracelets greets my ears, the sound shrill. "Okay, drive safe Alecsander." She hangs up.

As I speed my car down my drive and onto the road, my mind races. Where is Katherine? This isn't like her, especially if she had a planned date day with her best friend. I don't know much about Marisol, but I know enough about their friendship. Katherine wouldn't leave without telling her. She wouldn't ignore her, that's for damned sure.

I do my best to settle my racing heart and mind. I fail, but I avoid a speeding ticket on my race to Kirby's apartment. The drive takes half the time and I'm thankful I arrive in one piece.

The apartment building looks nicer than it used to, but I know that's thanks to Dominic. He bought it. He didn't think to mention it to me personally, but I saw the bank statements.

He failed to mention his purchase of the whole damn building. I know he bought it because of Katherine. There's no denying that part of the equation. I'm not that stupid.

I leave my car by the curb, locking it as I stride up the stairs. The building even smells nicer. I'll have to hand it to Dominic when I see him next. He's done a good job here.

I find Marisol leaning against Katherine's door, her ass firmly planted on the ground. "Marisol?" I ask as I slowly approach her, keeping my hands palm out and facing her. "It's me, Alecsander." I pat my chest. "You called me?"

Her face is blotchy and red. Her hair is tied behind her head in a haphazard bun with several strands sticking in all directions. She pushes herself from the ground. I can see the tear tracks on her cheeks.

"You've got to help me find Kirby, Alecsander."

"I can help, Marisol, of course." I scratch my head.

"I don't think she came back home after work last night," she whispers.

"Why not? Did she have plans?" I hope not.

Marisol shakes her head. "No, she didn't. She was going to go home and pass out."

"Then why do you think she didn't come home?"

Marisol rubs her eyes, her jacket pulled tightly around her. "Because, she still had a letter from her super taped to her door and it's dated yesterday. It must have been taped to her door after she left for work and since it was still there when I got here, she obviously wasn't here. She didn't make it home!" Marisol is near hysterics, her voice shrill with tears dripping from her eyelashes to her cheekbones. Her foot taps the ground rapidly.

I take her by the shoulders, using slight pressure to ground her. "Marisol, Marisol," I say, looking into her eyes. "Listen to me. We are going to find her. I'll get my best people on it."

She nods. "You're sure? You're going to find her and bring her home, right?" Her lower lip pouts.

"One hundred percent Marisol. I will find Katherine and I'll bring her straight to you. I promise."

Marisol collapses against me. She sobs into my shirt while her tiny fists grasp it. I pat her back soothingly.

There are a lot of things that I need to do.

After several moments of Marisol sobbing on my shirt, her cries quiet. She pulls away. "What now?" she asks, her voice shallow.

I sigh, running my hand through my hair. "I'm going to take you home, Marisol. You need to rest. Then I'm going to go to my office and make some calls."

"You'll keep me updated?"

I nod absentmindedly at her. "Yes, I will."

"Okay," she says. "Thank you, Alecsander."

I shake my head, mostly at a loss for words. My mind continues to race with thoughts of Katherine speeding by.

Where could she be?

It's a short drive to Marisol's home. I watch as she unlocks her door and disappears inside. Once she's out of the way, I drive to my office. I keep the radio down low, instead focusing on pulling up numbers of the people I'll need to call once at the office.

I need to get an assistant. If I had one, then most of this work could already be done and I would be even closer to finding Kirby. *Fuck!*

I park my car and climb out, nearly tripping over my damned feet as I rush to my office.

I spend the next few hours making countless calls. I call in favors that are owed to me and rack up new ones that I will owe. Nothing is going to stand in my way of finding Katherine. I have watched her walk out on me twice now, and I'd be damned if I'm going to let her leave completely. Not this time.

I will find her, and I will bring her home. Even if I have to kill everyone that stands in my fucking way.

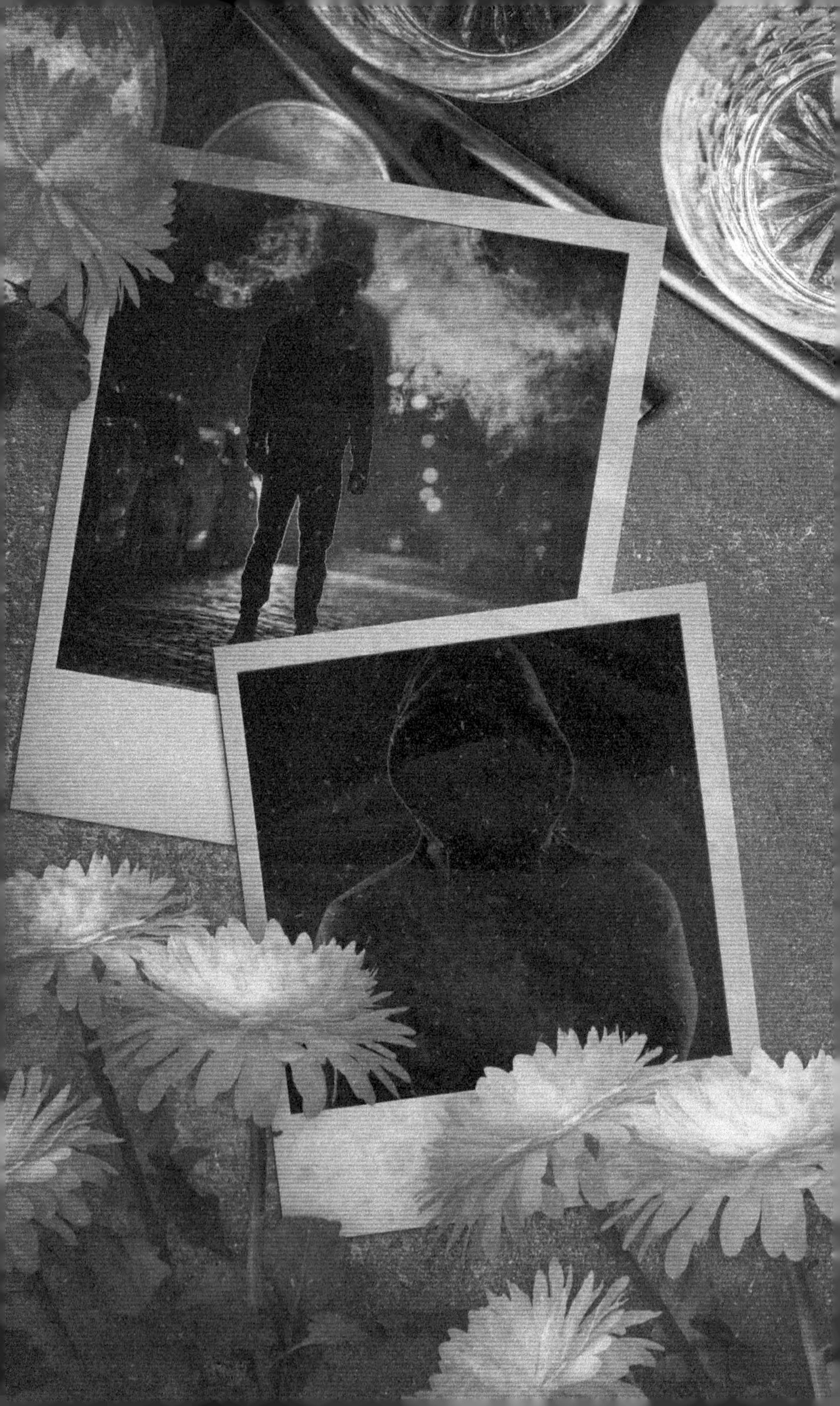

Twenty-Six

KATHERINE

The sun's delectable rays kiss my cheek. My toes curl in the warmth as I stretch my arms above my head. My fingertips find a satin pillowcase that melts into my hair.

Wait, satin pillowcase? I don't have a satin pillowcase. Motherfuckers are too expensive.

I rapidly sit up, my hands drawing the downy comforter closer to my hips as I stare at my surroundings in shock.

Where the hell am I?

I rub my eyes, my vision going dark and static-y for a sliver of time as I remember last night. I'm assuming it was last night anyway.

Walking home from the bar.

Agreeing to meet with Marisol the next day, today?

Getting clothes-lined and picked up like a sack of potatoes.

The shiny glint of the needle as it plunged into my arm.

I rotate my shoulder, the stiffness of a recent injection taking hold of my muscle. Shaking my head, I plunge my feet from the confines of the comforter to the cold, tiled floor. The room is lit with the sun's rays. They cast dazzling rainbows that flit from one corner to the plains of the tiles. I pivot, seeing the large, four-poster bed shrouded in downy and thick sheets. It's piled high with numerous pillows in various sizes and colors.

The chill from the tile causes gooseflesh to erupt up my shins and legs. I'm wearing a thin nightie that barely slaps against my mid-thigh. What the fuck?

I run my fingers through my hair. The strands rush through my fingers as I grab ahold of the base and strain.

My clothes have been changed.

The room has a large door on the far side, nearly twenty feet from the bed. Is this a fucking mansion? There's no way a room this size fits in anything less. But where? Who?

The golden doorknob taunts me in the sun's glow. I race to it, desperation clinging to my heels as my bare feet slap the tile. I jerk against the knob, the large wooden door not budging.

I'm locked in.

I bang on the door, at first using my open hands. My palms kiss the wood. My palms curl to fists rapping against the wood until it groans. Or I do. I can't tell. I bang on the door until my hands are bright red. Small bruises rise to the surface.

"Let me out!" I scream over, and over again. My throat constricts. My voice strains, growing weaker with each sentence.

Minutes?

Hours?

Hell, it could be days later. I'm sitting on the floor, my back pressed against the cool door. My legs are kicked out in front of me. My hands are in my lap, keeping the nightie in place.

My eyes are dry despite the tears that continually flow from them. My eyelashes matt together. There are clumps in the bottom and top of my vision. I sniffle, dragging my arm across my nose.

I sit on the floor long enough for my back to ache. The kink in my shoulders worsens the more I slump over.

Heavy footsteps pound in the corridor behind the door. I

scramble to my hands and knees before rising to my full height. As soon as the balls of my feet become steady, the door pushes open.

My eyebrows lower. My mouth nearly drops to my toes. "Milo?"

Milo has the decency to look down, his face growing red. He walks into the room, softly clicking the door shut behind him. He halts in front of me, a mere few feet separating us. I scan his face, willing myself to discover the answer to all of this. His face remains purposefully blank, void of emotion besides the red flush to his cheeks.

"Katherine-," he begins, but I don't let him finish.

I launch myself at Milo, crouching slightly so my shoulder dives into his torso. I take him by surprise. I hit him hard enough that we both go sprawling against the tiled floor. I land on top of him and use that to my advantage. I straddle his waist.

He grabs at my arms, trying to wield them to keep himself safe. "Katherine, listen to me!"

"No, you fucking asshole!" I rip my wrist out of his grasp, rearing it back and planting it squarely against his jaw. His face rocks to the side. His eyes widen, clearly surprised at my strength because I know I'm surprised. "Fuck," I mutter, not hesitating to withdraw my hand once again.

I squeeze my thighs tighter, trapping Milo between them. A small dribble of blood leaks from the corner of his mouth and I feel gratified.

How dare he?

How *dare* he? I wrap my hands around his wrists, pinning them to the ground by his sides. I crouch lower, my face only inches from his.

"Tell me what the fuck is going on. I swear to God, Milo," I seethe at him. My teeth crack against one another as I clench my jaw.

Before Milo can answer me, strong hands wrap around my waist. I'm tugged from my grip on the man who kidnapped me from the street. I thrash, not looking or caring who or what my limbs collide with. I kick and claw and pinch and scratch. I scream the entire time it takes for the stranger to dislodge me from Milo and throw me onto the silken bed. I bounce slightly when I contact the rumpled sheets.

My face burns from exhaustion, anger, and embarrassment. My cheeks are wet with hot tears, my hair sticking to any moisture. I'm panting. My chest rises and falls rapidly in time with my erratic heartbeats.

Moments bleed together until my chest finally settles into a normal rhythm. I open my eyes, taking in the room around me. Milo is sitting up on the floor rubbing a hand along the underside of his jaw. I instinctually flex my hand, feeling the cramps beginning in my knuckles and spreading into my palm and wrist. I hit him hard, yes, but it also means that his face collided with my hand. My hand aches. I bring it to my chest and cradle it with my free arm.

Someone clears their throat to the side of me, drawing my attention away from Milo to...to Dominic?

I blink furiously, trying to dispel the image in front of me. Surely, it is some type of mirage? An optical illusion perhaps? Maybe Dominic has a secret twin brother and he's the one standing before me?

The clack of his dress shoes against the sterile tile brings my attention back to him. His blonde hair curls against the nape of his neck before caressing his collarbone. Dark swirls of endless tattoos erupt from the collar of his suit jacket, bleeding onto his neck and jaw. They curve onto the plains of his face.

I stare at him for ages. He breaks the silence. "Katherine," he sighs my name. "I'm so glad you're awake and feeling better." His eyes rake over my body. "But we can't have you attacking my men, especially Milo."

I blink. Surely, I'm not hearing him correctly.

Right?

"Are you fucking kidding me, Dominic?" I yell. My chest flushes.

Dominic looks toward Milo. He nods then takes several steps away from the monstrous bed.

Milo is standing and walking toward me. Another man, one I've not seen before, opens the main bedroom door and clamors in. His steps are loud.

The new man has a sweater vest on and nice khaki pants.

"This is Doc; he'll be helping you, uh, settle in," Dominic says, all emotion void from his voice. His eyes are dark.

Doc steps next to me and takes my arm in a rough hold by my wrist. He pins the arm against my body while also using his body weight to keep the limb where he wants it.

He tucks a hand into his pocket, smoothly withdrawing yet another syringe that I carefully eyeball. Doc brings the syringe to his mouth, gripping the safety cap between his teeth before plucking it off.

"This shouldn't hurt," is all he says before the syringe is plunged into my bare upper arm. Flashbacks flood my mind as the memories rush back from last night.

Before I can bitch and scream at Dominic and Milo, my lids flutter shut. I'm trapped in a vast, dark void of slumber.

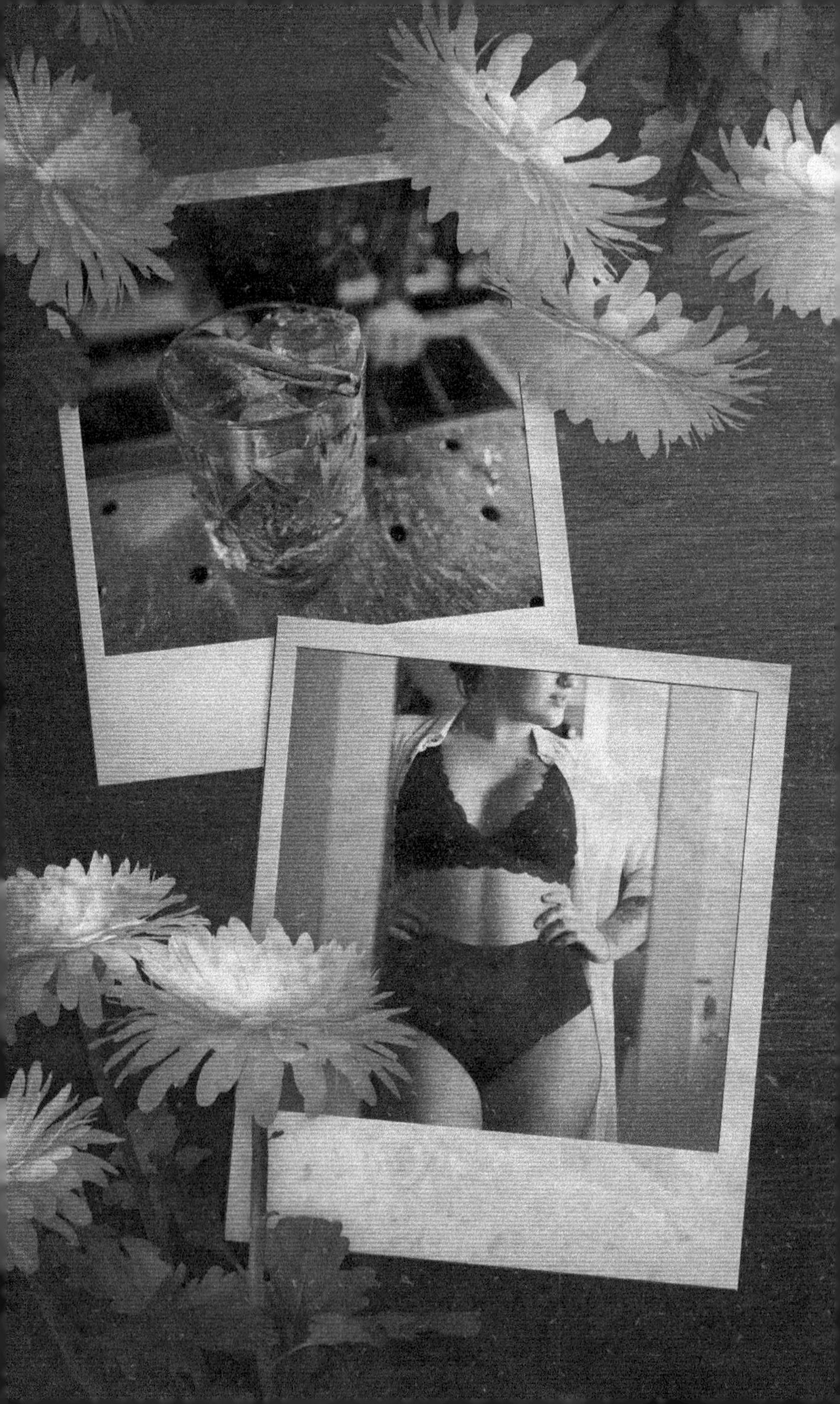

Twenty-Seven

DOMINIC

I bite my nails as I sit at my desk. Multiple monitors sit before me, all switching from camera to camera. I was focused on Point B, but now my cameras are in my own home. Down the hall, behind a large wooden door, awaits my Katherine. She lies on the four-poster silk bed like an angel waiting to be delivered to heaven.

After Doc gave her the sedative, he placed her on the bed. Her body was limp, and her eyes were closed. After I showed him out, I nearly tripped over my feet going back to her room. I gently plucked her from the bed and laid her on the pillow, tucking her under the sheets snugly.

I caressed her cheek with the back of my hand as her eyelids fluttered. Releasing a sigh, I sped back here, to my office, to watch and wait.

And wait longer.

I instructed Doc to give her a mild sedative, something that would wear off within a few hours. I had much to do, and Katherine needed to join me. But, no, I was waiting on the sedative to wear off. It's been twelve hours, and her eyes are still closed with her chest going up, then down rhythmically.

The door to my office creaks open. Milo slowly shuts it behind him. His face is worse for wear, the wrinkles in his forehead more prominent.

"Milo? What do you need?"

He gives me a look that can settle debts for a dead man before answering. "I don't need anything, Dominic."

I steeple my fingers. "Then why are you here? I thought you went home hours ago?" I double-check the time.

Milo sighs, the breath long, hard, and guttural. He plops himself into the armchair that resides in the corner. The patent leather creaks as he adjusts himself. Rubbing his face, he stares at me. "You know I don't agree with this, Dominic."

I tense. "Agree with *what*, Milo?" My hands are flat on my desk.

"You know damn well what! You had me *drug* her, Dominic! Does that not register with you?" His face grows redder with each word.

"Milo, Milo," I say gently, trying to ease him from the cliff he so dangerously rides. "Don't worry. Katherine is unharmed, and she most likely won't remember the interaction."

"Won't remember the interaction?" Milo screams, the veins in his neck bulging. "Have you already forgotten that she tackled me and tried beating me to death?"

I chuckle lowly. "Beat you to death? What are you? A teenage boy? You easily could have pushed her off if you wanted."

"You're an insufferable bastard," he spits.

I stand from my chair as a laugh tumbles from my lips. "Milo, I'm going to tell you something and I'm only going to say it once, got me?"

Milo continues staring. He hasn't stood up to meet me head-on. He stays seated, acting like he doesn't give a single fuck about what I have to say.

It pisses me off even more.

I scoff at his disrespect. "You're either on board with what I do, and I mean *any*thing I do or you're not on board at all." I pause, straightening the hem of my jacket. "So, either support my decisions and shut the fuck up or spend your last few days or hours down in the fucking basement like the rest of the filth that gets dragged there." I level him with a glare. My eyes are unmoving as he slowly brings his elbows to his knees, propping his chin on his hands.

Milo shakes his head slowly. "I never expected you to stoop so low you'd threaten me, Dominic," he laughs, a thing of cruelty. "But I shouldn't be surprised, should I?" He stands and goes to the door. "You did have me kidnap and drug a woman you claim to love more than life itself and then you had her drugged again when she wasn't fitting into the mold you've made in your head." He fondles the doorknob, teasing his departure, but not stepping through the threshold. "Maybe you *should* let the Sandman have her. He did have her first, and you've never liked leftovers." Milo exits before I can pick up and throw the crystal ashtray at him. It crashes against the wall next to the door as the knob clicks into place.

I breathe heavily. My mind fogs. Does Milo truly think awful things about me? Perhaps. I did threaten him, I suppose. What else could I have done? He was teeming with unease and disrespect and the combination of the two in this world, in our syndicate? I had to put my foot down or I'd be putting him down against my wishes. Protocol and standard would call for it.

I slump back into my seat, wringing my hands. I slide my chair to face the screens that hold my Katherine. I scan through the bedroom where I left her, feeling my pulse jump. I scan the hallways near her and the doors to the bathrooms. My heart drops to my stomach.

Katherine is gone.

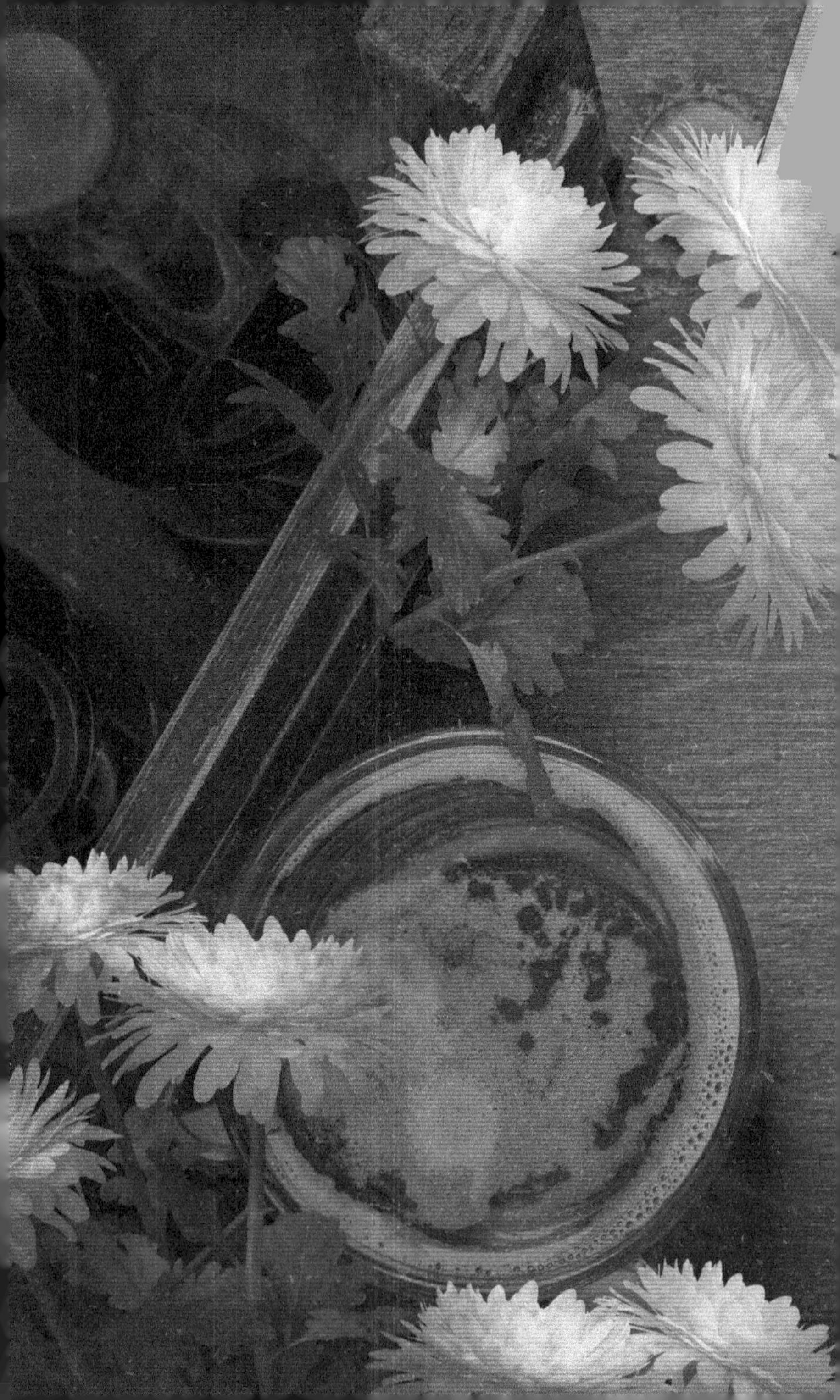

Twenty-Eight

ALECSANDER

The wait finally paid off.

One of my contacts, whom I now owe a large as fuck favor to, came through.

What they found though? Concerning, to say the least.

When my team scanned all the cameras near Katherine's house, they came up empty. There was no dice in finding her or even catching a slight glimpse of her.

But my contact's team? They found her, immediately. And the kicker? My team had checked that location.

Which leads to one, unfortunate, conclusion.

Someone on my team kidnapped Katherine or they were covering for whoever did. Either way, their day would end with a death sentence. I might deliver the blow myself, or I might pawn it off to Dominic since he seems to enjoy the act of killing. I'll let it be a gift to him or something.

Unlike Dominic, I don't keep close friends in the business. He has Milo, whereas I have only myself. So, I do the work that an assistant or right-hand man could do. I don't necessarily mind it, but I get irritated when I can't find the information I want quickly enough.

Thankfully, today is working with me rather than against me.

KATHERINE

I'm balled up with my knees curled against my chest. I'm against the back wall of the enormous closet of my new prison. I woke up and a rising panic crashed against my breastbone. It had me flinging the covers of the bed and all but scurrying away. I tried to pry the door open again, but of course it was locked. The bathroom was the obvious next choice, but it was too bright.

I need darkness.

I need it to surround me and envelop me in its cold embrace. There is a light in the closet, but I didn't bother flicking the switch. I found the furthest wall from the door and stumbled my way to it. Sinking to the floor felt therapeutic.

I'm sitting on the carpeted floor. The carpet is plush against my bare legs. I want to pick it, like I would pick the grass at recess when I was in elementary school. I resist the urge, however strong, and instead wrap my arms around my torso, giving myself some much-needed pressure therapy.

I rub my arms, soothing the ache that transpired from being injected more than once. My nose warms, the tell-tale sign that tears are forthcoming. I swallow repeatedly to push them away.

It only works for a few minutes before the first hot tear escapes and runs freely down my cheek. As soon as the first droplet hits, the dam is broken and I'm ugly sobbing on the floor of an overly opulent closet that feels too much like a prison cell to really appreciate.

When my eyes are blurry, I look around without feeling ashamed that I'm intrigued by what's in the closet.

Each wall has three levels of racks, each filled to the brim with any type of clothing imaginable. There are sweaters, crewnecks, tee shirts, long-sleeved and short-sleeved everything, tank tops, blazers and matching pants, blouses, dresses, several bagged dresses that make me think they're gowns of some sort. There's so much excess that the room starts to shrink. The weight of the clothing itself is bearing down on me, pushing me onto the floor.

My mind races. Tears slope onto my neck and collarbone. I'm a mess, but I don't bash myself for it. What other kind of reaction should I have if not this one? I've been kidnapped for fuck's sake. Sure, it was Dominic, but does that make it any better?

Fuck no, it doesn't.

I stand on shaky legs, using the wall for support as I seek out the softest sweater I can find within an arm's reach. Whose clothes are these? Upon further inspection, all the tags are still located on each item. Everything is brand-fucking-new. I want to scoff at Dominic's audacity, but I can't even manage that.

The softest sweater happens to be a light peach color.

I hate the color. It makes me look half-dead. I drag the hem of the sweater to my face, feeling the plushness of it as it caresses my cheek. I use it to wipe away all my tears, fresh and old. I wipe my eyes and nose and drag it down my neck, collecting tears as if they're possessions and now this sweater owns them all.

Once my face and neck are dry and I'm feeling more like myself, I adjust the sweater to hang how it was before I disturbed it. The light peach of it is now stained with remnants of my mascara. The fabric darkens with the tears and emotions it holds.

I'm about to exit the closet and crawl back under the silky duvet of the bed when I hear the door to the suite burst open. It hits the wall and bounces back several times.

"Katherine!" Dominic yells through the suite. I stay in the closet, tucking myself against the wall to make myself smaller.

"Where the hell are you, Katherine?" Dominic's voice isn't any lower. The pitch and deepness of it is intimidating and foreboding,

What do I do now?

I risk a step to the left, seeing through the crack in the closet door. Dominic stands in the center of the room. His hands grasp at his scalp as he grabs and pulls his hair. His face is red, showing more emotion than the last time I saw him.

I spy on Dominic (the irony) as he treats the bathroom door the same as the main door. He throws it open like it isn't heavier than any other door I've ever seen. He disappears into the bathroom.

I push the closet door open. Once it's open enough for me to slide through, I race out. I try my best to not fall. I clamor to the bed, racing up it with speed I've never felt. I shimmy up to the headboard and press my back into it. I finagle the sheets to sit over my crisscrossed legs as Dominic barrels out of the bathroom. I swallow thickly to halt the panting.

His eyes are red-rimmed, and I want to laugh at the idea that we've *both* been crying. What the hell does he have to cry about? Instead, I keep quiet as I stare at him. I will him to see me.

Shock shrouds his face when his eyes land on the bed, with me suddenly in it. Dominic rushes to the end of the bed. He comes to a halt as he pushes his palms into the blankets. "Where the fuck have you been, Katherine?" His teeth clash as he talks.

I grab a strand of my hair, casually twirling it between my fingers. "I don't know what you mean, Dominic. I've been here?" I say the words flippantly, sweetly. Why not gaslight the king of gaslighting?

Dominic's eyebrows go up, back down, then up as his brain races to figure out the truth. He's at a loss for words for a microsecond before his face flushes once more. He points an angry finger at me from the end of the bed. "You weren't here, Katherine," he pleads with me, his voice dropping to match his drooping eyebrows.

I cross my arms over my chest, hiding the ample cleavage that the nightie leaves me with. "So, fucking what, Dominic? I was in the damned closet losing my mind for a minute. Why the fuck do you care?" I glower at him.

Dominic stands there, his mouth opening and closing like a stupid fish. "Katherine, I," he begins, but I cut him off.

"No, shut the fuck up, Dominic. I've had enough," I hold my hand level with my head. "Of you telling me what to do and where to be and now you think you can, what? Kidnap me?" I chuckle darkly at him, my eyes never leaving his face. I rise on the bed, my knees sinking into its plushness.

"What the *fuck* is your problem, Dominic? Why would you do this to me?" I feel my chin quiver but bite the inside of my mouth to tamp it down. "Why would you *steal* me?"

Dominic's chest heaves with deep, erratic breaths. "You had to come here. You wouldn't see it my way." He looks around, like he's looking for something particular but doesn't find it. "I have to make you see, see what it's like here, so you'll want to stay."

"Stay?" I ask him, astounded. "You want me to *stay* here? With you?" I blink at him, wondering exactly what the fuck is going on here.

"I want you to stay here with me Katherine. It's been years in the making, since that first day I saw you at Point B." Dominic plants a knee on the end of the bed, his arm stretching out to hold himself up. "I saw you come around that fucking bar and lost it. I lost myself to you. *You* did this, Katherine." He says my name like it's a prayer, like he needs me to survive.

He doesn't, though.

"Dominic, I barely recognized you a few weeks ago when you helped me out with that customer. I don't know what you think." I truthfully don't. He's making up scenarios in his head that haven't happened.

"Katherine," he pleads, sinking his other knee on the bed. "The five years is almost up; the deadline is approaching."

I sink back on my heels. "What the fuck are you talking about Dominic? What deadline?" I have no idea what this man is talking about. Dominic's knees brush mine. His face is a mere few inches away from mine. His pupils are blown and wild. Dominic's never mentioned drugs before, but why would he?

Is he on something right now?

His hands reach toward me, and I instinctually flinch backward. His hands halt immediately. He settles by placing them on his legs. "We made a deal five years ago, me and the Sandman."

Gooseflesh peppers my arms as my mind stalls. *The Sandman.*

"We merged our empires, and we made a deal. We shook on it."

I have no idea what this motherfucker is talking about. He's unhinged as he sits right in front of me, his hands splay and curl on repeat. My mind can only focus on who he mentioned.

"We promised each other that we would find wives within five years. Each of us having wives would secure our future as an empire. We'll have heirs. Our children will run it together, but we aren't getting any younger. We need wives and children and that five years is basically gone now."

I hear what he says about the deal and merger. But my mind doesn't register what it all means and how it affects me. No, I'm stuck on the *who* of the situation. *The Sandman.*

The Sandman.

"You should have known better than to fuck with the Sandman."

Rhett.

But what does Dominic have to do with the Sandman? Why would they merge their empires? Why do they need wives? The questions in my brain are countless, but they keep hurdling toward me. I sit there, staring at Dominic with wide eyes.

"Why do you need me here, Dominic?" I'm afraid I already know the answer, but I want him to say it. I want him to tell me how this is going to be my prison forever.

Dominic touches my shoulders. I don't flinch but I don't lean into him, either. I'm stoic, cold, hard.

His fingers dig into my shoulders, not enough to cause physical pain but enough for me to know he's not letting me go. "Katherine," he says, his voice breathy. "You're here because you're *mine* and you're going to fall in love with me."

"Dominic," I start.

He shakes his head hard. "No, Katherine. You're not leaving. You're going to marry me before Alecsander can get you."

What? "Alecsander?"

"The Sandman won't win you; I refuse to let it happen."

Pieces begin clicking together, all of it spinning in circles around me. Alecsander? He must be the Sandman that Dominic mentioned. But they made a pact? Years ago, to find wives and have children. Did Alecsander fool me again?

I think of my past, the years I spent in foster care. The one foster family that had a boy my age. My wonderful, precious Rhett.

I loved Rhett and he loved me, fiercely. We had so many plans for *our* future.

Then he was stolen from me.

The news reporters called it a stray bullet.

It wasn't a stray bullet, though. I was there. I saw the man hang out the window of a beater car, the gun in his hands.

My eyes start to water, the tears escaping.

I quickly swipe at my eyes, catching the tears on the back of my hand. I refocus on Dominic. He hasn't noticed my delayed silence or my tears.

"Wait," I say, his words catching up with me. "What do you mean we're getting married?"

He grips me harder. "We're going to be married in a week's time, Katherine." Dominic licks his lips. "Then you won't ever leave me."

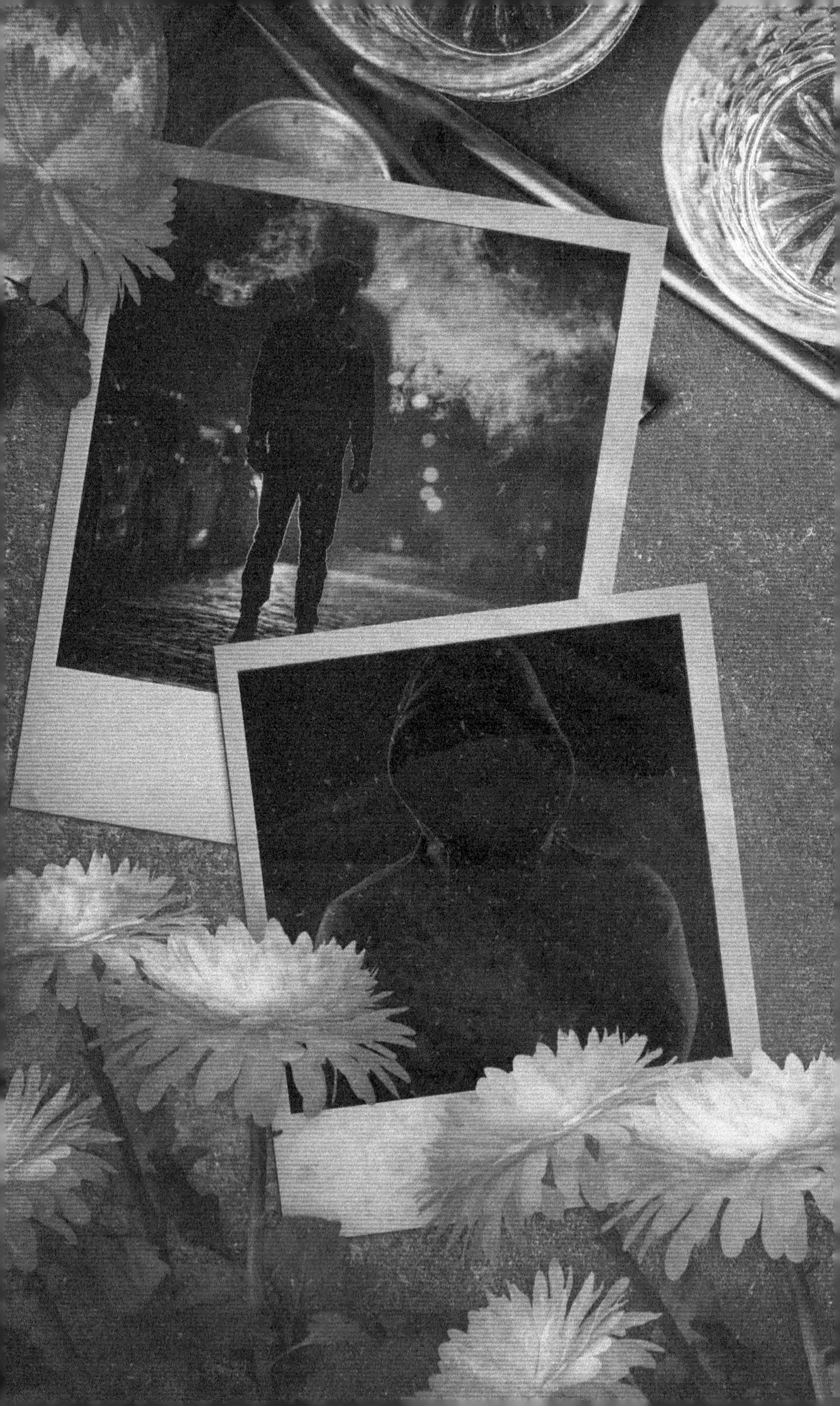

Twenty-Nine

KATHERINE

It's official. Dominic scares the shit out of me. He's really keeping me locked in this room. He wants me to *marry* him within seven days?

What the literal, *actual*, fuck?

He left a while ago, having leapt from the mattress to answer a piercing phone call. He'd cursed at the screen and didn't say another word.

He hasn't returned.

My thoughts are rampant. Any moment of fleeting awareness is crushing and all-consuming. Though I sit rigid on the bed, my heart hammers relentlessly. A distant cool breeze, probably from a vent somewhere, licks at my skin slick with sweat. The tiny hairs stand on end.

I bounce between the thoughts of my fate and Alecsander – the Sandman. My eyes are too dry to cry now, but there's a tight aching in the back of my throat. The man I'd fallen for, the one I'd gotten so close to letting inside, betrayed me. Alecsander killed Rhett. He *murdered* my first love.

A sudden cramp locks my fingers and I gasp, breaking from haunted thoughts. I'd gripped the sheets so hard that the blood in my fingertips fled, leaving them ghostly pale. I watch the red seep back into its place, clenching my jaw.

I don't know how – I don't know when – but the Sandman will pay for his crimes. And I will inflict as much suffering, if not more, on him than he did to me.

But first, I have to figure out how to get the fuck out of here.

I STARE UP AT THE GLASS CHANDELIER ANCHORED INTO the ceiling. It's a gaudy thing. The nightlight in one of the corners offers a miniscule glow. The glass from above scatters the light in pebbles along the walls and sheets. They imitate stars. I try counting them, like sheep, to induce sleep, but my body refuses.

I am viscerally aware of the slightest creaks in the hall outside the door and shifts in air flow.

I lay flat as a board until the sun peeks through the heavy curtains. Most of the room is still shrouded in subtle shadows. My spine aches from hours without movement, so I finally prop myself up on my elbows. The door swings open.

My heart leaps into my throat and I back into the headboard. Though the shock quickly boils into white-hot rage upon recognizing the man who quickly seals the room behind him.

"Milo?" I murmur, twisting my legs over the edge.

His expression remains locked in neutrality this time, eyes dissecting my disheveled appearance. My hands tremble, aching to crush his windpipe beneath them. "I've brought your breakfast," he states plainly, lifting a metal tray I hadn't noticed yet.

The rage is widely foreign to me. It takes up so much space. I was angry, utterly destroyed, when Rhett was stolen from me. I've slapped, punched, and kicked handsy men in the past and cussed out slow drivers. But nothing compares to this scalding ire. Looking at Milo, I know without a doubt I want to *kill* him.

Given the change, I know I will.

He kidnapped me. Drugged me.

Milo slowly approaches a table near the door. The tray clinks against the surface. He never turns his back fully, pinning me in place with constant glances over his shoulder. As he steps aside, I finally peel my gaze from him to examine what he brought.

There are several decanters filled with iced water, orange juice, and what appears to be coffee. Near the decanters are small bowls. Some are filled with a variety of berries, and another has granola with a tiny yogurt cup on the side. There's toast, accompanied by a pinch of dark jam.

The sweet and savory aroma strikes, and my stomach reacts like a caged beast. I won't give in. My arms fold over my chest. "How do I know you didn't poison it?"

Milo stares, standing stiffly, like I'm another task to be ticked off his daily chore list. After an agonizing moment, he grabs a decanter, popping off the top. He gulps the orange juice, eyes never leaving mine. His throat bobs as he returns the juice to the tray and tastes the others just the same. Satiated, he steals a couple blueberries from the bowl and bursts them between his teeth.

"I wouldn't poison you, Katherine."

"But you'd drug me, right? You'd attack me in a fucking alley and shove a fucking needle in my arm."

He has the decency to look down at his feet, shifting his weight. "I didn't want to do that either, Katherine." His voice is low, barely audible.

I scoff. "Oh, fuck you. Leave me alone."

To my surprise, he doesn't leave immediately. His lips part, as if he's grasping for something to say, but nothing comes.

I thrust my finger toward the door. "Get out!"

Milo ducks his head once before pivoting and quitting the room. The door clicks shut and I'm alone again.

I release a held breath and ease off the mattress. My feet slap against the floor as I survey the array of food. While I wish I could be fortified and not need sustenance, I must eat to maintain any semblance of strength. The stronger I am, the sooner I can escape.

I devour the berries and yogurt, making myself a shitty parfait topped with crunchy granola. I scoop the gooey mixture into my mouth in four bites and then munch on toast. Coffee washes the grit from my tongue but leaves a bad taste in the back of my mouth. I switch to the ice water, tipping the decanter against my lips and savoring the sharp chill as it glides down my throat.

Once finished with the prison meal, I leave the empty containers on the tray and find the adjoined bathroom.

The shower cubicle spans the entirety of one wall. The one in my apartment could fit inside with room for another. I ache for a hot shower. Dominic has watched me for a while. I know he has, especially at work and in this prison cell. He noticed when I wasn't in the bed and was in the closet. He came crashing in here so fucking fast.

A chill scurries up the back of my neck.

There are cameras everywhere. At Point B. The nightclub. The city streets. In that bedroom. Does he have access to them all? He'd owned Point B for years before approaching me that night. Exactly how long has Dominic Alcutti planned my imprisonment?

I study the shower drain, stand on my toes to peek into the corners, search the closet shelves and the cabinet beneath the sink. The sick bastard must have a camera hidden in here, too. Hell, cameras can be the size of a fingernail these nails. My breaths come swiftly as I search, ripping plush towels from the closet and opening shampoo bottles.

I come to an abrupt halt, taking in the absolute destruction in my wake. Is this what he wants? Dominic wants me to break—become easier to mold to whatever he plans me to be.

My throat bobs and I force my lungs full. I must maintain my composure. No matter how stir crazy or paranoid I become, I must remain sane.

I crack the door and peek into the bedroom. No one has come banging in to check on me. I ease the door shut and face the mess. It takes less time than I expected to refold the towels and return everything to its original pristine location.

I would not be caught off guard. Never again. Not if I can help it.

I know I need to form a plan, but I can't hide in the closet for more than ten minutes without Dominic tearing the door down.

I grab a towel from the rack, throwing it over my arm as I tiptoe across the bedroom and into the closet. If these clothes are for me, then I might as well find something to wear whilst I'm here. I can't keep wearing the same nightie. I hate the fabric and the fact that someone else put it on me.

Thankfully, there are plenty of pajama options in the large closet. Most are more revealing than I like, but I do find a pair of fluffy pants and a matching top folded in one of the many drawers that line one wall. The set is black and the only thing that matches my style from what I can see.

I'm in and out of the closet within five minutes, hoping to avoid alarming Dominic so he doesn't come rushing into the room for fear of me escaping or whatever the fuck he was talking about yesterday.

And then I sit on the bed and wait.

And wait.

And wait some more.

I pace the room, leaving no tile left behind.

I scour the corners and the walls for tiny cameras but manage to find a total of zero.

I scan the bathroom for cameras, even checking in the tank of the toilet.

And then I wait, wait. WAIT.

I'm so frustrated by the time night begins to fall that I stand in front of the window. I peer out at the sun as it sinks lower and lower to greet the horizon. I've spent a whole day here, alone. Milo never brought any lunch or dinner. I finished the last few room temperature berries earlier whilst pacing.

I stare at the sun sinking to the horizon.

I long to be that sun.

Sinking into something I've missed for so long, even after one hard day of work.

I long to be like the sun, caressing the horizon, Alecsander, as I come home from work or as he comes home.

I think of him.

I can't stop once I start. I haven't spoken to him in a few weeks.

Immediate guilt rushes to my chest, crawling up my throat like acid, clawing and scraping as it gets closer and closer to my mouth.

I push a hand against my lips as I rush to the bathroom. I barely make it in and flip the toilet seat lid before I vomit, the guilt emptying out of me like hot coals. Tears burn my vision, more guilt falling out. I retch a few more times, mostly stomach acid pooling in the water below me.

How dare I think of him! I hate him! I hate them both!

Rhett would know what to do.

I rinse my mouth with water from the sink, using my finger to roughly brush my teeth haphazardly before re-entering the bedroom. I avoid the window, the sun now at home and gone.

I sink into the bed, turning to my side to pull my knees closer to my chest. They don't quite make it all the way up due to my thick thighs and stomach, but I hold them, nonetheless. The tears are still falling, slowly and languidly. I stare at the wall.

And I wait.

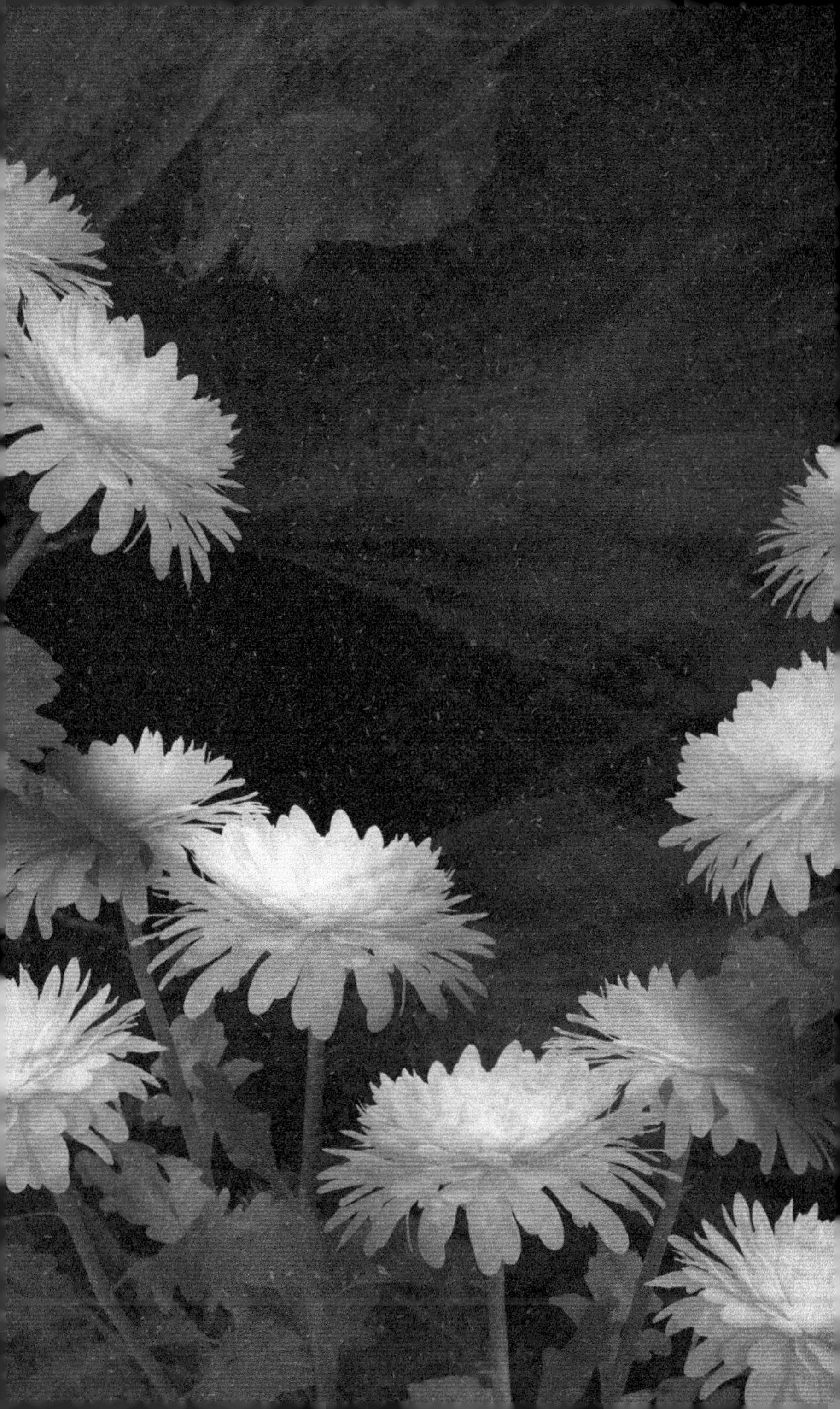

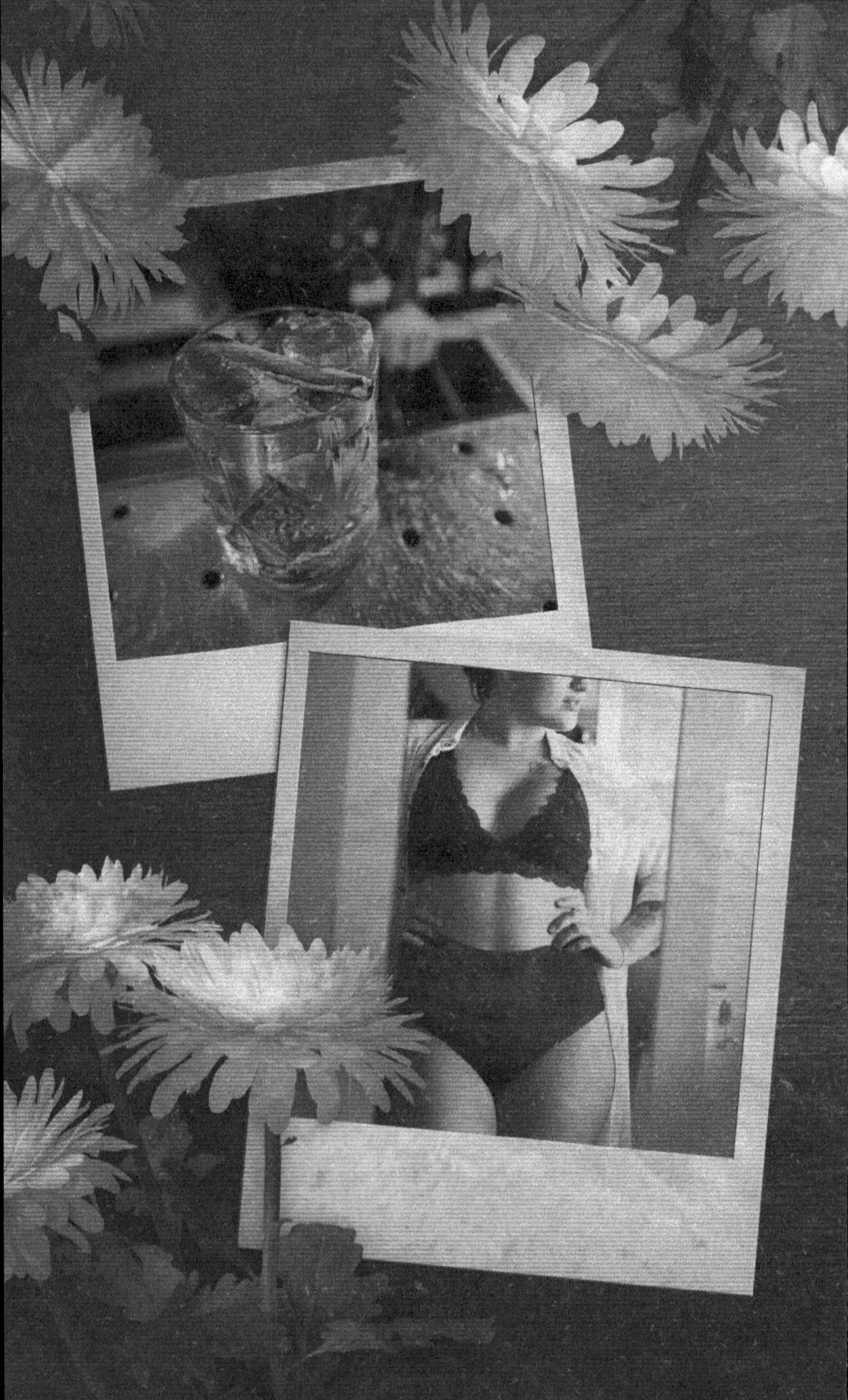

Thirty

ALECSANDER

I'VE SPENT THE LAST DAY, NO, MORE THAN A DAY AT THIS point, questioning all members within my ranks. I've concluded that it wasn't one of my guys who did something to my Katherine.

But it is someone in the organization. Which leads me to where I'm standing.

In front of Dominic's house. I need to speak with him, see him face-to-face, to show him the evidence my contact uncovered. He needs to hear it from me, not someone else. As much as I dislike that he likes Katherine, I have to admit that he feels something for her. And he deserves to know that she's gone— missing. Someone close to him stole her straight from the sidewalk. Near *his* bar.

I knock on his front door, the elevator behind me. I clench my fist in my pocket and do my best to keep my face neutral. I didn't let him know I was on my way. I didn't tell him a god damned thing, honestly.

After several knocks, the door finally opens, revealing Dominic with his eyes wide and red. I focus on his face for a moment, noting the dark circles under his eyes and the way his hair is mussed and tangled around his ears.

"Are you alright, man?" Concern laces my voice.

He shakes his head rapidly, side to side. "Yeah, I'm good." He peers through the crack in the door. "What's up with you, Alec? Why are you at my house? I can't remember the last time you showed."

He isn't wrong. I don't think I've been to his condo since he bought it all those years ago, but then, I was only here for business. This is a more personal call. "I have news I must discuss with you."

"It's late, Alec. Can't this wait until tomorrow?"

He's acting slightly suspicious, his eyes darting to and from me. "It's urgent. It's about Katherine."

That has his eyebrows raising. "Katherine?"

"Yes. It's important and we need to talk. Now," I urge him to open the door wider.

After several moments, Dominic concedes. He opens the door wide enough for my body to fit through. I inch inside, nearly colliding with him.

"Come into my office and we can discuss what you mean about Katherine," Dominic tells me, already walking in the direction I assume his office is in.

I follow him through a long corridor, up to a closed wooden door. Dominic palms a key and unlocks the door swiftly. Upon entering his office, I notice the dark tones of the walls and desk, how they mingle and mesh together to fit into a theme of dark and gloomy.

Hands in my pockets, I watch as Dominic rounds his desk. I opt not to follow him to give him a feeling of privacy and respect. He takes his seat and stares at his computer for a few seconds before clicking around it a few times, after which he finally settles his gaze to mine. "So, about Katherine?" he asks, his voice nearly breathless.

I smooth my shirt, glancing at the chair in the corner. I nod toward it. "Mind if I sit?"

Dominic approves, so I take my seat.

"A few nights ago, one of Katherine's friends called me. You might know her as she also works at Point B. Her name is Marisol, a redhead." Dominic nods again, signaling for me to continue, "Anyway, she called and long story short, she was supposed to meet Katherine at her house for a girls' day, but Katherine wasn't at home, wasn't answering calls. Nothing."

"Maybe she went somewhere for a few days?"

I shake my head vigorously. "No, Katherine doesn't leave town and not tell Marisol, especially when they had plans already. Marisol was in near hysterics when I picked her up to drop her off at her own home. Katherine's gone, Dominic."

"What are you trying to tell me here, Alecsander?"

I don't like his tone. I grit my teeth, staring at him coldly. "I'm telling you this, Dominic, because I thought you felt something for Katherine. I thought you would care about her well-being."

He scoffs. "Of course I care about her well-being."

"You're not acting like it right now. It's suspicious, honestly. Especially with the news that one of my contacts delivered to me."

This has Dominic's attention. "What do you mean, information? What do you know?"

I sigh, collecting myself. "My contact found surveillance footage of Katherine being taken when she left Point B, down the sidewalk from there, actually."

"How good were the cameras?"

What an odd fucking question to ask. I'll come back to that later. "Good enough to catch someone's face. My contact ran them through facial recognition. You're not going to believe who was a match for it."

"Tell me, tell me who took my Katherine!"

I want to snarl at him, tell him that she isn't *his* Katherine, but *my* Katherine. But truth be told, Katherine wasn't either of ours.

Not really. She belonged to no one but herself and I will respect that choice of hers until my dying breath. If she wanted to continue a relationship, or anything, with me after all this was over and through, then I would leap for joy. But if she decides to wash her hands of me for the rest of time, then I'll respect it. But my heart and mind will ache for her until my last day. I'll never take another.

"A close associate of yours kidnapped Katherine. Footage captured him injecting her with something. I assume it was a type of sedative to calm her down or completely knock her out."

Dominic smashes his palms to his desk, rising from his throne. "Tell me who the fuck took Katherine!"

"Your friend Milo took her. And I have the recording to prove it."

DOMINIC

Fuck. Fuck. *Fuck.*

Things are spiraling out of my control faster than I can handle.

Alecsander showing up to my house, unannounced, is uncommon. Yet, here he is. Telling me about Katherine as if I don't already know exactly where she is.

I won't let him know that truth, however. I don't want to throw Milo under the bus, but will I need to in order to keep my secret?

My skin itches. I want to claw my arms, dig my nails into my flesh to relieve the burn I feel. But I don't. I keep my hands, palms down, on my desk, narrowing my eyes at Alecsander.

Alecsander feels less and less like a partner in a business than he has since the official start of our merger. We haven't been close in a decade, but this? I was finally starting to feel a kinship with him, until this resurgence of Katherine became a thing once more.

And now here we are in my office. He's telling me my best bud took Katherine. He did it under my command and my watch. Alecsander will never find that out, though. He can't.

He won't see Katherine until weeks after our impending nuptials. I plan to take her on a proper honeymoon. Somewhere down south, maybe the Bahamas? I haven't fully decided yet.

"I don't need to see Milo taking Katherine," I tell Alecsander.

"Don't you want to see it to make sure it's truly him? My contact is thorough, but I figured you would want to see it for yourself. That's why I brought the flash drive over."

Alecsander brandishes a small, black flash drive in his hand. "I can plug it into your computer, it won't take long." Alecsander's rushes.

He walks to my desk before I can apprehend him. His arm is outstretched, holding the flash drive, coming toward the computer and tower. "No, here. Let me," I try telling him, but he's already around the side of my desk, in view of my monitors.

I move my hands, grab the mouse, and attempt to click *something*. Why did I leave the window open?

But it's too late.

Alecsander's eyes are glued to the screen. I watch as his eyebrows inch closer together and pull downward. His eyes crinkle in disbelief. His face is aghast with ire, his lips thin until they're barely visible.

I raise my hands. "Alecsander, I can explain," I start as Alecsander slowly turns his head.

"Do you want to explain why in the *fuck* you have Katherine in a bedroom with a camera in it?" He seethes, his jaw taut. He steps closer. I take a step backward.

Alecsander closes the small gap between us in one step. I stare into his eyes, realizing why people are terrified of the Sandman. He's never looked at me like he's looking at me at this very moment. It makes me want to shrink back. I want to put space between us, but his hands are grabbing my shirt.

I want to wince but refuse to show him any vulnerability. I stare back, doing my best to keep my face blank.

"Maybe start with explaining why the fuck Katherine's here, in your house, after Milo, your friend, mind you, fucking stole her off the damned street?"

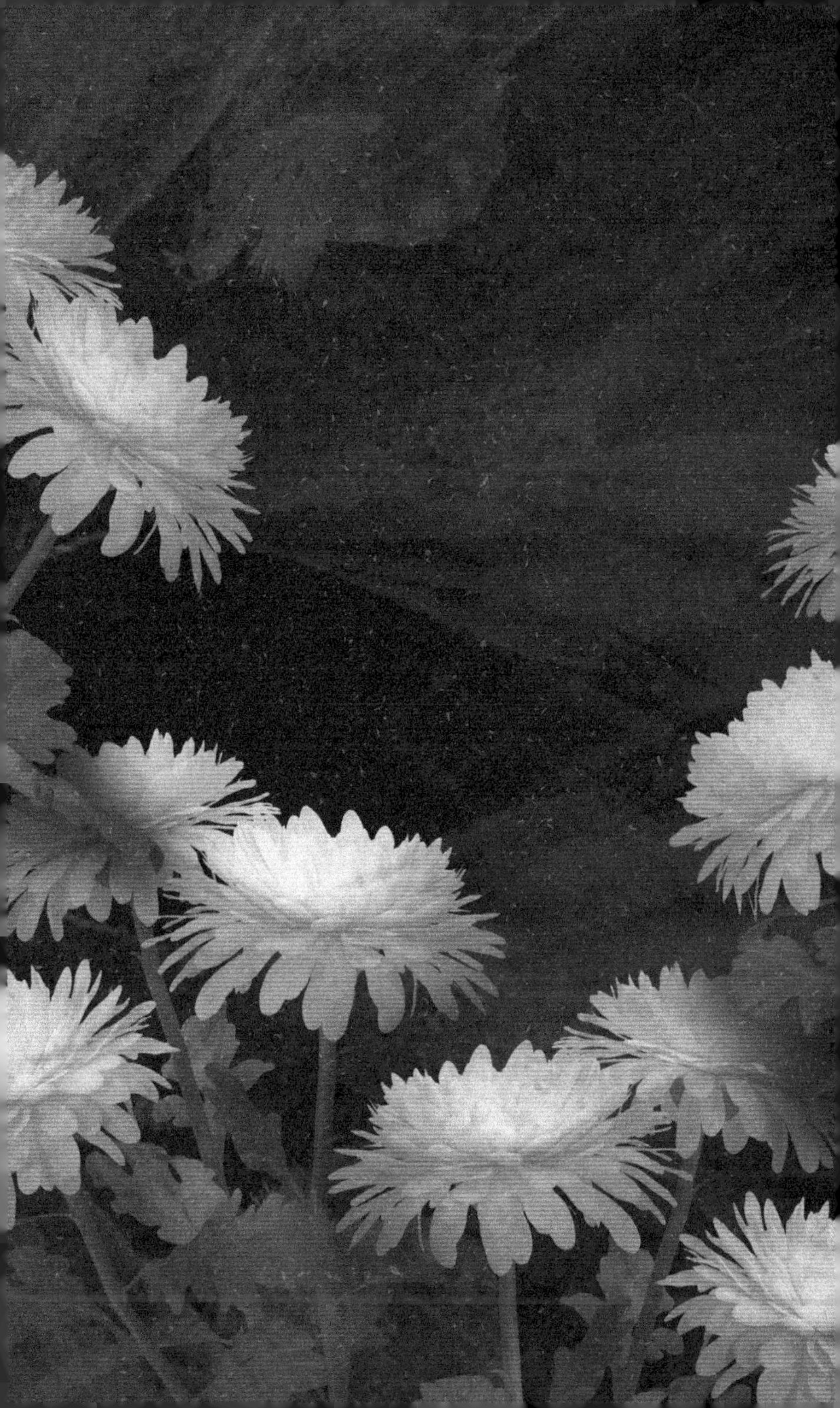

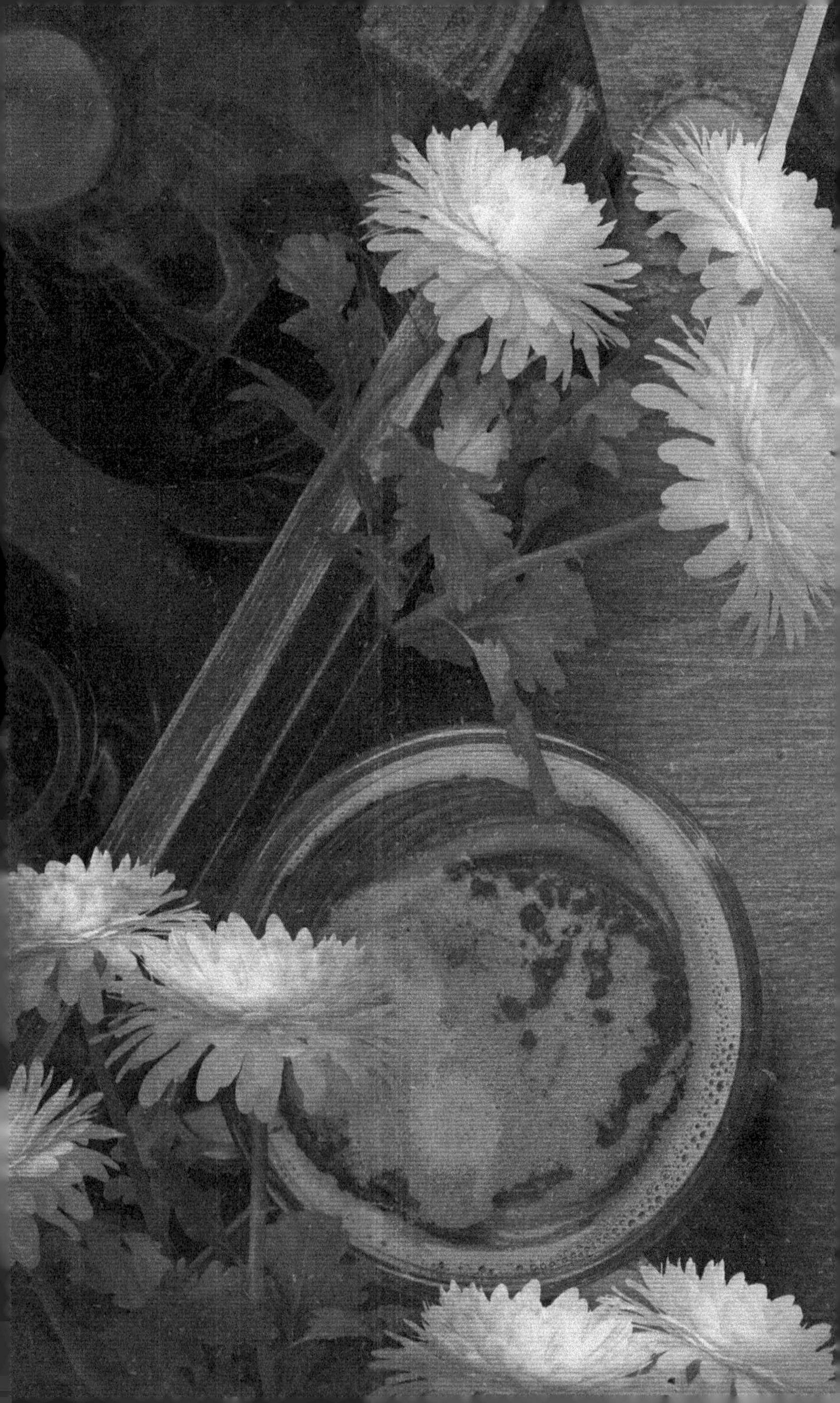

Thirty-One

ALECSANDER

Dominic is stupid. Egotistical and willfully *stupid*.

It's the only explanation I come up with when I see the screen of his monitor. The screen where I can barely see Katherine sprawled across a four-poster bed. The camera is high definition, leaving nothing blurry. It might be in black and gray, but I know instantly that it is her.

There's no mistaking her beauty, the way it permeates the wavelengths separating her and I. I grip Dominic's shirt tighter, using my arms to realign both of our bodies so I can see the monitors once more.

Katherine's chest rises and falls. She's alive. Thank fucking God.

I stare at Dominic, looking down my nose at him through narrowed eyes.

I hate him.

I hate him so fucking much in this moment. My hands itch to

release his shirt and crawl to his neck, strangling him until his face turns purple.

"Did you have Milo steal her for you?"

Dominic tries to pry my hands from his chest, but my grip is solid. I'm not leaving. Not until I know what the fuck is going on. "Fucking tell me, Dominic, or I swear to God," I threaten.

Dominic's whole demeanor changes instantly. His face falls expressionless. He no longer looks ragged, though the dark circles under his eyes don't magically disappear. He straightens his back while I hold him still.

"I don't have to tell you shit," he grits. His teeth are clenched, his jaw tightening in displeasure as he continues staring me down.

I shove him backward until his back hits the wall. I push into him until he's flattened against it. I bring my mouth close to his ear. "Why the fuck is Katherine here?"

Dominic shrugs. "We're to be married," he calmly states.

I loosen one fist from his shirt, pulling my hand back, and throwing it forward. I connect with his cheek in one swift movement. Dominic crumples. He tries to cup his face, but I use my other hand to keep him in place. My taller body keeps him in position as I punch him again, and again.

After three hard hits, his nose is bleeding and the dark circle under one eye grows darker. He glowers at me, but I ignore him. My thoughts race. "There's no way she's marrying you, you piece of shit," I snarl at him.

Dominic chuckles lowly at me, wincing a bit as he grins. Blood stains his teeth. "We're to be married in five days. Her and I. Then we're leaving for a few weeks for a proper honeymoon." He grabs the wrist of the hand that still fists his shirt.

"I was going to invite you to the ceremony." He glances at my hand that continues holding him hostage. "But given how you're acting now, I think your presence would only upset my Katherine."

"She's not your Katherine!" My face reddens as I yell, the blood vessels in my neck and forehead straining against my skin.

Dominic looks around me, moving only as much as I allow. "Come on in," he says.

I glance at the door, seeing Milo walk in.

Milo.

Milo stands in the room with us.

I release Dominic quicker than I grabbed him.

I cross the room in three large steps, bringing my arm back again and letting it fly as I reach Milo. My fist connects directly to his jaw, sending him careening to the side. He holds his jaw and I relish the feel of the bones snapping under my knuckles.

I'm seething, my teeth grinding hard enough to chip a molar. A tiny piece of tooth floats alongside my tongue. I quickly spit it out onto Dominic's floor, not giving a shit about it or the small throb of pain that lances my jaw with each inhale.

"You took Katherine," I say, lethal calm seeping into my words as I stare down the motherfucker who hurt my woman. "You plunged a needle in her arm, rendering her unconscious. What the fuck else did you do while she was out, huh?" I accuse.

Milo is still clutching his jaw as he looks at me, his eyes wide.

I don't give a fuck. "What did you do to her? Did you enjoy her while she couldn't fight back? What kind of man does that to a woman?" I'm in his face now. My nose nearly brushes his.

"I was gentle."

"Gentle? Gentle as you stabbed her? Gentle as you fucking clotheslined her, catching her by the fucking neck?" My blood is boiling, heating me and fueling my anger.

I shove Milo. He stumbles, landing in the chair that's adjacent to him. He catches himself at the last minute.

"She's so much fucking smaller than you and you felt the need to nearly choke her?" I want to pull at my hair like a crazy man, but I maintain my anger. I direct it at the fool who deserves it.

"Leave him be, Alecsander," Dominic says.

"You," I point my finger at him, barely turning. "Shut the fuck up." I stare at Milo, leveling a gaze as he still half sits, half stands by the chair. "You're going to get what you deserve."

I lean over, my body heaving with anger as I grab Milo by the scruff of his shirt, pulling it around the collar. I lift him out of the chair and help him to his feet. As soon as he's sturdy enough to stand on his own, I yank my leg and knee him directly in the balls. I watch as he crumples in on himself, grasping at his cock as the pain hits him.

"Alecsander," Dominic continues. "I hired him to do it, paid him. He was merely doing his job," he clarifies.

"Doing his job?" I spit. "His job was to hurt Katherine? That's what you pay him to do? Hurt your alleged future wife? What kind of fucking husband are you going to be?"

Before leaving Milo to groan through his pain, I give his stomach another hook with my boot. It sends him flying backward until his back hits the wall. He looks up, blood on his face. "I'm not fucking through with you yet," I promise.

I inch closer to Dominic once I know Milo isn't moving. I point my finger at Dominic's ugly mug. "I'll tell you what, Dominic," I get in his face again, my hand going to his throat, grasping it and squeezing until I can see his veins bulging and straining. His neck flushes scarlet. "You're going to be a shitty as fuck husband," I laugh cruelly. "And that's *if* I let you live long enough to do it."

DOMINIC

I'd be pissing myself if I were Milo. I steal a glance at him, and he's beside himself. I don't pay him any mind as I return my stare to Alecsander. He's still standing in front of me, basically toe to toe, as if that alone could change my mind.

It won't, but it's fun that he thinks so.

Katherine is here, in the room I curated for her. And she's staying here. We will get married and then we'll leave.

I long to kick his ass once and for all. I laid him out in his own club.

But he's gotten stronger, more brutal, than I remember. It's why he can fist my shirt with one hand and use his body for leverage to keep me against the wall or in one place. I won't let him see that he's getting to me.

"Dominic, what the fuck is going on?" He asks, like he wants to understand. He doesn't. He can't understand. He'll never be able to understand what Katherine and I have, what we are to one another. He won't get the privilege of even asking her. I'll make sure of it.

I smile, my hand yearning as it curls into a fist. I'm about to swing it backward when a noise from my computer system disrupts us. It's a shrill noise, one that sounds eerily like a scream.

There's only one person who could be screaming.

Alecsander comes to the same conclusion because we're tripping over one another trying to edge closer to my desk. I shove him back as I push around him. "This is my fucking desk. Get the fuck back!"

"Where the fuck is she, Dominic?" Alecsander asks, his voice higher pitched than usual. "Where the hell is she? That was her screaming a second ago!"

I wave a hand. "I know it was her. I heard it too. I don't see her, though. She might be in her closet and there isn't a camera there," I explain.

Alecsander's finger hovers into my vision, pointing at a smudge on my screen. "What's that? Zoom in," he demands.

I huff but comply, seeing a puddle. It wasn't there earlier, and it isn't water as it colors my screen a dark gray. I squint at it, trying to get a better look to determine what it is.

"It's fucking blood," Alecsander breathes behind me. My eyes snap to his, then dart to Milo, who is now standing. He clutches his side and face.

"You get the fuck back!" Alecsander roars. "She wouldn't even fucking be here if it weren't for you!"

Milo retreats as Alecsander stares at me, brows knitted together. "That's blood, Dominic. It's obvious."

I nod, thinking the same. "I know it is," I say somberly.

"So, who took her, Dominic? Where is my Katherine?" he pleads with me, sinking to his knees on my office floor. Alecsander holds his head in his hands, clutching his hair as he sobs viciously into his palms. "Where is she, Dom?" He cries.

"Where's my Katherine?" He asks over and over until he can hardly breathe through the tears and snot pouring down his face.

It's then I make several startling realizations.

Alecsander loves Katherine and loves her deeply. I've never seen him so distraught in all my life. He loves her. He loves her more than I do, in a different way than I do.

It doesn't change that I brought her here, however. She's still *mine*. But I need to let them see each other, even if it's only one more time. If I don't, then she'll spend her whole fucking life pining over him, never fully loving me.

But who has her now? She was secure in her room, the door and windows locked. I had a few men stationed in the hall. I scratch my head when no immediate suspects pop into my head.

I sink next to Alecsander, clutching his shoulders in fake solidarity. I bring my forehead close to his ear. "We're going to find her, Alecsander, I swear to fucking God. We're going to find our Katherine."

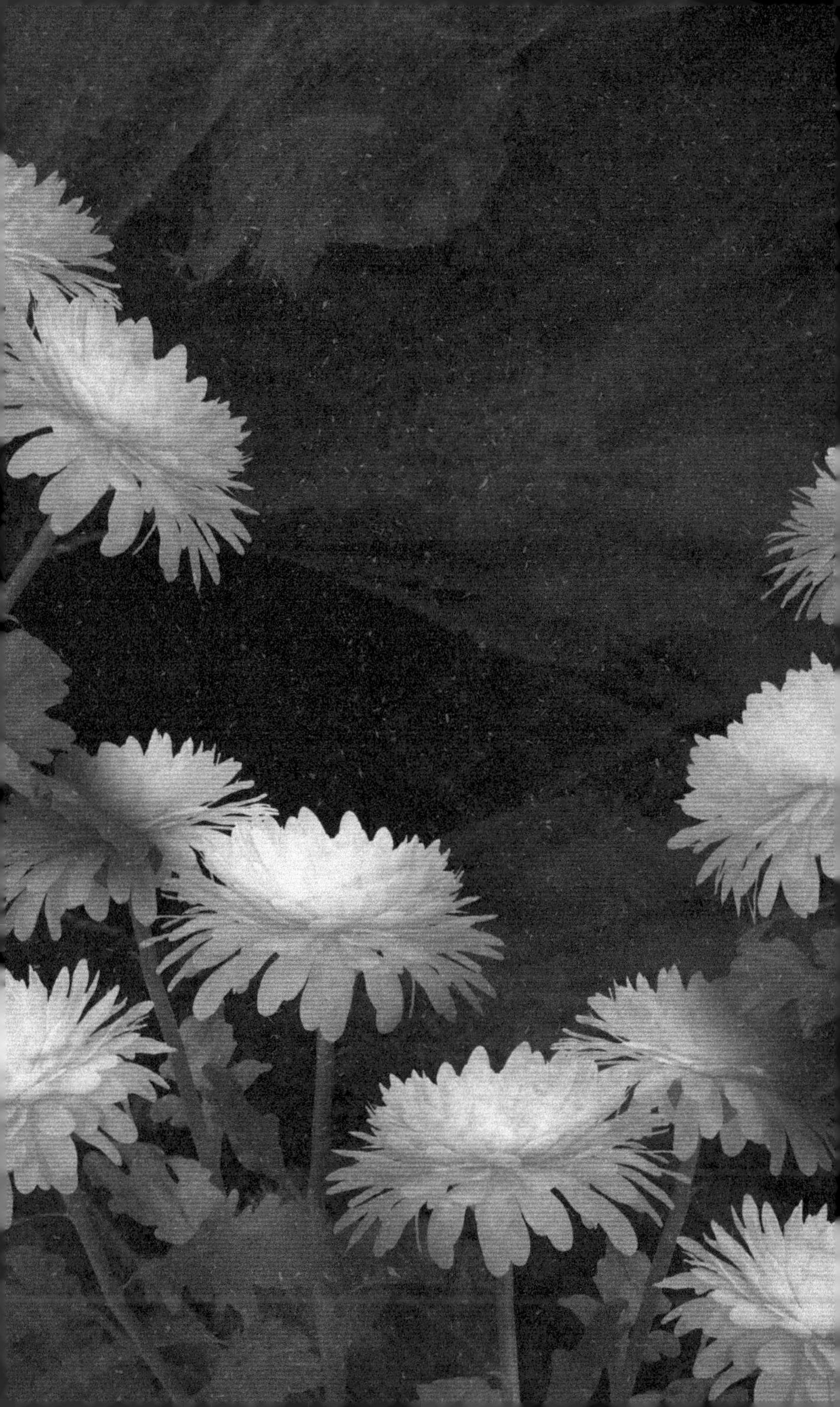

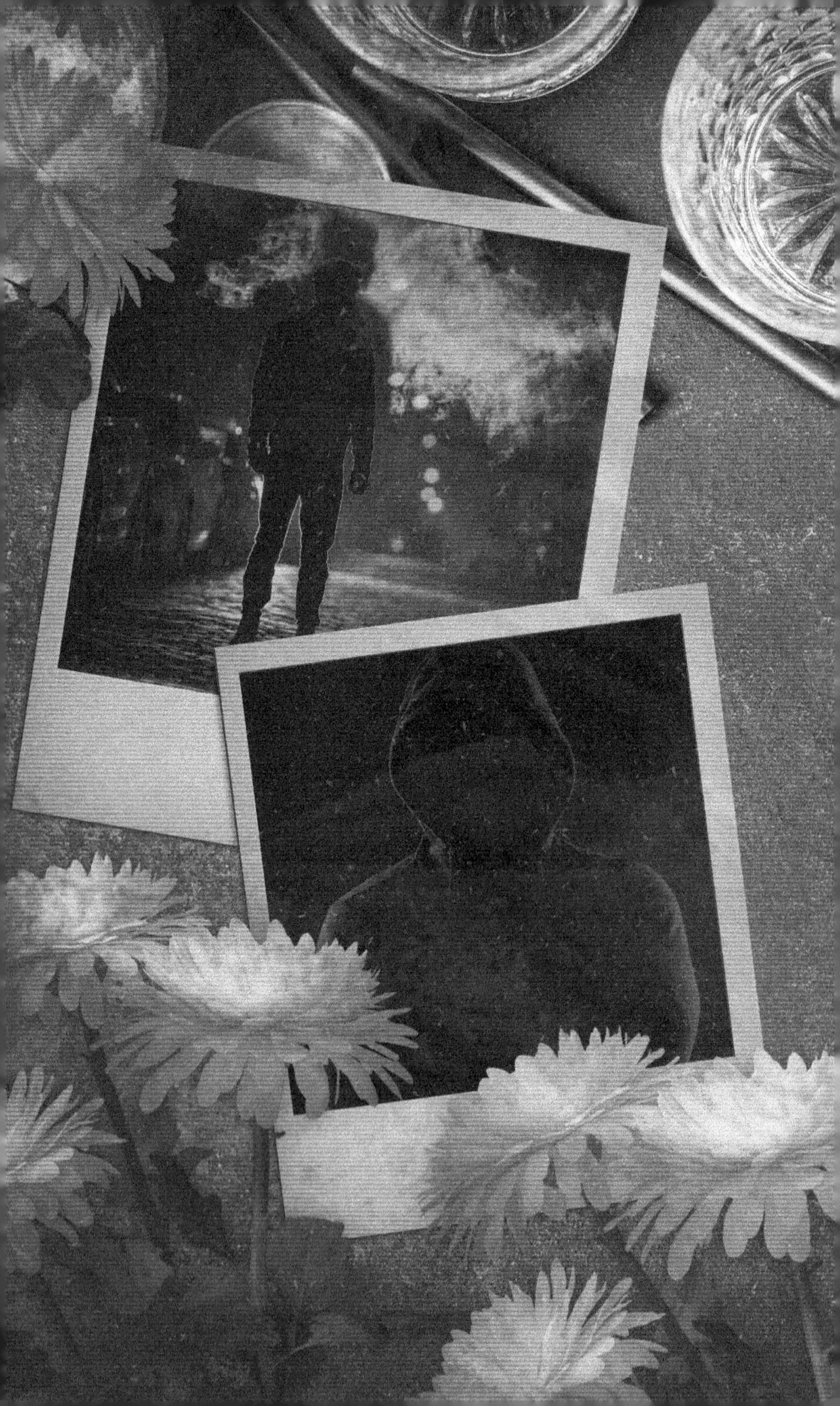

Thirty-Two

UNKNOWN

The Sandman pays Dominic a visit and my plan escalates. What a perfect distraction. I wait, only a floor down, in a barren room with only makeshift tables and computers.

Dominic leads Alecsander to his office. He's had the floor replaced and cleaned since I last saw him in person. I scoff, rubbing my chest as the scar pulls at the tight skin.

I take several moments to click and choose options, disabling several outlier cameras. Then I upload and use the footage of the past hour to create a seamless loop in the girl's room. I set it on a timer, so they'll know she's gone when I want them to know she's gone.

When the Sandman lands several punches, I take my leave of my makeshift office and head upstairs through the side staircase that no one uses. It was originally created for the maid service of the complex. Since Dominic's owned it, it's been mainly idle.

Until now.

The staircase leads to the side of his apartment, away from his front door. It comes to a small, side door that is sealed shut.

Or it was until recently. I've chipped away at the seals just enough the past several weeks to make a difference.

A few soft kicks and the door juts inward, the rusty bolts on the side not doing much to hold its weight. I breathe a sigh of relief when I grab the knob and force it open a bit more so I can easily slip through.

Monitoring the halls, I take note of two men. They have their heads pointed down at their cellular devices. New recruits then. I know the type.

They think they're better than they are, that they're worth more than they truly are.

No one is worth much in the eyes of the syndicate.

Dominic would do best teaching them. If they were my men and they were callously disrespecting their orders, I'd have them bloodied and beat senseless in the concrete basement.

I do the next best thing, though, and slide up behind one, wrapping my arm around his neck until its nestled in the crook of my elbow. I place my other hand along the side of his face and neck, giving a hard squeeze and a rough twist. I feel his neck snap beneath my skin, the sound jolting and making me crave more.

I ease the man to the ground silently. The other guard down the hall none the wiser as I place his head on the ground.

I repeat the process with the second guard, sliding behind him and dropping him within moments. Two cracked necks later, I edge down the hall until the door in question looms before me.

Her door has a latch on the outside, but that's all it is. A latch. I slide it unlocked and the door creaks open.

The room is dark, save for a small night light plugged in. How old is this woman that she needs a night light? I shake my head, not giving a shit either way. She's in bed, the blankets pooled around her body as she slumbers.

I approach the bed on light feet, my years as the head of the syndicate fueling me. As I see the woman's face, my chest throbs.

She's a gorgeous woman; she would have made Dominic happy eventually. Too bad she won't get the chance too.

As I sat in empty rooms the past few years, biding my time and coming up with dozens of plans to eliminate Dominic, I never saw this screw ball heading my way. The perfect way to break Dominic, something that would be more painful than his own death.

Something that would make him *crave* his own death.

My hand hovers above the girl's face. Her eyes pop open. Wide open. Her pupils dart around frantically, noticing me and going impossibly wider. She yanks her arms and tries to get up, but I slam a hand against her cheek. My silver watch smashes against the delicate skin of her cheek.

She scrambles more, rushing to her knees and flopping backward, going to the other side of the bed in a move that I wouldn't expect someone of her size and stature to be able to handle. I grimace as her feet hit the floor.

"You filthy bitch, get back here!" I demand.

She spares me a glance as she stumbles to the door. She's nearly there, but the seconds she wasted on looking back catch up to her as I pound my hand against the door. I keep it wedged closed as my body pushes into her soft flesh. I root her to the door, no gaps between us as I glare down at her.

"You're even more delectable in person, aren't you?" I ask. Her face is ghastly in the dim room. Her eyes continue flickering back and forth around the room, looking for an escape route that we both know isn't there.

"W-who are you?"

I only smile as I ease back a step, giving her a modicum of room. She mistakes my generosity and lunges forward.

I use her momentum against her as I push my fists into her back, between her shoulder blades. She folds and falls, headfirst, onto the tiled floor. Her head gives a definitive *crack* as it slams into the floor, the noise ricocheting off the walls as she manages to choke out a cry.

As soon as her head hits the floor, however, her cry dies. Her body goes limp. The blood oozes from her scalp for several moments, enough to leave behind a subtle pool. When I'm satisfied with the size of it, I grab her limp body. It's heavier with the dead weight, but I heave it over my shoulder. I don't care if her shoulders or hips knock on the door frames as I carry her through the exit. I lug her body down even more stairs until we hit the basement, cozy with its concrete.

Once in the basement, I throw her onto the floor, the sand no doubt embedding into her exposed flesh. I take my time tying her wrists and bolting the chains, pulling them tightly and securely, to ensure the most ache when she rouses from her unconsciousness.

I give her leg a swift kick, ensuring she's still out before I leave her in the small room. I lock the door and push the key deep into my pocket, making my way back to my makeshift office to watch the drama unfold between Dominic and the Sandman.

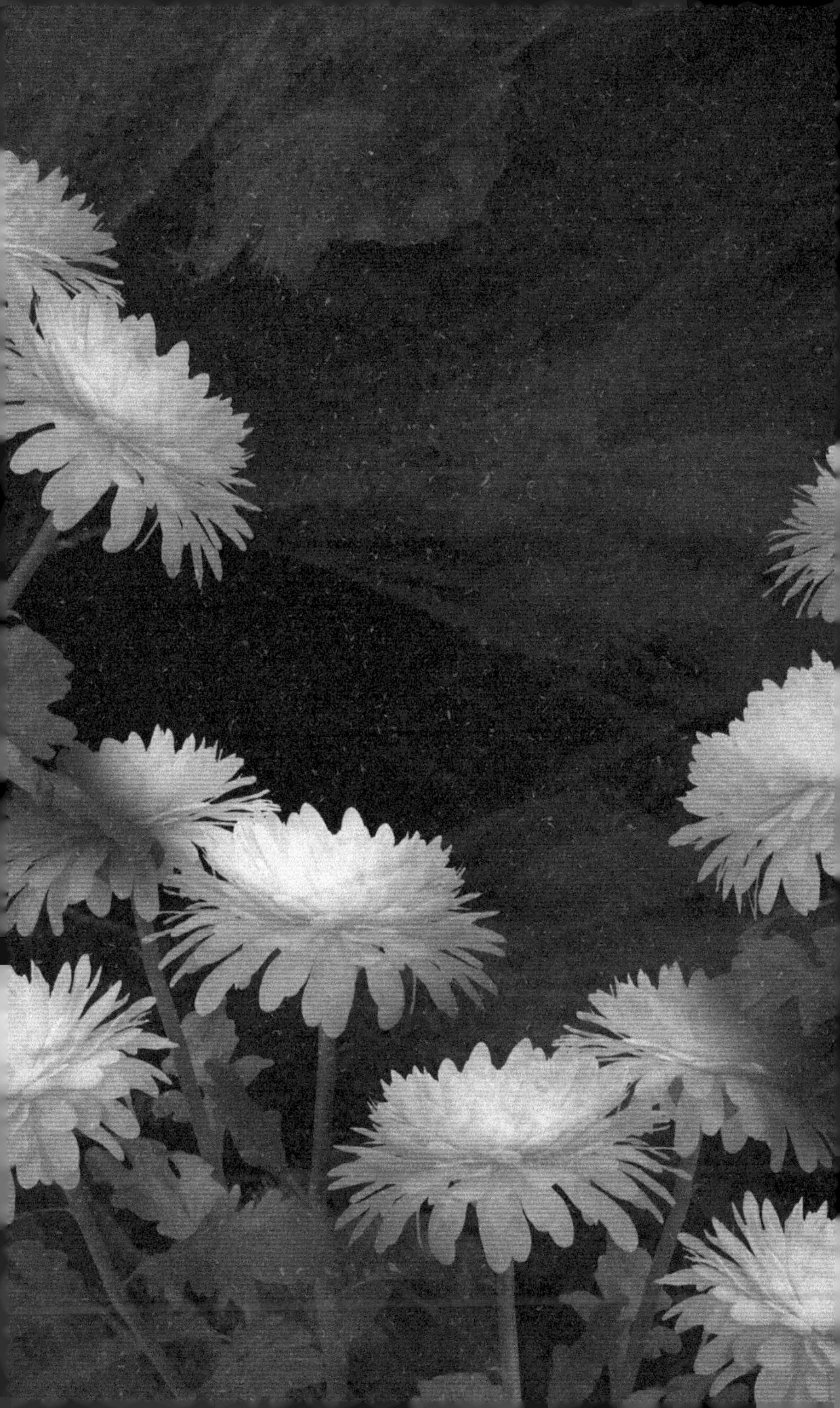

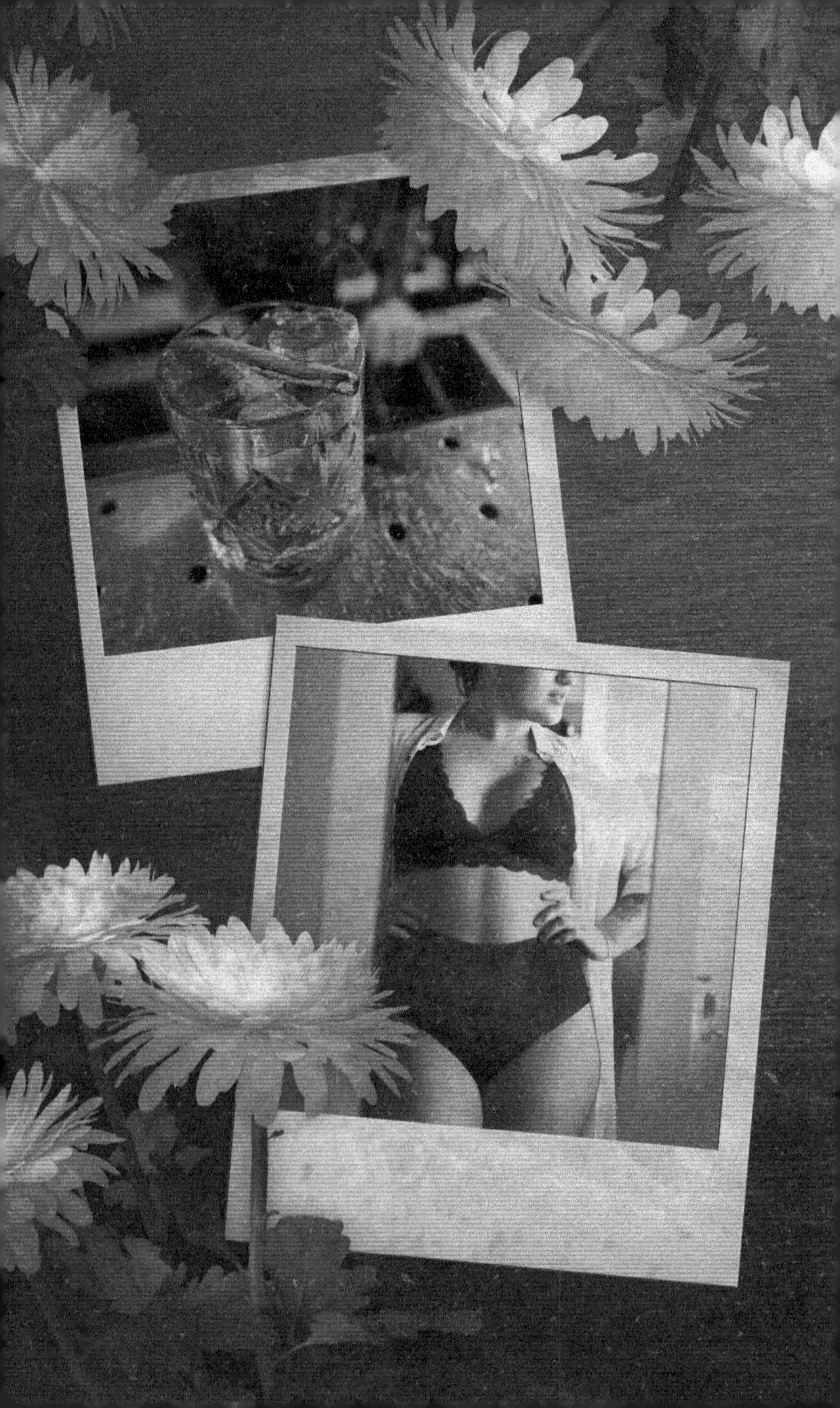

Thirty-Three

KATHERINE

My eyelids weigh against my cheeks. They're too heavy to lift.

I open my mouth to scream, but my throat is too scratchy and dry. My vocal cords are raw and abused. My mouth is also parched.

How long have I been here?

Is it even the same day? Has my forced wedding day passed?

I have no idea with no way to tell the passage of time. My limbs ache, my back bent oddly against a wall that I can only assume is concrete based on the semi-smooth finish with sandy edges.

Sand, sand, more sand. My eyes feel like they're made of sand.

I flex my fingers, or at least I think I do. The grit of the sand beneath me runs across the pads of my fingers, leaving micro abrasions in its wake.

There are micro abrasions everywhere.

My eyes finally deem me worthy and blink open, shrouding my sight in dim grays and deeper blacks as the shadows crowd around me, begging me to succumb to them.

I refuse, but the option is tempting. I'm alone, stolen, lost in the dark.

I've blinked at least two dozen times, and my vision slowly becomes sharper with each shutter. I take in my surroundings for the first time.

The concrete wall was a good guess and right on the money. The sand beneath me is real and damp with my perspiration. My pajama pants are ripped at the knees.

Did I fall?

I take stock of my arms, legs, and torso. My hands are chained at the wrists, the large metal cuffs flowing behind me into the concrete. I'm stuck. My ankles are similarly shackled, but those chains lead to a hefty pillar about three feet away. The room is tiny, so close and small that the pillar is in the middle.

The chains are so thick that I have no hope of raising my arms or moving my legs much more than a few inches.

My head thuds against the cold concrete. I hope the small thump will dislodge any ill thoughts.

It doesn't and they hit me rapidly.

Questions upon questions. With no answers in sight.

Where the fuck am I?

How did I get here?

Surely Dominic didn't put me here? Is this his doing?

It must be. He's only getting more brazen and more dangerous. This is a scare tactic, I'm sure. And, I'll be damned, it's fucking working.

I want to cry, but my eyes are bone dry. There's no moisture left in my body. It yearns for water and Alecsander equally. I need both to survive and I'm not sure if I will survive whatever hellhole I've found myself in now.

Then I recall my realization from earlier. Alecsander is the fucking Sandman. *The* Sandman, the one and fucking only.

I inhale and exhale, taking deep breaths because I start to

hyperventilate. I stare around the room, trying to see if there's an air vent or any kind of air ventilation system in place.

There isn't.

My cubicle is solid concrete, the door so tightly fitted against its frame that no light shines through. My breaths quicken and stutter from my lungs.

In through the nose and out through the mouth, I remind myself.

Over and over until it feels like it works. My breaths are still too fast, but at least a little slower.

I sit, shackled and growing colder by the minute, for what must be hours. My ass is completely numb, my legs and arms slowly following suit.

BRIGHTNESS FLOODS THE SMALL ROOM. MY EYES flicker open. Where's the light coming from?

I blink rapidly, my eyes attempting to adjust to the sudden change. A man stands in the doorway, that much I can tell for sure. His identity, however, is lost on me because I've never seen the man.

He's older, at least in his sixties, with sparse graying hair. His face holds wrinkles that must fight me in age. It's his eyes, however, that keep me breathless and silent.

They're dark, hard, and cold. He's staring down his nose at me, like I'm only an ant he's come to extinguish. I gulp.

"Nice to officially meet you, Katherine," he says, his voice gruff and gravely. It's evident he's been a lifelong smoker. "I've been waiting years to finally meet you in person rather than catching fleeting moments of your life through the cameras."

The man steps fully into the concrete room, nearly taking up one whole side. He looks at the pillar, then down at my manacled ankles. He takes one of his leather-clad feet and gently pushes at my leg with his toe. "I didn't want to put you in these, but I saw what you did to that lad Milo, and I have to say that there's better things for me to be doing than to have you tackling me," he laughs.

"You'd deserve it," I croak, my throat burning. My tongue is heavy in my mouth. How long has it been since I've taken a sip of water?

The man crouches, propping his elbows on his knees as he stares at me. "Katherine, Katherine, let's get on the same page, shall we?"

I don't respond. I don't think he wants me to.

He puts his knees on the ground and reaches out to grab my ankles, right above the heavy-duty chains. He yanks hard enough to bring me a few inches closer. My arms strain behind me, their own chains pulling and having no give to them whatsoever.

I groan as the pain washes through my wrists and flows into my shoulders and joints.

He laughs at my groans. "I've heard enough from you already, Katherine." He says darkly as he tugs my legs a little harder.

I bite my lip to suppress my grunt of pain as his grip tightens.

Overwhelming helplessness overcomes me. My chest is leaden with dread for whatever is to come. I stare at the man, unabashedly and unashamed.

He smirks in response. "He thought he killed me, those years ago. But I'm stronger and cleverer than he ever was. Even as a boy he wasn't much. Didn't do well in school, didn't play enough sports, and didn't take to business like I expected him to. But what can you do with kids these days, huh?" He stands, shoving his hands in his pockets as he paces from one wall to the next, keeping his eyes on mine.

"He thought he threw my body in the ground. But not deep enough it turns out." He chuckles. "My own son tried to kill me and then attempted to bury my body."

"Of course, with him being the son I knew, he didn't do it well enough. Didn't aim for the heart. Thought he did, that's for sure. But I knew it, I knew it as soon as the bullet hit my skin that I was going to live."

I follow the man's actions as he takes his hands out of his pockets to squeeze his fingers together then replace them in his pockets. He keeps repeating the action, over and over.

"Which gave way to the best plan I've ever had. I'll let my boy think he killed me. Hell, I let him bury me alive for Christ's sake!"

"The plan was," He looks at me, once again sinking to his knees and gripping me by the ankles. "To let him believe me dead for all these years. You can't be a threat if you're dead!" He smiles a toothy grin, his teeth yellowing and chipped.

"And when you entered the picture, it all came together. Viola! I'd lie in wait, until he got you and then I'd strike. I'd steal *you* from *him*."

"Who are you?" I have a sneaking suspicion.

"My name's Mark, Katherine. But you can call me Mr. Alcutti." He scans my face, looking for a reaction that I'm tamping down.

Dominic's father lives?

And he's stolen me from the son that stole me first.

"What are you going to do with me?" I shudder.

He grips me tighter, pulling me closer to him, his grin widening at my question. "I'm so glad you asked, Katherine. I'm going to keep you down here in the dark with me."

My heart accelerates.

I thought Dominic was crazy? That was an introduction course to legitimately crazy.

Mark stares at me, licking his chapped lips. I cower internally but hold my physical form steadfast. He won't break me. I won't let him.

"Oh, and one more thing, Katherine, dear." Mark smiles a saccharine grin. He digs into his pocket before holding a closed hand toward me. "I thought you might like this...welcome gift." He unfolds his fingers. A crumpled and semi-wilted dandelion floats onto me. I stare at the weak, green stem.

I don't have time to formulate a response before his voice scratches at my ears once more. "That's your favorite flower, yes? A tiny, worthless dandelion?" He stands, shrugging his shoulders as he stares down at me. He turns to the door, opening it. "Rhett told me they were your favorite when you were kids." He chuckles as he steps through the threshold. He shuts the door behind him and slides the locks into place.

No, no. There's no fucking way. Tears threaten to spill from my exhausted eyelids.

I can't afford to think about Rhett. Or the Sandman. Or even Dominic. I can't afford to think about any man besides Mark.

I won't let him break me. He can hurt me, sure, but I won't break.

He'll keep me in the dark, but I'll be coming to light sooner than he wants. That's for damn sure.

To be continued...

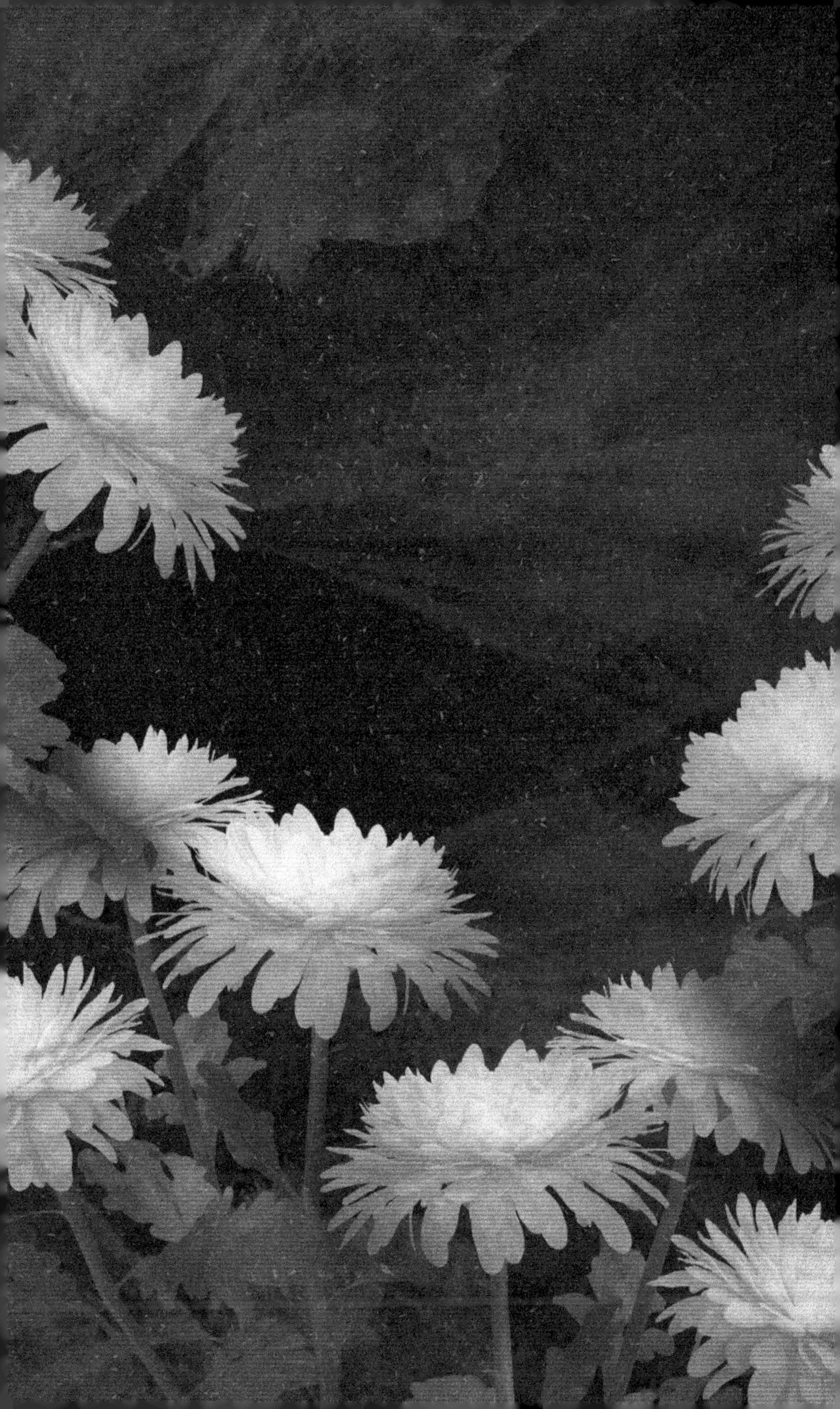

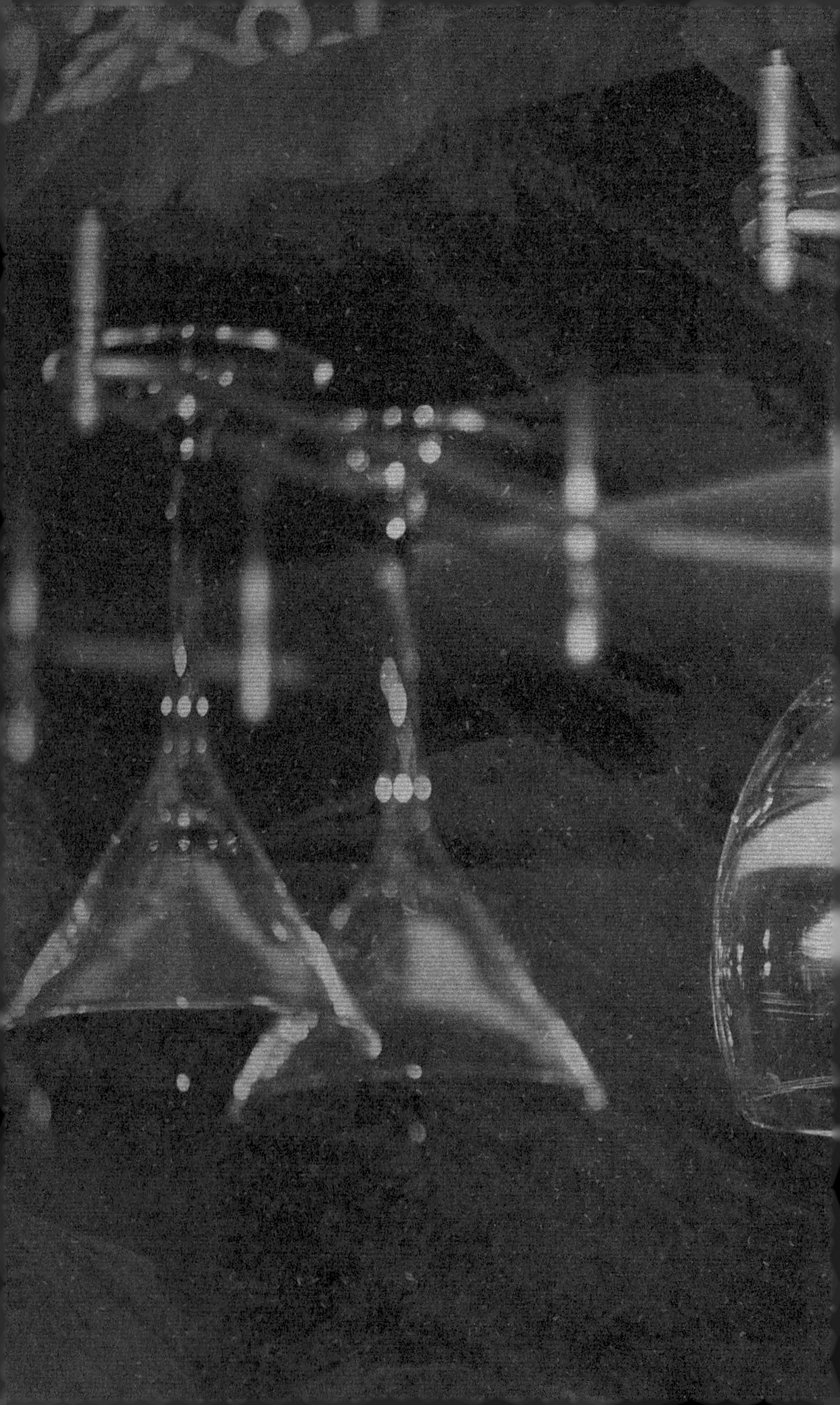

Acknowledgments

First and foremost, I must thank my two best friends: Jordi and Eilis. Without the two of you, this wouldn't be out in the world. Our weekly writing group has helped me immensely with staying on track and actually doing the whole writing part of writing a book. Funny how that works, eh? I appreciate the two of you endlessly. I look up to both of you and your writing. I cannot wait until I see one of your books on the shelves.

I also want to give an extra thanks to Eilis for writing the blurb for this book. I could not, for the life of me, figure out how to even write it. Whenever someone asks me what this book is about, my mine short circuits or something because I never know what to say. But, Eilis, you are a natural storyteller, and it shows. Thanks, again.

And to my bab, Zach— thank you for being the most supportive partner anyone could ask for. You've only had positive things to say, and you continue to push and encourage me when it comes to any of my creative endeavors. Without your endless support and praise, I don't think this book would have been completed. I truly cherish and love you to fucking pieces.

Thank you to Ashlyn Harmon, the wonderful woman who helped me edit this book by giving me a kickass editorial assessment/letter. You had such great insights and I greatly appreciate all the work you put into the responses you gave me.

And finally, I would be remiss if I didn't acknowledge the wonderful person who not only designed the amazing cover, but also completed the interior formatting for this book! Shay from Disturbed Valkyrie Designs, you're so much fun to work with and I adore all the little things you've done for me throughout this process.

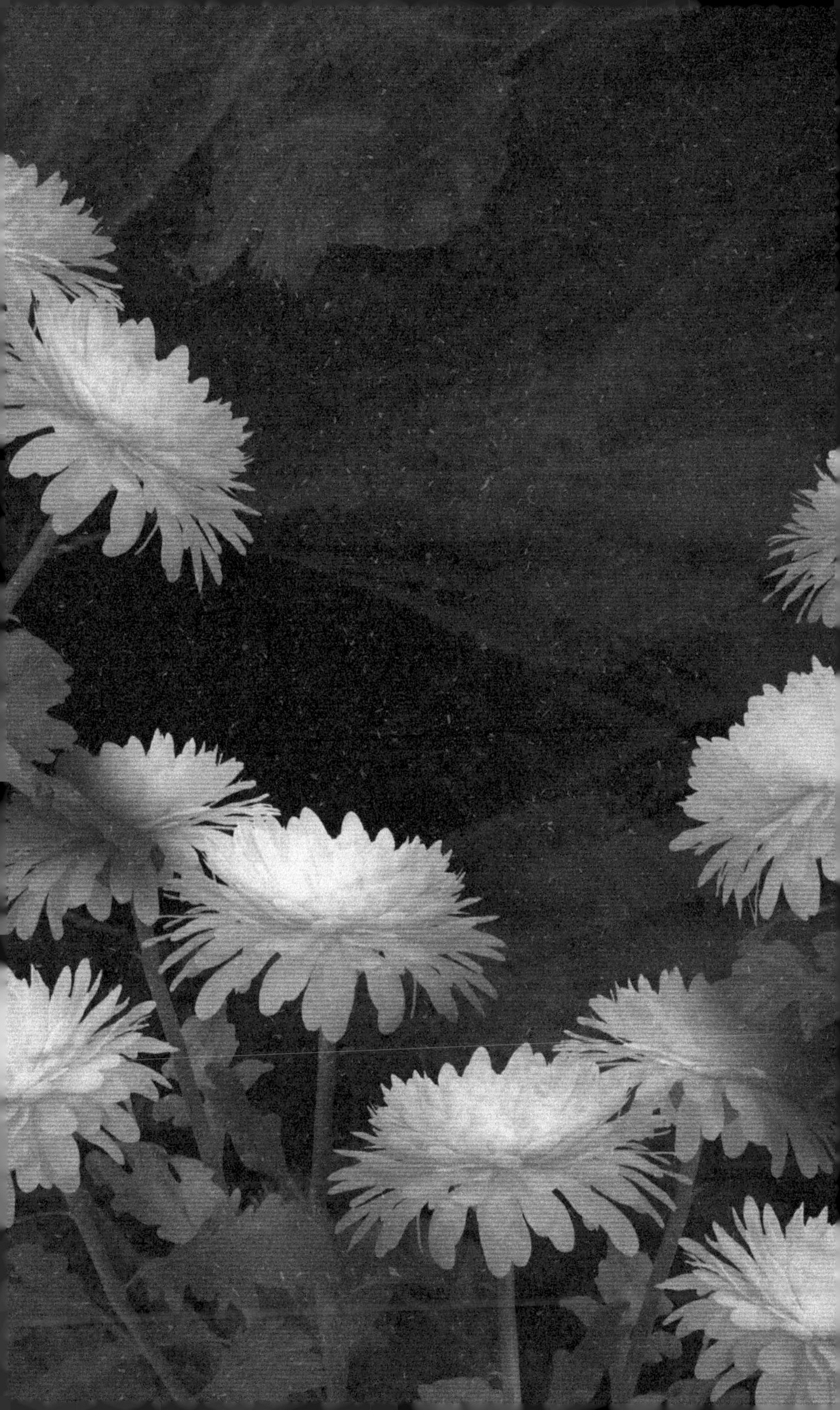

Stalk Me

Threads:
britt bee 🐝 (@britt.bee.books) on Threads

Facebook:
https://tr.ee/smyrRXlNvC

Pinterest:
https://www.pinterest.com/brittbeebooks/

Patreon:
http://patreon.com/BrittBeeBooks

Instagram:
https://www.instagram.com/britt.bee.books

TikTok:
https://www.tiktok.com/@britt.bee.books

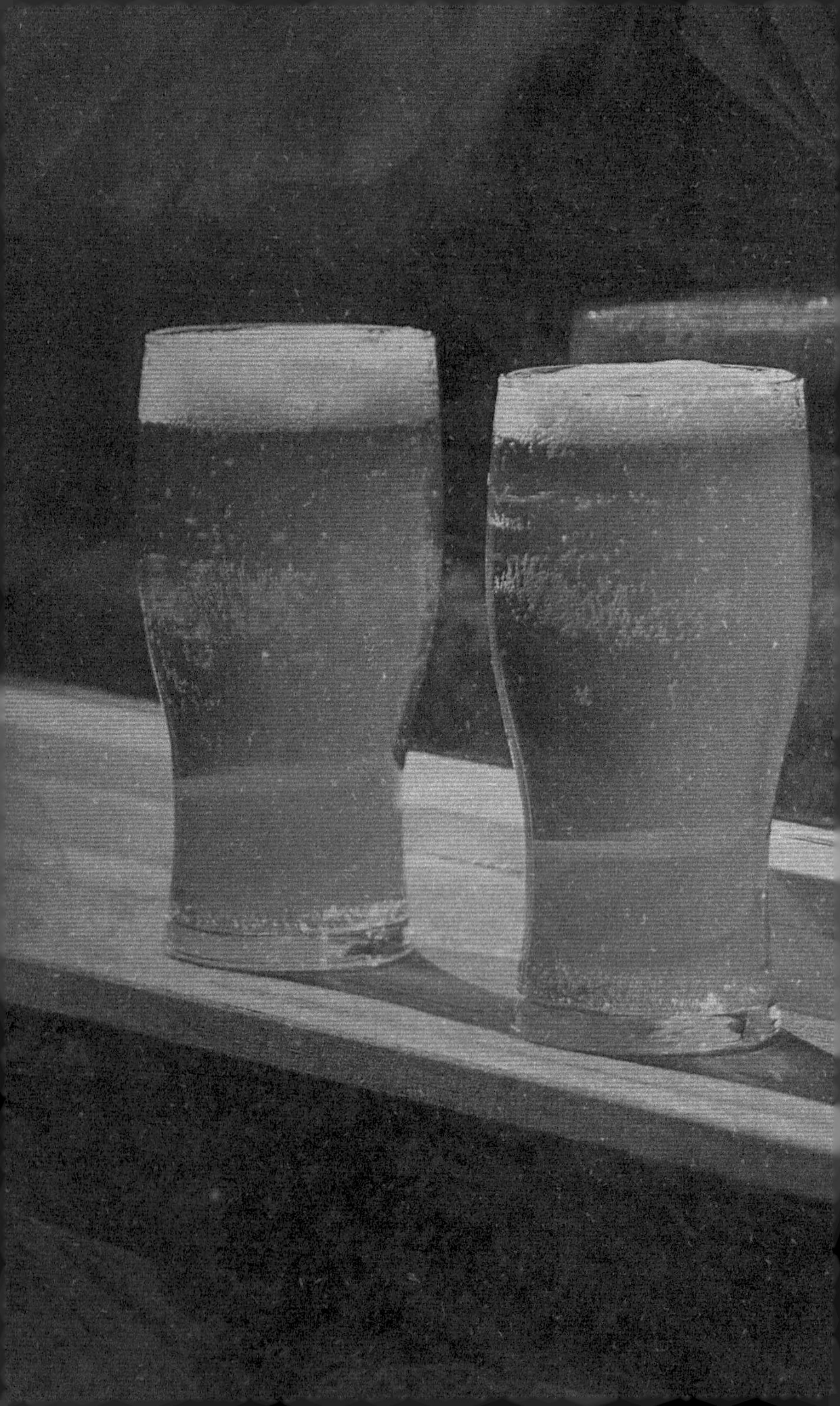

About the Author

Britt Bee is a twenty-something-years-old woman who resides in Indiana. She enjoys writing romance almost as much as reading it. She lives with her fiancé, two dogs, and three cats (yes, there's fur everywhere). She spends her weekends working her "normal" job and her weekdays writing, reading, spending time with her family and two friends, and crafting.